UNTIL THE NIGHT

BOOKS BY GILES BLUNT

The John Cardinal series

Forty Words for Sorrow
The Delicate Storm
Blackfly Season
By the Time You Read This
Crime Machine
Until the Night

Other novels

Cold Eye
No Such Creature
Breaking Lorca

UNTIL THE NIGHT

GILES BLUNT

RANDOM HOUSE CANADA

PUBLISHED BY RANDOM HOUSE CANADA

 Published in 2012 by Random House Canada, a division of Random House of Canada Limited, Toronto. Distributed in Canada by Random House of Canada Limited.

www.randomhouse.ca

Grateful acknowledgement is made for permission to reprint lyrics on page vii from the following Leonard Cohen song: WINTER LADY, © 1968 Sony/ATV Music Publishing LLC. All rights administered by Sony/ATV Music Publishing LLC, 8 Music Square West, Nashville, TN 37203. All rights reserved. Used by permission.

Library and Archives Canada Cataloguing in Publication

Blunt, Giles
Until the night / Giles Blunt.

(John Cardinal series ; 6)
Also issued in electronic format.

ISBN 978-0-679-31435-6

I. Title. II. Series: Blunt, Giles. John Cardinal series ; 6.

PS8553.L867U57 2012 C813'.54 C2012-902030-3

Cover design by Leah Springate

Cover image: Jim Brandenburg/Minden Pictures/Getty Images

Printed and bound in the United States of America

2 4 6 8 9 7 5 3 1

For Janna

Well I lived with a child of snow
When I was a soldier
And I fought every man for her
Until the nights grew colder

—Leonard Cohen

UNTIL THE NIGHT

From the Blue Notebook

We heard the plane before we saw it. The storm that had howled around us for three days and nights had finally limped away, leaving a thick cloud cover over the stillness that unfolded in its place.

Hunter had been out all morning ploughing the runway, if that is not too grand a word for the strip of ice that ran straight as a spoke from the lab at one end to the last of the beacons at the other. This was the pale blue gateway to Drift Station Arcosaur.

Wyndham and I had left the lab to come out and watch the plane land. The Twin Otters that arrived every two weeks were our only source of supply and we looked forward to them with pathetic eagerness.

Our coordinates by then were 82°28'N 55°20'W. We had drifted more than ninety geographical miles from our initial position in the Lincoln Sea, carried rudderlessly on the Arctic gyre. Two weeks previously we had passed the Alert defence installation. We actually put in a request to be allowed to use their airfield, instead of Resolute's, for our resupply point, but they responded with a curt negative. Vanderbyl was indignant for days.

Kurt Vanderbyl, our chief scientist, was at this moment tending to a crop of waist-high radiometers and sensors. He was the oldest among us, a silvery, ascetic Dutchman who moved among the instruments like a priest administering Communion. His grad student, Ray Deville, had been at his side all morning, a walking clipboard with sunglasses and blue down jacket. At the sound of the plane, the two of them stopped and turned to look, both shading their eyes despite the clouds.

The plane dropped into view, surprisingly close. Anyone new to the Arctic might have thought the pilot was in danger of overshooting the runway and ploughing right through the lab. I had had a pilot's licence myself for years, but Arctic pilots are a breed apart and I still marvelled at their skills. The Otter set down on its skis and pounded toward us, coming to a stop less than fifty metres away. The pilot climbed out and waved.

Wyndham snapped a harness around his chest and I hooked him up to the sled. As we headed toward the plane, a passenger stepped out.

Who the hell's that? I said.

Rebecca Fenn—Kurt's wife.

His wife? I heard they split up.

They did. She's here on her own project. Strictly professional—at least to hear Kurt tell it.

What a terrible idea.

I don't know. He wouldn't have agreed if he thought it would jeopardize anybody else's research.

Vanderbyl got to the plane first. He took a suitcase from her, but they didn't hug or make contact of any kind.

I think you know Rebecca, he said to Wyndham as we approached.

Yes, of course. Hello, Rebecca.

Hello, Gordon. Nice to see you again.

She reached out a hand, and Gordon took off his mitten to shake it. Vanderbyl turned to me.

And this is Karson Durie, glacier man, otherwise known as Kit.

Ah, yes. Heard a lot about you.

We shook hands. Hers was slim, and warm from the plane.

She put her mittens on and stood with hands on her hips and made a quick survey of her surroundings. Wow.

I hope that's a good wow, Vanderbyl said as Wyndham and I started offloading supplies onto the sled.

I don't know, she said. She had a low voice, a velvet delivery that gave her every utterance the air of a confidence. I was just reading about the first party to land on an ice island, she said. Some U.S. military thing led by a general. The first words out of his mouth were "Obviously no man can survive here. We must leave at once, if we can."

All us old-timers know that quote, Wyndham said, slamming a box labelled Patak's Curry Paste onto the sled. It's exactly the kind of common sense that always gets completely ignored up here— which is the only way to get anything done.

Wow, she said again. This place is . . .

I'll show you your lab, Vanderbyl said.

The two of them walked toward the camp, and something in the way they moved together would have told even the most casual observer that they were man and wife.

It's stupid to bring her here, I said to Wyndham.

Why? Everyone's got plenty to do. She has her own research, and God knows Kurt has enough to keep him busy.

I just don't want any Sturm und Drang.

There won't be any. Rebecca's a good researcher. Lovely girl, don't you think? Woman, I mean.

What I think doesn't matter.

1

A WILD WIND BLEW ACROSS Lake Nipissing, so loud it woke John Cardinal up and got him out of bed before his six a.m. alarm had even gone off. The sun was nowhere near getting up, but there was a big moon that lit the frozen lake and the trees that bent and swayed before it. As always at this time of year, the surface was studded with ice-fishing huts. Small branches blew across the lawn behind his building, a garbage can lid flew into sight and crashed into a tree. It rolled like a coin across the yard and out of sight again.

"I don't believe it," Cardinal said. He switched off the kitchen light to see better. He had been born and raised in Algonquin Bay and, except for a dozen years or so in Toronto, had lived here all his life. "The Bay," as it was known to locals, was only 340 kilometres north of Toronto—nowhere near the Arctic—but its idea of winter was severe. Cardinal had seen a lot of unusual weather phenomena over the years, but he had never seen anything like this. The fishing huts—not all of them, but some—were migrating, dislodged from their moorings by this implacable wind and travelling across the ice.

His phone rang and it was Chouinard telling him not to bother coming in, he should head straight for a crime scene out on Highway 17. By the time Cardinal was in the car, the wind had blown away across the hills.

~

The motel was located on a slight rise, and was almost hidden by a copse of trees except for its garish sign. Cardinal parked the car just behind the coroner's BMW and switched off the engine. He set the handbrake and looked at Lise Delorme, but she was already getting out.

Dawn breaking, clear and windless. January sun barely clearing the trees. They walked uphill past the other vehicles—the cruisers, a couple of unmarkeds, the ident van—toward the motel.

Delorme pointed to the sign. "Would you want to stay in a place called Motel 17? Really, what was the guy thinking?"

"If you like Motel 6, you'll love Motel 17," Cardinal said. "Simple math."

A uniformed policewoman posted in front of the crime scene tape waved them past.

They joined a knot of people in the parking lot. Two were kneeling. The grouping reminded Cardinal of a Christmas crèche. Detective Constable Vernon Loach stood up. "Perfect day for it, right?"

"Minus twenty-eight last I heard," Cardinal said.

"You see the march of the fishing huts?"

"Yeah. Guess there's a first for everything."

"I didn't know what I was seeing. Invasion of the porta-potties. I lead on this one, just so you know."

"What?" Delorme said. "How do you figure that, Constable?"

"Take it up with Chouinard."

Delorme whipped out her phone and walked away from the group. When she came back, her face was locked up tight.

Loach spoke to the coroner. "Couple of late arrivals, Doc. You wanna bring 'em up to speed?"

Dr. Barnhouse was wearing a fur-lined pilot's cap that made him look like a cartoon animal. He was a bad-tempered Scot whose mood was in direct correlation to the temperature. "Perhaps you'd like to schedule a matinee performance as well, Sergeant Loach."

"Detective Constable," Delorme said, "not Sergeant."

"Let's just get on with it," Loach said.

"Are we all quite ready, then? Everyone use the toi-toi? Everyone got their pencils sharpened?"

"You could be finished by now."

Cardinal was trying to keep an open mind about Loach, a recent import from Toronto. So far, the only interesting thing about him seemed to be that he didn't care whether anybody liked him or not. An attitude that might be useful when you're working narcotics in a metropolis like Toronto. Working a homicide—anywhere, let alone in a small northern city—it could prove a liability.

"Well-nourished Caucasian male," Barnhouse said, "early forties, been out in the elements approximately eight hours, possibly as much as ten. Extreme cold precludes even a rough guess at time of death.

"Cursory inspection of lividity shows he died right here, in this position. Mechanism of death is most likely asphyxiation. No ligature marks or sign of finger or thumb marks, but the hyoid is crushed and we've got petechial hemorrhaging in the eyes. Whoever killed him probably stood on his throat. You can make out a tread mark or two."

"Nice," Cardinal said.

"Let's go inside," Loach said. "We commandeered one of the rooms. Note the two vehicles on your way in."

They left Barnhouse filling out his paperwork, and the three of them walked to the room next to the motel office and went inside.

"Did Ident get pictures of his throat?" Cardinal asked. "Might be able to match those marks to a particular boot."

"Good idea," Loach said, and Cardinal wasn't sure if he was being sarcastic or not. He asked about the two civilian cars in the lot.

"Right. Get your pencils out, we got a lotta names. Black Nissan belongs to a local woman named Laura Lacroix, who is not here and not at home. She's married to but separated from one Keith Rettig, who still dwells in your fair city. Our fair city. The throat is one Mark Trent, administrator at the hospital and owner of the green Audi parked in front of room seven. Evidence in said room indicates the two were having an affair, and the manager confirms he's seen Trent before, and both the vehicles, although he never saw the woman. I suppose they were being discreet. Textbook tells us suspect number one is the former husband. You know how it goes: you discover the wife's unfaithful, you're ticked, there's really nothing left except to do a tap dance on some poor bastard's throat."

"Was he married too, the victim?" Delorme asked.

"To Melinda Trent, also a hospital administrator. According to the dictates of gender equity, Mrs. Trent is also a prime suspect. She called in a missing person report to the detachment this morning, but she hasn't been informed yet. I'll be doing that"—Loach pulled up the sleeve of his parka to look at his watch—"imminently."

Outside, a tow truck driver was slipping a harness under the Audi, wading through clouds of exhaust.

"So Ms. Lacroix is missing," Cardinal said, "but her car's still here. There any leads on a third vehicle?"

"None. No snow on the drive, no tracks. Speaking of which, what is it with the wacky weather up here? We get more snow in Toronto than this. I only came here for the skiing, as you know."

"Head ten kilometres north—they've got tons of it."

"Like I say, wacky. Where was I? Manager. Manager lives in the house behind the motel. Says he was in bed and didn't hear a thing. No other guests and no witnesses of any kind that we know of. Our theory so far—my theory—is that our two lovers call it a night. Laura Lacroix leaves first, still trying to be discreet—her coat's gone, but Mr. Trent came out in his shirt sleeves. We found a small bracelet near the body and I figure she forgot it and he rushed out to give it to her."

"You're quick," Cardinal said.

"That's a good thing, right? Seems likely somebody jumped her as she was getting into her car. Otherwise, what vehicle did she leave in, and why? Trent comes out with the bracelet, perp takes a negative view on potential witnesses and kills him."

"If it was the angry husband," Delorme said, "Trent may have been next on his list anyway. May have been first, in fact."

"Quite possible."

"You're talking to Trent's wife," Cardinal said. "You want us to take Mr. Rettig?"

"Yeah. And if he doesn't have a rock-solid alibi, bring him in and we'll sweat him. Cuz if it ain't the angry husband, I got a feeling this one could turn into an out-and-out mystery. And I hate mysteries."

They stood there for a full minute as Cardinal stared into space. Loach glanced at Delorme and said, "Detective Cardinal has a contemplative look. I believe he is being visited by a thought."

"Not much of one," Cardinal said. "Just that none of this—an affair, possible jealousy, the fact that the woman's missing—means she's actually been killed. It's possible she hired somebody to do it and staged her disappearance as cover. More likely, she's been abducted by some third party, though for what reason . . ."

"Exactly," Loach said. "Investigation like this, a cop's best friend is a dirty mind."

~

Keith Rettig lived in a white bungalow on one of the small streets off Lakeshore. He was a lot older than Cardinal had expected, maybe early sixties. He answered the door in a paint-spattered sweatshirt and jeans.

Cardinal introduced himself and Delorme and asked if they could come in.

"I'd rather you didn't. I'm in the middle of painting."

"Mr. Rettig, do you know where your wife is?"

"Well, she's not here. She doesn't live here. Why are you looking for her?"

"Her car was found abandoned at a motel. A man was killed there and we think she may be in danger herself."

"Killed? Wait—killed who? Is Laura okay?"

"The man is dead. Your wife is missing. She may still show up for work, but she's not at home and, as I said, her car is still at the motel."

"This is hard to take in."

"I know it's a shock," Delorme said. "Can we come in and talk?"

"I'm sorry, yes, of course." He stood back and held the door for them.

They stepped in and slipped their boots off. Strong smell of paint and newsprint. Newspapers and drop cloths spread over the floor.

"Come into the living room," Rettig said. "It's the only room that isn't in chaos. I just moved in a week ago."

The furniture looked expensive, but it was too big and there was too much of it. Cardinal and Delorme sat on the couch. Rettig sat in a leather club chair, much worn, with a brass reading lamp beside it. "Jesus. This is a shock. I knew Laura was seeing someone. This man who died, was his name Mark?"

"Mark Trent," Delorme said. "Did you know him?"

Rettig shook his head. "Laura told me his name. His first name, anyway. He's the reason we're not together anymore."

"Can you tell us where you were last night?"

Rettig looked at Cardinal and back to Delorme. "Um, sure. I was here all night. All day, too, except for trips to the hardware store. I painted the hallway, hung a couple of mirrors, and then I vegged out in front of the TV."

"Can anyone vouch for any of that?" Cardinal said.

"I didn't have a painting party, if that's what you mean. Well, hang on—I was watching pay-per-view. I watched four episodes of *Mad Men*, one after another. The cable company will have a record, won't they?"

"They should."

"And I did call a friend around nine-thirty, see if he wanted to go for a beer. That was a short call, though."

"Still," Cardinal said, "we'll need his details."

"Shouldn't you be out looking for Laura?"

Delorme sat forward on the couch. "There's some indication your wife was attacked first, Mr. Rettig. Mr. Trent may have been trying to intervene."

"Indication? What, like blood?"

"No. I don't mean to make it worse than it is. She may turn up unharmed, but so far we don't know where she is, and she hasn't used her cellphone, her credit cards or her car."

"You knew she was having an affair before you broke up," Cardinal said. "That must have hurt."

"Hurt? No, I wasn't hurt. I was devastated."

"Laura's, what, thirty-seven, thirty-eight? And you've gotta be, what, sixty?"

"Fifty-eight. Yeah, yeah—big age difference. But we were together eight years. It's not like anything changed or I hid anything from her. I thought she was happy. She seemed happy. Until about a year ago."

"Age difference like that can make a guy feel pretty insecure."

"I never did. Laura never gave me any reason. Until she met that guy."

"That was a year ago?"

"More like eight, nine months. Then everything turned to shit pretty fast."

"You must have been angry."

"Who wouldn't be? Angry was only part of it. Depressed. Humiliated. I was a lot of things. This isn't exactly what I envisioned for myself." He gestured at the tarps, the cramped little room. "I certainly hated this Mark character. But I never met him, never saw him, and I certainly didn't shoot him."

"Nobody said he was shot," Delorme said.

"He wasn't shot? Well, what happened?"

"We won't know until there's an autopsy," Cardinal said. "How much do you weigh, Mr. Rettig?"

"How much do I weigh?"

"How much do you weigh? About one fifty?"

"About one forty-five or so. Why are you— Is this even relevant?"

"It may be."

Delorme stood up. "Mr. Rettig, you mind if I use your bathroom? Lot of coffee this morning."

"Go right ahead. Door on the right, just before the kitchen."

"I realize your life is in turmoil right now," Cardinal said, "but it's essential we have a list of all your wife's contacts—friends, relatives, work people—everyone."

"Well, I'll give you whatever I have, of course, but her laptop or phone would be a better bet for that kind of stuff."

"Did she have any enemies that you know of?"

"Enemies? Laura's a nurse, she doesn't have enemies."

"Well, you may not be aware—the man she was seeing, this Mark Trent, was married. So Mrs. Trent, for example, might not be too fond of her."

Rettig placed his hands on the chair arms, looked up at the ceiling and shook his head. "Laura never told me the guy was married. That's just so crazy. So pointless. Why leave a husband who loves you and looks after you just to . . . Well, you don't need to hear it."

"What about stalkers—old boyfriends, perhaps an angry patient? Anyone like that?"

"Not that I know of."

Delorme reappeared in the doorway.

"All right," Cardinal said. "Just give us all the names you can—that's all we need for now. You understand we're going to have to ask around about you and your wife. We're not looking for dirt, but sometimes it can be unpleasant."

"Just don't get me in trouble at work. I'd like to retire on a full pension, if you don't mind."

"Where do you work?"

"Brunswick Geo."

"Mining?"

"I'm just a CPA. Mostly I deal with the regulation side of things. It ain't cheap being green." He stood up and pointed to a wall of boxes behind Delorme. "I may have an old address book of Laura's. In there."

"While you're looking," Cardinal said, "you mind if we take a look at your car?"

"My car? Jesus." Still, Rettig took the keys from a hook in the vestibule and handed them over.

Cardinal and Delorme went outside and checked Rettig's Prius. There was no sign of any struggle, nor was it excessively clean. Cardinal opened the trunk. He lifted up the carpeting and said, "You find anything interesting during your convenient trip to the washroom?"

"Mr. Rettig is subject to indigestion, gas, diarrhea, constipation, headache, backache, hair loss, anxiety and insomnia."

"You may be mixing it up with my medicine cabinet."

"No," Delorme said, "I'm not."

—

Traffic was slow along Twickenham, owing to a water-main break. Cardinal could feel Delorme looking at him. Not saying anything, just looking. It took ten minutes to get to Algonquin, and once he'd made the turn he said, "All right, what's going through that devious little mind of yours? You think I should have been harder on him?"

"Not really."

"You seem tense. More than usual, I mean."

She loosened her seatbelt and turned in the passenger seat to face him. "Let me ask you something. Do you honestly think Vernon Loach should be lead on this case?"

"Whoa. Okay. Change of pace, there. No, I don't, Lise. You've got the seniority, obviously."

"So why is he?"

"You need to ask Chouinard that."

"Chouinard will say he's an extremely experienced homicide investigator—"

"Which is true—"

"And the only reason he's at constable level is because *everyone*, no matter how experienced, has to start out at constable level."

"Which is also true. Loach has ten years with Toronto Homicide. It'd be dumb to waste that."

"So you *do* think he should be lead."

"No. You have the seniority, not to mention the experience."

"So why'd Chouinard do it?"

"Well, the Toronto thing carries a lot of weight. And apparently Loach did a great job on the Montrose murder down there. Nobody thought they'd get that guy, and he nailed him. I mean, if you're going to apply for a job, that's the way to do it, right after you clear a case like Montrose."

"If he's so damn hot in the big city, why come to Algonquin Bay and start back at detective constable again?"

"Hey, I came from the Toronto force, remember?"

"When you were, what, thirty? Loach is forty-five."

"I believe his wife is from up here originally."

"She lived here for like a week when she was ten. Did you know he's coaching Chouinard's son's hockey team?"

"Chouinard is not gonna let something like that sway him. He's just seeing the Montrose thing. Don't take it personally."

"You know my record, John."

"I do, and I agree it's not fair."

"Really?"

"Of course."

"But you agree with the D.S. that Loach is some kind of super-cop? Pick of the litter?"

"Too early to say."

"So to get taken seriously, I just have to crack a high-profile case."

"Apparently."

"And be male."

—

Laura Lacroix did not show up for work. The entire staff of CID spent the rest of the day interviewing people who knew her. No one had any idea where she might be.

Cardinal ate dinner alone at his kitchen table. Afterward, he went over to Delorme's place and they watched a movie together. They had been doing this for well over a year now, and sometimes Cardinal worried it might be a bad idea. On the other hand, there was no law against being friends with your colleague.

Delorme had rented *The Mission*, Jeremy Irons playing a Jesuit priest who tries to save the souls—and the lives—of the natives he has come to seventeenth-century South America to convert. When the movie ended, they sat in silence for a while watching the final credits roll.

Cardinal turned to Delorme and was halfway through saying he thought it was a pretty good movie before he realized she was crying.

He didn't know what to do. Or if he should do anything at all. Finally he came out with "Really got to you, huh?"

Delorme shrugged. She sat forward on the couch and hid her eyes with one hand and cried harder.

"Lise . . ."

Cardinal went to the kitchen and found a Kleenex box and came back and tapped her knee with it. She clutched at it blindly and pulled out a handful of tissues. She wiped her eyes and blew her nose and said "God" a couple of times, shaking her head.

Cardinal said nothing.

Eventually Delorme said, "I don't think it's the movie."

"No?"

"This Loach thing. Must have hit me harder than I thought. Guess I didn't realize what kind of ego I had—until it got wounded." She took another Kleenex from the box and blew her nose again. "And now I'm going to feel even worse for having cried in front of you."

"Forget it, Lise. We're friends first, colleagues second."

"On the other hand, it could just be hormones."

"Yeah," Cardinal said. "I get those too."

From the Blue Notebook

Before relating exactly what happened to the Arcosaur project, I should say a little about the terrain.

Drift Station Arcosaur (Arctic Ocean Synoptic Automatic Resource) was located on an ice island designated T-6, the T being short for "target"—a taxonomic legacy of the Cold War. We were living on what used to be part of the Ward Hunt Ice Shelf until it snapped off from Ellesmere Island in the mid-fifties and itself became an island. For more than three thousand years it had been attached to Canada, but by 1986 it had circled the polar cap many times, drifting aimlessly—but always clockwise—with the Arctic gyre. It was well to the east of its starting point when we first pitched camp on it, but the grooves and furrows of the surface left no doubt as to its origin: they all ran in the same direction, what used to be east–west when the island was stationary.

Twenty kilometres long and riding ten to fifteen metres higher than the surrounding ice pack, our ice island was selected by the Polar Research Institute because it was big enough to land planes on. Every now and again we would get lodged in the ice pack, only to become mobile with the first change in wind or current, or the first hard knock from another floe. But our radio beacon made us easy to find.

(Point of history: It was thought that Robert Peary mistook an ice island like ours for actual land, which he named Crocker's Land and put on the map. Some have hypothesized that Peary was misled by an Arctic mirage, but such mirages are commonplace and he was far too seasoned an explorer to make that mistake. Just as paleontologists like to discover species, explorers need to discover land. Crocker was Peary's patron. In any case, some years later an exploration party perished as a result of finding nothing at his coordinates but open water.)

Three of us—Wyndham, Vanderbyl and I—had been here since April, along with a few support staff. The others joined us in July. Elongated freshwater lakes—called leads—had formed in the island's grooves, some as long as ten kilometres, and these were a subject of intense biological research. Their blue colour is of a specific tone and brilliance I have seen nowhere else. The eyes of certain Nordic movie stars come to mind.

People who hear about Arctic research—that is, winter research—for the first time express wonder that anyone can stand the isolation, let alone the extreme temperatures. And the prospect of spending months on end in twenty-four-hour darkness they find terribly depressing. But it's actually the Arctic summers that test one's inner resources, at least on an ice island. Even though the temperature may never rise much above freezing, the twenty-four-hour sun turns the surface to slush, sometimes as deep as two feet, making all outdoor activity much harder. Supply planes can no longer land, dramatically increasing the isolation factor, and then there is the sun itself. If an Arctic researcher is going to snap, it will most likely occur on a summer day of blinding light, when he is exhausted from struggling to move equipment even a short distance, when he is wet (and as a result far colder than he ever was in winter) and when restful sleep is a receding memory.

But summer was still months away when Rebecca arrived. The surface was still firm; one could still believe in solidity. I had no reason to be thrown by her simply entering the same room.

Sitting around with Wyndham after dinner one evening, I said, Before I die, I would like to taste Shackleton's whisky. (A crate of it had been discovered beneath the floorboards of his shack.)

They won't allow it, Wyndham said. It'll be preserved for posterity.

He would have wanted us to have a drink.

Wrong pole. Anyway, doesn't enter into it, what Shackleton might have wanted. Didn't realize you were such a lush, he added with a smile.

No human being could dislike Wyndham. Even in the academic/scientific community, so rife with competition—for jobs, for grants, for recognition—so awash with rivers of bad blood, you never heard a bad word about Gord Wyndham, nor did he ever speak harshly of another human being. For that alone he was remarkable, but he was also a first-rate scientist, open-minded yet skeptical, precise, conscientious, generous.

About his family life I knew nothing first-hand, but he was always telling us about his wife, whom he found humorously, delightfully unscientific, and his two young boys, about whom he related stories as if they were anecdotes from the field. I told him he should write a monograph in the style of the old Geographical Society: Some Observations on the Curious Behaviour of Prepubescent Males in the Ottawa Valley. He spoke of them with such a charming combination of love and awe that even I, a person bored to petrifaction by people's families, remember his stories of Phil and Milo—even those names!—with pleasure and affection.

Eleven bottles wrapped in straw and paper dating back to 1907, I said. The Nimrod expedition. A brand no longer in existence. Mackinlay's, if I remember right.

Shame the poor guy never got to drink them himself.

And then:

The smell of Rebecca's hair when she sits in the chair next to mine. Mint and rosemary? Thyme? Some herb or other. She ignores me, as she has been doing the whole first week of her rotation. She has been perfectly friendly to everybody else, and especially to Wyndham, but with me it's been strict radio silence.

I lean toward her, and when she finally registers this invasion of her space and turns to face me, I look her in the eye and call her, ever so quietly, Vostok.

Vostok? She addresses the question not to me but to Wyndham, who is scribbling equations of some kind beside the remains of his scrambled eggs. Why is he calling me Vostok?

Wyndham flips his pencil around to make an erasure and recalculates some figure. Pens tend to be useless up here; ink turns to sludge. He looks up with a startled expression and says, Vostok? Coldest place on Earth, Vostok.

I thought that was Oimyakon in Siberia.

Vostok's the coldest uninhabited.

Rebecca looks at me again. She's wearing a big Irish wool sweater, dark curls spilling over her shoulders. The ivory turtleneck gives her a nunlike air.

Minus 128 degrees F, I tell her. Without the wind chill.

Makes this place seem positively sweltering, Wyndham adds, chasing the last of his eggs round his plate, but Rebecca has left the room.

2

ALL THROUGH THE MORNING MEETING, Detective Sergeant Chouinard sat on the edge of his seat, tapping his ballpoint on his legal pad. One by one the detectives summarized their interviews with the friends, relatives and co-workers of Laura Lacroix. McLeod and Szelagy had talked to people who knew Mark Trent. Cardinal had the impression Chouinard was only half listening, as if he had something he would much rather be talking about.

"Only thing we could find," Szelagy said. "Mark Trent used to work for the We Are One charity foundation in Ottawa. Remember they had that scandal a couple of years ago? He was never charged, but people went to jail. There might be something there."

"Let's follow that up," Loach said. "I can't quite get a reading on Trent's wife. She was so hysterical yesterday I couldn't tell if she was faking or not. My impression is, she knew hubby was screwing around and she was none too happy about it. She's got no alibi, and I'll be talking to her some more. Standing on someone's throat seems personal to me—doesn't seem like something you do to someone involved in financial peccadilloes."

"Is she heavy enough?" Delorme asked.

Loach nodded. "Lady's huge."

"Standing on the guy's throat," Cardinal said. "I've only heard of one case of that. Happened in the psychiatric hospital."

"Good thinking." Loach snapped his fingers. "McLeod, give 'em a call and see if anybody's AWOL."

"Already did," McLeod said, and added, "Your Highness."

"And?"

"All lunatics present and accounted for."

"Fine. Lose the Your Highness shit."

"Right away, Your Majesty."

"I wasn't thinking mental hospitals per se," Cardinal put in. "I was thinking prisons. It's the sort of murder you get when there are no weapons handy. Which would go against the idea it's personal."

Loach shrugged. "Possibly. I still like personal. Guy comes to do Trent. Woman is there and he takes advantage of the unexpected opportunity. At least then we have a motive for her."

"It could be the other way around," Cardinal said. "Guy is lusting after Laura Lacroix, is in the process of abducting her when Trent appears. Kills Trent and takes off."

"Either way, someone had to be keeping a close eye on at least one of them," Loach said. "We've still got lots of people to talk to, so keep going down your lists, and please—everyone—really lean on the idea of followers, stalkers, old boyfriends, girlfriends. Also strangers hanging around asking questions. Ident is still working the scene. With any luck, they'll come up with something that gives us some traction."

Szelagy and McLeod got up to leave.

"Whoa, whoa, whoa," Chouinard said. "Let's not forget we have other cases to work on, people. Szelagy, you've got your construction site thefts. Nobody likes missing dynamite. McLeod, you've got the property damage over on Woodward. Delorme, what do you have on your battered woman?"

"Doesn't want to press charges. Won't tell me the guy's name. Won't even admit she's getting beaten."

"Talk to her again."

"D.S., she doesn't want to talk. You know how these women are."

"Listen to her," McLeod said. "If it was me said that, you'd be calling me a sexist pig."

"For sure I would. And it would be true."

"Enough," Chouinard said. "And while we're talking about battered or missing women, let's not forget Marjorie Flint. The senator's wife disappeared in Ottawa ten days ago and nobody has a clue where she is." He held up an eight-by-ten photo. "You've all seen this. Last seen wearing a black cashmere coat, Hermès scarf, high-heel boots."

"She have any connection to Algonquin Bay?" Loach asked.

"None. But she's a senator's wife. That makes her national. Keep your eyes open, people."

~

As far as Lise Delorme was concerned, one of the most annoying things about Loach having been imported was that they really needed another woman in CID. Being the only female meant Delorme was automatically assigned all the sexual assaults and all the battered wife cases, and she was frankly sick of them.

When she first joined, she had looked forward to being a champion of victimized women, and indeed over the years she had had the satisfaction of locking up several abusive husbands and at least three rapists. But there had been two big shocks in store for Delorme. First was the number of cases where the woman (girl, more like it) was actually lying; there was no assault, she was just angry and out for revenge. The saddest effect of this was that it tended to undermine the credibility of genuine victims.

The other shock was the number of women who chose not to press charges—and not only not press charges but to go back to the men who beat them, to go on living with them in the hope they would change. Delorme knew about the syndrome but she could not get over what a grip it had on women who in every other way seemed, well, rational.

Miranda Heap was forty-five and good-looking, and she ran a business services concern that so far had managed to thrive in a niche that was too small for the big-city competition to bother with. She did most of her work out of her home office, and that was where Delorme found her.

"Your face looks much better," Delorme said.

"Yes, not so much like a raccoon now. Amazing what a little foundation can do. Would you like a coffee? I'm about due for a break."

"No, that's okay. I just stopped by to see how you were getting on."

"I'm fine. Really, I think I kind of overreacted."

"No, you didn't. He hurt you. You should tell me his name so we can press charges."

"He didn't mean to hurt me. He's just a passionate guy, that's all. That's part of the attraction, you know? A big part. It's hard for you to understand because you've never met him."

"Tell me his name, I'll go meet him right now."

Miranda laughed. "You'd probably get along great. You're obviously passionate too."

"Passionate is not the same as violent. Are you gonna let him keep hitting you just because he's good in bed?"

"You've only seen the very worst of him. He hates that part of himself too. He's so ashamed after. He purposely waits until he knows I'm out and then he leaves these incredibly long, heartfelt phone messages. Really. His apologies are masterpieces."

"I imagine he gets a lot of practice."

"You would never guess from meeting him that he could lose control that way. He's so intelligent, so generous—a good, good man in lots of ways."

"For all the difference it makes. Did you ever contact the therapist I recommended?"

"I did, I did. And she's great. I've been seeing her twice a week. I know she's doing me good, so I have to thank you for that. Really."

~

"That's the thing about women," Delorme said when she met Cardinal at the coffee shop. "We have an endless capacity to fool ourselves. To see what we want to see—and nothing else—especially when it comes to men. I do it myself."

"No, you don't." He might have said a little more on the subject, but he could see she was in no mood. "Listen, I had a very interesting name come up in one of my interviews."

"Who've you got?"

"Were you going to order a coffee?"

"Lineup's too long. Tell me on the way."

They went outside and got in the car and Cardinal drove up toward Airport Hill. "I finally got to speak to Laura Lacroix's best friend—Mia

Neff? Hasn't heard from her. Has no idea where she might be. She's the most upset of anyone I've seen so far. Says this is totally out of character—the vanishing, that is, not the affair. Miss Neff knew all about the marriage breakup and the fling with Trent. Turns out that the love affair wasn't so out of character."

"Oh?"

"Apparently the former Mrs. Rettig had another love interest before she took up with Mark Trent."

"That who we're going to see?"

"Leonard Priest."

"You're kidding," Delorme said. "Are you serious?"

"I've got no reason to doubt this woman. Everyone agrees she and Laura were best friends. She said right off no one else knew about it."

"Leonard Priest," Delorme said. "Wow. This just got a whole lot more interesting. Man, I would love to nail that bastard."

"Tell me about it. I thought I had him for Choquette."

Régine Choquette had been murdered in a boathouse on Trout Lake. She was found chained to an overhead beam, and nude, except for a zippered leather hood that covered her face. The weight of the evidence suggested that an evening of highly charged sadomasochism had got out of hand and ended in her being shot between the eyes with a Nazi-era Luger.

"I never understood why the Crown didn't charge him. It was Garth Romney, wasn't it?"

"Assistant Crown. Yeah, it was Garth."

"I remember that picture of him holding up that mask. Fighting the forces of evil."

"Don't get me started. Take a look in that envelope on the back seat."

Delorme undid her seatbelt and reached around. She opened the envelope and took out two eight-by-tens.

"See any resemblance?"

"Both long blond hair, wavy. Both have brown eyes, natural eyebrows, good cheekbones. Could both definitely appeal to the same guy."

"Both small framed as well. Five-two for Régine, five-four for Laura Lacroix."

"But I thought Priest sold his house up here—after all the trouble."

"Nope. And apparently he was in town this weekend. Miss Neff saw him at the Quiet Pint on Friday night."

"Leonard Priest," Delorme said again. "Wow."

They drove up Airport Road and then took a number of smaller streets until they got to a dead end called Crosier Place. There was only one house, a tall cedar A-frame that to Delorme's eyes looked as if it belonged in Switzerland. A Jaguar X-Type gleamed in the drive.

Cardinal pulled in and parked behind the Jaguar and switched off the ignition. Usually the two of them would decide in the car who would do most of the talking, but she got out and went straight up to the side door and pushed the doorbell.

Cardinal came up behind. "You in a rush?"

"Aren't you?"

The door opened and Leonard Priest was there, holding a cellphone to one ear and looking annoyed. He snapped the cellphone shut and slipped it into his shirt pocket. "Yes?"

Delorme started to introduce herself, but Priest recognized both of them before she finished.

"No, thank you," he said. "Don't want any."

Delorme stopped the door with her foot. "We just need to ask you a few questions."

"I don't care. Move your foot, you're freezing the place out."

"About Laura Lacroix."

"I still don't care. Now do me a favour and fuck off out of it." A dozen years back in Canada had done nothing to soften the London accent. Not to mention the rock-star attitude.

"Mr. Priest, it's just a few questions. A woman has gone missing—under violent circumstances—and we're talking to everyone who knows her. Why make it such a big deal?"

This time Priest spoke to Cardinal. "You tried to put me away. And now you come round here expecting me to be delighted to see you?"

"No, I expected you to behave like an asshole," Cardinal said. "You're not disappointing me."

Priest took out the cellphone again and pressed a button. "I have my lawyer on speed-dial."

"Really," Delorme said. "You must be so proud."

—

"We'll never get a subpoena with what we've got at this point," Cardinal said in the car. "A single person's hearsay that he once went out with Laura Lacroix."

"I know. He knows it too. He has a great accent, though, I'll give him that."

"You know he's actually from here originally, right? Moved to England with his parents when he was a kid. Moved back here after his band broke up. It's funny who moves back here. Guy like that, you'd think he'd stay in London or Los Angeles or somewhere."

Cardinal made the turn and headed downhill. He had to stop again at the highway intersection. It was a long light and they sat there in silence. Then it was finally green and they were on Algonquin.

"I seem to remember Priest made a pass at you during the trial," Cardinal said.

"More than one."

"Yeah, I think you might be his type. Régine Choquette and Laura Lacroix? You have the same colour hair, same colour eyes, about the same height. Same age too, pretty much. And look at their last names."

"Choquette. Lacroix. *Bon, donc, nous sommes toutes les trois Canadiennes-françaises. Trois soeurs.* All French Canadians look alike now?"

"No, but all three of you do look French-Canadian."

"You think I should cozy up to him? Dinner and a movie and wearing a wire the whole time?"

"Hell, no. He'd find the wire too fast."

"Very funny."

From the Blue Notebook

There is something ludicrous about a man shovelling snow in the Arctic. Wyndham had a photograph tacked above his desk of him and me doing just that. We were out there day and night, along with one or two of the others, sometimes with shovels, other times on our knees poking about with implements smaller than kitchen spatulas.

Snow cover on T-6 averaged about three feet. And yet the polar ice cap is a desert. Most areas receive less than eight inches of precipitation a year, but whatever comes stays. Snowstorms are most often a matter of blowing snow, not falling snow, but they can play havoc with a runway. Keeping the huts and equipment in running order fell to old Arctic hand Murray Washburn, but keeping our landing strip clear was the responsibility of Hunter Oklaga, an Inuit and former Army Ranger who was possibly the only man alive—and certainly the only man among us—who had parachuted into both the Antarctic and the Arctic, feats none of us yearned to duplicate. If anyone voiced discomfort with the environment, he would say, You're crazy, man. You should try Laurie Island. Antarctica? Now, *that's* cold. This is Miami we're in here.

We were less than eight hundred miles from the Pole.

"Hunter" was a translation of a nine-syllable name no English-speaking person could even remember, let alone pronounce. Hunter told me it actually meant "hunter with impressive penis" but he hadn't liked to adopt the second noun for everyday use. He was a cheery, chatty sort, always showing me photographs from the

Antarctic and other expeditions he'd been on. I think it was because he knew I was a former bush pilot and was under the mistaken impression that I was cut from the same rough-and-ready cloth. All his photos had been taken on sunny days.

There aren't that many photographs from Arcosaur, and most of the ones I've seen look black-and-white. But they are not; it's simply a reflection of the weather, which was so often overcast. The tallest object in every shot is the sixty-foot radio mast, barnacled with instruments. One becomes inured to the crudeness of an ice station. I don't notice it in memory, only in photographs. Empty fuel drums. We made no effort to corral them. They got blown from place to place like so much tumbleweed until they got snowed into place, some canted on end, others lengthwise.

We set boards on top of spent drums weighted with sea water, creating an elevated walkway between the radio shack and the lab and the sleeping quarters. Even so, we sometimes had to clear away high drifts. I remember a shot of Rebecca—it must have been a warm day—sitting on the walkway, the antenna rising like an ugly Eiffel Tower in the background. She is eating an apple and mostly has her back to the camera. Her red down vest the only colour in the picture. Dark hair lifting in a slight breeze.

There's another one of Ray Deville, looking shaggy and unshaven in front of one of the AARI buoys. He's going down on one knee, arms spread wide in the classic posture of the big Broadway number, huge grin on his face. Next to the buoy sits a Nansen sled loaded with crates of dynamite destined for the seismic ridge and a series of reflection experiments. The picture is the only instance I can think of where Ray is smiling.

Somewhere online there is a shot of the supply plane landing. Sky pale grey at the zenith, deeper grey at the horizon. The snow and ice scalloped and torn into strips of grey on grey, almost white in the foreground. The whitest object is a cloud hugging the NE horizon. It isn't a cloud at all, of course, but a windstorm. Wyndham stands in the middle of the shot cradling a twelve-gauge. We were having a lot of trouble with bears at the time.

Rebecca. Seated in the pale wash of light from one of the porthole windows. It's not a photograph—I was never a photographer and have frankly never understood shutterbugs—but the image is as fixed in my mind as a studio portrait: Rebecca in jeans and that ivory turtleneck, reading a volume of poems. I'm noodling calculations in my notebook. I've been growing increasingly alarmed at some of the findings, and I'm trying, not very hard at this moment, to find the errors.

I don't know anyone who reads poems, I say.

She doesn't respond. The place is silent except for the thrum of the generator. It's early in a new six-week rotation and everyone is somewhere else, perhaps watching a video of a ball game that took place weeks ago. Perhaps working. People fall into odd patterns when there is no night. The first day there is a kind of exhilaration at the unlooked-for escape from the dark. Many stay up until fatigue finally drives them to bed and a fitful sleep. Scientists go out at all hours.

I put aside the notebook and stand before her and slip my hand into the masses of curls. The warmth of her face against my wrist. She doesn't move. Doesn't look up.

Do you always just take what you want?

I can't, in this case. That would be your heart.

It's taken.

That's not how it looks.

Lots of things are more complicated than they look.

She has her finger under the next page, ready to turn. The paper trembling. There are pencil marks next to a couple of lines of verse: *Let me break/ Let me make/ something ragged, something raw/ Something difficult to take.*

I remove my hand from her hair and lean down. So close I can smell her hair, her skin, the ghost of cedar from her sweater. I know she can feel my breath on her ear as I whisper one word.

Vostok.

3

Assistant Crown Attorney Garth Romney took a stack of files from a cabinet and put them into a cardboard box that was open on his chair. After eight years as a prosecutor, he was being elevated to the bench of the Superior Court. "I can't tell you how good it feels to transfer these cases to someone else. Two more weeks here and then I have a month in Tuscany," he told them. "And next time you see me I'll be on the bench, with a very good tan."

Cardinal told him why they were there.

"You're nowhere near a subpoena. The fact that you had a date a year ago with a woman who is now missing does not make you a suspect, even if you're Leonard Priest."

"The missing woman looks a lot like Régine Choquette."

"Ah, yes. Régine Choquette." Romney moved the box of files to the floor and sat at his desk. He opened a manila folder and quickly closed it again. "Régine Choquette broke my heart. I would've loved to nail Leonard Priest for that—if we'd had the evidence."

"I thought we did," Cardinal said.

"I know you did. But you're not the one whose ass is in a sling if the judge decides the Crown has brought a meritless charge."

"We had an eyewitness who put Priest at the scene. He saw Priest and Reicher coming down the path to the boathouse just as he was leaving."

"You're referring to Thomas Waite. But Thomas Waite did not see Régine Choquette. He *claimed* he saw Leonard Priest and Fritz Reicher. And then his memory got mysteriously foggy."

"Yes, because a few weeks earlier, Leonard Priest had Reicher dress up like a Nazi and tie the guy up and beat him within an inch of his life. Priest's idea of foreplay. Waite was convinced he'd be dead if he hadn't managed to escape."

"Prior action. Not admissible unless the defence brought it up, and Priest's lawyers were far too smart for that. Plus Waite did not report the incident when it occurred."

"That's not unusual for victims of sex crimes," Delorme said.

"Look, the guy changed his mind and there's nothing I can do about that. It's irrelevant now anyway, seeing as he's dead."

"What? When did this happen?" Cardinal said.

"I don't know, six months ago. Blood clot, apparently."

"But there was Fritz Reicher," Delorme said. "In his statements to us he said the whole thing was Priest's idea. Priest ordered him to shoot."

"Courts are extremely reluctant to convict where the sole evidence is the testimony of an accomplice—especially a murdering accomplice. And that's when they're under *oath*. Fritz Reicher was not under oath when he made those statements, and you seem to forget that he recanted and then refused to ever open his mouth against Priest again."

"We had Priest's prints at the scene," Cardinal said. "That alone—"

"From a previous *occasion*," Romney said. "Priest never denied being there. Never denied having sex in that horrible place. He just denied being there on the night in question."

"We could have gotten Reicher to turn," Delorme said. "To go back to his initial statement. You could have offered him a better deal."

Romney laughed. "Did you ever meet Reicher?"

"Once in chambers for depositions, that's all."

"Fritz Reicher—aside from having a remarkably low IQ—was a known fantasist, and that's putting it kindly. All sorts of claims about his background and huge ideas about the future, both unencumbered by any connection to reality. He would have made the world's worst witness—he had the affect of a zombie and an accent right out of the Berlin bunker."

"The Luger was found at one of Priest's sex clubs," Cardinal pointed out.

"A club where Reicher was *employed.* He had twenty-four-hour access to the Ottawa club. And they were Reicher's prints on that gun, not Priest's. Please. I know you both as first-rate investigators, but it was a weak case against Priest two years ago and it's a lot weaker now." Romney stood up and transferred the cardboard box back to his chair. "I frankly don't even know why you're here."

"Because you and I have presented a lot of cases together," Cardinal said, "and we usually see eye to eye. It wasn't like you to give Priest a free pass."

Romney slammed a stack of files into the box. "The Charter of Rights and Freedoms gave him the free pass. The facts gave him the free pass. Do you seriously think I'd not press charges if I thought we had a case? You think the guy paid me off or something?"

"I might," Cardinal said, "if it was somebody else. But you enjoy winning too much."

"Exactly. And now I get to enjoy judging."

~

Delorme had been in front of the mirror for more than half an hour, going systematically through the work side of her wardrobe. She pulled out one of her more sober ensembles. Grey suit, white open-collar blouse—probably the most unsexy outfit in her possession. She had worn it to court more than once.

She considered the effect.

She took off the jacket and exchanged the blouse for a silky dark top. Still prim, but with a lot more neck and throat. She changed her mind again and went for severe.

~

Leonard Priest was mostly known for his former association with an English fusion band called Ward Nine. He was not the front man—that honour had belonged to a berserker named Patch who had died of a heart attack at the age of thirty-two—but Priest had been a solid rhythm guitarist and the only member with the slightest head for business. Ward Nine's flame had burned but briefly, and once Patch was gone the flame expired and the fans went home.

After Priest moved back to Canada, he turned his business acumen and entertainment know-how to the creation of a series of highly successful nightclubs in Toronto, Montreal and Ottawa. Other types of clubs followed, and one or two restaurants. His business presence in Algonquin Bay amounted to a single enterprise, a modest English-style pub called the Quiet Pint. The local paper had interviewed him when it opened and asked him why a nightclub mogul—a man with flourishing enterprises in big cities—would choose to come back to the north, even if he was from there originally. He wanted a refuge, he had said. He loved the quiet of the north. It reminded him of his childhood.

The pub was on a side street, a few doors from the public library. The small parking lot was empty and Delorme parked right by the building, under a sign that promised *No Television!*

She had come to the Quiet Pint once in the course of the Choquette investigation, never as a patron. It hadn't changed: dark wooden booths along one wall, scattered tables in the centre and a couple of plush banquettes at the front. A gas fireplace put out considerable heat. Two young couples were giggling in one of the booths and a middle-aged man sat at a centre table, but the only other people in the place were the bartender and a waitress crisply turned out in a white blouse and a very short plaid skirt. A jukebox was playing Blue Rodeo at low volume. Quiet pint indeed.

Delorme sat toward one end of the bar under a hanging light and ordered a glass of red wine. She pulled a sheaf of papers from her briefcase. She read a memo on staff parking, another on cubicle decoration, and an office circular, impossibly prolix, concerning a New Year's charity event.

"Can I buy you a drink?"

It was the man from the centre table. He had an elongated, hound-dog face, with the eyes of one who expects rejection.

"No, thank you," Delorme said, and patted her papers. "I really have to read this stuff."

"Why would anyone try to work in a pub?"

"It's where I want to work."

"Uh-huh. Sure."

The man went away and Delorme watched in the bartender's mirror as he left the pub. Another couple joined the four in front and the noise level went up a notch. The music had switched to Sarah McLachlan and Delorme was on her second glass of wine when Priest came in. She remembered this about his routine from two years ago: nine o'clock he would come in and sit at the end of the bar for an hour.

She didn't look up as he greeted the bartender and ordered a Guinness. Cold air wafted from his coat as he removed it and hung it on a hook under the bar. The bartender brought his beer and they talked about the day's receipts and some inventory issues. Then the bartender went to make drinks for the waitress, and Delorme, although she was half turned away from him, sensed that Priest was looking at her.

She took a sip of her wine and turned a page. She reached for her briefcase and pulled out a ballpoint and made a note on the paper.

Priest came over and stood beside her. "What are you doing in my pub?"

"I thought *pub* was short for *public*."

"You're not public, you're police. What are you doing here?"

"I'm not on duty, if that's what you're worried about."

"Bollocks. The briefcase? The don't-fuck-with-me suit? You look like you're about to tell a lot of lies under oath and sell some poor sod down the river."

"That isn't what I do for a living."

"You going to harass me at my place of work? Is that your plan?"

"At the moment, I'd say it's the other way around. I don't see you cross-examining the group up front."

"They're not the Old Bill, are they. You've never set foot in here before. What are you doing here now?"

Delorme lifted her papers. "I'm reading some stuff I've been putting off for weeks and I'm having a glass of wine. I was actually enjoying it until you came along—the wine, anyway."

Priest folded his arms and went completely still, looking at her. His eyes scanning Delorme's face, the topography of her deception. Priest's own face was angular, expressionist: twin deltas for eyebrows, architectural cheekbones, his eyes high-intensity blue.

Delorme turned to her papers again and reread a memo on the protocol of assisting the Children's Aid Society in the removal of children from abusive homes.

Priest pointed at Delorme's wineglass and said to the bartender, "On me, Tommy."

"No, no." Delorme's hand automatically covered her glass. "That's all right."

"Thought you were off-duty."

"I am. I just prefer to buy my own drinks."

"Course you do. Evidence is useless if you've been accepting favours. Otherwise, why turn down a friendly gesture?"

"It isn't friendly."

He turned his face to the bartender again. "On me, Tommy. Anything she leaves is yours."

He went back to his Guinness at the end of the bar.

Delorme shook her head at the bartender and he shrugged. He was just a kid. College age.

Delorme stared at her papers a while longer, and came to the conclusion that coming to Leonard Priest's bar was one of the most boneheaded ideas she'd ever had. She took out her wallet and asked for the check.

The bartender smiled and shook his head.

Delorme put fifteen dollars on the bar and pushed it toward him. She put her papers in the briefcase and reached for her coat and put it on. When she turned around, Priest was in front of her.

"You want to talk about Laura Lacroix?"

"Like I said, I'm not on duty . . ."

"You want to talk about Laura Lacroix, we'll sit at that table and do it right now." He pointed to a small table beside the gas fireplace.

"All right."

Priest went to the table and pulled out a chair for her. Delorme took off her coat again and sat down. Priest gestured to the bartender for drinks and sat down.

"I don't need any more wine," Delorme said.

Priest paid no attention. "I know very little about Laura Lacroix. I saw her exactly four times. What do you want to know?"

"When was the last time you saw her?"

"I'd have to look up the exact date, but it was about a year ago, maybe a little less. At Club Risqué in Ottawa."

"Your sex club."

"One of them." The bartender brought their drinks and put them on the table. "Thanks, Tommy."

"Did she go there with you?"

"Get your hand off my cock."

"Pardon me?"

"Get your hand off my cock, you trollop."

"You think I'm wearing a wire?"

Priest smiled and folded his arms, muscles at ease under a tight ribbed sweater. Delorme could see why women went for him. He was a compelling presence.

"As far as I know, Laura arrived on her own—unaccompanied women have no trouble getting into the club. I had already told her I didn't want to see her again. I don't have sex with the patrons of my clubs—not at the clubs, not when they're paying. It's too complex legally." He took a sip of his beer and placed it back on its Guinness coaster. "She arrived alone. I did not expect to see her there and I was not happy about it. She wanted to talk, but I said no, I'd made my position clear and I had work to do. Have you been to the club?"

"I've seen it," Delorme said. "Not when there were people there."

"Had to add that, did you? Case I might think you actually had sex?"

"To let you know I haven't seen your club in operation."

"What did you think?"

Delorme shrugged. "It was nicer than I expected. Physically."

"Morally, of course, you found it repugnant, good Catholic girl like you."

Delorme shook her head and took a sip of her wine before she remembered she wasn't going to drink any more. "Did you ever play with magnets as a kid? You know that feeling when you try to put two positive poles together? Or two negatives? You can't make them quite meet? That's how it felt."

"I think that's called nerves."

"It's called knowing who you are."

He lifted his glass, as if to toast self-knowledge. "So I made myself busy in the office for a while. I avoided the woman for the next couple of hours, all right? She had a bit to drink, but we do not let our patrons get drunk. We don't want people passing out or claiming they weren't in a position to consent.

"Next time I saw her, she was in the Tudor Room with one guy fucking her from behind while she sucked the guy in front of her. There were three other fellas all stroking themselves, and two or three couples on the sidelines who stopped every once in a while to watch. Have you ever watched people having sex up close?"

"Let's stick to Laura Lacroix."

"You're asking me about sex. Why can't I ask you?"

"You did ask, and I answered."

"You've wanted to. You've thought about it. Probably dreamed about it. Maybe listened to another couple at one time or another. You do admit to being human, right?"

"My ideas on what's human are probably different from yours. Are you going to finish telling me what happened? Because it's getting late and I do have to work tomorrow."

"You're joking. You wouldn't miss this for anything. Because I'll tell you something, darlin', you may not be wearing any perfume, and you do a reasonable pretence of being totally unacquainted with sexual desire, but you absolutely reek of ambition. It comes off you like a pheromone." He raised his chin and closed his eyes as if sampling the nose of a fine Bordeaux, nostrils flaring. "Yes—ambition. Definitely. Lusting to trap the big bad wolf, protect the innocent little virgins of this world. Admit it."

"It's my job. I try to be good at it."

"I enjoy my work too." He shook his head as if to clear it. "The men took their turns. Each one would fuck her for a while, then they'd move around, so she must have been tasting a good deal of herself on those men—that's a turn-on for a lot of women, as I'm sure you've noticed. And then eventually she sat back in a receptive position and they gave her the seminal equivalent of a tickertape parade."

Delorme rested her forearm on the table and leaned forward. She spoke quietly, evenly, trying to say only what she intended and nothing more. "This person you're talking about, Laura Lacroix? She's missing. There's good reason to think she has been murdered or soon will be, and I have to ask you to please—please—not dishonour whatever small part of yourself may still be at risk of such a thing by lying about her."

Priest's eyebrows shot up. "Lying? This was a year ago, nigh on—there's no reason to lie."

"I'm just asking you not to exaggerate for effect. You're obviously enjoying trying to make me uncomfortable."

"The subject matter does that all by itself. You can't blame me."

"Were you surprised by her behaviour?"

"Totally. I had sex with her exactly twice. Plain vanilla. But she started making a pest of herself, phoning me, showing up here—I didn't like it.

"As for her performance at the club—maybe she thought she would make me jealous? Or maybe it was just that once she started fucking around on her husband, she couldn't stop? Or maybe she thought she could pique my interest with a display of virtuosity? You're a woman, you tell me."

"Can you give me the names of the men who had sex with her?"

"You're clinically insane, you are. People who come to the Risqué clubs do not expect to have their names bandied about in a cavalier manner. I didn't recognize any of the men involved, I've no idea if they arrived in a group or separately, and I wouldn't give you their names if I knew them. You think some stranger who fucked her in a club a year ago suddenly decides to come up north and carry her off? You're not getting any names from me, sunshine. End of story."

Delorme held up her hands in a "stop" gesture. "Off-duty, remember? I didn't ask you to talk to me. You offered."

"Because I don't want junior detectives hanging round my bloody pub, do I? Or did you think I just fancied your gorgeous arse?" Priest dipped his head slightly, flecks of firelight in his eyes. "D'you like it up the arse, by the way?"

"Did Laura ever mention a guy named Mark Trent?"

"French-Canadian girls love it, in my observation. Legacy of the Vatican. Nothing like a taboo to get people hot and bothered. And you do have a gorgeous arse, must be said."

"Pretty childish, talking dirty all the time."

Priest leaned forward and spoke in the urgent whisper of one imparting confidential information. "It won't be gorgeous forever, will it? So may as well make the best of it while you can. My official diagnosis? ODD. Orgasm Deficit Disorder. Left untreated, it'll only get worse. You'll end up a bad-tempered old crone reeking of mothballs and cat's piss."

"Are you going to tell me how you met Laura Lacroix?"

"Sorry." Priest stood up and turned to the bartender. "If she tries to pay, smack her."

—

"Tell me something," Ronnie Babstock said, pouring more wine into Cardinal's glass. "Do you believe in ghosts?"

"No. I don't believe Elvis is alive, either."

Babstock turned his glass, as if considering all the colours in the burgundy spectrum. "But don't you ever think about it? I never did until Evelyn died, but I do now. I sometimes wonder if she's . . . I don't know. Don't you wonder about your wife?"

Cardinal and Babstock had been friends in high school—always on good terms, although never close. They had lost touch for many years. Cardinal became a cop in Toronto and later in Algonquin Bay, and Babstock had gone on to a glorious career in industry, eventually founding a robotics company that had been a prime contributor to the space shuttle programme and the exploration of Mars. It was one of the few companies in Ontario that still actually employed people to make things.

Cardinal was once again struck by the variegated nature of those people who chose to come back to Algonquin Bay. In fact, Cardinal's own decision to return, after ten years with the Toronto police, had surprised him. And who would have expected the likes of Leonard Priest or Ronnie Babstock?

Babstock had stunned the high-tech world by moving his company to this pocket of the near north, more than ten years ago now. He hadn't got in touch with Cardinal at the time, and Cardinal didn't even consider contacting him; his old schoolmate had moved into a different class.

But then they both became widowers within months of each other, and Cardinal had been surprised—and touched—to receive a sympathy card signed *your old friend, Ronnie Babstock*. A couple of months later, Babstock had called him at work and they went out for a beer and a burger.

Cardinal didn't expect much; they'd led such different lives. But they were both newly widowed, both with grown daughters, both in their late fifties—and they discovered they enjoyed one another's company. They found they could even talk politics, something Cardinal avoided with pretty much everyone.

"You know, you're amazingly liberal for a cop," Babstock had said.

"And you're amazingly liberal for a businessman."

"That's Evelyn's influence. And Hayley's—my overeducated daughter. I'd probably be a lot richer if I never listened to them, but I'd've been a lot more miserable too."

Babstock had become known as a philanthropist and had put his money behind major international initiatives as well as local improvements to the main street and the waterfront. Cardinal had come to have tremendous respect for him.

"I'm glad you called me, Ronnie," Cardinal had said when they were parting that first time. "Why did you?"

"Hell, I don't know. Suddenly you're fifty-eight and you haven't paid any attention to friendships for thirty, forty years and you wake up in the bloody Yukon—psychologically, I mean. That's probably why I called you, to be honest. Gets fucking lonely."

It sent a chill through Cardinal to hear a man admit to loneliness. He never used the word about himself. But he knew what Ronnie meant. Friendships suddenly matter a lot more when you live alone. He didn't know what he would have done if Delorme hadn't somehow managed to become his buddy over the past two years.

"You're ignoring the question," Ronnie was saying now. "If I tell you I sometimes think Evelyn's trying to contact me, you just think that's nuts, right? You never wonder that way about . . . ?"

"I miss Catherine. I miss her every day. I don't suppose that'll ever stop. But we had our life together and now it's over and . . ."

"And what?"

A pretty young woman came into the dining room and asked if they would like more dessert.

"No thanks, Esmé. That was delicious. Just clear everything away and you can be off."

Cardinal had been having dinner at Babstock's place once a month for going on a year, and he still wasn't sure if Esmé was a maid or a caterer or a niece. Babstock always treated her with respect but betrayed no interest beyond that. Caterer, Cardinal decided. The meals were always perfect, and he enjoyed their quiet conversations before the others—one the architect who had designed Babstock's house, the other a major at the local radar installation—arrived after dinner and proceeded to beat both of them at stud poker.

"Fabulous meal," Cardinal said. He tapped his wineglass with a fingernail. "Wine too."

"You never thought Catherine might be trying to get in touch with you?"

"No, Ron. Why, has Evelyn been phoning you?"

"Phoning, no. But I hear her voice sometimes. I think I do. I mean, it's bad enough I even saw a doctor about it."

"What did he say?"

"Stress, of course. Overwork."

"Well?"

"Okay, I'll stop. I'm being silly. Let's move."

Cardinal followed him into the game room. Babstock's house was a series of rectangles, mostly glass, overlooking Lake Nipissing. The lights of Algonquin Bay glittered across the frozen lake, making it look a much larger city than it was. Babstock had another house in town, but Cardinal had never visited him there.

They sat at the poker table and Babstock patted his pockets for his reading glasses. "Oh, listen—before I forget—I want you to come to my party."

"It's nice of you to ask, but I'm really not a party person."

"I don't want party people. I want real people. Feel free to bring someone, of course. Are you seeing anyone?"

"Not just at the moment."

"What about that detective colleague you told me about? Why not bring her? You said you like her."

"Lise is even less of a party person than I am."

"All the better. Be good for both of you. Listen, what did you make of that case in California? That little girl missing for eight years."

Babstock made a charming effort to be up on crimes Cardinal might be interested in—no matter how far afield they had occurred. This was a California case in which a child had been abducted at age two. Her mother recognized her eight years later, now age ten, at a playground in a different city. DNA tests confirmed her identity, and the couple who had stolen her were now in federal prison. Cardinal hadn't paid much attention.

"Of course, what I really want to ask you about is this motel murder. But I know you can't talk about it."

"'Fraid not. Ongoing investigation."

"I know, I know. There's the doorbell. Come to my party, John. Meanwhile, get ready to part with a serious amount of cash."

From the Blue Notebook

Back in the winter, when the plane deposited Wyndham and me and the construction crew on T-6, we had somehow contrived in that polar darkness to assemble the prefabricated structure of the mess hall in such a way that it ended up with an extra stub of a room, a kind of alcove. I had dragged one of the more comfortable chairs into it and stacked some of my books around it. I liked to sit there at night and read.

Rebecca (this was weeks later) was doing a crossword in the mess. Of all of us, Rebecca was the one most able to keep to a regular schedule despite the unending twilight. When she was finished recording and sorting her data for the day, she devoted her evenings to crosswords, board games or reading. I was in my alcove, from where I could see Wyndham but not Rebecca. He was tinkering with his laptop, trying to improve the insulation pack around his jerry-rigged car battery. We weren't supposed to do such things in the mess, but Wyndham always did.

I don't know which of them started it—probably Wyndham, who was always good for a philosophical ramble—but they were talking about different kinds of cold. For some reason their easy conversation put me in a sneering mood and I couldn't focus on my book. Rebecca told a story about a young monk who travelled thousands of miles to study under a great Zen master.

Rebecca's voice in the twilight:

The master told the student to sit still and meditate. Told him to meditate every day. Told him to meditate his every waking hour, to ignore everything else in the world except for the demands of nourishment and sleep.

I couldn't see her, but I pictured her face, her mouth. Full lips forming the words.

So the student meditated for months on end—until he was exhausted, wasting away. Time and again he would go to the master and say, Why have I not attained enlightenment? I have done everything you say. The master grew angry and told him not to come bothering him with any more complaints. Not to come to him at all until he attained enlightenment.

I know how this ends, I thought. I was half tempted to heckle.

The student went away and managed to stick with it for another month. Then he climbed up the hill to the master once more, and all he wanted to ask was, Am I nearly there? Am I making any progress at all? Is there the slightest hope? But the moment he began to speak, the master pulled out his sword. With a single motion—it flashed just once in the sunlight—he cut off the student's finger.

Stunned, howling, the student staggered back from the master, turned and stumbled down the hill. He hadn't gone far when the master shouted his name. The student stopped, clutching his bleeding knuckle, and looked back up the hill. The master slowly raised his hand and, with a smile of utter bliss on his face, wagged his own index finger.

Rebecca paused, and I knew she was demonstrating to Wyndham. Wyndham looking up from his task to see her imperturbable face. Beautiful slender finger wagging at him.

And at that moment, she said, the student attained enlightenment.

Ah, yes, said Wyndham, a very different kind of cold.

My regard for religion, any religion, has always been low, but Zen Buddhism—perhaps because it is fashionable in those urban enclaves where fashion is everything—seemed to me particularly bogus, precious, its masters the spiritual equivalent of mimes. As for sub-zero pedagogy, the High Arctic is the coldest teacher of them all—I have lost far more than a finger under its instruction—but I have yet to attain even a modicum of wisdom, let alone enlightenment, for all its fabulous array of blades.

Not like Vostok, Wyndham added.

Rebecca's laugh, brief, throaty. Not like Vostok at all.

Oh, smug! Oh, Annex! I thought, my sneering still at full roar when it was blown from me as if by a sudden blast, a shock wave that rolled outward from their easy concord. It had been stupid of me to imagine Rebecca and I sharing the warmth of that unspoken *contra mundum* attitude that seems to envelop certain couples.

A few days later, I changed my mind yet again. We had a globe at Arcosaur, quite a big one. Close to the poles, there's nothing like a globe to give a proper sense of geographical relationships. But I had another globe of my own that I kept on display in my area of the lab. It was a scruffy, disreputable-looking thing I had picked up at a flea market. (I am a frequenter of such places when in a big city, not because I have any expertise or love for antiques, but because I have a certain affection for things that survive, especially if they survive for no apparent reason.) The market stall had two globes on display, high school models of the same vintage. One of them was the familiar blue and white sphere interrupted by nations of less natural shape and colour, many with vanished names. Siam. Yugoslavia. The GDR.

Someone had painted the other globe, an identical high school model, matte black.

How much is that? I said to the vendor. It looks like something they'd use in a TV version of *Hamlet*.

He looked at the black sphere and back at me. Three bucks.

My black Earth went with me on all my travels after that. Whenever people would ask me about it, and they invariably did, I would give them different answers.

What is that? Rebecca was standing behind me in the lab. I could smell the faint cucumbery scent of her hand lotion.

My mother, I said.

It's like something from *Hamlet*, she said. If it had been written for television.

4

DELORME PARKED IN THE LOT of the Algonquin Bay Public Library and got out of the car with her hood up. She took her briefcase from the back seat and shut the door. She walked as far as the sidewalk and looked across the street. A half-dozen cars were parked behind the Quiet Pint, none that she recognized. The night was cold, snowless. From somewhere, the repeated grinding of a car engine refusing to start.

She crossed the street and entered. Two young men with long hair and nose rings were chatting in one of the booths, a paperback copy of *The Corrections* between their pints. The fireside table where she had sat with Priest last time was occupied by a couple. The woman stared at the tabletop while the man traced her hand with a fingertip. Illicit lovers, Delorme thought, or perhaps just a couple recovering from a quarrel.

Priest himself was hunched over a newspaper at the bar. Delorme sat a few stools over and ordered a glass of red wine. "I'll pay now," she said when Tommy brought it.

Priest glanced over, then turned his face right back to his newspaper. His cellphone was on the bar beside a half-empty pint of Guinness.

Delorme took out several papers from a conference she had attended months ago and opened the top one. "Developments in Case Management—A Success Story."

"You intent on making this your home office?" Priest said without looking up. "That your plan?"

Delorme turned to him and raised her glass. "I'm fine, thank you. And how are you this evening?"

"Sod off."

"Here's to British hospitality."

They sat in silence for a few minutes. Even the jukebox was silent. Murmurs of conversation from the two occupied tables. Priest folded his paper. *The Guardian*. He picked up his phone and swivelled on his stool, facing Delorme. He keyed in a number and put the phone to his ear. "Yes, I want to report an incident of police misconduct, please." He kept the phone to his ear, looking at Delorme the whole time. "Yes, Sergeant, I wish to report a case of police harassment . . . At a pub. The Quiet Pint. Yes, that's right . . ."

Delorme kept her eyes on the case management study. *The institution of new protocols over the course of several months resulted in significant upward deviations in clearance averages.* She read the sentence several times. If Priest was really calling the station, it could be embarrassing.

"Delorme . . ." Priest said into the phone. "I don't know her first name. She says she's off-duty, but she keeps coming round here asking questions. I've asked her to stop, but she refuses . . ."

Delorme turned a page. *Precincts where protocols remained unchanged reported lower clearance averages or similar averages with less desirable outcomes.*

"No, I think what it is, Sergeant, is she's one of those cunts who thinks she's so bloody hot she can do whatever the hell she wants and the blokes'll just fall all over begging for more . . . Certainly . . ."

Priest got off his stool and came over to Delorme, holding the phone out. "He wants to speak to you."

Delorme took the phone and glanced at the little screen, but it was blank. She could hear a man's voice, and put the phone to her ear. "You work hard all day," the voice said, "and now it's time for some serious relaxation. Call 970-COCK and we'll lick your pussy for as long as you want. Talk to real live studs, with massive erections ready to serve you—anywhere you want it. Any way you want it. Just open your legs and dial 970 . . ."

Delorme handed the phone back. "I think it's your dad."

Priest placed the phone on the bar and slid it down toward his newspaper.

"So tell me. What do I have to do to get rid of you?"

"I'm a paying customer—trying to be. Why do you want to get rid of me?"

"You know why."

Delorme shrugged. "And you know how."

Priest turned his back on her, went to the end of the bar, collected his phone and his Guinness, and went to an unoccupied booth and sat down. When Delorme didn't move, he held out both his palms and raised his eyebrows. Well?

Delorme put her papers into the briefcase, picked up her wine and brought them over to the table. Her knees brushed his as she slid into the booth, and she wished they hadn't.

Priest half stood and reached across the table for her briefcase and placed it between their glasses. He leaned forward and spoke in a low voice into the handle. "Thirtieth January, two thousand eleven, interview with Leonard Priest in the matter of Laura Lacroix, disappearance of. Present, D.C. What's-Her-Name and God knows who else."

Delorme stood awkwardly and opened the briefcase, tilting it toward him. "No microphone."

"Could you open your shirt as well, please?"

Delorme sat down and placed the briefcase on the seat beside her.

"It's open to the third button already, I notice. Freckles, I see—very nice."

"How did you meet Laura Lacroix?"

"Come on, then. Just one more button."

"How did you meet Laura Lacroix?"

He closed his eyes and leaned forward, and the wide nostrils flared. Then the vivid blue eyes opened, taking her in once more. "Incredible," he said softly. "You actually use Ivory soap."

This was true, as it happened.

"Should I come back another day?"

"I'll tell you how I met Laura Lacroix. But I have to be sure you're not wearing a wire between those tastefully freckled tits. Are you going to show me or not?"

"No."

"We appear to be at a standoff, then, don't we."

Delorme reached for her briefcase. "I'll just come back another—"

"Wait." Priest grabbed her forearm and squeezed.

Delorme froze, looking at his hand until he let her go.

"I've thought of a way. I'll tell you what you want to know, but first you have to ask if you can suck my cock."

"Oh, for God's sake." She got up and went across the room for her coat.

"You won't leave," Priest said after her. "Laura's been missing—what?—three days now? And you're afraid of words? So repressed you'd screw up a case rather than say a few little words Sister Mary Tightarse wouldn't approve of?"

Delorme took her coat from the hook and struggled into the sleeves.

"She could be tied up somewhere. Or lost in the bush. Freezing to death. But you can't bring yourself to say a few little—"

Delorme came back, coat and all, and sat down opposite him, banging his knee hard. She grabbed hold of his turtleneck and pulled him closer and looked into those gleaming blue eyes. "Oh, please master, please master, please, mister British rock star master, won't you please let me suck that huge cock of yours? Please? Please? Won't you, huh? Huh? Oh my God, it's so big. It's so huge. How do you even get around? Really, something that size, you ought to get it fitted for a shoe. Maybe build it its own garage." She pushed him away and sat back.

Priest frowned at her and half stood, twisting a little to see himself in the mirror. He fussed with the material of his turtleneck for a minute, then slid back down to his seat.

"Are you really that pathetic?" Delorme said. "Is that really what you need to hear?"

"As a matter of fact," Priest said, "I think this is going very well."

He signalled for more drinks, and when they arrived he began to talk.

—

Eleven months earlier. He said he remembered because he had just returned from Christmas vacation with the aged ones in London—Hampstead Garden Suburb, to be exact. Then to Algonquin Bay to get in a little skiing and northern solitude before venturing back into the belly of the monster in Ottawa and Toronto.

"I was invited to dinner at a friend's place. Fella named Brian I met at the squash club. I forget why Laura was there—they weren't trying to set me up. I think she works with Brian's wife up at the hospital. Pleasant evening, blah blah. Anyway, few days later I head back to Ottawa and—"

"Where do you live, exactly? Here? Ottawa? Toronto?"

"Ottawa. I've got my Swiss cottage here and a loft in Toronto, but the Toronto club runs itself at this point. It's Ottawa I got to keep an eye on—thanks to your colleagues. Believe it or not, police investigations do tend to have a negative effect on the libido, as well as everything else."

"Doesn't seem to have affected you."

"Yeah, but I'm exceptional." He took a sip of his Guinness and contemplated the glass. "So I'm back in Ottawa a couple of weeks and I get a call from Laura. In town for some kind of conference. Wonders if I have time for a drink. Not dinner. Not coffee. Drink. I know what that means, and so do you. So, fine. We meet at the Shadow and we have a drink."

"I'm sorry—the Shadow?"

"Yeah, the hotel. Shadow Laurier. Oh Christ, you're not taking the piss about my accent, are you?"

"I thought you said Shadow. I thought it might be another club."

"Non, c'est une plaisanterie. Que tu es snob! Tu penses que t'es tellement supérieure? La petite Pepsi avec son accent qui donne l'impression d'une chatte en chaleurs? C'est insupportable." His French was infuriatingly good.

"First point," Delorme said, "you've never heard my accent. Second point, did you actually call me a Pepsi?" It was an age-old put-down of uncertain derivation for French Canadians, especially dizzy young girls.

"I did. And I notice you're sticking to English. Bit self-conscious, are we? Let me give you some advice, darling—never get between an Englishman and his accent. We grow up with a hundred of 'em buzzing in our ears, each with its own little class marker—and believe me, every one of us learns to negotiate that minefield very quickly indeed. That's why we produce the best fucking actors in the universe."

"So why do you sound the way you do?"

"If I felt like it, I could sound like Bertie Fuckin Russell, but I prefer to sound like someone with a dick between his legs. Awright, sistah?"

"So you met for a drink."

He nodded. "Laura'd already had a couple. She was fun in a small-town kind of way. Very innocent. Marriage was in trouble, told me that straight off. And she pretended to be concerned that she was feeling sexually restless. Sexually restless—I'd never heard it put quite that way before.

"So I take her back to the Lord Elgin, where the conference was, and I know this will shock you, Sister Delorme, but, well, I'm afraid we went to bed together. I cannot tell a lie. Would you like the details?"

"No."

"I had the impression her nipples had been shamefully ignored. Very responsive, she was, in that area—quite electrified, really. And apparently no one of even average sexual IQ had addressed themselves to her clitoris. Amazing what women have to put up with. Men are terrible lovers, as I'm sure your own researches will confirm."

"How can you make the comparison?"

Priest laughed. "You're kidding, right?"

"You're saying you've been in bed with lots of men?"

"Correct!" He touched her hand, a brief pressure, then gone. "You are truly amazing. Have you ever even seen a penis?"

"Could you just stick to the story?"

"Week or so later, she looks me up here. Right here, same as you. Took the same seat at the bar, waiting for me to notice. So subtle. We have a bit of a chinwag and she casually mentions some married git she's shagging. Didn't stop her from coming on to me again. Only this time I wasn't having any."

"Why not?"

"Because I look at someone like Laura Lacroix, I see tears and phone calls and overdoses and lots of just plain not-worth-it. Very attractive woman, Laura—looked a bit like you, frankly—but unfortunately a bit clingy."

"Did you see her again?"

"Yeah, I told you. Ottawa. When she showed up at Risqué and got fucked silly. You ought to try it sometime."

"You've said in the past you like sex games. Tying people up. Role playing."

"It's called fun, sister. It's not my sole occupation."

"And you also like sex outdoors."

"You're taking a suspiciously deep interest."

"So let's say you were going to abduct a woman for sexual purposes. You'd—what?—take her to someone's backyard and do it out by the garage?"

"I don't abduct women. I've no interest in abducting women. Seducing women, yes. Allowing women to express their own sexual nature, yes. Abducting, no. Not my style."

"What if it were your style?"

"It isn't. But I can tell you a very nice place for it. You know the former Deep Forest Lodge?"

"It's not former. It never opened."

"On a moonlit night, I can tell you, there's nothing like it. Like doing it in a haunted house, but outdoors at the same time."

"Sounds horrible."

"Some women like horrible. Like to be tied up. Like to be scared." He waggled long fingers at her and made a ghostly sound, "*Wooooo . . .*"

"You think women like to be beaten and killed too?"

"I said *scared*. It's called a *frisson*—or is that word not available in your FC *vocabulaire*? Must say, I thought at first you were just tightly wound, a little repressed, a little starved for it. But on closer acquaintance, I'm beginning to think you're just dead fucking boring."

Delorme stood up and slapped a twenty on the table. "This round's on me, Romeo."

"Oh, Christ—D.C. Delorme's been watching cop TV."

"It's Detective Delorme, or Sergeant Delorme, when I'm on duty."

"Well, promise me one thing, Sergeant. Promise me you won't come back unless you really do want to suck my cock."

~

Ronnie Babstock woke in the dark. Earlier, the moon had lit the room like a street lamp, but now it had moved on. He was in the old house, in town, the house he had shared with Evelyn. He had intended to sell it, had even bought the new place out on the lake, but somehow he couldn't bring himself to leave this place. He slept better in this house. Usually.

He rolled over and tilted the alarm clock on his bedside table. 3:22. Hiss of air from the heating vents. The house was not ancient, but all houses make noise, especially in the cold. Something metal was ticking at odd intervals.

Insomnia had troubled Babstock much during his younger years, but now, nearing sixty, he generally slept through the night. It wasn't supposed to work that way, but he wasn't complaining. So what had woken him at 3:22 on this particular night? He didn't need the bathroom, and the house was not unduly cold even though he kept the thermostat pretty low for sleeping.

There were wakings that felt bad—a sudden yell in a dream that tears you from sleep, or the phone going off in the hollow of the night—and yet you could turn over and be right back to sleep. Other times, your eyes open for no reason at all but sleep is out of the question. He lay still, trying to take the measure of his own response.

After a while he got up and put on his bathrobe and went down the hall to the bathroom. He opened the cabinet and took out a prescription bottle, opened it and tapped out a single pill. He broke it in half and put one half back in the bottle, then poured a quarter of a glass of water and took the other half. As he was closing the cabinet door, he froze.

Please help me.

It sounded like a young woman, a girl even. He spun around and leaned slightly to see around the bathroom door frame and down the hall. Night light glowing at the top of the stairs. That ticking sound again. He stood waiting.

It couldn't be neighbours. Babstock's property was large; he had no neighbours. It must be the memory of a dream.

Oh, God, I'm so cold . . .

"Who's there?" He had to clear his throat and repeat it. "Is there somebody there?"

He knew it wasn't Evelyn, despite what he had said to Cardinal. Although which of us can say if the voice survives the trip across that threshold? He turned on the hall lights, upstairs and downstairs. A weapon of some sort seemed advisable, but he was not a hunter and owned no guns.

He went down the stairs and walked swiftly through all the rooms, one after another, switching on light after light. Nothing. No one. No furniture disarranged. Windows and doors secure.

I'm losing my mind, he told himself. The voice was in my dream and now my dream life is leaking into my real life.

The voice again. *I'm going to die. I know it.*

Not a dream. The voice was in the house. He went into the hall and opened an ornate wooden box that had been in the family forever. Then the armoire. He opened the vestibule door and felt the wall of cold from outside.

He looked behind the couch. He climbed the back stairs and checked the other bedroom. Closets. No one.

The words had been so disconnected, so discontinuous, he could not even be sure of their direction.

Night terrors, he told himself. You haven't had night terrors for fifteen years. Dementia, could be. I'm losing my mind.

He went downstairs and pulled a bottle of Highland Cream from the liquor cabinet. He reached to the top shelf for one of the really expensive crystal glasses—in times of stress he took comfort in material reminders of his wealth—and poured himself two fingers. He took a swallow. Another. The quivering in his knees began to subside.

He stood in the kitchen, glass in hand, listening. He turned forty-five degrees to the right. Nothing. Then to the left. Silence. Just that metallic ticking—irregular and, in normal circumstances, inaudible.

He went into the living room and sat in his favourite leather chair and opened the Le Carré novel he'd been reading. He wanted the company of a man who understood paranoia. The dangers of delusion.

From the Blue Notebook

The first time I stepped onto ice pack above 80° N, I was utterly vanquished by the immensities of white and blue. A voice not my own reverberated in my skull and rib cage both: *You should not be here,* it told me—*no one should be here.* A friend of mine who is a neurosurgeon had the exact same thought the first time he inserted a gloved finger into the cerebral cortex of a living human being.

It costs a small fortune to keep a man alive in the Arctic for any length of time, and governments and funding agencies like to be sure that anyone they put there is capable of completing a mission. We all had to undergo not just physicals but psychological exams before we were cleared. It was also for that reason that Arcosaur enjoyed the services of Jens Dahlberg, an expert in Arctic medicine and nutrition, as camp physician.

I do not belong here is an idea that can very rapidly turn crippling. Many an Arctic adventurer has had to make the humiliating call for rescue in a matter of days, undone not by the cold but by looking into the face of what might have been called—before overuse rendered the word useless—the awesome. Air so preternaturally clear that you can see the curve of the earth. And in all that vista nothing but snow and ice and, in summer, veins of open water. Even the most thoroughgoing atheist can be destabilized by setting foot where only gods should walk. In that white desert, the only thing worse than a crack opening up beneath your feet is a crack opening up in the psyche of the man next to you. Arctic missions rely on people like Jens to weed out such risks.

We each had our area of expertise. Vanderbyl was oceanography, a man who mapped mountains and valleys no human eye had ever seen. I was ice, Wyndham snow. Rebecca was clouds. Her tools were radar, lidar and radiometers, and she spent many hours a day staring at readouts and computer screens in an effort to define the vertical structure of cloud water contents. She measured the size of droplets and crystals, properties that determine how energy is exchanged between the Arctic surface and the atmosphere.

She was embarked on a long-term project to measure how clouds interact with aerosols, and how they change with the seasons and from one year to another. At some point in the future her findings would be correlated with mine and Wyndham's on seasonal meltage. Already by this time, which was 1992, much research had been done on global warming, and the models were predicting an especially high rate of warming in the Arctic. But so far (surprisingly, given the dolorous certainties to come) we had found no hard evidence of it.

And I hoped desperately we wouldn't find any. I had nightmarish visions of oil platforms and tourists overrunning the only place on the planet I felt at home. Of all of us, Wyndham was the most pessimistic. When depressed, he would spin scenarios of catastrophes—of floods and cyclones and mass migrations. I wasn't willing to call him paranoid, as some of the others did. Instead, I chose not to think about it, the way one chooses not to imagine the death of a spouse.

What happens in your ideal world? I asked Rebecca one day.

My interest was entirely selfish, of course, and there may even have been a touch of irritation in it. It should not be possible for a woman to be such a dedicated scientist, such a humble and reliable trader in hard fact, and yet have such a beautiful neck and throat. I was not usually one to notice these things. When it came to the appreciation of female beauty, I had always been strictly an impressionist. But Rebecca taught me to be a detail man. I thought about the elegant and shifting columns of tendon and cartilage. I thought about her way of blinking exactly once whenever I spoke to her, as if capturing my remark like a lattice of crystals for later analysis. I thought about her fingers, slender and tapered, the nails perfectly formed, neatly shaped. Her skin was darker than mine, not quite tawny, and I had to suppress the desire to touch her hands as she typed, despite the wedding band.

My ideal world?

I had spoken to her from the doorway of her office. Only three of the scientists had private offices: Dahlberg, Vanderbyl and Rebecca. In Rebecca's case, it was a matter of getting her instruments as far from the power shack as possible, because the generator tended to interfere with her readouts. The space was not much bigger than a graduate student's carrel, but it had a porthole window over which she had hung a towel to keep the glare off her screens.

My ideal world?

She didn't turn to face me but spoke to my reflection in her radar screen.

In my ideal world, we don't have a sea station here, a drift station there, we have an international network of cloud observatories: Tiksi, Hammerfest, Alert and Barrow—at least those four. And every day I get to chat with Russians and Danes and Americans about Arctic clouds. And you?

It must be wonderful to be so easily amused.

Now she did turn to face me. Why ask, if you're only going to make fun? A coordinated network of stations is what we need. It's going to take a lot more than a drifting dysfunctional family to figure out what's going on up here.

I didn't respond, only stood for a few moments reading the Ice Island Regulations that were taped to every door in the facility.

> Please appreciate that this camp is in a very remote location. In the event of an accident, every effort is made to evacuate the injured party(s). However, we cannot control bad weather or radio blackouts, which can last up to 10 days. Exercise extreme caution and good judgment in your daily work and activities during your stay on the Ice Island. Thank you for your co-operation and have a pleasant stay.

A few days later, I stopped at her door again. The temperature had dropped ten degrees and there were loud cracks and pops from outside. Ice contracting.

I'll tell you about *my* ideal world, I said. My ideal world is one where you turn around the moment you hear footsteps, because you hope it's me.

She shook her head, not looking. You can't talk to me that way.

You and Vanderbyl are breaking up. You've already broken up.

She shook her head again. You can't.

But I am. I think you want me to.

She removed her hands from the keyboard and folded them in her lap and looked down at them. When she looked up again, she pointed at her lidar readout. The screen resembled a spray of yellow and red confetti.

You know what that is?

No.

You've just come in from outside. How would you rate ground-level visibility?

Right now? If it wasn't for the curve of the earth, you could probably see Denmark.

Clouds?

None. Not one.

That—she tapped a trim fingernail on the screen—is a cloud. It's not visible to the naked eye. It's not visible to a telescope. It's not even visible to infrared. I'm looking at a cloud here and I have no idea what it's made of. I'm going to be analyzing these readings for the rest of my life. I wouldn't want also to be trying to figure out if you love me or hate me. There's only room in a life for so many mysteries. I couldn't face coming home to another.

A wave of bitterness took me by surprise. Don't flatter yourself, I said. I just want to sleep with you.

She gave me one of those single blinks. Data received. There was always the risk with Rebecca that you transmitted more than you knew. She raised her hands once more to her keyboard and resumed typing.

If I thought that was true, she said, it might stand a chance of actually happening.

5

DELORME'S ALARM WOKE HER AT four a.m. She patted the bedside table to shut it off, cursed, and sat up on the edge of the bed. It was cold in the room and she was wearing nothing but the long T-shirt she slept in. The alarm was on the chair where she had put out her clothes the night before, placed there to ensure she got out of bed.

She hit the button to silence the alarm and closed the window and went still for a minute. Fragments of a dream. A highly graphic scene involving Leonard Priest. "Oh, please," she said aloud. "*Gah.*"

Lifting her T-shirt over her head, she caught the fragrance of Ivory soap and resolved to switch brands. She put on the clothes she'd laid out and went to the kitchen, where her coffee was waiting. She poured it into her thermal cup and put the lid on. She ate a bowl of Grape-Nuts standing up and put the bowl in the sink.

She strapped on her Beretta and sat down to pull on her big boots. Then the blazer and finally the big parka. She closed the inner door of her vestibule—her airlock, she called it—and stepped outside into the dark. Black sky, crescent moon, and air so frigid her lungs refused the first breath entirely, making her cough. She locked the door and went down the steps, then went back up and opened the door. She picked up the tool kit she had put there the night before and shut the door again.

Her Volvo was facing the street, the trailer and snowmobile already attached.

—

Black streets. Empty. Soft roar of the Volvo's heater.

Ten kilometres north of the city, almost as if she had crossed a border, the world turned white. Snowbanks, shoulder high, lined the highway, and boughs hung down under their burden of snow. Delorme made a left at a sign that announced a series of recreational trails. The parking area was empty. She got out and unloaded the snowmobile. When she climbed on and started it, the noise was shattering. Thirty-five years she'd managed to live in Algonquin Bay without owning a snowmobile, but the previous year she had caved in and bought one. The winters were long in this place, and if you let them imprison you, it could make you crazy. She had joined a club, paid a fee, and got a trail map and a schedule of events. She had attended exactly one. The racket was unbelievable and the entire membership appeared to be twelve-year-old boys.

The trail wound away from the road and past a tiny frozen lake. That was it for open country. Trees and brush whipping by. The ruby numerals of the speedometer showed forty, but being inches from the ground gave a tremendous sensation of speed. Snowmobiling at four-thirty in the morning—it's crazy in fifty different ways, Delorme thought. Is this how you get a promotion? Or is this how you get a reputation for being a little "funny," with colleagues rolling their eyes when your name is mentioned?

The Ski-Doo's headlight threw long shadows shuddering into the woods. The engine's roar ensured the absence of wildlife. She came to a fork in the trail and kept to the right. The map showed a dotted line, meaning an unofficial trail, coming up. Half a kilometre farther, a small gap opened in the trees. Unofficial indeed. But the snow was packed down and chomped by snowmobile tracks, so she steered up and over the verge and into the woods.

The engine blared louder. The front blades slammed over rougher terrain. Then a steep rise and she crested the old railbed. She had to do a two-pointer to orient the machine, and then followed the railway line. It wasn't far now. Ancient utility poles tilted at angles; others, felled by beavers, sagged almost parallel to the ground, supported by smaller fir trees.

The railbed ran for fifty or sixty kilometres, but Delorme kept an eye on the passing trees for another gap. When it came up on the right, she turned and the machine clattered onto even harsher ground. At one time this would have been a construction road, but that was short-lived and nobody had kept it up since.

A few more bone-rattling minutes and then there it was.

When the tracks were torn up, the developer's plan had been to build first a road and then a "winter recreation lodge" right here in the middle of the woods. But he underestimated the kind of delays that can ensue when you're dealing with three levels of government, two or three public utilities, at least one defunct corporation, and a population of aging boomers who just wanted the woods left alone—but with nice cleared paths for skiers and snowmobilers. In a fit of defiance, he had begun construction and worked at great speed, perhaps counting on a *fait accompli* to sway fortune in his favour.

Delorme was looking at the result now. Whatever rustic glory the developer may have had in mind, what he'd actually left was a concrete-block rectangle. Half of this was covered with split pine cladding and a sharply peaked roof. The rest was bare concrete.

He had intended to call it Deep Forest Lodge, but it was known to cross-country skiers as the Ice Hotel. It was set on the crest of a long slope that faced south, so it caught the sun all day, even in winter. Any snow that fell on it melted and dripped down the walls, where it froze into a sheath of translucent, impenetrable ice.

The place couldn't be torn down until armies of lawyers had finished wrangling—much to the chagrin of the provincial police. Although they tried to secure it, it was impossible to keep teenagers away. The place was dark, unfinished and unsafe. Every year the OPP had to rescue some kid who had climbed inside, only to end up with a broken leg.

DANGER: KEEP OUT. TRESPASSERS WILL BE PROSECUTED.

The usual signs were prominently posted, and just as prominently defaced. Delorme regarded the ruin with a shudder. *Some women like to be scared.* It wasn't the place that frightened her so much as the idea that anyone would fantasize about bringing a woman out here and doing God knows what.

She left the snowmobile running to have the benefit of its headlight. She took up the tool kit and flashlight and walked toward the fence, her shadow totemic against ice and concrete. The gate was padlocked, but ten metres to the right someone had clipped the chain-link fence—none too recently by the look of it, and high enough that you could slip through without great difficulty.

She forced the fence back even more and managed not to rip her parka climbing through. She walked up to the wall and shone her flashlight upward to where the concrete wall became a glacier wall. Entrances had been bricked up, but there were gaps. She climbed through one, turning her ankle on the jagged detritus underneath the ice so hard that she gasped.

The snowmobile's headlight was no help here. She looked up. A thin cirrus dimmed the stars, but the crescent moon hung low and bright just above one wall. No glimmer of daylight yet. She played the flashlight beam over what looked like a small prison yard. A perfect square of white ground, with a frozen white wave of snow about two feet high curling up against one wall, giving the whole a tilted effect. No tracks of any kind. Solid concrete block on three sides, then on Delorme's right the partially collapsed building.

The cold was getting to her and she wanted to keep moving. She pushed on one boarded-up window, but there was no give in it. She tried the other window. Someone had put the original three-quarter ply back in place and wedged a two-by-four over it, but there was nothing securing it. Delorme pulled away the two-by-four and dislodged the plywood without even opening her tool kit.

Utter blackness inside. Shadows veered and lurched in the flashlight beam. Exposed struts and temporary plywood flooring, curled and separating at the edges. Delorme got up on the ledge and examined the flooring below. She turned around and lowered herself to test it with one foot. She lowered her other foot, holding on to the window ledge.

She wished Cardinal was with her. The cold seemed worse in this darkness. She moved slowly, sweeping the flashlight beam from side to side. Graffiti jeered from the walls. Old cigarette packs, beer bottles and candy wrappers littered the floor. Whoever liked this place, it wasn't health food addicts.

A square of emptiness opened up in the floor ahead of her, a concrete stairwell that looked like an invitation to hell. She was tempted to call out, make her presence known, but the thought of how it would reverberate dissuaded her.

She went halfway down the steps and shone the flashlight around. Forest of I-beams. Could anyone—even Leonard Priest—conceivably come out here for sex?

Not far from the stairs, a sleeping bag, much stained and torn, lay in a twisted heap. Nearby, the charred remains of a small fire and a pile of feces, thankfully frozen. In a corner, a dead fox lay on its side, small white teeth exposed.

Graffiti everywhere. Many sexual invitations, many phone numbers. An individual of loftier ambition had written in letters three feet high, *Become Your Dream*. And Jenny P, whoever she might be, was apparently blessed with a "hot vag," which to Delorme sounded like something you'd find in the produce section. Clearly, in the minds of many, sex and isolated ruins were a natural combination. A longing overcame her to be inside her car with the heater going full blast.

Ambition like a pheromone. Is it just ambition—or are envy and resentment making me stupid? She stood outside again and swept the flashlight beam over the walls, the snowdrift, the rest of the emptiness. She was glad she had not called Cardinal to come with her on this jaunt. He wouldn't have anyway, she told herself, because he would have realized it was dumb.

At the break in the wall, she reached through and set her tool kit down on the far side. She turned and made one last sweep of the courtyard and the long curl of the snowdrift, which ran the length of the wall about knee high. Toward the far corner it rose higher, and now, as she held the beam steady, she saw that there was something in it. Some material partially exposed. Impossible to tell the colour.

She crossed the white square on a diagonal toward the corner. Probably another sleeping bag. She leaned closer, and now, in the more intense light, she could see that the fabric was blue, and more like a jacket than a sleeping bag. She reached with her big snowmobile mitten and brushed at the snow. It was crusty from melting and refreezing and she had to break a piece off.

A shoulder, a scarf, hair.

Delorme took off her mitten and worked her fingers under the crust of snow and broke more off. The powder underneath slid away. She went down on one knee to get a closer look.

A woman's face, eyes closed, white crescents of snow clinging to the lashes.

Delorme reached into her parka and pulled out her cellphone. It took a while for Cardinal to answer.

"You're not gonna believe this, John. I'm looking at a dead body. A woman . . . No. That's the incredible thing. It's *not* Laura Lacroix."

From the Blue Notebook

It is possible in the Arctic—possible sometimes—to mistake oneself for a superhero, one's faculties, one's perceptions can be so transformed. Such is the array of optical and acoustic phenomena. It is a special moment, the first time you realize you are overhearing a conversation taking place more than a kilometre away. Distances of three kilometres are not unusual, depending on temperature, wind speed, surface conditions. In contrast to temperate climates, Arctic air is coldest close to the ground; it refracts sound waves downward instead of upward.

That moment has the quality of an excellent dream—the feeling of vindication and exhilaration one sometimes gets from a gorgeous subconscious narrative: Yes, of course! This is who I am! I've always been infinitely more perceptive than others!

Wyndham, guileless Wyndham, reported such a dream to me once, over a midnight breakfast.

I was with Isaac Newton, he told me. At his lodgings in Cambridge. We were doing differential calculus together, performing it as if we were playing a duet. We had an enormous ledger open on the table before us. There was a cat sitting next to it, watching us with the greenest, most intelligent eyes. And we were doing these equations—incredibly intricate, incredibly precise—and they just flowed effortlessly one after another, and we took turns writing them out. I was filled with this incredible joy. The two of us were best friends and always had been. And I was thinking, How did I forget this? How did I forget that Isaac Newton and I are best friends and do equations together?

A sadness crossed Wyndham's face.

When I woke up, I was thinking, you know, I really should give Isaac a call. And I couldn't accept at first that it wasn't real. That it was just a dream. It seemed so perfect. So right. And I lay there with reality seeping into my brain like dishwater, dirty and grey, and I felt utterly bereft. I was depressed for days.

So it is for some men, some researchers. They come back from the Arctic, where their superhuman visual acuity has shown them sun dogs and halos. Fata Morgana. Yes! It was always thus! My powers have come into their own! Only to return to their real lives in Calgary and Edmonton, Peterborough and Waterloo.

Such people, after less than a week at home, before they've even written up the data they've just brought back, start scrambling for the next possible research grant.

From the tinkle of candle ice on the shores of Lake Hazen to the subtle beauty of a fog bow—colourless owing to the fineness of the vapour—to the shattering storms of Tanquary Fiord, the High Arctic is a place to go mad in. A place to fall in love. A land of mirages.

In a sense it is all mirage, with the odd pocket of reality. The Antarctic may be more wild and more bitter—though opinions on this vary—but at least it offers actual solid ground somewhere beneath one's boots. There is no land at all at the North Pole, just an unending frozen sea, so that even one's footsteps are a kind of lie.

I told Rebecca one day that I had come to understand she was simply a mirage.

Thanks. And I suppose you're real.

Completely. Utterly.

She gave a little snort of derision.

You misunderstand. I just mean at times like this you seem almost attainable. As in a superior mirage. Light warps in the cold and things appear on the horizon that aren't really there. Or aren't there yet. You're on my horizon, but never quite in reach.

I just swallowed thirty millilitres of your semen, Karson. I'd say that's within reach.

She was still calling me Karson at that point, not Kit. I turned away and lay on my back and sighed. Petulant. Childish, even. But this is the truth of the matter. I am—was—someone who chose a solitary life. Not womanless. Not gay. Solitary. The emotions and how we deal with them are every bit as Darwinian as fins, genitals, tentacles. We all find our mechanism of survival—or not. Mine was monkish solitude. It worked for me. Had done for more than a decade. I was frightened by my loss of equanimity.

After a while Rebecca turned on her side, propped up on one elbow, and looked at me with the intensity she brought to her cloud formations, her readouts and water droplets.

You're hurt? Is that possible?

Look, I said, I'm not a poet. I don't have words for this.

She ran her index finger along my cheekbone. I don't want a poet. I want Karson Durie, ice physicist and seducer. You don't have to fancify, just tell me. I don't have a radar for you. I don't know what you want or what you feel or where you're going unless you tell me. Directly. No mirages.

I was trying to.

Trying not to, more like it.

You can't expect me to express any feelings at all if you sneer at them.

She shifted in the bed, took hold of my face, her palms hot, and shook her head. Eyes the green of stadium night games. Not sneering, love. Please. Try again. I'll listen, I promise.

All right, I said. I'll try a quote. A song. Don't worry, I won't attempt to sing. But there's a line I've never forgotten. It goes through my head a lot. I try to make out like I really don't care . . .

She shook me a little by the shoulders, breasts pressing into me. And?

I try to make out like I really don't care. And the way that I do it is I really don't care.

The briefest pause.

This is what you're struggling to tell me? That you really don't care?

No. I'm saying not caring has been my mode of existence. It's what I'm afraid of losing. You can't blame me for that, surely. I lose it and then I finally reach the horizon only to find . . .

I was a mirage.

Well, a superior mirage.

Of course.

Goes without saying.

She pushed herself up and straddled me, knee on either side of my chest, hands pressing down on my shoulders. She reached out with one hand to steady herself against the wall behind my head. A few more adjustments and then she is there. My nostrils fill with the glorious, intoxicating scent of her. I raise my face and kiss her cunt, a flurry of kisses, but she moves again and presses me against the pillow.

Oo, you need a shave.

So do you, I said with some difficulty.

Pervert. Not a chance.

She rubbed herself over my face in a kind of dreamy delirium. Let me know, she said, when I'm real enough for you.

Afterward, I fell asleep, and when I woke up she was reading a fat hardback by Robertson Davies. I watched her for a while and she pretended not to notice.

You're the only person I've ever met, I said, who's as Canadian as the CBC.

She smiled her cat's smile but kept reading.

You're a curling rink, I said. You probably have pyjamas with matching toque and mittens.

She was making an effort not to laugh, but she refused to look away from her book.

You gorge on poutine, I said. You wolf down donuts and peameal bacon when no one's looking. You have a complete set of Tim Hortons mugs.

Go away, she said, exasperated.

I got dressed and tossed on my coat and left her reading. I crossed the slushy rectangle between the huts and went into the mess, where Wyndham, Vanderbyl, Dr. Dahlberg and Ray Deville were all sitting around the table like figures in a painting. Cups and mugs and magazines were spread out along with the remains of their various dinners and snacks. Mozart on the sound system, lanyard clanging on the flagpole outside. We often hung around the table after dinner, not necessarily talking.

This fresh? I said, lifting the teapot.

Reasonably, Wyndham said. He was the only one who didn't seem to be doing anything. Perhaps he was just listening to the music. Vanderbyl was reading a biography of Niels Bohr, his professorial pencil poised to correct even published material. Ray Deville was rewriting a paper he was preparing to submit. And Jens Dahlberg was tormenting himself with a Rubik's cube.

I took the empty seat between Wyndham and Dahlberg. I said to the doctor that I thought those colourful cubes had disappeared from the face of the earth.

I'm a firm believer, he said, twisting the thing, turning it, twisting again, in attempting to do things you're not good at.

Sounds painful, I said.

Uncomfortable. Not painful.

I reached for a plate of cookies and dunked one in my tea.

Ray had put down his pen and was staring at me across the table. I twiddled my fingers at him and smiled.

His expression changed to stern disapproval. He gathered his papers, stood up and left the room. The Arctic attracts eccentrics, but Ray Deville was strange even by the standards of graduate students. A bit of a lurcher, Ray was. A starer and a blurter with an extreme accent.

I turned to make a light-hearted comment to Vanderbyl but found he was staring at me too. His face, that fair Dutch skin, was a deep, stinging red. He pushed back his chair, almost falling in his rush to flee.

Then Dahlberg. He placed the cube neatly on the table, took his plate to the sink and left the mess.

All right, I said. Apparently I have leprosy.

Don't be an idiot, Wyndham said. I mean, really, Kit. How far do you want to push him?

I realize every expedition has its designated pariah, Gordon. Call me obtuse, but I would have put odds on young Deville of the thousand-yard stare. You might at least explain why this time the mantle has fallen on my shoulders.

He turned to me, eyes shadowed by the overhead lamp. Your aftershave might have something to do with it.

Aftershave. I don't wear any aftershave.

Your face, man, your face. You reek of pussy.

I raised a hand to my cheek, still warm from bed.

That's right, Wyndham said. That wonder of nature we all know and love and adore. Fabulous. Miraculous. Bully for you. But Rebecca is the guy's wife, man. She's the guy's wife. He's trying to play the Stoic, the picture of calm reason. He's lead scientist, for God's sake. But he's utterly torn up over the idea of her sleeping with someone else. And if you can't see it—or won't see it, pardon me—then you're just an out-and-out bastard.

6

Bob Collingwood was removing snow from the dead woman with a fine brush. Gradually the brittle blond hair was revealed, the fine blue veins beneath the temples, the thin lips almost as pale as the snow. Frozen eyelids oblivious to the scene man's brush. Silent Collingwood showed no more reaction than the woman.

Cardinal looked at Delorme, her movie-star sunglasses looking back at him, fur trim of her hood a fiery halo.

"Marjorie Flint," he said. "How does a senator's wife end up in this godforsaken place?"

"You maybe get the feeling it wasn't her idea?"

"Last anybody knew, she was heading home to make dinner. So how does she get from Ottawa to Algonquin Bay?" Cardinal pointed to two small peaks of snow on either side of the head and shoulders. "Bob, can we get a look at these?"

Collingwood removed the snow one thin layer at a time. A bolt and then a steel ring became visible. A chain.

Cardinal pointed to the chain. "Let's follow that."

Collingwood's brush flicked at the snow, the chain appearing link by link. He could move faster now, since he was not touching the body itself. The chain was about three feet long and ended in a steel cuff, a padded cuff that encircled the woman's wrist.

"Jesus," Delorme said. "Why?"

The hand itself was clenched, and tightly wrapped in thin rags.

"Let's see her other hand," Cardinal said.

Collingwood changed position and worked with his brush. Again the blue sleeve, the cuff, the wrapped hand.

"What's that?" Cardinal pointed to a slight rise in the snow beside the hand.

He and Delorme watched the brush, the gleam of metal as it appeared.

"Is that a Thermos?"

"That's exactly what it is," Collingwood said. "You believe that? She's holding a Thermos."

The three of them went still: Collingwood crouched, brush poised above the dead woman's hand; Delorme, arms crossed in front of her, chin down; Cardinal with hands in pockets, shoulders hunched.

"I'm wondering about that jacket," Cardinal said.

"You want me to get at the label?"

"What bothers me is it's not the coat she was wearing."

"The MP report listed a black cashmere coat," Delorme said, "not a blue down jacket."

"I don't want to mess up your routine, Bob, so I'll just ask if we can get a quick look at her wallet, if there's one there, and then her boots. Then we'll leave you to get on with it."

Collingwood photographed the Thermos and took several exposures of the area where it seemed likely a wallet might be. He broke off some crust and started brushing, eventually reaching inside the jacket.

He extracted a wallet and handed it up.

Cardinal flipped through it, riffled the bills. "Lots of ID. And there's at least three hundred bucks in here. Well, scene like this, robbery's not the first thing crosses my mind."

They waited while Collingwood cleared the snow from her feet.

"Good hiking boots," Delorme said as the sole began to appear. "New, too."

"The report said high-heel boots," Cardinal said, "and I'm betting her hands weren't wrapped in those rags when she left home, either."

~

They found Paul Arsenault, the other half of the ident team, culling the snow some distance outside the scene perimeter. He was on his knees under a birch tree, working with hand implements.

"Why are you way out here?" Cardinal asked him. "I think Collingwood can probably use you about now."

"You're just in time," Arsenault said. He got to his feet, holding a shard of black plastic by the edges.

"What have you got?"

"Piece of snowmobile cowling is my guess." Arsenault flipped the plastic over. It had a slight curve to it and showed a network of surface scratches. Part of a word had snapped off, leaving only the letters *rb.*

"*Rb*," Delorme said. "What do you suppose that used to say?"

"I don't know," Arsenault said. "You tell me—you're the snowmobile maven."

"Me? No—this is like the fourth time I've been out. And mine just says Ski-Doo."

"Are you sure this is connected to the crime?"

Arsenault pointed to the trunk of the birch tree, where a gouge had peeled away the bark. "That looks pretty recent to me. The victim vanished ten days ago. Plus I checked weather patterns for the area? In the past two weeks, they've had freezing rain twice—once twelve days ago, once three days ago. This was between those two layers of glaze."

"You checked the weather patterns?" Cardinal said. "You can do that on your phone?"

"I checked 'em before we got in the truck."

Cardinal and Delorme looked at each other.

"I *am* good at this, you know."

"We've noticed," Delorme said. "Now all you have to do is run it through the snowmobile database."

"Ah, yes," Arsenault said, "the famous snowmobile database."

Cardinal and Delorme stayed for several hours, but thorough processing of the scene was going to take days. D.S. Chouinard was demanding a command performance, and Cardinal eventually found him waiting in interview room three, a comfortless chamber the size of a jail cell.

"Why are we meeting in here?" Cardinal said.

"My office has sprung another goddam leak, and the chief has the meeting room booked."

Cardinal sat on a plastic chair that was usually occupied by criminals.

"Let me get this straight," Chouinard said. "We've got a woman chained up outdoors in minus thirty degrees, and she's got a Thermos in her hand?"

"Smelled like coffee," Cardinal said, "but obviously we're going to need the lab report. Same with the traces of food we found beside her."

"Someone chained her up outside like a dog?"

"Seems whoever did it either failed to return for some unexpected reason or just decided he wanted to make sure she died of cold, not starvation."

"Other than the body itself, we picking up anything useful out there?"

"Arsenault's keen on a piece of snowmobile cowling he found under the snow."

There was a rap at the door and Delorme came in. "Why are we meeting in here?"

"Don't ask," Chouinard said.

Delorme sat, holding a notebook and pen on her lap. Her face was still pink from the cold.

Chouinard tapped the tip of his ballpoint on a notebook. "You rang Cardinal at five-thirty a.m. Pitch dark. Middle of winter. Call me nosy, but what were you doing out in the woods at five-thirty in the morning?"

Cardinal could feel Delorme glance at him, but he ignored it. She was on her own this time.

"I went out there on the basis of information received."

"Cut the shit."

"I bumped into Leonard Priest off-duty. He started opening up to me for some reason, and in the course of our conversation he mentioned that if he was going to have sexual relations with someone outdoors, he would take her to the Ice Hotel."

Cardinal could hear in Delorme's voice that she had rehearsed this answer. No doubt Chouinard could too.

The detective sergeant made circular motions in the air with one hand, as if erasing a blackboard. "Back up a minute. You thought Leonard Priest might be confessing? He gets through a full-blown investigation without a scratch and now, two years later, you're thinking he killed Senator Flint's wife, and he just happens to tell you where you'll find the body?"

"No, I was thinking Laura Lacroix. Two years ago, Régine Choquette was abducted and killed outdoors. Leonard Priest was our number one suspect. And now it turns out Leonard Priest went out with Laura Lacroix. I thought he could be involved. You did too," she said, looking at Cardinal.

"We got the information from Laura Lacroix's best friend," Cardinal said.

"I don't know why Priest told me about the Ice Hotel—aside from the fact he talks about sex non-stop—but I thought it was worth checking out."

"At five-thirty in the morning."

"It was a long shot," Delorme said. "I wanted to check it out myself in case I was wrong."

"You *were* wrong. It's Marjorie Flint on her way to the Ottawa morgue, not Laura Lacroix. You *were* wrong."

"Come on, D.S.," Cardinal said. "She just broke this case wide open."

"This case? Last I heard, we had *two* cases here. Okay, Laura Lacroix's friend says she had a fling with Leonard Priest. We still can't even say for certain any *crime* was committed with her. We got no *body*. And how does it link Priest to Marjorie Flint? It never occurred to any of us—or to the Ottawa police, I can tell you—to question Leonard Priest about Marjorie Flint. So he tells you the Ice Hotel's a great spot for sex—but this woman's fully dressed, right? What's the evidence that sex in fact took place?"

"None yet," Delorme said. "But I'm betting the autopsy will show it."

"Great spot for sex. Leonard Priest is not the first to notice it, by the way, from what I hear. Did you take notes at the time he told you this?"

"As soon as I got home."

"And did you advise Mr. Priest of his rights?"

"I was off-duty, D.S."

"Then why did you take notes?"

"Because I didn't want to forget, obviously."

"No, what you mean is, you took notes because it's proper investigative procedure. And if you were investigating Mr. Priest, you were under an obligation to inform him of his Charter rights. You went to his home." Chouinard shot a glance at Cardinal. "I assume you went with her?"

"Yeah. But he hates me. He refused to talk to us."

"Help me out here, Delorme. Where exactly did you talk to this man?"

"At a pub. The Quiet Pint."

"Oh, Jesus."

"I just stopped in for a glass of wine and—"

"This just gets better and better. The Quiet Pint is not *a* pub, it's *his* pub. You show up at the man's place of work and you start firing questions at him and you don't advise him of his rights?"

"D.S., I wasn't questioning him. He *offered* to talk to me. Was I supposed to say no, I'm not interested?"

"No, you were supposed to Charterize him."

The D.S.'s voice had gone quiet. Cardinal began to count the seconds until the explosion.

"It was a *conversation*. I was off-duty."

"And out of the blue he tells you he knows this great place to take abducted women."

"*No,*" Delorme said. "It wasn't like that."

Don't lose your cool, Cardinal thought. Don't make things worse.

"He was annoyed I was there," Delorme said. "I said it's a free country. He said, 'If I tell you about Laura Lacroix, will you leave?' And I said sure. We were joking, sort of. I thought we were joking. But he told me how he met Laura Lacroix and a bit about their relationship. This guy is totally wired to sex. You wouldn't believe some of the stuff he said to me. Sex with women, sex with men, sex in public, sex outdoors . . . So I said, 'If you were going to abduct someone for sexual purposes and take her somewhere, where would it be?'"

"And he said Deep Forest Lodge."

"Not exactly. What he said was, 'I don't abduct women, but if you want to have sex outdoors, there's no place better.' He said it was like being in a haunted house but outside at the same time. I said that sounds horrible and he said some women like horrible."

Chouinard was shaking his head.

"Two years ago we thought we had him for Régine Choquette," Delorme said. "Well, we thought he was worth checking out about Laura Lacroix. We can't get a subpoena. I had the opportunity and I asked questions and now we've found Marjorie Flint, D.S. *We've found Marjorie Flint.* That's more than the RCMP and the Ottawa police could do."

"And what's your theory as to why he told you?"

Delorme sat back. "I don't know. I really don't."

"It has nothing to do with, say, your physical appearance? Or how you were dressed, perhaps?"

"What did you say to me? What are you—"

"D.S.," Cardinal said, "really."

"What *really*? Don't get all equity on me, I'm simply taking into account an officer's appearance. A huge cop enters a room, it has an effect. A mousy cop enters a room, different effect. A highly attractive female—off-duty, at that—has another effect. Let's not be stupid and ignore it."

"I was wearing a grey suit that I wear to court. Hardly provocative."

"That's a matter of opinion. Some people find nuns pretty hot. Were you trying to turn his crank?"

"I'm not even going to answer that, D.S. And frankly, you'd better not ask it again."

"You watch your tone, Sergeant. Don't you try going head to head with me."

"Most likely just coincidence," Cardinal put in. "Why Priest told her about the Ice Hotel? It had to be coincidence."

"Come again?" Chouinard said. "Tell me you're kidding."

"Despite how it may look," Cardinal said, "I don't think Priest had anything to do with Marjorie Flint's murder. If he did, there's no way in hell he's going to tell a cop where to find her. No way in hell. My guess is you're right: Detective Delorme, through no fault of her own—did everyone hear that? *through no fault of her own*—gets Mr. Priest's motor going. He was playing with her, trying to get a rise out of her. There's no way he knew what he was stepping into. Because, like you say, nothing connects him—so far."

"That sound credible to you?" Chouinard said to Delorme.

"Yes," Delorme said. "But I wish it didn't."

"All right. Loach is running Lacroix."

"Oh, for Christ sake," Delorme said.

"Cardinal, you're gonna be lead on Flint. But I—"

"D.S., Lise got this whole thing rolling. You can't—"

"I just did." He got up and pointed his pen at Delorme. "And you know why. You want to run an investigation for me, you learn to do it right. In the meantime, consider yourself lucky you're still on any case at all."

From the Blue Notebook

There is a night within the night. Even in the temperate latitudes, even in nights of the duration we would consider "normal," there can be a time, an hour or two, that might be called the night within the night. The hour when a wife discovers she can no longer pretend to love her husband. The hour when a young man judges that the world is not going to hand him the life he yearns for, and it seems preferable to end the one he has.

It was early April. Arcosaur was still jammed in the ice pack. Arctic dawn was yet to come. We were a skeleton crew, the first rotation of scientists having yet to arrive. Before Rebecca, in other words.

Wyndham, Vanderbyl, his grad student Ray Deville, and myself. Beyond this, we had Paul Bélanger the cook, Murray Washburn, our facilities manager, Hunter and, of course, Jens Dahlberg. It had been a long day. We were in the mess. If we hadn't had Paul there to make meals at regular hours, we probably would have warped into a forty-eight-hour cycle, which ends up being less productive than it sounds.

The weather had been foul for days. Horrendously cold, with a wind that could not be borne. But now the wind had dropped and the stars came out in their millions. The cold was deep and vast. Finally we could work outside again.

We put on many layers and our thickest downs and thus broke a cardinal rule of Arctic labour: if you're warm when you venture outside, you will soon be too hot. We overworked and sweated hard all day, eventually staggering into the mess one by one, stinking and exhausted and damp. We probably consumed three or four thousand calories each at dinner.

Paul gave us a long and obviously prepared speech about pitching in to do dishes because we were eating as if we were three times our actual number. Paul himself had been working with stove and oven all day, and now his pies and cakes were vanishing before his eyes. As he lectured us, he bundled himself into his parka and raised his hood, wrapping the lower part of his face in his scarf. He looked like an astronaut going EVA, even though he and Hunter shared a cabin between the mess and the radio shack, which meant he had to travel about ten metres.

Jens Dahlberg sensibly went off to bed soon after, but the rest of us sat on, not talking. We were in a group lassitude brought on by shared exhaustion and the heat of the stove. We had passed that point where exhaustion skirts the edge of weeping and goes beyond it. Even Vanderbyl, who had reserves of energy that made one occasionally suspect a secret supply of Dexedrine, sat angular and expressionistic, one elbow on the table, cheek to palm, and the dead stare in his eyes of the terminally numb. Wyndham was asleep, chin on chest, quietly snoring. Ray Deville was scribbling urgently in a notebook, the sound of his pencil like the scurrying of a mouse. I've no idea what he was writing, but I suspect it was not academic.

Had one of us fired a shotgun into the air, I don't think the effect of what happened next could have been any more drastic. A pounding, satanically loud, shook all four walls of the mess. The four of us stared at the door, its sturdy construction suddenly enfeebled. Vanderbyl, not a man given to cursing, sat straight up and yelled, *Jesus Christ.* Ray looked like a cartoon image of alarm—goggle-eyed, mouth open.

It came again. We were immobilized, dumb as figures in a natural history tableau.

I nominate Ray to answer the door, Wyndham said quietly.

Ray shook his head. He seemed to be getting smaller in his chair, as if he would sink under the table.

I got up and approached the door. Jens?

The mad thing on the other side pounded again.

I opened the door and an enormous Inuit man, rounded, solid and monolithic as one of their sculptures, was bathed in our light. The depth of his hood made his face a black circle.

Welcome, I said in Inuktitut. Undoubtedly this represented a naked attempt to hide my fear, not good manners.

He crooked an arm much rimed with snow, beckoning. He was enveloped in the cold of hell.

Honour us, I said, and gestured toward the stove, the table. Quickly, if you would.

He stepped inside with the lumbering gait of Arctic dress. He was clad head to foot in sealskin and wolf hide. I closed the door.

My name is Karson Durie, I said. Will you have some tea?

In another country one might offer vodka or brandy, but there are communities where the offer of alcohol is received as an assault, and not for religious reasons.

He pulled back his hood. The ageless smooth face of an Inuk in his prime. He was the tallest I had ever seen. My head came to his shoulders.

Karson Durie, I said again. How do you call yourself?

He received my words like a plate of stones.

Come in, Vanderbyl shouted down the length of the mess. He was fluent in Inuktitut. Let your testicles hang low.

No change of expression, no sign of recognition. He pointed to the door, crooked his head toward it.

Vanderbyl turned to me. "Where the hell's Hunter?"

I don't think this fellow speaks Tuk, I said.

What do you think he is, Romanian? Come in, Vanderbyl yelled again, you are welcome to our food and our fire. Come and share a story.

I don' see why we 'ave to invite 'im in, Ray said, if he don' even try to be frien'. Ray's face was drained white; he looked in danger of fainting. And 'ow did he get here in da first place?

There must be quite a jam behind us, I said.

From the Inuk, no shadow of a response. I had an unnerving sense of figure and ground, as if the air in the mess had turned solid and the figure before me were empty space. It pointed at the door and again crooked its head. I retrieved my parka from a hook.

Jesus Cry, Ray said. Don' go widdim.

This is great, Wyndham said. I love this. Good luck, Kit. Don't forget to write.

I put up my hood and opened the door. The Inuk went out ahead of me. The generator suddenly seemed terribly loud, our camp lights as gaudy as Times Square.

How had we not heard his dogs? A full team lay crouched before a traditional Inuit sled. The whites of their eyes flashed as they looked up. Why had our own dogs not been roused?

The Inuk didn't wait for me, didn't speak—to the dogs or to me. He went to the sled and pulled away the side panel. A heap of sealskins. He reached down and pulled back the layers. The face of a young man stared up at the stars with milky eyes. His features were dark, and at first I thought he was of some exotic race, but of course I was looking at the effects of extreme frostbite.

Not ours, I said.

The Inuk flipped hides away. He bent and reached down and waited.

I took the feet and we lifted the stony weight of him from the sled. The Inuk backed toward the mess.

Wait.

He stopped and we lowered the boy to the ice pack. The clothes were odd. Buckskin jacket, trousers of some material I didn't recognize. High boots of sealskin, hand-sewn with gut.

I was reaching for the door when it opened. Kurt Vanderbyl took one step outside and stopped. Wyndham and Deville bumped into him from behind. Four of us in hoods and parkas looking down at the dead youth.

Who is he? Kurt said.

I don't think we're going to know any time soon, I said.

Where can he be from? We're the only group for twelve hundred miles or more.

Yes.

We can't have him inside. He'll thaw. Where did you find him? he said to the Inuk.

The Inuk, still as a sculpture, said nothing.

He had to be sheltered somewhere, I said. Perhaps a glacial cave.

The bears would have got him. Foxes. He looks totally undamaged except for the frostbite.

'Ell wid dis, Ray said, stepping around Kurt. Why you come and bodder us like dat? You imagine you're de only people on de planet?

Stop, Kurt said, and put a hand out to hold him back.

'Ell wid dis, Ray said again. Dat guy 'as something not right widdim.

Squeal of boots on snowpack as Ray walked away from us, one hand touching the wall of the mess as if he were on board ship. He muttered curses in French as he went.

Look at his clothes, I said, pointing at the dead youth. He's not contemporary. Not even this century.

Incredible, Wyndham said.

We'll put him in one of the unoccupied huts. We've got an Otter due in five days. They'll have to take him back.

Grab an end, Vanderbyl said. We'll put him in Paris.

Some camps do this—they give whimsical names to various locations so that it's easy to explain where things are. No one knows who started it, and not all camps do it, but ours did. My cabin was called Pluto because it was farthest from the mess.

And so Kurt and I lifted the boy and carried him to Paris, his body having no more give than stainless steel.

For some reason—and barring a high wind—an unheated interior space always feels colder to me than the outdoors. It was only on stepping into that darkness that I remembered it was near fifty below zero outside. My face, despite the hood, was on fire.

We decided against waking Jens Dahlberg, there being nothing in his medical bag that was going to be of use to this young man, and tramped back toward the mess. Ray had thankfully gone to his cabin. The dog team lay in quiet formation in front of the sledge.

I asked Vanderbyl how it was that our own dogs had not woken up.

It's strange, he said, the smoke of his words issuing from his hood. The whole thing is strange. Christ, it's cold.

He won't sit, Wyndham said when we were back inside. I invited him to, but he won't. Won't even warm up by the fire.

The Inuk stood in the shadows by the door, his hands, encased in enormous sealskin mittens, folded before him.

Wyndham had pulled his own chair over to the stove. The kettle whistled and he got up and poured hot water into four mugs flagged with teabag labels.

Vanderbyl hung up his coat and went to stand beside the man, taking, as it were, his point of view. It's a thing I've noticed with some of the more isolated peoples: they prefer to talk side by side rather than face to face, sharing a point of view even in disagreement.

Thank you for bringing this boy to us, Vanderbyl said. It cannot have been easy for you. His family will be very grateful. A plane will land here in a few days and take him to a place where he can receive a proper burial.

The Inuk bowed his head. Impossible to tell if he was nodding in agreement or merely ruminating or registering nothing at all. If this sounds like the cliché of the silent Indian, it is. In my time, I have met the stereotypes of the absent-minded professor, the hot-blooded Latin, the stiff-upper-lipped British officer, and it just can't be helped. This was his behaviour.

The Inuit in general are not particularly quiet people. Hunter Oklaga could make a story last all night, if you let him, and his wife was the same. I had dinner at their home in Resolute one evening and was thoroughly exhausted by the experience. His two teenage daughters gave an impromptu throat-singing recital, an eerie Inuit custom. Two females—it's always females—stand face to face, lightly gripping each other's elbows. One begins a rhythmic bass line consisting of a phrase that may or may not be nonsense, while the other develops a sort of spinning, buzzing melody line above it. The sound is closer to that of two mating furry creatures, or even to a didgeridoo, than to anything recognizably human. They look intently into each other's eyes or at each other's lips, standing only inches apart, and combine the sounds with a shuffling dance. The effect is slightly erotic but the intent is amusement—the object being to see who can last the longest without giggling.

But this solid ghost who stood before us, threads of steam rising from his sealskins, was a different creature entirely. It was as if he lived in a different medium. It was like talking to a fish, a flash of silver below the surface, a hydrodynamic shadow in the depths. It seemed idiotic to speak at all, let alone expect a response.

Vanderbyl told him he was welcome to stay the night, or longer if need be. We would be happy to feed and shelter his dogs as well. He spoke in Tuk and repeated it in English.

Wyndham carried over two mugs of tea and offered one to the Inuk, who ignored it. He handed the other one to Vanderbyl and came back and sat beside me.

He doesn't understand a word, Wyndham said.

He's Polar Inuit, I said, from the tip of Greenland. They don't get out much.

That's four hundred miles away. What the hell would he be doing out here? Vanderbyl said, warming his hands over the stove.

Lika-Lodinn, I said.

What?

In the Norse sagas, Lika-Lodinn collected the frozen bodies of adventurers and returned them to the people they came from.

Well, he's making it pretty clear he wants nothing to do with us, so what's he doing hanging around in our mess?

He's waiting to be paid.

7

When they got to Ottawa, it was grey and just above freezing, with a cold rain falling. Technical difficulties had delayed their takeoff, and by the time they arrived at the Forensic Centre on Vanier, the autopsy on Marjorie Flint was over and they had to have the pathologist paged.

Dr. Motram was a young man who chewed gum constantly while he listened to them and even between his own sentences. Cardinal had an irrational prejudice against gum chewers and had to remind himself that it didn't mean a person lacked intelligence. In the pathologist's case, it might represent a token defence against his sometimes fragrant clientele.

"She's still on the table," he said. "Would you like to see her?"

The autopsy suite was like all such places except a lot bigger. There were eight tables, though only one was occupied.

Dr. Motram pulled the sheet back. A moment you never quite get used to. Pitiless Y incision coarsely sewn. As Motram spoke, he pointed to various parts of the woman's body, points of interest on a map.

"As you can see, we have frostbite to both hands, even the nose and ears. Those violet-coloured patches over the hip joint and over the knees are called frost erythema—probably caused by capillary damage from the cold and plasma leakage. Ottawa's one cold city, surrounded by rugged country, and we've got the same homeless problems as anybody else, but I've never in my life seen frostbite this bad. She was out there a long time before she died."

"She went missing nearly two weeks ago," Cardinal said.

Motram nodded. "There's post-mortem damage as well, notably a skull fracture from freezing of the brain. Internally, we've got Wischnewsky spots on the stomach mucosa. Those, in combination with the frost erythema, make hypothermia the cause of death. The electrolytes get totally out of whack and you end up with a ventricular fibrillation. That's finally what killed her."

"What day do you think she died?"

"The freezing makes it impossible to be precise, but I'd say she's been dead five or six days."

"So she lived through the cold for several days," Delorme said. "He left her food and coffee. He wanted to make it last."

"Or maybe he didn't really want her to die," Motram said. "Maybe he thought someone else would come along."

"You didn't see where she was found."

Motram folded his arms and chewed his gum for a moment. He pointed to the wrists and ankles. "Restraint marks obviously—padded restraints is my guess. They would have contributed to the advanced frostbite in the hands."

"You see any signs of struggle?" Cardinal asked. The body—reddened here, blackened there—showed no slash marks, no scratches.

"She struggled against the restraints, certainly. But you mean a fight?"

"Yes, a fight."

"On that score, I'd have to say no. No defensive wounds, no scratches. No sign of sexual trauma, or recent sexual activity of any kind for that matter. Nothing under the fingernails, what's left of them. Clearly she was tearing at the restraints, whatever they were."

"Cuffs," Delorme said. "Padded steel cuffs."

Motram regarded her, stopped chewing. "*C'est triste, non?*"

Delorme nodded, looking at the thing on the table that had recently loved, wept, had hopes. Marjorie Flint heads home to make dinner for her senator husband, with no idea of what the night will bring.

Motram turned and snapped on the light box and pointed to one of the images that showed a clear fracture. "She was a skier. Couple of old injuries to the ulna and clavicle, but this one—that's the left tibia. She fractured her shinbone trying to break out of those cuffs."

He gestured to the row of large glass jars, their organic contents suspended in fluid. "She was a healthy woman for fifty-five. Major organs disease free. Arteries, heart and lungs clear. You can see the hemorrhagic spots there. Stomach contents indicate her last meal was about twenty-four hours pre-mortem."

"How accurate is that?" Cardinal asked. "She was pretty locked down."

"I'm taking that into account. Twenty-four hours, give or take two hours. Digestion was long over. But I'm saving the best for last."

He snapped off the light box and the three of them turned once more to the body. He pointed to the graceful region behind the clavicle where shoulder joins neck. "See those?"

Cardinal and Delorme leaned forward together.

"Needle sticks," Motram said. "As you can see, whoever administered it was no expert. Took more than a couple of stabs at it. In fact, you asked about struggle, and I guess that could be a sign she was struggling when she was injected. Hard to tell. Anyway, subcutaneous residue shows traces of ketamine."

"Is that long-acting?" Cardinal remembered the hospital room, the smells of plastic and disinfectant, his mother half devoured by disease.

"Not really. He's not hitting veins, so he'd have to reinject. I have the report from toxicology in my office, and I'll give it to you when we go up. The findings indicate it would have worn off long before she died."

~

Cardinal and Delorme went to the evidence room, where Marjorie Flint's clothes were spread out on a table.

"There was more than three hundred dollars in her wallet," Cardinal said. "And there's no sign of sexual assault. No robbery, no rape. What are your thoughts so far?"

"On motive? I don't think the person who did this had any motive. The only motive is he wants her to die—slowly, painfully—and it makes me sick. A woman will kill you. A woman will have a rage and kill her husband, her child even, but something like this? Only a man would do this—it's always men brutalizing women, and I just get so sick of it. You see a crime like this, does it ever occur to you that maybe there are just too many men in this world? Not too many people—too many men."

"Yes, it does, Lise. What can you tell me about the clothes?"

"The jacket we know—it's a North Wind, goose down, of a very popular blue colour. Not the black cashmere she was last seen wearing. The blouse, sweater, underwear—all good labels. A senator's wife, what do you expect?"

"You can give me more than that. I mean, the boots alone . . ."

"Exactly, John. The boots alone. What are the chances that a woman who wears Hermès, Holt Renfrew, a Patek Philippe watch is going to go walking around the nation's capital in a pair of Kodiak boots?"

"I know," Cardinal said. "If it wasn't for the fact she was chained up, you'd think the guy was concerned for her safety."

"Amazing what a difference a few chains can make. And no gloves?"

"Yeah," Cardinal said, and picked up one of the rags—parts of a torn shirt that had been wrapped around the victim's hands. "And where did she get these?"

"The Ottawa guys say the husband didn't recognize the jacket or the boots. Someone went out and bought them for her, John. Went out and got outdoor clothes in her size. I don't think it was out of kindness."

"Lise . . ."

"What?"

"Take it easy. We're in this for the long haul."

"Forty below, John. Forty below."

"I know. I get it. There's a man out there who should not be at large. And a woman is dead who should not be. But there are things we can do—things for *her*, Lise—and if we do them right, we'll come up with an answer here and an answer there and sooner or later those answers will put us on the right road. At the end of that road, we find our man and we get him off the streets for good."

"And everything is wonderful and the world is a good place."

"No. We lock him up and go after the next one. Anything else is just a one-way ticket to misery."

—

Cardinal dropped Delorme off at the Ottawa police headquarters, where they'd been allocated a desk and not much else. The rain looked like it was about to freeze. He drove through town to Rockcliffe Park, listening to the French-language CBC. He had been trying to learn French off and on for a couple of years now, something he had not mentioned to Delorme because he suspected she would laugh. The announcer was talking about climate change and sea ice, he could make out that much—but only because he'd read the same story in the *Globe and Mail* at the airport.

Cardinal had never been to Rockcliffe Park before. Right in the middle of town, and yet it had patches of what looked like a private forest. There were no sidewalks and lots of walls and many of the houses were not even visible from the road. He passed one that appeared to be constructed of glass and gold.

The Flint house was more modest, a three-storey mock Tudor with grounds the size of a small game reserve. Cardinal pulled into a semicircular drive and parked near a garage that was bigger than the house he used to live in. He switched off the car and picked up his briefcase and thought a minute about what he would say. Cardinal had talked to a few MPs in his time, but never to a senator. In the dark forests of Canadian politics, senators are mythical creatures rarely seen, their powers (if any) uncertain. Cardinal did not know what to expect.

He got out and went up the front steps in the cold drizzle and rang the bell. The door was answered by the senator's daughter, who was on her way out.

"He's expecting me," Cardinal said. "I phoned ahead."

"He's in mourning, for God's sake. He's already talked to the Ottawa police. Can't you come back?"

"Someone has done a terrible thing to you and your family, and I want to put that person where he belongs. I'm pretty sure your father will want to help."

She scanned his face and opened the door wider. Cardinal stepped into a vast foyer composed entirely of oak panelling and works of art. She took his coat and Cardinal heeled off his galoshes.

"May I give you a little tip, Detective?"

"Please."

"Despite my father's manner, he's not the tough guy he may appear. It's easy to misread him."

"Thank you for telling me."

He followed her down a short corridor to a small room where her father was watching a flat-panel TV. A black-and-white movie.

The senator got up and shook hands. He was about Cardinal's age, but he steadied himself on the arms of his chair as he sat down again. Hollowed out with grief, as if he might be blown away by the slightest breeze. Skin tone the shade of grey that speaks of extreme stress. White-collar criminals turn that shade after their first week in jail. And people who have lost what they most love.

The senator clicked off the TV sound but left the picture. Edward G. Robinson in a priest's outfit, looking dyspeptic but caring.

"First, let me say I'm very sorry for what you're going through, Senator."

"Thanks." The senator looked at him, the whites of his eyes webbed with red. "Siddown. And call me David."

Some kind of western flatness in his voice. Cardinal remembered that Senator David J. Flint had grown up in the Yukon.

"I'll tell ya, a time like this, whatever else it is, is utterly fuckin exhausting. I hope you don't mind a little cussing."

"You swear all you want, Senator."

"Nobody's got the least crumb of an idea what this is like. Not one fuckin micron. Couple of my friends, sure, their wives have *died*—but this is just a whole different . . . I just—this is not somethin a man can prepare for."

"I know," Cardinal said.

The senator closed his eyes, and Cardinal knew what he was thinking. Before he opened them again, Cardinal said, "My wife was murdered too."

The senator opened his eyes. "Really."

"A couple of years ago now."

"And you're still walkin around."

"I don't know what else you can do."

"You tell that to a lot of people you deal with? Bereaved people? Gain their trust?"

"You're the first. It's not the kind of thing they recommend. You'll either trust me or you won't. I don't expect to earn it with a few words."

"Well, you talk good. You want some coffee?"

"No, that's okay."

"Fuckin cold rain out there. Warm you up. Let's hit the kitchen."

The kitchen was large, mostly white tile, with a round pine table in one corner. A pair of French doors looked out on snowdrifts pocked with rain.

The senator opened a cupboard, got a coffee filter out and put it in the basket. He opened the fridge door and spoke to the interior. "People seem intent on provisionin me. Bringin me so much food, I can't find anything. Nice of 'em, though. Real nice."

He brought out a can of President's Choice coffee and filled the basket and switched on the machine.

"Better put some water in that."

"Water." The senator snapped his fingers. "Right." He dealt with the water and sat down. "You got questions, you better get at 'em. I don't promise to be coherent."

Cardinal took him through the usual questions, ground the Ottawa police had already covered. Senator Flint made no complaint about repeating the answers. It took half an hour.

"Just a couple more points, Senator, and then I'll leave you alone. Your wife's car was left at her therapist's office, the last place she was seen. Appointment finished at four p.m., and this was a regular thing she had, right? Weekly, I think you said?"

"Marjorie was forever tryin to fix herself. She didn't need fixin, but she imagined she did. She was a busy woman, charity work every which way, and three unpaid positions. I think she just needed the reprieve—a little sliver of time that was hers and hers alone. An hour of reflection never hurt anyone. She liked her therapist."

"It's very unlikely we're looking at a chance encounter here. Your wife's abductor seems to have known her schedule, meaning this was either someone already familiar with her routines or someone who had tracked her movements for a time."

"I'm not aware of anyone who would wish Marjorie harm. You could not hope to find a less contentious person. Generous. Kind. Jesus . . ." The senator pinched the bridge of his nose. He shaded his eyes with his hand. "Sorry. Uh, try to collect myself here."

"Take your time."

The senator dabbed at his eyes and blew his nose. "I'm not generally an emotional person."

"Human, though."

"*Hah.* All too."

"I know I'm repeating myself, but are you absolutely sure there were no unusual visitors to the house leading up to your wife's disappearance?

Maybe some unexpected workmen? Some survey takers? Jehovah's Witnesses? Strangers of any kind?"

"I don't stand at the window lookin for strangers. And I don't stare into my rear-view neither. No doubt that'd make me a terrible detective. Anyways, neither me nor Marjorie is home that much. Someone could have got in here, I don't know. Didn't see any sign of it. Christ, you think someone planned this? In God's name, why? Why Marjorie?"

"If I could answer that question I could probably tell you who killed her. Keep in mind it could've been you they were after, Senator."

"That would at least make sense. I piss people off now and again. Sometimes I don't even intend it. But I got to tell you—I'm a senator, not an MP, and senators in this country are appointed, not elected. It's undemocratic and frankly it's outright dumb, but one thing it means is you're freed of a whole lotta political nastiness. Senate's a collegial bunch. Used to be, anyway."

"What about from before? You were an electrical engineer?"

"Power systems. Micro-power systems. Fortune favoured me in my work life same as in my home life. I don't know why. Couple of patents came my way and paid for all this extravagance. We don't live high, but I won't deny we're fortunate. Wealthy. I retired at fifty, ran for office, failed at that right quick. Worked for a couple of candidates behind the scenes after that, did my rain dance for 'em, and voila—Mr. Flint goes to Ottawa. Ridiculous, but it may as well be me stedda some of the yahoos they appoint. Ain't got the sense of a doorknob, most of 'em. I'm just prayin Dear Leader sends up a bill to abolish me and the whole bunch of us. I'll rubber-stamp that puppy in a flash. Opponents, yes. But outright enemies? No."

Cardinal reached into his jacket and pulled out his wallet, opened it and took out a ticket. "This was in your wife's wallet."

The senator took it and contemplated it. Turned it over and looked at the number. "It's from a fundraiser."

"You need a ticket for that?"

"Naw, they always have a giveaway of some sort. You pay your thousand bucks to attend and you get a chance to win something—artwork, signed first edition, whatever. So you hang on to the ticket."

"And the number on the other side? Number 25?"

"Table number. This one was at the Château Laurier. World Literacy, if I recall. I'd a never thought of it, but Marjorie would." He handed back the ticket.

Cardinal opened his briefcase and dropped the ticket inside, along with his notebook, and snapped it shut again. "Senator, thank you. Once again, I apologize for intruding at a time like this."

The senator waved him off. "I'm just sorry I can't be of more use."

They went out to the foyer and the senator stood looking out the sidelights of his front door while Cardinal put on his galoshes and coat.

"You ever find the guy that killed your wife, Detective?"

"Yes, I did. He's doing life in Kingston."

"I'm glad. And what about this bastard now?"

"No guarantees. I'll do my best."

"Listen, I don't want to interfere or nothin, but could you use the RCMP on this?"

"We're already using their forensic services, and they've offered further assistance if we need it. The Ottawa police are being very helpful too."

"Well, let me know if I can help any other way."

"If it's all right, I'd like to take a look around your property."

"Fine with me. You've been very understanding, Detective. I appreciate it."

Cardinal didn't know what to say to that. He asked a question instead. "Do you have any connection with a woman named Laura Lacroix? Or do you know if your wife had any?"

"Laura Lacroix? I don't think so. Mind you, I meet a lot of people. Too many people." Flicker of a smile, a memory passing by.

Cardinal pointed at a life-sized portrait of the senator's wife. It was big and colourful, but it looked like a sketch. She was laughing, a boat and a lake in the background. "That's beautiful."

"Charles Comfort. You heard of him?"

"My wife would have."

"He rented the cottage next to ours one summer. Lugged that over the day he left. Worth a buck or two, actually."

"Generous guy."

"Something I've noticed—when you have a lot, people are always giving you things."

"So you don't mind if I take a look at your garage, the rest of your property here? It might help me get a handle on this guy."

"Help yourself, Detective. Ottawa police did all that, of course, but you're welcome to check it out—anything that'll help."

Cardinal took out a business card and wrote on the back of it before handing it to the senator. "This is not because you have a lot. That's my personal cell number. In case you think of anything else. I mean it—call any time."

The senator held the card in two hands by the corners and looked at it. "I have a notion this is another of those things they don't recommend."

From the Blue Notebook

And what is the going rate for dead Victorian teenagers? Dahlberg inquired. As his red beard grew thicker, he was taking on something of the look of Robert E. Lee.

I told him how Vanderbyl had presented two large hams to the Inuk, who cradled them in his arms like twins. How Vanderbyl had opened the door and released him once more into the night.

What does Hunter have to say about all this?

He's beside himself that he slept through it. I guess we should have woken him.

Dahlberg was down on one knee beside the cot where we had placed the dead youth. This fellow can't be from the Franklin expedition, he said. We're nowhere near their last known location.

We talked about the various expeditions. The stray graves and markers. The three headstones on Beechey Island.

His clothes look too early for the Greely expedition, Dahlberg said. That was the 1880s—and didn't they end up eating each other?

Frostbite had turned the boy's face and hands deep purple.

Do you suppose others found him and took his outer garments? Dahlberg said. He can't have lasted long like this.

Whoever he may have been, I said, you can't do much for him now. But you need to look in on Ray. He's acting a little . . . unsteady.

Dahlberg glanced at me over his shoulder. I can't discuss him with you. He's a patient.

I'm surprised Vanderbyl hasn't said something.

If he had, I couldn't discuss it with you. Dahlberg felt in the boy's pocket. He pulled out a tiny coin and held it up in the window light. Sixpence, 1832, he said. He felt in another pocket and pulled out a compass. This time he stood up and we both examined it.

A Tinsly, Dahlberg said. They went out of business before the Gutta Percha Company. He opened the case and the needle swung first one way, then the other.

Wouldn't have been much good, I said. Too near the magnetic pole.

Fire and food would have been the only things of use to him, and I don't think he had either, poor bastard.

Dahlberg fussed with a camera for a few minutes. When he finally took an exposure, the flash left an afterimage, the dead boy's face adrift in the frigid air.

8

THE GROUNDS OF SENATOR FLINT'S estate were beautiful even in the sombre light of mid-afternoon. The air smelled of wet snow and woodsmoke, and among the old oaks and maples there was a rustle and click of bare branches. Now, in the dimming of the day, the windows of the house were dark.

The garage, with its former chauffeur's apartment, now a storage area, was a likely vantage point, but the family had noticed no unexplained footprints in the snow, and Ottawa detectives had found the alarm in working order, the locks untouched, the dust undisturbed. Cardinal had no reason to suspect them of incompetence.

The patio at the back of the house was partially cleared off. Cardinal stood between the recycling bins and the ambiguous shapes of furniture shrouded with snow. The property extended some five hundred metres, the rolling landscape interrupted by outcroppings of granite and stands of pine, the entire vista surrounded by a two-metre stone wall. To see over it, you'd have to be in a tree or a lineman's cherry picker—distinctly uncomfortable prospects in the middle of an Ottawa winter. There were no houses close by. Through the trees beyond the garage he could make out just a single gable.

He went out through a side gate and walked along a winding road under a tracery of black branches. School was out, and the sounds of children and barking dogs carried over the stone fences, the wet roads. He rounded a curve and saw that the structure he had mistaken for the gable of a neighbouring house was actually an elaborate tree house, or rather what remained of one. The children for whom the structure had been built had no doubt long since gone away to distant schools, distant cities. He thought about his own daughter, pursuing an art career in New York, and the kinds of distance you can't measure in miles.

He climbed up on the low stone fence. There were depressions at the base of the tree, foot tracks, since snowed over and rained over, that could be from the Ottawa police, or from someone else. There was no tree house mentioned in the scene reports they'd showed him. He hopped down and cursed as snow slithered into his galoshes.

From the far side, the tree house looked even more decrepit. One whole wall was gone, another sagged almost forty-five degrees away from the frame. The frame itself, at least from below, looked solid and well made. Access consisted of a series of wood blocks attached to the tree trunk with rusted spikes. Some of the lower ones were missing.

Galoshes proved to be less than ideal climbing footwear, and Cardinal had to take it slow. He paused on each block, hugging the wet tree. It was only when his head was just below the tree-house floor that he could see over the senator's stone wall. Even then, the back of the garage blocked any view of the house.

Cardinal pulled himself up, the edge of a one-by-eight digging into his knee, and then he was kneeling on the floor. No sway, no creak. A couple of floor planks were missing, and he got to his feet and tested the others before putting his full weight on them.

There was no view of the Flint residence. It was blocked by the one wall of this spavined structure that remained completely solid. Off in the opposite direction, where the wall was missing, he could see a mansion of brick and stone. Cardinal was not a man who nursed any interest in how the wealthy lived, but he was—or had been for many years—a man with a passion for woodworking and cabinetry. After Catherine's death, with the move from their house to an apartment, he had put his tools in storage, unable to part with them for good. Well-made things spoke to him, and he allowed himself a moment of envy of whoever lived in such a beautifully constructed house.

A piece of tarp hung from a small hook that had been screwed into the old four-by-four of the frame. The hook looked new, as did the tarp when Cardinal lifted it up. Matching hooks, three of them, had been screwed into the opposite post. He stretched out the tarp and hung it by a corner grommet from the top hook. It made a makeshift fourth wall that hid him from view. He was now the sole tenant of six square feet of country property. Handyman's dream, as the real estate ads liked to put it. Amenities included a two-plank "table" supported by two diagonal planks underneath and a crippled chair with a rush seat, usable in an emergency but badly in need of more rushes.

The winter light was draining away and with it Cardinal's interest. Whether standing or sitting—gingerly—he could see nothing of the Flint residence. He could peer over the tarp if he wished. And through the sagging wall on his right he could watch the headlights on Rockcliffe Road. The solid wall was covered with childish drawings and lettering. ALEX, HELP! MARNIE WAS HERE. It was hard to make out the smaller scribbles.

He unhooked the tarp so he could see better. Pictures of Charlie Brown and Lucy and Snoopy and Garfield and many highly active stick figures. Charlie Brown looked as if he had just had brain surgery and the cap of his skull had been reset a half-inch off-kilter. Same with Lucy's haircut.

Cardinal touched the board second from the top. It was loose. A slight nudge to the left rendered Charlie and Lucy whole. He pulled the board right out and put it on the table. Through the space where it had been, he now had a clear view of the senator's house. He could see one whole side of the house as well as the front entrance. Beyond the top of the garage, the iron gates were just swinging open in front of the senator's car as it rolled down the drive away from the house. Cardinal watched the gates close behind him.

A box seat. Best view in the house.

Cardinal leaned close to the slot where the board had been. There was something written on the exposed wood of the frame. He pulled out his cellphone and held the screen close. In the pale glow he could see the number 25. There were no numbers on the other exposed struts, nor on the back of the removed plank. He snapped several pictures of it and of the tree house itself, then dialed the Ottawa squad and Delorme.

~

Delorme had arranged to meet Cardinal at Café Max, a small Parisian-style bistro just off Rideau. She ordered a bottle of Cabernet Sauvignon and a basket of bread and sat back on the banquette reading the menu. Some of the dishes were French Canadian, but she didn't recognize a lot of the others. Parisian dishes, she supposed. She had never travelled to France, let alone Paris. At one time, in her late teens, she had been keen on the idea, but over the years the urge had faded.

Cardinal came in and sat down and she poured him a glass of wine. He put on his glasses to read the menu.

"What do you think?" Delorme said. "Too rich for expenses?"

"It's fine."

"My mom used to bring me here when I was going to Ottawa U. I asked them to bring you an English menu, but they seem to have forgotten."

"I'll manage. The wine's good."

The waiter came and told them the specials in French. A Québécois, Delorme noted with pleasure. Waiters who considered themselves *vrai français* always asked her to repeat everything.

Cardinal surprised her by ordering in French as well. Beet salad and the steak frites. He did very well, even managing the French usage of *entrée* for appetizer, but then the waiter posed a supplementary question. How would *monsieur* like his steak prepared? Cardinal was decisive: he would like his steak half-baked.

The waiter smiled and said in English, "Did you mean medium?"

"Medium, yes." And when the waiter was gone, "Isn't that what I said?"

"It's *médium*, not *mi-cuit*. But I'm impressed you've even heard of *mi-cuit*. Have you been reading Julia Child?"

Cardinal muttered something unintelligible and asked about her afternoon.

"Oh, it was exhilarating. I read the entire case file, all their reports, from end to end. Police are not great writers, you ever notice? Doesn't look like they were getting anywhere, but they've saved us a lot of work."

"Well, they should have their scene men all over that tree house by now. If there's anything there, they'll find it. What do you make of the number 25?"

Delorme suddenly felt a little oppressed, she wasn't sure why. She didn't want to talk about the case, but Cardinal was bright-eyed and eager. Of course, that was one of the reasons she and all the other detectives liked to work with him: it just never occurred to him to get tired of a case.

"There wasn't anything in the reports about '25,'" she said. "Guess you'll have to take it to a numerologist."

"It might be nothing. On the other hand, there were no other marks like it. The scene guys should be able to tell how recent it is. What's up? Are you pissed off with me for some reason?"

"Where's our food, for God's sake?"

Cardinal looked down at the table and tapped his fork on the checkered cloth. He always turned away when she was upset, as if she was just too pathetic to contemplate. The guy lives with a wife who was in and out of psychiatric wards all her life and he doesn't bat an eye. Me, I get a little annoyed and he can't take it. Of course, Catherine had been beautiful and talented and not his boring colleague.

"So, one of us had a productive afternoon," she said. "Must be nice."

Cardinal looked up. The little-boy eagerness all gone, replaced by Mr. Calm and Inscrutable.

"John, did you ever think for a moment that I might have liked to be in on the interesting stuff? Why do I get sent to the file cabinet while you get to take a close look at the killer's possible hideaway?"

"Hey, careful." Cardinal looked around to see if anyone was within earshot.

"You agree with Chouinard, is that it? Anybody—even a guy like Loach—is preferable to having me on a case?"

"What's Loach got to do with anything? We had to split up the work, that's all. I wasn't expecting to find anything at the Flint property. It may still turn out to be nothing."

The waiter brought their food and Delorme observed her own transformation into a normal, polite human being. She even offered a few unnecessary pleasantries in French. When he was gone, she said, "Don't shut me out of the interesting stuff, that's all I ask."

"That's it," Cardinal said. "From now on, you're McLeod to me."

"McLeod. Really. Now I'm fat and racist?"

"Prickly and unpredictable."

"That's not fair. McLeod is completely predictable."

They ate in silence for a while. The food was good, but Delorme couldn't bring herself to say so. She wished, as she did all too often around Cardinal, that she wasn't so childish.

When they got to the hotel, Cardinal went to his room on the fifth floor and Delorme went to hers on the seventh. She took off her coat and boots and got undressed and put on the extra-large T-shirt that was her nightgown. She sat on the end of one of the double beds and thought about calling Cardinal's room and inviting him to watch a movie.

She contemplated her reflection, a grey wraith in the television screen. "I don't want to watch a movie," she said.

From the Blue Notebook

Twice a week, Vanderbyl would set off on his skis for the seismic hut. This was several kilometres away, toward what had been the western end of the island but, owing to headwinds, encounters with other islands and underwater shoals, was now the southern end. He had government funding to complete the mapping of the Alpha Ridge, the hope in Ottawa being that it would prove to be firmly connected to Canada and not to Greenland—or, worse, to Russia. Kurt would sleep at the hut in order to begin blasting as early as possible.

Sometimes, when the others were safely engaged in their separate pursuits, I would go to Rebecca's lab. Despite how it may appear in the movies, desks and countertops are not ideal surfaces for lovers' encounters, even without all Rebecca's electronic gear. Sometimes I would sit myself on her task chair and she would straddle me, and I could lose myself in the scent of the hair at the nape of her neck, the taste of her sweat.

On nights when Vanderbyl was gone—this was May, when the nights were still extremely long—we could still use her cabin. But if Vanderbyl was in camp, she would come to my hut, my dwarf planet, as she called it, and we would lie in each other's arms. Afterward, it was a struggle for her to climb out of bed and venture once more into the sub-zero darkness. But we felt safer there, because there seemed little likelihood of Vanderbyl visiting me.

One night I was in bed and I put my book aside. It was another novel Rebecca had thrust on me, a "coming of age" story about a

Pakistani boy growing up in Muskoka. His experience was remarkably similar to that of the Catholic girl in Newfoundland in the previous book she had lent me, and I resolved to accept no more. There's a factory somewhere turning these things out, I had said to annoy her.

Why does everybody have to be kooky? I yelled in answer to the soft rapping at my door. Why does everybody have to have a heart of gold? Come in, for God's sake. I want to berate you.

But it was Vanderbyl who opened the door and came in and quickly shut the door behind him.

He removed his gloves and pushed his hood back and stood there in his stooped way. His face looked as if it had crumpled with exhaustion and subsequent attempts to smooth it out had been unsuccessful. Dark circles under his eyes, points of white at the corners of his mouth. A man to whom sleep was a stranger.

I apologize for the disruption. May I sit down?

He removed his boots and sat on my desk chair in his parka. He stretched his hands out before him as if checking the lengths of his arms, then let them rest in his lap, a collection of long fingers, bony wrists. He lapsed into stillness.

There was nothing for me to say under the circumstances. I sat back against the wall, wrapped in my sleeping bag that smelled of Rebecca.

A rustling of parka as Vanderbyl roused himself. I thought he was going to go hurtling back out into the night, but he went down on his knees. He clasped his hands in front of his chest and shook them before me as if they were chained.

Is this what you want? he said.

Kurt, for God's sake.

If this is what you want, you have it. All right? You have it. It must feel good, right? Must fill your heart with joy?

Of course not. Please get up.

But you're the one who put me here. You must want me here, isn't it?

No.

You and my wife. Together, you have crushed me into nothing. She had reasons, you have none.

Kurt, you split from her. You left her. You're separated.

A trial separation. I wanted her to realize she wants to stay with me. It turns out I am the one doing all the realizing.

That's the trouble with experiments. They rarely yield the data we expect.

Is it because of the hiring committee? Is it because you didn't get tenure?

That was years ago, Kurt.

You must realize that was nothing personal. There was simply a more suitable candidate.

That's debatable.

It was duly debated. It was not an easy decision. Nor was it unanimous. But in the end—for a number of reasons—Klimov was the committee's choice.

You were chair. You had ultimate control.

And here I am.

He held his clasped hands out to me again. Even on his knees, Vanderbyl was looking down at me.

I was angry then, I said. Full of resentment, perhaps even hatred. But I'm perfectly content at Carleton, and I don't believe in revenge.

Are you so certain? I didn't believe in jealousy.

He got to his feet and reached for the chair. For a moment I feared he was going to raise it over his head and smash my skull with it. He dragged it closer and sat down.

But now I do. Proved upon the pulses, as the poet says. How ridiculous that I—I, who pride myself on nothing so much as my reason—should see that reason overthrown by a simple fact of anatomy. All logic, all judgment gone from me, leaving me reduced to whatever is left when they are gone. I am yearning and appetite, loneliness and lust. I am rage and grief and helplessness, the whole sorry—no, the *mere* sorry, the *merest*, weakest, sleepless sorry thing. Amusing for you, of course—to see me devoured alive.

No, Kurt. I'm sorry you're in pain.

Yes, yes. Of course you are.

Well, that's the nature of jealousy, isn't it? Keeps you at the centre of the story?

When you're being eaten by a shark, it's difficult to see it from the shark's point of view.

I'm in love with her, Kurt.

Then I ask you, as a man in love, to recognize what I am going through. And if revenge is your motive, I am here to tell you the knife is in my heart and yours is the hand twisting it. I am on my knees before you. Begging you to stop.

Kurt.

We have worked together many times. We do not know each other well, but well enough. You know that I have a large ego. Such an easy target. I ask you to measure my words to you now against that nature and calculate what it is costing me.

Kurt.

I don't come here empty-handed. Brenner is retiring next year. You'd start with full tenure.

I have tenure at Carleton.

You'd have almost no teaching, no committees. Full research sabbaticals. And the salary would be higher. We could probably make it as high as mine.

Jesus, Kurt.

If I had money of my own, I would give it to you, but you probably have more than me. I am not a wise investor. Perhaps we could come to some quiet arrangement.

Kurt, she isn't mine to sell.

She isn't yours at all. Rebecca is my wife. Do you know what that means? Do you have any idea? It's not a piece of paper. It's not a matter of a ceremony. It means I have watched her grow from a graduate student, still a girl really, into a fully mature and wise woman. I have been there in the big moments of her life—achieving her master's degree, the day she defended her dissertation. I have been there for the disappointments, the setbacks. I have watched her walk face first into the most cruel academic traps. She thinks everyone is her friend, everyone wishes her well, until they don't.

That was not my experience of Rebecca, and I said so. Whether he heard me or not, I've no idea.

I held her at her mother's funeral, he said. I have heard her talk in her sleep, stroked her hair when she woke up from some nightmare.

Driven her to the emergency room and sat with her hour after hour. I've never seen anyone so sick. They gave her five bags of fluid, Durie, five bags of saline. It caused her temperature to plummet and she shook on the gurney as if possessed by epilepsy. And the car accident—did she tell you about the car accident?

I said no, but it hardly mattered. He didn't hear me.

Norway. We were going far too fast. Terrible weather, fog and sleet, and the driver lost control and we woke up in some tiny little outpost clinic, not a hospital. I received a broken arm only, but Rebecca had a deep gash in her leg and desperately needed a transfusion. I woke up covered in her blood. They had a line in my arm and took my blood for a transfusion—we have the same type. She is literally of my blood, Durie, that's what the word *wife* means in this particular instance, in case you don't happen to know or care.

I tried to speak some calming words, but he was raving now.

It means also, yes, I have hurt her. Because I am a man and I am vain and stupid and weak. I have hurt her and felt her tears soak through my shirt when I have given her my abject apologies. But it isn't just that. It is not such big things always. Not so long ago I was looking for a stamp or some scissors or something and I opened her desk drawer and you know what I found? I found a ticket, a torn ticket, for an evening of Bach concertos. No great virtuoso, no acclaimed orchestra, but it was the first place we had gone together, and she had kept the ticket and glued it to a piece of fine paper and written the date underneath in her beautiful handwriting, with the words *The first place I went with Kurt.*

Kurt, please. It's late. Let's just work together as best we can.

I have heard her giggle on the phone like a schoolgirl, I have heard her singing off-key at the top of her voice when she thought no one was home. You think because you fuck her you're somehow closer? Yes, sure, look away, I don't blame you. And it's not just the little things either, it's the less than that. The nothings. I get up in the morning and she is there, Durie. She is there, you understand. Year after year, day after day. This person I know I don't deserve, every day.

Was there. You took her for granted, Kurt.

Yes, of course I did. I'm selfish and vain and not very noticing of things. But it's not all bad, you know, taking each other for granted. You get used to each other, as you get used to a landscape—living on the plain or in Toronto or in the shadow of some mountain. Yes, they are your landscape, they surround you, you forget they're there. In a way, taking a person for granted is a mark of love.

Good night, Kurt.

A mark of trust.

He swiped at his tears with the sleeve of his parka. God, I'm a stupid man. Of all the people to ask! I've long known you for a cold person, Durie, an unfeeling person. But it would take a microscope to measure the distance between unfeeling and cruel. Sometimes to be cruel requires no action at all, just the willingness to stand by and do nothing. I am a man engulfed in flame, begging you to piss on me, but of course you won't. Give her back? God, I'm an idiot. You'll never give her back.

Kurt, I'm not trying to hurt you. You say you love her. Is it so hard to believe I love her too? Why is it so impossible that I should love Rebecca as well—maybe more than you ever did?

He was struggling with his boots now. Muttering. Yes, it's impossible. I'll tell you why it's not possible. It's not possible, Durie, for the simple reason that you don't love anyone and never will.

Honestly, Kurt, I don't think psychology's your strong suit. You talk like some half-educated priest.

Kurt opened the cabin door and the polar night rushed in. He went out and slammed the door behind him. I listened to his footsteps recede, then switched out the light and crawled deeper into my sleeping bag. In his rage and impotence Kurt imagined that his words had made no impact on me. But his claim of intimacy, true intimacy, with Rebecca had wounded me. I breathed in the scent of her—took it deep into my lungs, my antidote, my morphine. And I wondered once more if I was a bad man or simply a man of no moral import either way. I have never suspected myself of being good. If I have any virtue, it must be my not claiming any.

9

SHE CAME OUT OF THE Thomas Fisher Rare Book Library and trotted down the front stairs, enormous backpack bouncing with each step. Red mitten in the air as she waved to someone heading upstairs. Pretty smile.

A winter evening at the University of Toronto. Crowds of students flowed across the intersection in currents that shifted with each change of the traffic lights. They chattered to each other, their faces alive with the effortless beauty of the young, eyes shining in the street light, their cheeks lit by cellphones. Amid all this, one man, his features shadowed by a hood, made a very still point.

He watched as the young woman reached the bicycle rack, hair whipping across her face. Between the backpack slung from her shoulders and the helmet dangling from one hand, she looked more student than teacher. She put the backpack into her carrier, removed one mitten, and held it clamped between her teeth as she put the helmet on and fastened it. She bent to undo the U-lock and snapped it onto the frame and, still with the mitten in her mouth, unzipped a pocket of the backpack and reached inside.

A red light throbbed in her hand. She attached it under the bicycle seat and fixed another one—white, not flashing—to the handlebars.

Mitten on, she walked the bike over the curb, climbed on and pedalled west along Harbord.

The bicycle made her difficult to follow by car or on foot. Not that it mattered ultimately. Nothing mattered ultimately.

He watched as she joined the line of cyclists waiting at the next light. A confident woman, unfazed by snow squall or rush-hour traffic. Intrepid. She evoked in him a kind of awe. It is a tremendous thing, when you are composed of nothing but the past, to behold a creature, effortlessly beautiful, who is all future.

~

"And what am I supposed to wear to this thing?" Delorme sounded a little panicky on the phone. "How formal is it?"

"I don't know," Cardinal said. "He didn't say. Ronnie's not a formal guy."

"But he's rich, no?"

"Yeah, but—"

"Okay, so formal. He knows this isn't a date, right? We arrive together, people are going to think we're a couple, and I don't want to be explaining all night."

Cardinal had been a little nervous about asking her to Ronnie Babstock's party, especially after she had been so annoyed with him in Ottawa. When she answered the door, he couldn't shut up about how great she looked.

"Have you been drinking already? It's just a little black dress."

"No, it's not. You've got shiny things on, too."

"Shiny things. Great. Anyway, since when do you notice what I wear?"

Cardinal thought about that as they drove out to Ronnie Babstock's house. Delorme was right that it was out of character. Of course, it was also out of character for her to look like a total knockout. But it was more than that. It had been two years now since his wife's death, and he was aware of certain changes in himself.

Back before Christmas, he had been watching a movie with Delorme at her place. It was not a comedy but it had some funny bits, and Cardinal had laughed too loud. He heard it himself—he'd been doing it a lot lately—but he was defensive when Delorme remarked on it. She asked if he planned to become one of those laughers who annoy other people in movie theatres.

"It was just funny," he insisted. But he had been laughing too loud, and it had felt good, as if something inside him, not his heart but some lesser-known organ of feeling, long frozen, had somehow melted. The world began to seem a richer place; amusing things were more amusing.

And sad things were sadder. When Delorme had told him about her neighbours' dog having to be put down—their young daughter hysterical with grief—he had been quite upset. These were not even people he knew. Where did it come from, this burgeoning susceptibility? He was sure it was healthy—well, fairly sure—like recovering the feeling in fingers numbed with cold. It felt good on the whole, if slightly illicit. It only made sense that he was finally beginning to fully engage with the world once more.

Delorme had a lot to do with it. Their friendship was so free and easy, like no friendship he'd ever had. He never worried about Delorme. With Catherine, after her first breakdown early in their marriage, there was never a time when he was not worried about her. His love for his wife, though deep and loyal, had always contained a large element of protectiveness. Delorme was just a friend, he wasn't responsible for her, and she did not require anyone's protection, thank you very much.

When they arrived at the party, Cardinal enjoyed introducing her to Ronnie and his other poker friends, observing their reactions. Several of the women were wearing shiny things as well. Amid the candles, the ice buckets, the flutes of champagne, they took on the cheerful glitter of Christmas presents. But he felt no urge to leave Lise's side.

He was not generally much of a drinking man, but a bevy of highly groomed young women drifted among the guests, refilling glasses without asking. By the time dinner was served, he was discovering in himself hidden wells of amiability.

People asked about the Marjorie Flint case. A senator's wife had been murdered in their city, why wouldn't they? It was one of the things Cardinal usually hated about parties, people inquiring about high-profile cases when he couldn't say a thing about them. Tonight he refused to let it bother him. And in any case, Ronnie Babstock was running a kind of protective interference for him.

"Is it true she was chained up like a dog?" one woman asked.

"He can't talk about it," Ronnie said. "Case in progress."

Over dessert, another woman said, "Totally nude in sub-zero weather—it's unbelievable what that man did."

Actually, the fact that Marjorie Flint was warmly dressed was far more remarkable, but Cardinal said nothing.

"Rachel, didn't you hear? The poor guy can't talk about it."

"It's okay," Cardinal said. "People are bound to be curious."

"I mean, really," Ronnie said. "There's a limit."

The conversation turned to Ronnie's own work. Delorme mentioned the photographs that had been coming back from Mars, how Marti, the peripatetic robot, had lasted longer and travelled farther than anyone had expected. Cardinal realized she must have read up in preparation for the party, a courtesy that would never have occurred to him.

"You must worry all the time," she said. "All those billions at stake."

"Our test protocols are stringent," Ronnie said. "We put 'em through hell before NASA even gets a peek at 'em. And I mean hell."

"Does NASA get a warranty?"

"It's complicated."

"Well, there'd be rolling guarantees, I imagine."

"You know about contracts?"

"Lise is our white-collar-crime specialist," Cardinal said. "Don't let her near your tax return."

"There are various time frames with various liabilities," Ronnie said. "We're way above water on this one."

"Yes, I'd imagine so." Delorme raised her glass. "To Marti."

They toasted the robot, and then someone said, "A wife gets murdered, it's always the husband. And David Flint's known as a total bastard around the Senate."

"For Christ sake," Ronnie said. "They can't talk about it."

"Yes, but *we* can."

It was late when they said their good nights and stepped outside into the cold. Cardinal handed his car keys to Delorme, and she accepted them without comment. She took the slow route, along Lakeshore, probably because the lighting was better.

"I really enjoyed that, John. Thanks for taking me."

"I'm glad you came. I wouldn't have gone on my own." That didn't sound quite right to Cardinal's ear, he wasn't sure why. He reached over and turned down the heater a notch.

"Ronnie Babstock's so down-to-earth. Kinda cute the way he wouldn't let people make us talk about work. Like we were celebrities or something."

"Uh-huh." Cardinal was still trying to figure out what it was he had meant to say.

They drove the rest of the way to his apartment building in silence. Delorme parked in his spot and handed over the keys.

"I'll walk you home," Cardinal said.

"Don't be silly. It's two minutes."

Cardinal went with her. They walked uphill side by side, both with their hands in their pockets. A thin dusting of snow glittered in the street lights. Distant sound of a freight train heading south.

When they reached her house, Delorme stopped at the front path and started to thank him again, but Cardinal found himself speaking over her words. "I just have to say this," he said. "I'm really happy when I'm with you. That's all. Simple, true, and it's not champagne talking. I'm really happy when I'm with you."

Delorme squinted at him. Gave him the full Clint Eastwood he'd seen her use on thugs and lawyers, not to mention those colleagues whose commitment to honesty was imperfect. "What did you just say?"

"Nothing. I'll see you Monday. You're in Monday, right?"

"John, wait." Her voice softened. Her hand—gloved, small—alighted on his forearm, a touch barely perceptible through his parka. "I'm just not sure I heard what you said."

"I just said I'm happy when I'm with you, that's all."

"Oh, that's all."

"It just seems to be a fact. I guess it's obvious. It just suddenly struck me, that's all."

"Oh, that's all," she said again. Those skeptical eyes looking up at him, those lips slightly parted.

Cardinal takes hold of her shoulders and kisses her. In the cold of the night, the sudden heat of her mouth responding to him. Her hand reaching up and coming to rest on the back of his neck. And the whole time they're kissing, he has the feeling he's just stepped out of an airplane at thirty thousand feet.

—

In the course of her police career, Delorme had come across any number of paranoids. Her egregious colleague Ian McLeod was a prime example.

But before meeting Senior Detective Vernon Loach, she had never encountered a reverse paranoid. Loach seemed to cherish the delusion that people were out to do him good behind his back.

"No, I was talking to a producer at CBC," he was yelling to someone on the phone, possibly even his wife, poor woman. "And I think they're going to do a whole profile on me . . . like an actual biography thing."

Only if they're developing a satire, Delorme thought, and scanned an entry in Marjorie Flint's e-mail address list for the third time. Earlier, Loach had suggested to some unfortunate that Judge Roselyn Tate, the newest—and certainly the prettiest—member of the Superior Court, had a crush on him.

Loach was not bad-looking. Delorme could allow him that much. But he was one of those people who have regular features, a good build, a reasonable wardrobe, and no sex appeal whatsoever. Put him beside Cardinal and it was like he wasn't even in the room—except for his ego.

She thought again about that kiss. No telling where that was going to lead; they had ventured into uncharted territory. But she was feeling an excitement she hadn't experienced in a long, long time. It worried her a little—more than a little—and she told herself to focus on work.

She put her hands over her ears to block out Loach and tried to concentrate on the lists of contacts—names, numbers and e-mail addresses—that had once been the private property of Laura Lacroix and Marjorie Flint.

The senator's wife had lived in Ottawa, Laura Lacroix in Algonquin Bay; the chances of their having many people in common were slim. She did a search for 613 in Lacroix's address book and came up with three Ottawa phone numbers: a couple named Sal and Jackie Gottlieb, Club Risqué and Leonard Priest. None of these showed among Marjorie Flint's contacts.

Delorme worked her way through the entries one by one, marking off each one with an asterisk. Every now and then she'd get a flutter when there was a match between the two address books, but so far these had turned out to be national concerns such as Air Canada, the Bank of Montreal or Fairmont Hotels.

She tried to cheer herself up by remembering that even if she ruled out common connections, it was valuable information. Valuable, but not exciting. She kept wishing Cardinal would show up. They hadn't spoken since the party, and over the rest of the weekend she'd found a ridiculous anticipation building up. Sunday evening she'd called an old friend, Claire Nadeau, and told her what had happened.

Claire's enthusiasm was complete and unhesitating—surprising, since Delorme herself was far from certain this was a positive development.

"We work together," Delorme reminded her. "What if it doesn't work out? It'll be horrible."

"Don't be such a pessimist. Ever since the day you moved back to Algonquin Bay, you've been talking about this guy."

"As a colleague, not as a—"

"Bullshit, honey. You've always had this tone about him, how if only he wasn't married."

"I have not."

"Oh yes you have."

"I have not."

"Lise. Listen to your voice—you're totally thrilled. It's wonderful. Are you going to screw it up now by getting all negative?"

Delorme had tried to make Claire see that she was just being reasonable. Cautious. It's not like she was twenty-one, for Pete's sake. And yet here she was checking the clock every ten minutes.

At twelve-thirty, she put on her parka and went outside. Sunlight bouncing off the snowbanks made her eyes water. She was halfway across the parking lot when Cardinal called her name. He was at the side entrance, in shirt sleeves.

"Lise, where you headed?"

"I was just going to pick up a sandwich and bring it back. You want me to bring you something?"

"Hop in the car. We'll pick up something on the way."

"Way where?"

"Astor Bay. Arsenault came up with something good."

—

He told her about it on the way out to Astor Bay. Arsenault had finally managed to pin down the piece of snowmobile cowling. It matched an Arctic Cat 660 Turbo model produced between 2007 and 2009.

"Turbo. That's where the *rb* lettering came from?"

"Right."

"And how'd he get the date range?"

"In his words? 'Easy. They changed the font.'"

"Love that database."

"Actually, it's called Dents 'n' Dings. Place out on 63 sells scrap snowmobiles. He just went out there with that piece of plastic and browsed till he found a match. I've spent the morning going through reported snowmobile thefts."

"Are we sure it's stolen?"

"No, but it's a good bet."

"Where were you doing this?"

Cardinal looked at her. "Where?"

"You haven't been at your desk. I didn't even know you were in."

There was an odd tone in Delorme's voice. It made Cardinal a little nervous.

"I stayed in Ident," he said. "Collingwood's out, so I just sat at his desk and started running through what we had. Why?"

"Nothing. There must've been a ton of snowmobile thefts."

"Not of that model, not in black and silver. And I focused on a week either side of the day Marjorie Flint was abducted. That gives us three possibles. Printout's in my briefcase, top folder. I love it when footwork pays off, don't you?"

"You've got True North dealership as our first stop? If you want to steal a snowmobile, why would you go to a place that's well lit and has alarm systems and video cameras?"

"It's closest. We'll rule it out and move on."

—

The showroom of True North, with its gleaming Yamahas and Ski-Doos, was deserted except for the manager himself. Apparently the snow-poor season was raising his stress levels. When Cardinal and Delorme identified themselves, he put on an elaborate show of being surprised to see them.

"Two weeks ago I called. Two weeks, and now you show up? Guy could've driven the thing out to B.C. in that time."

Cardinal didn't want to get into it. "Your statement of complaint says the suspect took it out for a test drive. How'd he manage that? We haven't had any snow."

"Actually we had about four inches two weeks ago," Delorme said.

"Not that it stayed," the manager added with bitterness.

"Did you get some ID before you gave him the keys?"

"Two pieces. I can show you, but one's fake and the credit card's stolen. Believe me, afterwards I checked."

Cardinal pointed to the security camera above the counter. "You have the security tape?"

"We *gave* you the security tape. Two days after it happened. What's wrong with you people?"

The initial complaint had been taken by Ian McLeod. McLeod was a good investigator, except when a case bored him, which this one clearly had.

Cardinal apologized. "There was no note of it in the file, unfortunately."

"Typical. I *love* paying taxes, don't you? Luckily, I kept the original. You can watch it in my office."

He took them to his office and opened the safe. He pulled out the photo ID and handed it to them. Cardinal could see right away that a new picture had been rephotographed over the original. The manager put a disc into a player.

They watched a squarish, chunky man talking with a salesman, pointing to the window, the lot outside.

"He took the Arctic Cat, right?" Cardinal said. "Silver and black?"

"Silver and black. A 2008 model with barely a scratch on it."

Cardinal turned to Delorme. "Did you have any questions?"

"I think we have what we need."

It wasn't like Delorme to be so quiet during an investigation. Cardinal found it a little unsettling. He thanked the manager and promised to be in touch if they found anything.

When they were back in the car, Delorme said, "I can't see anyone who plans a murder of this kind putting his face on a security camera. I hope we don't have to go visit his phony address now."

"Let's get Sergeant Flower on it." Cardinal pulled out his cellphone and dialed.

Delorme shook her head.

"What? Flower loves stuff like this."

"Loves doing it for you, maybe. If I tried that, she'd snap my head off."

Cardinal was already speaking into the phone. He gave the address and a couple of parameters to follow, made a joke, and rang off.

He could feel Delorme getting annoyed. Whether it was at him or not, he wasn't sure. He thought again about their kiss of the other night. Exciting, yes, but he knew they had to talk about it. Probably she did too and it was making her edgy.

He wasn't used to being nervous with Delorme, and he was aware of his own peculiar reaction. It made him chatty, not at all his usual style, rattling on about what a great job Ident was doing, about the "snowmobile database," about the Ottawa people running down everything they could find on that tree house. "They've even got some cryptography guys at the RCMP looking at the number 25, seeing if they can relate it to anything to do with Marjorie Flint. You know, it occurs to me her table number at that fundraiser was 25."

"I'm sure that's the key, John. Take a week off. Your work is done here."

Cardinal glanced at her, but she kept her eyes on the oncoming traffic.

"Hey. It's called brainstorming, Lise."

"If you say so."

"You're usually the one with the hare-brained ideas—"

"Thanks."

"You didn't let me finish. The hare-brained ideas that turn out to be really smart. Are you annoyed about something? About the other night?"

"You seem hyper, that's all."

"You're right. I'll shut up. What's the number on Beachfront?"

Delorme glanced at the printout. "Twenty-five."

"No, it's not."

"One thirty-nine."

—

The woman who answered the door was holding a calico cat in her arms. "She runs out if I don't hang on to her," she said. "She'd kill every bird in this province if she had the chance."

To Delorme, the cat looked as if she had just swallowed three Valium, the way she was drooped all over her owner's chubby arm.

Cardinal asked about the stolen snowmobile.

"It's back," she said. "Returned of its own accord, believe it or not."

"I'll need a little more information than that," Cardinal said.

"In a way, it wasn't even stolen. My *son* took it. He's *supposed* to be studying journalism at Ryerson, but no, he just quit going and came back early. Didn't get around to telling us about it till a week later. In the meantime, he snuck into the boathouse and took the snowmobile for a wild time with his girlfriend."

Cardinal asked her for the exact date.

"Just a minute," she said, and closed the door. When it opened again, the cat was gone. "He brought it back January twelfth. Or rather, *we* brought it back—had to go pick it up at his girlfriend's place, other side of the lake. Some little skanky thing can't even *spell* college. Guess they had a great time till it run outta gas."

"Why didn't you let us know it had been returned?"

"To tell you the truth, I didn't think you cared."

"We'll need to see it."

"Why? The machine's not stolen anymore."

"It involves something else we're working on. Could you just show it to us, please?"

They got the key from her and opened the side door of the garage.

"It was returned before Marjorie Flint was even abducted," Delorme said.

The garage was large and neatly kept. The Arctic Cat was still on the trailer. The cowling showed no sign of damage or recent repair.

~

Next stop, the home studio of one Anne-Marie Caffrey, proprietor and yogi in chief of Namaste Yoga.

"Yes, they took the trailer too, I'm afraid. It was sitting right in front of the garage, so I guess we made it easy for them."

Delorme and Cardinal were seated side by side on a sofa while Ms. Caffrey told them about the theft of the family snowmobile. She was dressed for her afternoon yoga class in tights and a tank top, and although her hair was many different shades of silver, she had the body of someone half her age. Delorme thought this woman was the calmest person she had ever met. She promised herself to take up yoga within the week.

"I was of two minds whether to even report it," Ms. Caffrey told them.

"Why's that?" Cardinal's voice was softer than usual. Apparently her tranquility was contagious.

"Well, you know, it's possible the person just wanted to borrow it for a while and will return it of their own accord."

"It's possible. In fact, we had a case exactly like that, didn't we, Detective Delorme?"

"A family member took it," Delorme said.

Ms. Caffrey smiled. "Well, we don't have children, so that's not the case here. Anyway, it's not good to be too attached to things. My husband and I enjoyed the machine for a couple of years and now someone else is enjoying it."

"Someone who doesn't own it," Delorme said.

"Someone who didn't buy it, let's say." This delivered with a very slight, very tranquil nod. "I was never too keen on the thing. So noisy, and not exactly eco-friendly. But my husband wanted it, and it did get us out into the woods a lot more often than we would have gone otherwise."

Cardinal asked her if she had any idea who might have taken it.

A shake of the head. "Someone who needed a snowmobile? Or imagined they did."

"Did you see anything or anyone that might give you an idea who took it?"

"Not a soul."

"You teach yoga," Delorme said. "You have a lot of strangers coming to the house."

"I don't think of them as strangers, and I doubt any of them would borrow anything without asking. Mind you, I did see a van parked nearby a couple of times, not one we usually see around here, and I did vaguely wonder why. I mean, we know most of our neighbours, and it wasn't any of theirs."

"How do you know?" Cardinal said.

"It was a commercial vehicle of some kind—you know, like a contractor or a delivery van. Oh, and it was from Toronto. I remember thinking that was a little odd. It was white, very grubby."

"Old?" Delorme said. "New?"

"It didn't look new. The logo or lettering had been painted over—not very well. And it was so dirty." Ms. Caffrey looked grave for a moment, then brightened. "Of course, the fact that your van needs a bit of a wash doesn't automatically make you a snowmobile thief."

They got a few more details about the van from her. Cardinal sketched a rough outline of a van and got Ms. Caffrey to show him where the logo and lettering had been. She couldn't remember what it said, or the type of business, but she did remember it had no windows. Model or make? No idea.

"Do you think she's for real?" Delorme said when they were in the car again. "That stuff about how it's nice if someone else is enjoying her property?"

"It's one way of looking at it." Cardinal put the key in the ignition and started the engine.

"Make our jobs a lot different if everyone was a Buddhist." Delorme didn't know why she was going on about it; it wasn't what she wanted to talk about. There was only one thing she wanted to talk about, but Cardinal's streak of hyperchat was over, and now he was barely talking at all.

They got stuck in construction for ten minutes and still he didn't say anything. Just sat there tapping his fingers on the steering wheel and resolutely not looking at her.

If he doesn't say anything by Wal-Mart, she told herself, then I will. But Wal-Mart came and went and neither of them spoke.

If he doesn't say anything by the lights at Sumner, she promised herself, then I will. But he made the left at Sumner and they drove on past St. Boniface Church and the city jail and still neither of them spoke.

She decided the parking lot would be her now-or-never point. Cardinal made the left off Sumner and the right into the lot, but instead of pulling into his slot, he just stopped by the front entrance.

"I'll drop you off," he said. "I've got a meeting with the crown."

"You're seeing Romney again?"

"No, no. Hartman. My endless Wilkerson case."

"Okay. I guess I'll see you later, then. Or whenever." Delorme undid her seatbelt and grabbed her briefcase.

"Lise."

She turned to face him, one hand on the door handle.

"About the other night."

She waited.

"I think it was maybe a mistake. I mean, it was great, I enjoyed it, and God knows I'm attracted to you, but, you know, we do have to work together."

"Chouinard's wife works in the evidence room. Collingwood is going out with that blond beat cop, what's her name."

"Really? He's quiet about it."

"Of course he's quiet about it. He barely speaks."

"Well, it's different being on the same squad. If things went wrong between us, it could get pretty difficult working investigations together."

"I know that."

"It's not a small thing, Lise."

"I know."

"Besides which, I really like what we have. I love seeing you outside of work, the way our friendship has developed. It's important to me." Cardinal put a hand on his forehead as if checking for fever. "God, I never talk like this."

"It's important to me too."

"Well, I don't think we should jeopardize it. Let's face it—it was a party, we'd both had a lot to drink. This kind of stuff happens all the time."

"The office party, you mean. Get drunk, screw on the copy machine, et cetera."

"I'm not saying it's the same. I'm just saying it doesn't have to mean we blow everything up. Sorry, I'm not putting this very well."

"You're putting it perfectly well. We have a good friendship, we work well together, you don't want to risk all that over a single drunken kiss."

"Well, not drunk. A little light-headed maybe."

"Okay. You're right. It makes perfect sense. We go back to the way it was and make like it never happened. Have fun with the crown." She opened the door and got out.

"Not drunk, Lise."

"I know. And it wasn't just one."

10

"It's nine-thirty," Loach said. "Where the hell's Delorme?"

"Called in sick," Chouinard said.

"You guys do that a lot? Two murders, probably three, on the go—you get a headache, you don't come in?"

"Last time Detective Delorme called in sick," Cardinal said, "she had a fractured tibia and had just killed a guy who had the really bad idea of assaulting her."

Chouinard said, "Let's move on."

"SIU musta loved that."

"SIU had no problem with it. Proceed."

Loach was standing in front of the whiteboard, tossing a marker up in the air and catching it. "While you guys were vacationing in Ottawa and doing whatever else it is you get up to—"

"What's that supposed to mean?" Cardinal said, not loud. He didn't look at Loach, just kept his pen poised over his notebook. Nobody else moved either.

"What I meant? What I *meant* was exactly what the *words* mean. As in, I don't know what you and Delorme have been doing, because half the time you're not here. If you want to take it some other particular way—like the D.S. says, that's not my business."

"Watch your mouth," Cardinal said, still not looking at him.

Chouinard picked up a large dictionary and slammed it hard on the table. It occurred to Cardinal that it was the only reason the dictionary was kept in this room.

Chouinard looked at Loach. "Please continue."

Loach turned to the whiteboard and wrote the words *White Van*, putting them in quotation marks and adding three underlines. The marker squeaked with every move.

"Okay. Had an idea our hotelier friend at the illustrious Motel 17 was not telling us the entire truth. His register showed only a single room occupied. I ask myself, how does this man make a living?" He twirled the marker and caught it. "Turns out, upon closer questioning, Mr. Motel has a sideline with one or two ladies of the night—actually your standard MILF-next-door, who makes a little extra through the online personals. One Millie Pankowitz.

"I proceed to the domicile of said Millie Pankowitz and interview her about the night in question. Results of that interview are as follows: Millie was in room nine, where she had already entertained two delighted consumers of the male persuasion *seriatim*. That means one after another as opposed to—"

"Jesus," Cardinal said quietly.

"—as opposed to *not* one after another. She was waiting on yet a third prospect, who had an appointment for one a.m. She gives it fifteen minutes. He still doesn't show and she finally bags it. Goes out, gets in her car and sees the parking lot is about as busy as usual for Motel 17. Two vehicles in addition to her own. Laura Lacroix's black Nissan parked a couple of rooms over, another car—no doubt Mark Trent's green Audi—by the office. But get this: She gets in her car and heads out of the lot. She's rolling down the access road when a white van turns off the highway and comes *up* the access road. She stops at the highway, and in the rear-view sees the van pull into the motel parking lot."

"There's a murder two doors down from her," Chouinard said, "and she doesn't see fit to maybe mention this to the police?"

"Didn't occur to her, far as I can tell. Reason being, hubby works night security and is unaware of her nocturnal activities. She better hope he never answers her online ad."

"How do we know this white van wasn't her one a.m. john?"

"Because that guy's a repeat customer. She doesn't know his real name—she calls him Tom—but she knows what he looks like and she knows his car. He's maybe forty, got a beard and a crooked nose, and drives a Mazda3. This she remembers because she happens to drive a Mazda3 also. Now, she didn't get a good look, but the guy she sees in the van is late fifties, maybe sixty, clean-shaven."

"Still doesn't rule out her john," Chouinard pointed out. "He could have been in the back of the van. Or maybe he sent a friend as a proxy, so to speak. Bought someone a birthday present."

"Really?" Loach said. "You do that a lot up here? Anyway, at this point, Millie is too pissed off to hang around and find out if Mr. White Van is hoping to meet her. Van goes into the lot, Millie hits the highway, and that's the end of their brief encounter."

"Delorme and I came up with a white van too," Cardinal said. He told them about their interview with the serene Ms. Caffrey and held up his sketch for everyone to see. "She said it was a commercial van, no windows, some kind of logo painted out on the side. And from Toronto."

"This is getting interesting," Loach said. "Maybe we should get a police artist to interview these two ladies again."

"I'm on it." Paul Arsenault raised his coffee mug that said *Arsenault* in 20-point Helvetica. "I'll be doing the Identi-Kit with Millie Pankowitz this morning. I'll get more on the vehicle too."

"In the meantime," Loach said, "I want to look deeper into Mark Trent. I'm leaning toward the notion that he was the intended target and Ms. Lacroix, a.k.a. Ms. Rettig, may just have been in the wrong place at the wrong time."

"We have progress," Chouinard noted as they wrapped things up. "Definite progress. But it would be nice to have an actual suspect."

~

At the visitor check-in, Delorme had to hand over her Beretta, her bag and even her belt to the plump guard on the other side of the counter. He issued her a receipt for the items and said, "Welcome to Kingston Penitentiary Services."

As she went through the security gate, the alarm went off.

A massive guard with no discernible emotional life raised a hand in a "halt" gesture. "Notebook."

Delorme handed it to him.

A female guard stepped forward and patted her down with a thoroughness that in any other circumstances would have got her arrested.

"Hey," Delorme said, and stepped back.

"You got a problem?"

"Who taught you to give a pat-down—Paul Bernardo?"

The woman stepped close and looked into Delorme's eyes for a full fifteen seconds. Burnt coffee on her breath. "Undo your jacket."

Delorme unbuttoned her blazer and opened it up. The guard reached for the inside pocket and removed a ballpoint pen.

"Uh-uh."

"The prisoner will be manacled. They let me keep it at check-in."

"Do I look like I care?"

"I'm investigating a murder. I need to take notes."

"The pen stays at check-in or it goes back outside with you. Your choice."

The male guard handed back the spiral notebook. "This too."

Delorme returned to the check-in counter. The plump guard shook his head. "Sorry. Tear a few pages out of the notebook, and you can use this." He handed her a library pencil.

Delorme returned to the security gate and went through.

"You're lucky that ain't a underwire bra you're wearing," the female guard said, "or I'd a taken that too."

Yet another guard escorted her from security, unlocking and relocking each door as they went. The prison interior—this part of it, anyway—resembled a high school. Gleaming floor, the smell of cleaning products, and steel doors that almost looked like wood.

"How long have you worked here?"

"Too long."

Another door, another corridor. Halfway along, he stopped at a door with a small square of thick Plexiglas. It had been spat on and inadequately cleaned.

The guard opened the door and held it. "I know they told you the rules and I know you signed the visitors' agreement, but I will tell you again. You do not touch the prisoner. You do not give anything *to* the prisoner. You do not accept anything *from* the prisoner. Nothing. Do you understand?"

"I understand."

"Sit in that chair over there. You will find a panic button under the edge of the table. It's big enough you can operate it with your knee if need be. It rings an alarm out here that can't be heard in there and will bring me pronto. You find it?"

Delorme felt under the table. "Got it."

"All right, then."

He closed the door and locked it. Delorme tried to pull her chair closer to the table, but it was bolted to the floor. She wrote several single-word reminders on a sheet of notepaper, the soft lead smearing her attempts at neat strokes and loops. The chair was too far from the table, and in no time at all her neck started to hurt.

The clack of the lock made her jump. The door opened and the guard steered Fritz Reicher inside. The prisoner was manacled at wrists and ankles, the two restraints connected by a short chain that kept his wrists low and before him in a monkish attitude. He was thirty years old, six-three, with enormous hands. The manacles did little to diminish the impression of physical power.

"Fritz, you're gonna behave yourself, right?" the guard said.

"Yes, of course." The German accent was still strong, but Reicher had a pleasant voice, melodious and surprisingly soft for a man of his size.

"You know what happens if you don't, right?"

"Yes, of course."

"Yes, of course. Yes, of course. You got a way with words, Fritz." The guard had him lean against the wall. He knelt and unlocked the ankle manacles. He stood again and pulled the connecting chain through, turned the prisoner around, and unlocked the wrist restraints.

Delorme had expected the manacles to stay on. She thought about saying something.

"Sit."

Reicher sat and folded his hands in his lap.

"You stay seated throughout, understand?"

"Yes, of course."

"You don't move out of that chair until I come get you, understand?"

"Yes, of course."

"All right, then." The guard put his key in the door and looked back at Delorme. "I'll be right out here."

"Okay. Thanks." She wondered again if she should ask about the restraints, but the guard looked as if he knew what he was doing.

He went out and closed the door behind him. Bolts slid home. Then nothing. No sound of him walking away. No sound of anything at all from the corridor. From somewhere beyond the prison walls, a truck horn honked long and loud. Men's voices echoed along distant corridors, involved in a game or a fight.

Reicher remained still, a mild expression on his face. Even sitting down, he looked extremely strong. Years ago, at the academy, Delorme's instructor in hand-to-hand combat had stressed that physical power was not just a matter of muscle. "Big muscles are one thing, but they're not everything. You can get these big-boned guys, tall, wide in the shoulders, even if they're quite skinny—even if they never work out—with formidable advantages of reach, obviously, but also incredible grip, not to mention the kind of leverage that can snap a major bone like that." The snap of his fingers had reverberated around the gym.

Delorme introduced herself and told Reicher the reason for her visit. Loose ends on the Choquette case. If he was helpful, she would ask that his co-operation be noted in his file.

He showed no sign that he remembered her. That was not surprising, as her own involvement in the Choquette case had been peripheral, her testimony confined to minor matters.

She expected a demand for a more exciting quid pro quo—cigarettes, more privileges, the usual barter. A note in the file was pretty cheap.

"It's a mistake," Reicher said. He turned his head and looked at the door.

"What's a mistake?"

He turned his head back to look at her. "He should not have removed the manacles. This is not the way."

"I'm sure we'll manage."

"It's an error because of last week. My lawyer was here. For lawyers they remove restraints. It's proper protocol. This is not. I worked in security. This is bad security."

"Do you get the news in here, Fritz?"

"Ha ha. Yes, of course."

"Then you know about Marjorie Flint? The senator's wife?"

"Yes, of course. Poor woman, freezing to death like that."

"Do you know anything about her—or about the senator—besides what you may have read in the news?"

"No, I'm afraid, nothing."

"Are you sure? Her name never came up anywhere? Did you see her picture on the news?"

"Yes, of course."

"Did you recognize her?"

"No, I don't know her. Freezing to death like that, it's no joke."

"Would you actually tell me if you did know her?"

"Ha ha. Yes, of course."

"Fritz, are you on a lot of medication?"

"Do you think I am?"

"You repeat yourself a lot. You say 'Yes, of course' a lot. And you laugh at weird times."

"I see. Possibly I am being medicated without my knowledge." He pronounced it *nollich*. "They could give me things, I wouldn't know. I have to eat what they give me. Ha ha, you think I'm on medication. Interesting. Did someone inform you of this?"

"No. What about Laura Lacroix—does that name ring a bell?"

"Who?"

"Laura Lacroix."

He shook his head. "I don't know this name."

"You're sure?"

Reicher seemed to throw off his lethargy. He sat up and leaned on the table, the change in posture doubling his size.

"Do you half a dog, Detective? Did I already ask you this?"

"I don't."

"Damn. It's too bad."

"Laura Lacroix was Leonard Priest's girlfriend. Briefly."

"Ha ha. Leonard." *Lennet.* "Yes, of course. You know I can tell you nothing about Leonard. Some people, yes. Ha ha. Not Leonard."

"He claims she came to Club Risqué. I thought perhaps you might remember her."

Delorme pulled the photo from the file. Reicher reached for it but she pulled it back.

"Ha ha. I'm just trying to see."

"You can see." She tilted it to counter the glare.

"Pretty."

"Do you recognize her?"

"Not really. But she is Leonard's type. They all look the same, Leonard's girlfriends. The ones he really likes. She looks like you. Ha ha."

Garth Romney's position was beginning to make more sense. Whatever else Fritz Reicher might be, he was not a great witness, drifting in and out like a faint signal. Then there was his size, his accent, his air of aggressive indifference. Not to mention the stupid laugh. You might not automatically brand him as a murderer, but it was easy to imagine him standing by while someone else did the murdering. "Yes, of course," he would say. "Kill the lady, yes, of course."

Delorme started to ask him about the night of the murder, but Reicher's mind was elsewhere. "You don't half a dog, okay, it's fine. But perhaps you are knowing some veterinarian? Or the—what do you call it—the animal authorities. The shelter people? I want to walk dogs. It's my plan. For when I'm getting out. Leonard says he will help me do it. I want to be a dog walker. I lift for a time in New York City. There they half many dog walkers. Five on a leash—six sometimes—you should see. So funny."

"The night of the murder. In your initial statement, you said you drove Leonard Priest to Algonquin Bay to—as you put it— 'play some games.' That it was Priest's idea. That you were just there to role-play."

"Yes, but I was confused. I was high, you know, when I was arrested. I was confusing it with another time. Many times. Leonard was wanting me to play Nazi always. With people who like to be scared and so on. I didn't like to do it myself. I didn't like people thinking always Germans are Nazis. But Leonard luft it and so did many customers also. To me it was acting. Performing a part. Pretty convincing, too, I would say. You know, I studied acting."

"In fact, you terrorized people."

"Only people who wanted it so. Nobody was calling the police, something like that."

"Because they were terrified."

"Yes, of course—but like at the movies you're terrified. Frightened because you want to be frightened." He half rose from the chair and flashed his enormous hands. "*Boo!* Ha ha, you jumped." He sat back down. "But it's not like you're having a heart attack, something like that."

Delorme glanced at the door.

"He's not there probably. I think so."

"You can hardly call it a game, Fritz. The gun was loaded."

"Yes, of course. It's more frightening. Shoot a hole in the wall, shoot a tree. *Boom!* Then you are convincing people. When I was studying acting in New York, they used to say, 'Ya gotta sell da line.' Just like that, they would say. 'Ya gotta sell da line.' We were selling the gun, in that sense. Not really selling it, of course. Ha ha. Not gun-running."

"Do yourself a favour, Fritz. Tell me something I can use. There's no mention of you being high when you were arrested. You were a bartender, sometimes a bouncer—how would you get to know a customer so well that you could drive up to Algonquin Bay on your own for an encounter with her—let alone take her out to an abandoned boathouse for sex? It doesn't make sense."

"It was sex. To make sense is not required. I got carried away, that's all. I was playing my role, you know—Nazi bastard interrogating poor little prisoner and so on—threatening her. I'm drunk, I'm in character, a total Nazi bastard, and I did it. I'm sorry for it. I never wanted to kill her. I never wanted to kill anyone, never in my life. Always I am a peaceful person. It was just games and I had too much to drink. It went too far and I can't fix it."

"Except in your initial statement you said it was Leonard's idea, Leonard giving the orders. Leonard ordered you to shoot and you did."

"I was high. I was confused. It's wrong. Leonard didn't do it. I did it."

"So here you are for, what, another twelve or thirteen years."

"No, it's eight years total. So six more only."

"Really? Someone's telling you they give parole to a guy who takes a woman to an abandoned boathouse? Who slaps a leather mask over her face and terrorizes her for God knows how long? Threatens her with a loaded gun and then puts a bullet through her head?"

Reicher's face changed. His eyes stayed on her and Delorme pitied Régine Choquette if those were the last eyes she saw in this world.

"You're being harsh to me, Detective. But I'm having good behaviour. I'm taking courses. I will get parole." Even from across the table, Delorme could see the heat rising from his chest, up his neck, scorching the pale skin. His breathing had become rapid.

"Meanwhile," Delorme said, "the years go by. You're in here getting old, losing your good looks, surrounded by people a lot nastier than you are, and the man who ordered you to murder this woman is in one of his beautiful houses. How many houses does he have, by the way?"

"Okay, so life is not being all the time fair. Is life treating you all the time fair?"

"Fritz, it was *his* gun. Found at *his* club. *His* prints at the scene. Why isn't he in prison?"

"Leonard is trying his best to get me out. He's doing, you know, behind the scenes. It takes time. He's talking to the Ottawa animal shelter for me, too. He has a veterinarian friend in Algonquin Bay, too, he's talking to. He cried, you know. When he heard I got twelve years? Leonard cried."

"*His* gun. Found in *his* club."

"I was not thinking clearly. Hiding the gun at the club, it was not the best idea."

"All of this against him, and yet Priest was never charged. Don't you wonder why?"

"Leonard has money. Friends. People like Leonard."

"Fritz, I can name three millionaires who are serving time in this country. Money and friends don't get you off a murder charge."

"It's the women, with Leonard. I've seen it. A magnetism. And Ottawa, you know, powerful people. There's a woman who helps him."

"A lawyer? Who are you talking about?"

"I told him, Leonard, I said—one time he's coming to visit me—I said, 'It's amazing, I thought they would charge you. Why didn't they charge you?'"

"He came to visit you?"

"Listen about Leonard. If you are Leonard's friend, he stays always your friend. He's generous. He's kind. He understands. He told me, he said, 'Fritz, it's not fair'. He said he was just lucky. He had a secret weapon. A person, I mean. A secret weapon named Diane something. Deborah, something like. Darlene! That's it. Darlene. I never heard of any Darlene and I said Darlene who but he said it was better I'm not knowing. Well, you can look at me like that if you want, but it's true."

"Some lawyer in Ottawa. Darlene."

"Could be Toronto. Could be also Algonquin Bay."

"No. I'd know her."

"Toronto then. I don't know."

"This is bullshit, Fritz. You know it's bullshit. I don't believe in any magic 'Darlene' and neither do you. The reason he wasn't charged is because you changed your story. You took the fall. Do you have any idea how dumb that is? You could get years off your sentence if you told the truth."

"You call me stupid?"

"I just said taking the fall for a murderer who doesn't care is dumb."

"You think I'm stupid."

"I didn't say that."

The placid, indifferent features had rearranged themselves. Reicher unfolded himself from the chair and went to the door. He put a hand up to shade the Plexiglas. He made a *tsk-tsk* sound. "It's improper. It's bad security, don't you find?"

"Sit down, please, Fritz."

He turned his back to the door and leaned against it, folding his arms. "Look at you, so small. I could kill you right now. Imagine. And no one would know. No one would hear."

"That would be a really bad idea."

"I don't like it. Calling me stupid."

"Just sit down, Fritz. If that guard sees you're up, you'll get in trouble and that's not what you want."

"Do you see a guard? Do you see a camera? There is no camera. What's to stop me pulling you out of that chair, snapping you in half?"

"Fritz, I'm a cop. You're not going to touch me."

He showed her an enormous hand, just swivelled his arm out from the elbow like a gate, hand open, fingers aligned. He flexed it a couple of times.

Delorme pressed the panic button with her knee.

"Look at you. One hand I could wrap around your throat—one hand. You couldn't even scream."

"Unless I shot you first."

"Ha ha. You're not armed."

"You don't know that."

"It's not allowed. No one brings weapons in this place. Not even the RCMP."

Delorme put a hand inside her blazer. "Think about it, Fritz. Why would they take the manacles off if I wasn't armed?" She pressed the buzzer again.

"He won't come. It's change of shift."

Possible self-defence scenarios were flashing through Delorme's mind. A leap to the table, kick to the head.

"Let's get back to Laura Lacroix. She may still be alive. If you help us save her, that could look very good in your file." Delorme opened her folder, pulled out a photograph and held it up.

"What could you do if I decide to hit you a few times, ruin that pretty face?"

Delorme sat forward and tried to look bigger. "And what are you going to do when I tell them you made repeated threats? That you refused to stay seated? How do you think that's going to play at your parole hearing? I'll tell you exactly how it'll play: *Petition denied. Shows no remorse. Still a danger.*"

"I was not threatening."

"Do it again and I'll make sure you never get parole. I'll devote my life to it."

Reicher went to his chair and sat down.

"Press the buzzer, please. I don't like you. I want to go back."

"Tell me why Leonard Priest wanted Régine Choquette dead."

"He didn't. It wasn't intentional. I told you. I did it. It was an accident. Call the guard, please."

She pressed the buzzer yet again. Where the hell was he?

"Why are you protecting this killer, Fritz?"

"Leonard is not a killer. He is my friend. He looks after me. Takes care of me. Loves me, even."

"You think Leonard Priest loves you?"

"Maybe he doesn't say so in words, but I know he loves me. He gets me a lawyer I can't afford. Sends me money, packages."

"You think Leonard Priest loves you? He's the one who got you into this mess, and he's out there laughing."

"Okay, you want to play the nasty bitch?" Reicher stood up, flexing his giant hands. "You want to play this game with me? Fucking cop bitch, I'll—"

The clack of the lock.

Reicher lowered himself to the chair and put a benign expression on his face. Apparently the acting lessons had paid off; the transformation was remarkable.

A guard entered. A different guard.

"Please take me first," Reicher said. "I want to go back."

"Yeah? You in a hurry to get back to your cell?"

"Yes, please." He turned back to Delorme, suddenly chatty, friendly. "I don't want to miss *Days of Our Lives*. It's the best. There's a dog-walker character sometimes. Celine? She's going to turn out to be a blackmailer or an imposter or something, I just know it, but I like her a lot. She likes the dogs she's walking. It's not just a job, you know. It's a profession. To be good at it takes a special person."

"Nice talking to you, Fritz. I'll send you a dog book."

"Really? Ha ha. Games again. You're worse than me, Detective." He raised clasped hands for the guard.

"Jesus Christ," the guard said. "What'd you do with the bling, Fritz?"

"Johnson removed them. It's an error, obviously."

"Up against that wall right now."

Reicher got up and leaned against the wall.

"Make one move and I crack your skull wide open. Got that? One move and I turn you into an eggplant. Ma'am?" The guard jerked his head toward the door.

Delorme got up, cold with sweat, and went out.

The guard manacled Reicher to the chair, stepped into the hall behind her and locked the door.

"I'm glad it's you," Delorme said, "and not Johnson."

"Oh, yeah? Why would that be?"

"Because I would have killed him right here."

From the Blue Notebook

An evening lecture in the Arcosaur mess.

This was something we did twice a week. Partly it was a way of making our supply of VHS tapes last longer, and partly it was a way for us to keep each other apprised of progress on our various projects. The field of Arctic research is a small one and yet, within it, even within the same room at the same camp, it's possible to have two scientists sitting next to each other in mutual incomprehension.

The evenings were informal and more for the benefit of the junior researchers than the old hands. It gave them a chance to practise their presentation skills in front of people who might have some influence on their future—a chance to display their private data hoard.

The wiring in the mess was unreliable, especially when the temperature got much below minus thirty, so these talks were often bathed in candlelight. I was being visited by an uncharacteristic fit of benevolence. The faces of my colleagues hovering and glowing in the half dark. The precariousness of our existence thrummed within me, the sense of how little stood between us and certain death should our generator fail entirely, say, or our supply lines be cut off for a serious length of time. Such a sense can drive a man sentimental.

Ray Deville stood in front of a whiteboard lit by two standing flashlights. His talk was rambling, repetitious, almost incoherent, but his accent was entertaining. Vanderbyl, Ray's thesis supervisor, sank lower and lower in his chair, pressing his chin into his chest. He was possibly the worst adviser Deville could have had. A nervous soul like Ray needed the parental touch, motherly if possible. Rebecca would have brought out the best in him, but oceanography was not her field and her university was fifteen hundred miles distant from his.

Wyndham came up with a question for him, a kindness that got the young man on track for a few moments. His enthusiasm for his subject welled up and he spouted findings none of us would have been aware of.

I thought of the dead youth the Inuit "ghost" had brought us. We had heard back from researchers at Laval—terribly excited researchers—that they were pretty sure he was a member of the doomed Franklin expedition. The recent opening of three graves on Beechey Island had revealed that one of them, marked "Roger Arlington in his twenty-first year," was in fact empty. Their theory: Young Arlington had been banished from the expedition—effectively executed—for some unknown crime. The empty grave was an effort to avoid uncomfortable questioning upon their return.

It was thought best not to mention any of this to young Deville, who was already spooked enough. In any case, for those few moments under Wyndham's gentle prodding, the candlelight seemed to reach him, and he shone.

On clear nights such as this one, the stars were preternaturally bright, their ancient energy made new. When a few hours later I woke from a deep sleep, the walls of my cabin were glowing. I thought I was still dreaming, because my cabin seemed so absurdly colourful that it could occur only in a Disney film.

I sat up in my sleeping bag and looked out the porthole window. The night was awash with light. Some of the others were already outside: Rebecca and Vanderbyl, Wyndham and Dahlberg, four dark figures, faces to the sky in attitudes of amazement, as if all four were simultaneously receiving the stigmata.

High above, a waterfall of red poured down from the black heavens.

The next thing I remember, I was standing outside. The cold must have been blistering, but I have no memory of it. I stood like the others, drinking in the aurora. Red is the rarest, and this red was so brilliant and mobile it was as if an incision had been made in the exact centre of the sky and ruby light cascaded from the wound.

So incredibly red—I think it was Jens who spoke—I've never seen red before, never even heard of it.

It's at least two hundred kilometres up, I said. Solar wind colliding with high-altitude oxygen. Green and yellow are generated at about sixty kilometres.

I saw a blue one once, Vanderbyl said. They think it's caused by ionized nitrogen. I've only seen it that one time—in Svalbard. Our pilot actually wept.

Jens, ever practical, said, It'll kill our radio contact. We'll be blacked out for days.

The display curved away from us at its sides, shifting from a curtain shape almost to a funnel. A long crimson tail danced toward us, hovering on one side, then whipping to the other, a tornado of light.

And it's composed of nothing, Wyndham said. Just broken bits of atoms.

Words fled me. At that moment I understood the pilot who had broken into sobs. I yearned for a new language, an idioglossia to span the unbridgeable distances that separate one human mind from another. This was unlike me, and probably had more to do with Rebecca than the aurora.

I wanted to hold her close, feel her warmth and reality, the human scale of love and desire, the infinitesimal beauty in the brush of her eyelashes on my cheek, the heat of her breath on my neck. But at that moment, she too felt the need of contact. And there, silhouetted against the ruby light, encircled by its corona of stars, she reached to rest her hand upon her husband's shoulder, then tilted her head against him, Kurt's arm in answer reaching around her waist.

11

CARDINAL WAS LATE. HE STEPPED out of his car and took his parka off. Cold gnawed at his ribs, his belly, his nerves. He tossed the parka onto the back seat and opened a flat plastic package and took out a bunny suit. He walked over to the motel room and stepped into the suit just in front of the door.

Everything about the Broadview Motel was generic, even the pervasive smell of carpet, but the mirrors, the lamps, the TV screen were already speckled with fingerprints where the ident guys had dusted for latents. The desk was done, the phone, the television remote. Collingwood and Arsenault were now working silently at the bedside tables.

Loach was by the window, holding his phone out now and again at elbow level as if checking a compass reading.

"Reception sucks in this dump," he said to no one. Then, into the phone, "I'm very glad to hear you say that. I agree. It's crucial for law enforcement in this country." He clicked off, put the phone in his pocket and contemplated the plate glass window.

"You're late." The room was studio bright with Ident's lamps, and Loach had no trouble identifying Cardinal's reflection in the window and speaking to it.

"I wouldn't be here at all if Chouinard hadn't called me."

"Found it sooner than we expected. Narrowed it down to motels near Mark Trent's house, and when that didn't work, to places near Laura Lacroix. Manager says he stayed a little over a week. Paid cash. Description: Maybe sixty, slicked-back hair, in shape or at least not fat. No visible deformities, although manager did notice a limp."

"A limp. Like from an accident? A birth defect? What kind of limp?"

"He's a motel guy, not an osteopath. He says the guy has a limp. Left leg kinda stiff. Oh, and he wore gloves a lot."

"You'd never know it." Cardinal gestured at the storm of fingerprints.

"Yeah, well, who knows if any of them are his? You'd expect by this time the room woulda been cleaned up, except the grampa running the place saves money in the off-season by waiting till he's got half a dozen dirty rooms. Here's his sign-in." He handed Cardinal a flimsy sheet of paper. "Plate number's a phony. Manager confirms dirty white Econoline with some kind of painted-out logo, but the plate number doesn't check out. We already ran it down."

"Roger Arlington," Cardinal read. "'Arlington' could be fake too."

"Getting nothing from the records so far. Garbage cans are mostly McDonald's and Subway wrappers. And I nearly tossed out the Tim Hortons receipt too, until I noticed the date and location. Highway 17, Pembroke, twelve days ago."

"The day Marjorie Flint vanished."

"Good solid policing combined with good leadership—you can't beat it." Loach took his phone out and put it to his ear and turned once more to the window. "Hi, honey. Hey, just heard from a contact at the academy—they may fly me down there to give a talk on the Montrose case."

Roger Arlington. Cardinal made a note of the name and went over to Arsenault, who was photographing a print on the Gideon Bible. "How'd the Identi-Kit go?"

"Well, the one lady gave us good stuff on the van, but the other witness was a no-show."

"This was the hooker, right?"

"Turns out hookers are not reliable people. But we got the manager here, who's likely to do better, and a chambermaid also. Says she saw the guy a couple of times and he gave her twenty bucks to stay out of his hair."

"That's interesting." Cardinal glanced in Loach's direction. "Nobody told me that."

"Unfortunately, not so good on prints. Bob, you want to tell him?"

It was charming the way Arsenault always included his silent colleague. It was like trying to bring a Corgi into the conversation. Collingwood gave no sign of hearing, so Arsenault led Cardinal over to the front window. The glass was frosted at the corners and speckled with red fingerprint powder.

"We've got tons of partials, but I got a feeling they're not going to lead anywhere. Why? First, because they're all different and that makes me suspect they're old and not his. Second, because there are lots of smudges that don't show a single loop or whirl. See? Look here. And here." He pointed out a couple of blank smudges. "Even here." He pointed to two marks, about three inches long, that were slightly curved toward each other like parentheses. "Karate prints, like when you shade your eyes to see out a window?"

"Or in," Cardinal said. "How many thieves have we caught that way?"

"Exactly. But again, no skin lines at all. We're striking out here. I think this guy is wearing gloves everywhere."

"Yes, the manager said he wore gloves a lot."

"That's interesting." Arsenault glanced in Loach's direction and back again. "Nobody told me that. But check this out."

Cardinal followed him over to the desk. Cigarette burns and watermarks. Tattered Yellow Pages open to Chinese restaurants. Beside this, another crescent-shaped mark.

"The guy's not all that careful about being seen," Cardinal said, "and yet he's wearing gloves indoors. Is there any chance our boy has a prosthetic hand?"

"You read my mind," Arsenault said.

"This is good work, Paul."

"Thank you."

"I'm going to double your salary."

"Too bad you're not in a position to do that."

"But you know I would if I could."

"Will you throw in a Porsche as well?"

"Consider it done."

Cardinal went back outside. He took off the bunny suit and got in the car and started it. He switched off the heater; the sunlight was so strong it had warmed up the interior. He took out his cell and called Delorme on speed-dial. Then he remembered she was out sick and he hung up. He thought about maybe stopping by later to see how she was doing and then wondered if that might be a bad idea. He was pretty sure he'd handled things poorly.

~

The ARC hotel in downtown Ottawa. The kind of place where the staff all wear black and a visiting cop would never dream of staying. The room was small, the furniture minimalist to the point of severe. Delorme sat on the edge of the bed and gave it a testing bounce. Firm.

She took out her cell and checked the list of calls. Chouinard, Cardinal, Cardinal, Loach, Cardinal. You can damn well wait, John Cardinal. She dialed an old number she had for Leonard Priest. There was no ring, no response of any kind. She dialed Club Risqué and asked to speak to him.

"I'm sorry, Len is not in tonight. Perhaps I could help you?"

"I was told he'd be there."

"He was, but he took off for Toronto. Is there anything else?"

Delorme shut the phone book and opened the room service menu. The idea of eating in the room depressed her. A heaviness settled over her chest and stomach and she heard herself sigh. *Really* depressed.

A desk card caught her eye. It showed a woman wrapped in a towel with a dreamy smile on her face. Delorme picked up the desk phone and dialed. A recorded voice told her the spa was closed. She opened her overnight bag and hung a little black dress in the closet, placed her other items on the shelves.

She got undressed, put a shower cap over her hair and stepped into the shower. The pleasures of high water pressure and expensive soap. She resolved to change her shower head when she got home.

She dried off quickly and brushed her hair. She opened the closet again and put on her underwear. Her reflection in the full-length mirror nagged at her and she tried to ignore it. Then she couldn't stand it and turned to look.

Ugh. You used to have a good body. Where did that go? The twenty-year-old she had been would have hated her as she was now. Then again, that twenty-year-old bundle of ego was hardly her present-day idea of good company.

She slipped into the black dress that was shorter than the one she had worn to the party. She hadn't worn this one for, what, five years? She smoothed it over her thighs and submitted to a train of unhappy thoughts. It looked better with the shoes, but it would take at least two glasses of wine before it looked good. She had no credible reason to get dressed up in the first place. She would have dinner by herself and come back up to the room and watch some terrible movie on TV.

She went to a restaurant a couple of blocks away that she remembered as a lively place. Naturally, this particular night it was all but deserted. A trio of men stood at the bar, too busy jawing about sports to notice her or her vampy little dress. The waiter came and greeted her in French and English, and for reasons Delorme didn't bother to ruminate on, she chose to answer in English. Normally she was happy to speak French—it was one of the pleasures of visiting the nation's capital—but tonight apparently she was anglophone.

The waiter had asked only if he could bring her a drink to start, but she ordered the whole meal: steak frites without the frites, double the salad instead. No point in getting even more grotesquely misshapen.

The house red had no edges to it at all and went down too quickly. She was on her second glass before the steak arrived, just the right shade of pink.

The place had gone from subdued to tomb-like. Two of the men had left the bar, leaving the last one, who looked very French Canadian, to pick at his beer label. He had a good face and seemed about Delorme's age. A left-hander. Wedding band gleaming on the hand that held the beer. He glanced at her and her stomach tightened at the thought that he might come over and speak to her.

She ate her steak and thought about Leonard Priest and the questions she wanted to ask him. She remembered their last conversation and how he had said *cock* so many times. Not something men did, in her experience, outside porno films. The word repeated itself in her mind without her wanting it to.

The waiter brought the check for her to sign. The man at the bar was gone. The bartender scooped up his tip and the beer bottle with its half-peeled label.

Back at the hotel, she had to wait for the elevator. When the door finally opened, a young couple released each other, none too quickly. The girl's dress settled against her thighs as her lover withdrew his hand. Delorme got in and the three of them rode in silence to the third floor, where the couple got out. She heard them burst into laughter as the doors closed once more.

In her room, she took the bathrobe from its hanger and threw it on the bed. She took off her shoes and started to unzip the black dress. Then she folded her arms and stared at her reflection in the TV screen. A thinner, more ethereal Delorme stared back. According to her watch, she'd been wearing the dress for less than ninety minutes. She shook her head.

"Pointless," she said. "Totally pointless."

She sat on the end of the bed with her hands on her knees and thought about why she might be feeling this bad. John, of course. She thought about Loach and discounted him. She thought about Reicher and the depth of her fear in that locked room. It wasn't that. She dealt with lots of creeps. A little shakiness for an hour or so afterward, but that was it. A little anger at the idiot guard.

It occurred to her that she might have entirely misunderstood the word *loneliness*. She had always thought it just meant wishing there was a friend around to talk to. Especially when you were feeling bad about yourself, your character and your life. She'd felt like that often enough, but this crushing, nameless weight was new. This awfulness that seemed to fill not just her heart but the entire room.

She leaned forward and opened the mini-bar. Pulled out a bar of dark Swiss chocolate and a half bottle of Pelee Island red and put them on the bed beside her. She picked up the remote and turned on the TV. Crackle of static as it came alive. The movie selection was long, but most of the titles meant nothing to her.

She scrolled through eight iterations of *Barely Legal* alone, *Horny Housewives*, *Cum-Crazed Coeds*, *Gang Bangs*, *Ass Masters*, *Sweet Slavery*, *DP Debutantes*. The Info button informed her that *DP* meant "double penetration" and watching seventy-five minutes of this would cost $13.99. Titles, the screen promised, would not appear on her bill.

She switched off the TV and got out of her dress and hung it up. She slipped into the envelope of cool sheets and opened the paperback novel she had brought with her, highly recommended by Oprah. Page one struck her as less than engaging, and page two was worse. The prospect of losing herself in a story dimmed and went out.

She reached for the light switch and caught another glimpse of the woman wrapped in the towel, the dreamy smile. The whiteness of the towel, the smiling lips remained as an afterimage as she closed her eyes. She couldn't remember the last time anyone had rubbed her back.

I'm not supposed to be here. I don't even know what I'm doing here.

Two minutes, maybe three. She throws off the covers and switches on the light. The little black dress is still warm.

~

He was astonished by the simplicity of the place. A whitewashed attic, angular walls, slanted high ceiling, little more than one room, but whether through frugality or good taste she had managed to make it look large and inviting. She had painted the baseboards walnut brown and papered one wall with a spacious frond theme that maintained the brightness of the space but saved it from monotony.

The floor was covered with scraps of carpet in various shades of grey, fitted together in random squares and rhomboids. A single artwork dominated the place, a poster from the Musée de Cluny, bright red, showing a princess in medieval dress. Other than that, the most vivid object was a double bed draped in a spread of scarlet corduroy. Beside it, a wooden library table, with books packed into the shelves at either end. No television, no CD player, but she wouldn't need one. In the past five days he hadn't observed her more than twice without the white audio arteries of an iPod dangling from her ears.

An Apple laptop front and centre. He had followed her to Starbucks and watched her pull out a stack of papers to mark. It seemed early in the term for papers to be due, but perhaps she was earning extra money marking for someone else.

He had entered by the fire escape, the only way into what must be an illegal sublet. The door had a solid enough lock but he had managed to jimmy a window without much problem. It opened beside the galley kitchen, if that was not too grand a term for a built-in hot plate and sink. She had forgotten to switch off the overhead light.

The pay for a contract teacher, even at a major university, had apparently not improved much over the years. She didn't even have bookshelves. Instead, forty or fifty volumes were lined up along the baseboard. Chaucer,

Dante, Villon. Norton anthologies. Not following in Daddy's footsteps, obviously. Not living on his money, either.

The clothing in her closet consisted mostly of neatly stacked T-shirts. A few pieces suitable for lectures, two small dresses, nothing expensive. He made a mental note of sizes.

The bathroom had no door. It was separated from the rest of the space by a curved wall. In the medicine cabinet, birth control pills, a prescription cream for eczema, allergy pills. Nothing she would die without.

He went back to the desk and opened the laptop. E-mail from students angling for higher marks or to retake tests. A couple from her father. Her calendar was more useful. It gave course numbers and times; the locations would be easy to find. She had a conference coming up in Chicago in a couple of weeks. A doctor's appointment tomorrow. Spin class on Monday, Wednesday and Friday evenings.

A dark stairwell. Using his flashlight, he went down it and examined the door to the second floor of the house. Bolted from the inside. Dust on the doorknob and on the stairs themselves confirmed that the fire escape was the only entrance in use.

He was starting upstairs again when he heard a key in the lock. He drew back into the shadows. Sound of the door closing, keys hitting the counter, backpack hitting the floor. He lowered himself to sit on a step and waited.

Her boots hit the boot tray, her footsteps crossed the room. Rattle of hangers. He listened in his darkness as she undressed. And he listened for a long while after that, during which there was no sound. Above the stairwell, the lights remained on.

She was crying. Not loud, but unmistakable, the sound of sobbing, the rattle of mucus. Then her bare feet, the light, light step of a ninety-pounder, a hundred at most. Splash of the shower.

He moved soundlessly up the stairs. He opened the door and stepped out onto the snowy fire escape. Dull clang of metal steps as he descended. Rusted hinges squealed as he opened the rear gate. Snow swirling in the alley lights as he pulled his hood up and headed toward the street.

The sound of the young woman's tears stayed with him as he walked several blocks. It was with him still as he got into the van, and as he started it, and as he stopped at the first intersection, and as he crossed it.

From the Blue Notebook

Did you hear Ray last night? Rebecca said, twiddling a knob on her lidar unit. He scared me half to death. I thought some little animal was being tortured.

He suffers from nightmares, I said. Minute he touched down, I told Jens he wasn't suitable. Jens, of course, wouldn't discuss it. I think Kurt pressured him to accept his acolyte.

Kurt isn't like that.

No one is immune to worship. Except possibly you.

She ignored that. Kurt was looking for Ray earlier, she said. It's a good thing you weren't in here when he came by.

No doubt.

Ray does seem a little lost. Do you think he even wants to stay?

Wants? Maybe—if you can be said to want something that is killing you. He's staring into the jaws of failure if he quits—and God-knows-what if he stays. Annihilation, I suppose.

God, you're grim. Suddenly your ash-black globe makes sense. You're not one of those people who mistake being depressed for being intelligent, are you?

This is the dark side of the earth up here, in case you hadn't noticed. And anybody who loves it—in winter, at least—is not likely to be the life of any party one would care to attend.

Rebecca had removed the towel from her porthole window. She turned from her lidar readout and stared at the circle of fog pinned to her wall. The camp had been fogged in for days and nerves were raw.

Unlike you, I don't feel any urge to come up here in the dark of winter. I'm not even slightly attracted—emotionally, I mean—aside from my research interests. And yet I'm drawn to those who are. Kurt. You.

Opposites attract? That's your analysis? Eight years of postgraduate education and this is what we get?

I was leaning against her door, arms folded across my chest. There was nowhere to sit. I was smiling, but she wasn't looking at me and took me seriously.

She shook her head. Not opposites.

I took a half-step forward and placed my hands on her shoulders. She rolled her chair aside to escape.

There doesn't seem to be anything I can do about it, she said. I'm drawn to you the way you are drawn to the dark.

Then why do you pull away?

Don't be obtuse, Kit.

Tell you what, I'll put together a repertoire of jokes. I'll become the sort of person people call "a great storyteller." Remember in your high school yearbooks they would always say so-and-so "livens up any gathering"? So-and-so "really knows how to tell a story"? That's who I'll become.

Please don't.

Just for you. That's how much I love you. Karson Durie, raconteur.

I know this is your version of being light-hearted, but why is it every time I talk to you about anything serious it's like I'm feeling my way around the knife drawer?

My mother used to say something similar: You're so sharp you'll cut yourself.

It's not you I'm worried about. I don't think you should visit me here anymore.

Don't think—or don't want?

Just go, would you? I can't take this. I'll see you in the mess.

I opened the door and went out and the fog closed around me like a fist. The lights of the mess, not more than twenty metres distant, were a barely perceptible glow. I moved with one hand outstretched before me. The temperature was dropping. I could feel the difference in the texture of the slush beneath my boots.

I was startled by a loud crack. A slash of fire tore upward through the fog and vanished. I called out, What's going on?

Wyndham's voice came back, oddly close in the fog, though I could not yet make him out.

Ray's missing. We don't know what to do about it.

Thwock of the flare as it burst into a dandelion bloom, a dim throb beyond the fog.

Do you think he'll see that?

It's getting colder. The fog must be thinning in places.

My hand touched parka, but it was Vanderbyl. He stumbled a little to avoid me. I've been trying to radio Base, he said, but I don't think they're receiving me.

Wyndham said, Nobody's seen him since this morning, when he went back to his cabin to rewrite some material Kurt critiqued. That was when, Kurt? About nine-thirty?

Nine-thirty, yes.

I asked them if he was armed and if he had his radio.

As far as we know, Kurt said. Not that he's answering.

Hmm. How sharp was your critique?

The briefest of pauses before Kurt answered. It was a candid review. Not what you'd call harsh.

The two of them had searched everywhere: the radio shack, the power shack, the shop, kitchen, labs, and all the other huts. They had even radioed the seismic and core huts. Nobody had seen Ray Deville.

And so we hovered there, three disembodied voices in the fog, wondering where he might have gone. We didn't even bother asking why, at least not aloud. Ray and his radio silence. Sometimes a man can be so lost there's nowhere to look, nothing to be done.

We had a gloomy meal, a gloomy evening. People spoke but little. Wyndham attempted to lighten the mood by telling us a couple of unintentionally funny things Ray had said, these rendered in a note-perfect imitation of his franglais. He didn't get much of a laugh. The truth was, Ray and his manifest neuroses were hard to endure. One sensed that there ran beneath them a slick black river of contempt.

God, I hope he's all right, Kurt said later as he rinsed his dishes in the sink.

Wyndham listed the reasons for optimism. The temperature, at minus five Celsius, was crisp but far from severe. Ray's parka and scarf and boots were not in his cabin, so it was likely he would be warm enough. Our ice island was not vast, and in half-decent visibility he should have no difficulty finding his way back. He was armed, he had his radio . . .

Kurt opened the door, and his irritated response hung there in the mess with the cold air that rolled in: Then why the hell hasn't he used it?

In my narrow bed, I dreamed I had to climb a glass mountain that glittered in the glare of a savage sun. I was in the company of a man and woman who claimed to know the way but did not. Nor were they of any help when the mountain metamorphosed into a pure, unclimbable pyramid. It rose to a blinding point, and when I woke in the darkness, my eyes were wet as if I had been crying.

The fog had lifted and the hut was lit by a toppled pillar of light that angled through my porthole: they had left the floods burning on the Decca mast as a beacon. I lay there thinking about Ray Deville and imagining his encounter not with a bear or a walrus or a crippling fall, but merely with the Arctic in all its purity—an indifference that was boundless and exquisite, immeasurable to man.

After a time, I heard cries and answering shouts. Slamming doors and frantic voices—manly Vanderbyl and oboe-toned Wyndham. I hunched at my porthole, sleeping bag clutched around my shoulders. Wyndham was helping Ray across the last few metres of slush. Kurt waited, his back to my hut, erect and motionless, his shadow in the floodlight an endless black tangent. He said Ray's name.

The staggering, limping boy looked up, and I saw in the silvery light the blank, staring eyes of one who has blundered into God's private palace, who has looked his maker in the face and felt his marrow freeze.

12

ANOTHER MIRROR. DELORME STARED INTO the black depths and was aware that this was one of many reflective surfaces she'd studied in the past week or two. This one was an onyx panel, almost as wide as a movie screen, with half a dozen brushed-steel sinks before it and the flattering globes of dressing-room lights surrounding it.

"First time here?"

Delorme glanced at the reflection of a tall brunette who was leaning over the marble counter to examine herself close up. Delorme told her yes, and applied a little powder.

"You come alone?"

"Yeah. You?"

She nodded. "Are you as nervous as I am? I'm totally freaked out, and I'm not the freaking-out type."

The woman was about Delorme's age, but she sounded like the ingénue in some movie about show business. A backstage drama. It was hard to see clearly in the dark mirror, but perhaps that was the idea, to not look like yourself. The dark wig helped. It was longer than her own hair and felt reassuring as it brushed against her shoulders.

"Do you think everyone gets this nervous?" the woman asked her. This time she turned to address Delorme and not her reflection. Delorme did the same. The woman had fine, pale skin, opalescent.

"You'd have to be pretty strange," Delorme said, "to not be nervous."

"Maybe we should hit the bar together. For moral support. I mean, I'm not coming on to you or anything. Just might be a little easier."

"Let's say one drink," Delorme said. "Then we'll reassess."

"Cool. I'm not exactly a hundred percent committed to being here. Or doing anything with anyone." She went first to the door and held it open. "What's your name, by the way?"

"Stella." That name had been part of her role as an undercover hooker, as had the wig.

"I'm Heidi."

"Okay, Heidi."

~

Arriving at Club Risqué had been like stepping off a boat and sinking downward into the deep. The sense of pressure was immediate and building. Her lungs felt one-third smaller, as did her dress.

The smell of food was the first surprise. Delorme had forgotten there was a restaurant.

"Will you be having dinner?" the hostess said. Her smile was friendly, professional, nothing more.

"I think maybe just the bar. But I need the ladies' room first."

"Of course. Do you know how the club works?"

"You'd better tell me."

The hostess explained the etiquette of the different rooms and levels. She had an engaging manner and seemed to really want Delorme, and all her patrons—members, as she called them—to have a good time. The twenty-dollar fee afforded the place its designation as a private club, thus freeing it from certain legal restrictions on sexual behaviour.

The woman's positive demeanour, the inviting decor should have lessened the sense of walls closing in, but they only made things worse. The pressure wasn't coming from the place or the hostess, it was inside Delorme. She signed the little scrap of paper that listed the club's terms and conditions and headed for the ladies' room.

—

Now, in the first-floor bar, the music was low and the lighting dim, but there was still nothing sleazy about the place. Five or six couples sat at the tables and the bar, sipping cocktails or glasses of wine. Delorme couldn't see a single beer mug.

"Kinda surprising how normal it looks," Heidi said.

"Except there's no single men."

"They don't allow single men. Or I think only one night of the week."

"Uh-huh."

They didn't say anything for a while. Delorme had intended to ask many questions—of the hostess, the bartender, the other staff—but was silenced. The pressure in her chest wasn't fear. She knew what fear felt like: the sudden certainty that something terrible is about to occur and nothing will be able to undo it. Having that feeling on a regular basis was part of being a cop. But fear had an honesty about it, a directness. There was no certainty here.

Jesus, Delorme thought, I'm not even honest enough to know if I'm working or not. To know why I'm in this place.

"Don't look," Heidi said, "but I think the couple near the panther mural is sizing us up."

"We need another round." Delorme ordered two more, and when she turned to hand one of them to Heidi, the man from the couple Heidi had pointed out was standing in front of them.

"My wife and I were wondering if you'd like to join us." He had a shy smile and what Delorme thought of as a Superman curl.

Heidi bit her lip and looked at Delorme.

"I think maybe it's a little early for us," Delorme said. "For me, anyway. We just got here."

"Okay, no pressure. Join us later, if you feel like it." He looked at Heidi. "Are you Irish?"

"Not tonight."

The man laughed and went back to his table.

"I don't even know what I meant."

"I do," Delorme said.

"We probably should go sit with them. It's gotta be more comfortable than just wandering up to the second floor on your own."

The second floor. The second floor was where people started taking off their clothes. Full nudity acceptable but not required. Partial nudity expected.

"It says on the web page that nobody has to have sex, but that it's not a good idea to come here if you plan to say no all night."

"I think they were talking about the third floor."

"Actually, no. I believe they were talking about the club as a whole." Heidi's voice had lost the nervous-little-girl tone. The confirmation of her desirability seemed to have given her a shot of confidence.

"What made you come here, Heidi?"

Heidi looked at her martini. "I'm mad at someone," she said, and took a sip.

~

The ladies' room on the second floor had lockers.

"The only thing I can put in here," Heidi said, "is my cami. And then what am I gonna do if I go to the third floor—put the rest of my stuff in another locker?"

"Or you could come and get it and take it up there with you."

"I need another drink."

The bar was circular, surrounded by a series of alcoves furnished with long, low couches and tables. Couples were making out in several of these, including a man and a woman who were wearing only jeans. The light was dark and flattering, the music an ambiguous throb, as if the building were an engine of some sort.

There were no seats at the bar. Heidi and Delorme had an alcove to themselves.

"You're hot," Heidi said. "I bet they hit on you all the time at work."

"Not really. It's always the same—the one you want isn't interested and the ones you can't stand won't take no for an answer."

"God, does that sound familiar." Heidi raised her glass in a silent toast.

A couple came over from the bar. The woman had perfectly straight blond hair cut in a pageboy. The man looked a little younger, maybe mid-thirties, and more nervous.

"Do you mind if we sit here?"

"Of course," Heidi said. "Lots of room."

The woman sat beside Delorme. The man sat on the far side of Heidi.

"My husband," the woman told Delorme, "thinks he would enjoy seeing me make out with another woman."

"What a shocking idea," Delorme said.

"I think what he really means is he wants to do it with more than one woman at a time."

"No, no," the man said. "I don't necessarily have to be involved."

Heidi leaned into Delorme, a little too hard, her cold nose hitting Delorme's neck before she righted herself. She cupped a hand to Delorme's ear and whispered, "He's pretty cute, doncha think?"

"I think," Delorme said, "I'm going to save it for the third floor. Assuming I get up the nerve."

"My name's Janey, and this is Ron. We've never been up there," the woman said. She had a wide forehead and authoritative cheekbones, the sort of face you might cast in a movie as a senator or a judge. Not a Janey. "Maybe we could venture up there together—assuming, as you say, we get up the nerve."

~

When Delorme placed her foot on the bottom step of the stairs to the third floor, she had the sensation of something collapsing inside her. But she forced one foot in front of the other, following the woman, who was following the man.

"I'm staying behind you," Heidi said, "to make sure you don't chicken out."

In the ladies' room, with the locker door open before her, the collapsing sensation was replaced by something else. Delorme slipped out of her dress and hung it up, and it was as if a flock of birds had been released inside her chest.

"Are you sure you're okay with it?" Heidi was saying to the woman. "Won't it bother you to see your husband with someone else?"

"I think I can handle it."

"They're not married," Delorme said.

The woman laughed. "Guess it shows, huh?"

"Really?" Heidi tottered a little, pulling a shoe off. "Sometimes I'm so dumb I amaze myself."

"You gonna keep the underwear on?" the woman said to Delorme. "I think we're allowed to."

The third floor was designed for sex and nothing else. There were no chairs. All the surfaces were meant for lying down, not for sitting. The colour scheme was devoted entirely to the red end of the spectrum, the darkness relieved by sconces turned low.

Delorme thought she had thrown her numbness switch upon ascending to this floor, but the sight of a naked couple engaged in slow, quiet but unmistakable sex shorted that particular circuit. A hot blush, invisible in this place, spread upward from her rib cage. Her face burned with it and a fine sweat broke out across her shoulders.

Other men and women were arranged on the floor around the couple. None of the men wore clothes. Two of the women had tops on, the rest wore microscopic panties.

"Why don't we sit over there?" Heidi pointed to the far side, where there was a gap in the circle.

The fluttering in Delorme's stomach was not going to settle down. She had never even glimpsed a couple having sex before, let alone watched one. Thanks to the tastes of more than one boyfriend, she had seen porn movies. She had found them exciting in parts, though those parts depicted things she did not necessarily want to engage in herself, no matter what ideas the boyfriends might have had.

"Do they know each other?" she heard someone ask.

"Just met," came the hushed reply.

The couple were in their early thirties, and they went at it with a kind of solemn devotion, aware of their audience but focused on each other. They were lying on their sides now, facing each other. A woman in the outer circle reached out and caressed the man's back. If he made any response, Delorme didn't hear it.

Delorme was surprised at how unsexy it was. Perhaps this was due to the complete absence of fantasy. These were real people, and Delorme found their realness constricting in a way that fantasy was not. She found herself looking at the floor in an effort to avoid eye contact. She could feel the pulses in her wrists and ankles. How strange that, while seeing the couple engaged in sex was not wildly arousing, the *fact* that they were doing it was. The *fact* that this attractive young woman was opening her legs to someone she had just met. That this well-built young man, probably with a responsible job and a good income, possibly a good father and kind to animals, was willing to share the sight of his erect member in action with a group of naked strangers. It was not what they were doing but the *fact* they were doing it that was rearranging the tumblers in some heretofore unseen lock on Delorme's self-knowledge.

A cool hand touched her upper back.

"Okay?"

Delorme looked back over her shoulder. Janey was looking at her, eyebrows raised. Behind her, Heidi had fastened her mouth to Ron's, her bra already abandoned.

~

Bruce Turcotte stopped his snowmobile and sat for a few minutes just looking up at the magnificent fire tower before him. Middle of the bush, and here you have this perfect structure—not beautiful, but completely suited to its purpose, and built with an economy and integrity that spoke to the engineer in him. He had made his preliminary inspection a few days before and had been looking forward to the return trip.

Turcotte had been employed by the Ministry of Natural Resources for over twenty years, and in that time he had suffered his share of lousy assignments. He'd nearly frozen to death in James Bay one year, all but perished of boredom carrying out projects near communities so small they hardly deserved a name, and been driven half mad by blackflies more often than he cared to remember.

This assignment was a peach. In the days before satellites, the Ontario government had addressed the issue of forest fire prevention with the construction of more than a hundred lookout towers. Anywhere from eighty to a hundred feet tall, these mini-Eiffels were set atop the highest elevations in the province. The earliest ones were wooden and had long ago been torn down for safety reasons. During the fifties they had been replaced with steel towers, and these were the subject of Turcotte's current assignment, which was to inspect each one and make a recommendation based on his engineering expertise as to whether it should be torn down, preserved for restricted duty as an unmanned fire alert outpost (webcam only), or refurbished for recreational value in the ever-growing system of hiking trails that were replacing the province's extinct railroad, logging and mining operations.

The project required the collective wisdom of a small team of experts: a retired fire warden whose blood pressure gave him the face of a candy apple, a railroad executive whose first response to every request was *no*, and several representatives from Parks and Rec, including a dry stick of a woman, a vegan whose every utterance had the narcoleptic power he had formerly associated solely with the heavier opiates—not least because she spoke so slowly.

"Honestly," he told his wife, "when this woman starts to talk, I feel like I should go out, get in the car, drive to the beer store, maybe fill out a couple of lottery tickets, pick up the dry cleaning and stop off at the hardware store while I'm at it. And then maybe, just maybe, when I get back to the table, she'll have got to the end of her sentence. She must be from one of those planets that have an orbit of ten Earth years—and that's when she's talking about something *interesting*."

But the team entered the picture only after Bruce had come to his decision about structural safety, and to make that decision required a couple of solo trips. He had been to some wild places, seen many beautiful sights in his years with the ministry, but nothing had prepared him for how this new experience would resonate within him.

Each tower was crowned with a cupola, a more or less hexagonal structure with windows on all sides. The vistas he made him silent and thoughtful in a way nothing in his life ever had. "I'm a chatty guy," he said to his wife. "I don't have to tell you. Not the most introspective bastard you're ever going to meet . . ."

They were lying in bed and his wife had closed her Patricia Cornwell novel and turned on her side to listen to him. She touched his arm, encouraging him to continue.

"But something about these towers, the view from them, it shuts me right up. I just want to sit right down and think—except I don't actually have any thoughts. It's, I don't know—just suddenly I got a sense of how nothing I am. How small. The one I was in the other day—Algonquin Bay?—elevation puts me seven hundred feet higher than the town. Twenty-three hundred feet above sea level. All I can see, every direction, is sky and lakes, woods and mountains, and they're just standing up under all those winters and cold and . . . and *time*. And they go on *forever*. I'm talking sixty, seventy kilometres minimum. The scale of it. This is the earth I'm looking at, the way it was made, the way it was before I was born, the way it'll be after I die, the way it always was—well, for millions of winters anyway. And forty-seven, eh? I'm forty-seven years old, and for the first time in my life I know where they got the word *breathtaking*, because this tower, this view, it just took my breath. You think I'm being sappy?"

His wife had smiled at him, shaken her head.

He told her what was special about the Algonquin Bay tower, a "total honey," as he'd put it to his boss. It still had a table and chairs, still had the tower man's bunk, and even the plotting table with its turntable for triangulating the location of a fire or a wisp of smoke relative to the adjacent towers—adjacent in this case meaning forty kilometres away. The windows were intact and the hardwood floor in good shape.

He told his wife how the guys who had worked this one had been lucky. It boasted its own generator, and there was even a TV aerial attached to the roof a few feet from the anemometer. The place hadn't been manned since the fifties, and television wasn't much in those days.

"I'd like to meet one of these tower men," he said, "talk to him." You had to be some kind of philosopher to work in that beaut. You couldn't look out at the platinum plain of Lake Nipissing, the black gleam of highways threading through the hills, the clouds flat as tables over the valleys, and not become a thinker, even if you weren't one before you agreed to become a professional hermit.

The old Decca radio unit had looked as if it might crackle to life at any minute—beautiful thing. Turcotte had opened the back to look for tubes, but they were missing. The telephone was an old black dial type. When he blew the dust off, he saw that the number had only five digits: GRover 2-4348.

Now here he was once again at the foot of this tower, some twelve kilometres northwest of Algonquin Bay, sitting in the sudden silence that followed the roar of his snowmobile. Struts of galvanized steel glinted in the sunlight, the day so bright his eyes watered. He counted it a piece of excellent good fortune that his work required a second trip to install equipment.

He climbed off the machine and slung his backpack over his shoulders. It was relatively light, containing mostly a turret-mounted webcam system. This was just a test model. If it proved to be useful in filling in gaps in the satellite data, they would mount a proper all-directional system, replace the anemometer and get this place back online.

There was no question the Algonquin Bay tower would be a prime tourist draw. Aside from the spectacular view and the great condition, it was only a couple of kilometres from a main highway and not far from the old logging roads. Kids would love it. The vegan bore would probably declare it a global warming hazard, but by the time she finished making her point, everyone would be dead anyway.

Exhilarated by the crisp sky and the tart breeze, Turcotte actually spoke out loud. "You're a keeper, sweetheart. I'm gonna make you a star. But what I want to know just now, honey, is who cut this damn fence. I don't like it one damn bit."

It wasn't just the fence. Someone had managed to pull down the inner stairs, which you were not supposed to be able to do without the proper part—a removable crank. As he walked under the lower struts, Turcotte realized with a pang of guilt that he must have left the crank in place. And the hoist had been raised, too. The previous week it had been docked just above ground level; now it was way up beside the cupola door.

"So help me, if they've trashed the place, I'm going to bust some heads," Turcotte said. "I don't know whose, but heads will be busted."

He started up the stairs, patting his pockets for his cellphone. Then he remembered it was in his backpack. He unhooked it from his shoulders as he climbed, already beginning to sweat. He stopped a quarter of the way up and leaned against the safety rail to dial. Not much of a view from here, still below the treetops. When he got his boss's voice mail, he said, "Looks like someone has been up the structure. I'll call again when I get to the top."

He continued up the stairs, undoing his parka. He sensed the vista unfolding around him as he climbed, but he didn't look just yet. He wanted to save it for the top, to feel that feeling again. For now, he stared at his boots as they raised him step by step.

He had to pause halfway up, and again at three-quarters. An excellent way to give yourself a heart attack, he told himself. This is what comes of not going to the fitness club. Angina, tachycardia, and whatchacallits—infarctions. There's something you don't want to have. No one wants to infarc.

He didn't like the look of the door. Whoever had broken in had ruined the latch. It was not even fully closed. The window next to it had been smashed, the glass broken away right to the frames. I can understand all kinds of bad behaviour, Turcotte thought. Bank robbery, even murder if

I was mad enough. But vandalism to me is just an out-and-out mystery.

He sat on the top step, pulled out his phone and hit the speed-dial. "I'm about to go in," he said to his boss. "Just from the outside, we got problems. Some yahoo's been up here and screwed up the door and smashed a window to smithereens."

"Why the hell would they smash the window? You break into the place, presumably you don't want to freeze. You said it was in great shape last week."

"I know. Makes you sick." Turcotte looked out through the Xs of the struts into triangles of sky and cloud, too winded to appreciate them. "Hold on, I'm gonna go in. Christ, I hope they haven't emptied the place out. I mean, this is *history*. Hold on."

He put the phone, still live, in his pocket, pushed the door inward and stepped inside.

His boss, desk-bound seven floors above smoggy Bay Street in Toronto, squeezed the receiver between shoulder and ear as he packed hard copies of his PowerPoint presentation into his shiny ministry pocket folder. He had exactly seven and a half minutes to get to the fifth floor. "Bruce? Bruce, you there? Listen, I can't sit here. I have to go and impress a bunch of eco-freaks, and I—"

Turcotte was yelling at him now, cellphone overmodulating like crazy. He couldn't have heard him right. The man was up an abandoned fire tower out in the bush and he's yelling something about a woman.

"Throw the book at her, Bruce. Destruction of government property, trespassing, vandalism, the works. She's going to court and then she's going to jail. But I'm late, and I—"

But Turcotte—probably the most unflappable, down-to-earth, call-a-spade-a-spade kind of guy you could ever hope to meet—is telling him in tones of strangled hysteria that they won't be charging this woman with one damn thing, and the only place she's going is the morgue.

~

Delorme's house was dark, the curtains pulled. She always closed them early in the evening, even in summer, as soon as she got home. Her house was on a quiet little crescent, but the front window was wide and low and easy to see into.

Her car was in the drive, the afternoon snow on its roof and rear window undisturbed. No fresh tire tracks in the drive. No foot tracks either, on the front walk or on the stoop. Either she hadn't stirred all day or she had gone out in the morning—perhaps having been picked up by a cab—and had not yet returned. It could be someone else, it didn't have to be a cab.

Cardinal checked his watch. Nine-thirty is early to be in bed, though perhaps not if you're really sick.

The snow had stopped falling. He turned and headed back down the hill toward his place. He took off his glove, pulled out his cellphone and held his thumb over the dial button. He wanted to talk to her, see how she was doing, but he had a feeling she didn't want to hear from him right now. If she did, she would have called. He crossed Rayne Street and put the phone back into his pocket.

From the Blue Notebook

For the next forty-eight hours, Ray Deville remained curled up in his cabin.

Moment this bloody fog lifts, I want him out of here, Vanderbyl said.

I've already requested transport, Jens said without looking up. I didn't tell them who for. He was making notes in his group nutrition records, consulting Paul's recipes for the past few days and working out calories with a calculator.

It won't do his career any good, Vanderbyl said, but nobody wants him committing suicide either. He turned to Rebecca. When's this stupid fog going to lift? You're the cloud expert, tell us something useful for once.

Rebecca took her jacket down from a peg and left the mess.

That was uncalled for, I said.

Don't you tell me what's uncalled for, Vanderbyl said.

All right, all right, peacemaker Wyndham put in. Let's keep things civilized, shall we?

Too late for that, Vanderbyl said. Some people don't know what the word means.

Calm down, Kurt. It's just the damn fog getting to everyone.

Wyndham got Kurt's jacket and handed it to him—the temperature had warmed so much in the past few days that we had abandoned parkas for lighter clothing—and the two of them went out.

Jens, I said, did Kurt tell you what happened at the remote navigation shack?

Jens raised his Viking eyebrows. I've worked with Vanderbyl at half a dozen stations and I've never seen him like this. Don't you think you have rather a lot to apologize for?

I've never seen *me* like this either. Did he tell you about the navigation shack?

No.

They radioed in yesterday. One of them stumbled over—literally, that is—one of them stumbled over a dead polar bear. Nine bullets in him. That's a full clip.

Do we know Ray did it?

His automatic was empty when he finally decided to stagger back here.

Well, if his life was in danger . . .

He had a flare gun, he could have scared it off with that. Yes, I know—maybe it was past that stage. Except it wasn't. All of the bullets caught the animal in the back. It was apparently dining on a baby seal when Ray decided to kill it.

Dear God, Jens said. Well, he'll be leaving us soon enough. And I'm asking you and everyone else to be discreet about it. The pilot will be expecting a passenger, but he won't know why. Base doesn't even know why, other than "medical reasons."

Rebecca came to my cabin that night, the first time in more than a week. She made a valiant effort at passion and lust, tearing her clothes off without a word. And then, amid all the sweat and cries and breathlessness, she suddenly went limp and rolled away from me, sobbing into the pillow. Why does he hate me so much? It devastates me. He has nothing but contempt for me.

I held her lightly from behind and kissed the back of her neck. He doesn't hate you. He wouldn't be in such pain if he hated you. It's me he hates.

I've only ever wanted his love and respect. And for a time I thought I had it. I think I did have it. I did.

You mustn't mind what he says. He's in pain, that's all.

I know, she said, and wept again. That's the terrible thing—I deserve his contempt. If it were totally unjust, I could live with it, live with myself. But I deserve it. Why do *you* want me? You see how horrible I am.

No, I said, kissing her shoulder, I see how perfect you are—how tender and hurt and perfect and good—and I want to be with you always.

How does one measure love, the emotional current flowing through the connection of one human being to another? The instruments have yet to be invented. Were it to be measured in kisses, ours would not have come to much. But in tears . . .

13

ARSENAULT RELEASED THE BRAKE ON the hoist and the pulleys squealed as they began to turn. The body of Laura Lacroix, strapped to a pallet and shrouded in its dark plastic bag, swayed against the blue of the sky.

Everyone inside the turret—including Cardinal, Delorme, Loach and the two ident men—had stopped working to watch. Dr. Barnhouse tore off his top sheet and handed it to Loach. "Hypothermia is my guess, based on two things. First, the lack of lividity, which you get when the muscles stiffen with cold. Second, the lack of any other obvious cause. You're going to need the autopsy for anything more specific than that. Why Dr. Harris couldn't tell you this is a question for the medical college."

"Dr. Harris," Loach said, "never got above the first ten steps. He's afraid of heights."

"Whatever happened to normal?" Barnhouse said. "There used to be normal people in this world."

"Luckily we have you," Cardinal said.

Barnhouse tipped his fur hat and set it back on his head, then took hold of the safety rail before starting his descent.

Arsenault and Collingwood were poring over the bed where the body had been secured. They had tried and failed to get prints from the straps that had held her in place, and now they were examining the mattress. They had brought lights up on the hoist, but so far they hadn't needed them. Looking in some directions required sunglasses.

Loach hovered over them. "Are we locked-down, hundred percent sure we're dealing with the Flint doer here?"

"I've never come across another case where someone was deliberately frozen to death," Cardinal said. "Now we've got two. And once again she's wearing what appear to be brand-new clothes—at least some of them. Clothes that would keep her warm for a while, but not warm enough. He even broke the windows to make sure the sunlight wouldn't raise the temperature."

"Not quite thorough enough on that point," Loach said. "I'm gonna have to burn these goddam clothes."

"It's the same guy," Delorme said. "He left her food, same as Flint. He wanted her to last a while."

"Women are always complaining guys don't make it last."

"That's not actually funny," Delorme said.

"It is if you have a sense of humour."

"We need to figure out what these two women have in common," Cardinal said. "We're not dealing with crimes of opportunity—they were targeted. So far, the only thing they have in common is they fly Air Canada."

"I thought you liked this Leonard Priest character," Loach said to Delorme. "Fond of the outdoors, right?"

"Much as I'd love to put Leonard Priest behind bars, there's no sign of sexual assault in either of these cases. He has no connection to Flint that we're aware of, and no recent connection to Laura Lacroix or her husband, Keith Rettig."

"Take a look at this, guys." Arsenault was standing between the table and the bunk, a dark, pudgy figure against the brilliant window. He pointed at one of the few unbroken windows.

"It looks like a Volkswagen," Loach said. "Thank you so much for pointing this out."

"Not the cloud, the window. You have to be at the right angle."

They craned their necks at different angles and squinted.

"Call me crazy," Arsenault said, "but that looks like a 4 and a 5 to me."

"Me too," Cardinal said. "It was 25 at the tree house by the Flint residence."

"You think they're related? Anybody could've put that here," Loach said. "It could've been here for years."

"I know. It would be nice if we could rule out the numbers or rule them in."

"We'll take a closer look," Arsenault said.

Cardinal took Delorme aside. "This is too good, don't you think? Too organized."

"What?" Her mind seemed to be somewhere else entirely.

"He must have done this before. It's so well planned. And so was Flint. You don't get this good that fast."

"What's so good?" Loach said. "The vehicle's been seen. People have glimpsed the guy himself. We're not exactly dealing with Houdini here. He's leaving prints everywhere, for Chrissake."

"Smudges," Cardinal said, "not prints."

"Exactly. He's probably got a prosthetic hand."

"Which didn't pan out," Cardinal said. "I checked, and there've been no recent releases of anyone with a prosthetic limb of any kind. But I agree he's not making a huge effort to cover his tracks. It may be he's not worried about being caught."

"Everybody worries about being caught—except lunatics."

"Definitely not a lunatic—maybe just someone with nothing left to lose."

~

Business was slow. So slow, Larry Shawm was the only salesperson on the floor. Eleven-thirty, Rachel would be coming on for the lunchtime business, but until then he was on his own, unless you counted Myla on the cash. But Myla was like having nobody at all. Myla was the phone zombie to end all phone zombies.

Business had taken a dive since the move off Queen Street, but the lower rent at least meant he could count on a job for a while longer, which is more than you could say for a lot of retailers. These days, any store that wasn't a chain was living on a cliff edge.

"Please tell me I can help you," he said when the older guy came in. "It's a little slow today."

The man looked across the store and up the first aisle. The floor-to-ceiling shelves were intimidating to first-timers.

"Maybe I can interest you in a compass, first thing. Help you find your way around?"

"Just doing a little winter camping. Need a good short windbreaker, maybe a down vest, and a pair of boots."

The aisles weren't wide enough for two people. The man followed him to the rear of the store.

"How cold are we talking?"

"Minus thirty, thirty-five, thereabouts."

"We've got a wide selection of parkas and climbing jackets in that range. You trekking? Skiing?"

"Just a little hiking."

The man went over to the women's gear and lifted the sleeve of a climber's shell.

"Those there are women's. Is this for you?"

"My daughter. She takes a small."

"Well, your key, as you may know, is flexibility. So rather than go for a heavier item, I'd recommend a fleece hoodie under maybe something like this." He pulled out the BioFine Trekker, nice powder blue.

"Looks the right size."

"It's a small."

"Okay, I'll take that."

"She's going to need a thermal underneath it. This'll only protect you down to about fifteen below, depending on wind chill, sunshine and how active you're going to be."

"I'll just take this for now."

"She's already got some stuff, I take it."

"We're just filling things out a little."

"And boots, you said?"

"You have something that'll work for the city as well?"

"Here in Toronto? Kinda difficult. Anything that'll serve you in thirty-five below is going to be way too hot down here, unless she's just planning to wear them to get to work, then change into something else."

"What size are these?" He lifted up a pair of hikers.

"Never work for any kind of snow, even with snowshoes."

"Do you have these in a six?"

"Are you sure about the size? Those are gonna need double-layer socks to be any good in the kind of temperatures you're looking at."

"Sixes are fine."

Larry went downstairs and got the boots and brought them back up. The man had already moved to the cash. Larry wouldn't have pegged him for an outdoorsman, but then nowadays you got all kinds. Lots of hikers, even trekkers, were historians or biologists, ecology scholars of various stripes.

Myla rang up his purchases—once Larry had managed to glare her off the phone. Larry felt like reminiscing about his canoe trip down the Mackenzie, but no luck. The guy wasn't rude exactly, but he wasn't going to be engaged. He paid with crisp fifties, got his change and said thanks, shiny leather glove on his one hand the whole time.

~

Priest's car was in his driveway and Delorme could hear music from inside the house. She leaned on the doorbell a third time.

Priest answered the door wearing nothing but a T-shirt, beneath which his penis stood at half-mast.

"I need to ask you a few questions."

"I'm flattered. Please come in, you're freezing John Thomas." He stepped back, held the door open for her and closed it behind her.

In the shadows beyond the dining table, a woman on a couch clutched some clothing to her chest. "For Christ sake, Leonard, what the fuck."

Priest called to her. "Not to worry. As you were, darlin'."

"Put some clothes on," Delorme said.

"My house, I dress as I like, thanks. Feel free to shed some clothes yourself, though."

"We've found Laura Lacroix's body."

"That's very sad, but it's got nothing to do with me."

"I can see you're all broken up about it."

"Take your boots off, if you don't mind. You can take your jeans off too, while you're at it."

Priest's pale ass retreated to the living room. Delorme left her boots in the kitchen and went as far as the dining area.

"Melanie, this is Detective Delorme. My friend, Melanie Smith. Don't worry, she's not after you, Mel. She thinks I killed this woman who's missing."

"No, I don't. I think you killed Régine Choquette, who took a bullet through her skull. Ms. Smith, you might not want to hear all this."

Ms. Smith—if Smith was her real name—shook her head. "Len and I go way back. I've heard it all before."

"Are you going to put some clothes on?" Delorme asked Priest.

Priest put on the voice of a cross-examining attorney. "Detective Delorme, please tell the court what the defendant was wearing when you interviewed him. T-shirt and no pants, I see. And was his penis fully erect, to the best of your knowledge? Sort of half-and-half, I see. And in the course of your interview, did that change at all?"

"We have a witness now who says you ordered Fritz Reicher to shoot Régine Choquette."

"Melanie, could we get back to work, please? You don't mind if Lise watches us, do you?"

Melanie tossed the sweater aside and got down on her knees in front of him.

"Did you hear what I said?"

"*Yes, of course.*" His parody of Reicher's voice was perfect. "The only so-called witness who might say such a thing has already been convicted."

"Suppose he recanted his earlier testimony. His earlier plea."

Melanie's head bobbed up and down, dark curls swaying.

"Ooh, yes, just like that. Why don't you take your clothes off, Lise?"

"Tell me about Darlene," Delorme said. "Who is she, and where can I find her?"

"I don't know anyone named Darlene. Oooh, yeah. Oh my God. Come and join us, Lise."

Delorme went back to the kitchen and put on her boots.

~

Although Chouinard was always in charge of the morning meetings, Loach had lately become the dominant presence. He sat beside Chouinard looking as if he had just won several million dollars and was condescending to listen to the petty concerns of those whose net worth was stuck at terrestrial levels. Stereo speakers had been placed on the table on either side of him.

Arsenault and Collingwood talked first. Laura Lacroix, like Marjorie Flint, had been injected in the neck. They were waiting for the toxicology report from Toronto.

As to the number scrawled on the window, all Arsenault could say was that the five was similar to the five carved into the wood in the Flint case. "Both are perfectly closed at the top. But sorry, folks, we can't be sure when the window marks were made. Going by the other dust patterns in the tower, they could have been made any time in the past three or four months or so."

"Tell us about the clothes," Chouinard said.

"The down vest is new. But it's a popular brand available across the country. More than a hundred different outlets."

"Could she have bought that herself?" Chouinard asked.

"Possible," Arsensault said, "but it isn't what she wore to meet her lover. That was a medium-weight trench coat that was dumped in a Sally Ann donation box. Sharp-eyed volunteer found a credit card receipt in the pocket and recognized the name. Unfortunately, the coat hasn't generated any more leads. No hairs, nothing we can follow up."

"The vest looked like the right size to me," Cardinal said.

"And the point of this observation?" Loach wanted to know.

"If the killer bought it for her, it means he got very close. Possibly he was even inside her place. I think we should pursue the clothes, even if there are a hundred outlets. It's an older man buying a woman's item, probably somewhere not too far from here. We could get lucky."

"I'll tell you what," Loach said, "why doesn't everybody just listen up for a second and we might make some real progress." He got up and went to the lectern that was sometimes used for seminars. He slotted a flash drive into a laptop. "This was left on my voice mail last night."

There was some throat clearing. Sound of a microphone being jostled, rubbing against fabric. Music playing in the background—lots of strings, something classical. Then the voice, an older man with a strong French-Canadian accent.

Officer Loach, I saw you on da TV de udder night and now 'ere you are again and I just gotta call and congratulate you. So you fine your second victim at last—you must be ver' proud. I wondered 'ow long it would take you. I was worry I might 'ave 'id her too good. Of course, it wasn't you who discover da body. Dat would have require some intelligence. Forty-five years ol' and nudding but a small-town cop, you're not exactly da sharpes' knife in da drawer. You got lucky with dat forestry guy.

But not lucky enough, my frien'. Because me, I am not finish. I don't know about you, but I'm 'aving a lot of fun. And I can give you twenty-five different reason you'll never catch me, even if you live to be ninety-five. So I'm going to 'ave more fun—a lot more fun, maybe sooner dan you tink.

The atmosphere in the room had changed. Everyone had shifted position, sitting forward now.

"Obviously a major development," Loach said. "Let's listen to it one more time."

He fiddled with his trackpad and started the playback again. When they had listened all the way through, he shut his laptop.

"Like I say—major."

"It certainly is," Cardinal said, "assuming it's real."

"Are you saying it isn't?"

"I'm just saying we have to be sure."

"He comes up with the numbers 25 and 45 by accident? Where's he get those, if it's not real?"

"Well, one of them refers to your age, right?"

"I'm forty-six, not forty-five, or ninety-five, thank you. And how's he get the 25? I don't think that's coincidence, and we haven't mentioned either of those numbers to the media."

"You're forgetting your Montrose case in Toronto. You were in the news a lot with that. I'm willing to bet more than one of those stories mentioned your age."

"Well, that's true," Loach conceded. "I was forgetting about that."

"Let's cut to the chase," Chouinard snapped. "Do we think it's real or not?"

"We can't know for sure," Cardinal said.

"Exactly," Loach said. "Which is why I've already sent it to the RCMP profilers. In the meantime, we're gonna throw everything we have at this. The caller's French Canadian, obviously, with a strong accent—and we're gonna go right back to the next of kin and places of employment and get the names of any contacts with FC accents."

"People can fake accents," Delorme pointed out, "and that one's pretty extreme."

"Which doesn't mean it's fake," Loach said. "Maybe you don't hear it the way we do."

"French Canadians have a genetic defect? We not only talk funny, we're born deaf too?"

"I'm not even going to answer that," Loach said. "This is a hot lead and we're going to hit it with everything we've got."

Cardinal appealed directly to Chouinard. "D.S., we're better off focusing on something more solid. The sedatives, for example—they had to come from somewhere. We've got to run down drugstore thefts, veterinarians, hospital inventories. And the clothes, too. Older guy buying outdoor gear for a woman—someone might remember."

"Excuse me," Loach said. "We have a man's *voice*. We can run that voice right by the people closest to the victims. Someone's gonna recognize it."

"It's too much of a leap," Cardinal said. "Except for the two numbers, which *could* be coincidence, he doesn't say anything that isn't common knowledge. Also—let me finish—also, it doesn't jibe with previous behaviour. We *know* the killer followed or observed these two women very closely, without being observed himself. The crimes themselves were well planned and well executed."

"Not true. We have a recognizable vehicle. People have *seen* him. We're pretty sure he has a fake hand, for Chrissake."

"Point is, this is a quiet, concentrated, methodical person. Now all of a sudden he picks up the phone and calls us? Why?"

"To taunt us, obviously. Same as with the numbers themselves."

"Do they really qualify as taunts?" Cardinal said. "They're not in-your-face like the phone call."

"Think what you want. I'm running Lacroix, and the people on my team are going to get names—and recordings—of any French-Canadian males known to the victims. Work, relatives, professionals, I don't care. And we're gonna get voice prints." He put the cap back on his flash drive and stood up. "Arsenault, see what you can do to this recording to bring up that music in the background. Those violins or whatever—I'd like to know exactly what that is."

"Beethoven."

Everyone turned to look at Collingwood. He blushed and spoke into his chest. "Quartet in C minor, opus 18."

Loach pointed at him. "He always talk this much?"

"Bob was raised by a family of raccoons," Arsenault said. "We're happy when he talks at all."

Cardinal went to his cubicle, sat down, and stayed there exactly fifteen seconds before he got up again and went to Chouinard's office.

"Don't even bother," Chouinard said.

"D.S., we're going off on tangents. We can't have the case split up like this. Put me in charge of the whole thing."

"No. You look after Flint, Loach is looking after Lacroix."

"It's the same killer. It should be one case, one lead."

"Normally I would say you're right, but this department is a little too complacent for my taste. I think a little competition could do us a world of good."

"I just don't want anyone else to get killed."

"No one wants anyone else to get killed. Close the door on your way out."

From the Blue Notebook

Wyndham emerged from the lab and lugged his computer battery to a sled that was already heaped with equipment. Gordon had evolved a kind of mobile observation post that he painstakingly assembled and disassembled every other day in his obsessive pursuit of perfection. He was a compact, pocket-sized man, but his shadow as he crossed the ice must have been thirty metres long. The shadow of his heavily laden sled was not much shorter.

For some time now we had been bearing south along the western shore of Axel Heiberg Island, our ice island having been nudged by other floes into the Sverdrup Channel. It was a beautiful day and nearly everyone was working outdoors to make the most of it. We had abandoned our heavier parkas for down jackets or fleeces, although the slush necessitated knee waders. I checked my AARI buoys, which gave continuous readouts of drift direction and speed, details of water currents, temperature and so on. My fans and scoops and sensors were at the end of a narrow drive shaft beneath ice that was over seventy metres thick.

Wyndham had passed our radio mast and had nearly reached his first observation post, trudging in the peculiar head-jutting way of anyone who is man-hauling anything heavy. The sun was low, and half obscured by a lenticular cloud that swept upward like a solid brushstroke from the horizon. The light was the colour of a blood orange.

We were spread out across our table of frozen sea like markers on a board game. Most of the buoys were fixed into the ice directly north of the lab, and normally that's where I would have been at that time of day. But I was getting an anomalous readout from a buoy half a kilometre to the west, so that's where I went. I was cranking my sensors toward the surface while watching Wyndham.

Rebecca was farther from the central building, between me and the landing strip. She genuflected and aimed her camera into the cloud, into the sun. Probably shooting infrared. Her passion for documenting the invisible.

Hunter was riding his tractor, doggedly ploughing the landing strip down to something approaching solid ice. The Twin Otter was scheduled to pick up Deville and drop off some supplies in three days. The temperature was expected to drop before then. Even so, landing a Twin Otter on that surface was going to be dangerous, and I was thankful once again that I had quit the flying business for the relatively tranquil requirements of research.

Vanderbyl was making adjustments and checking readings from his hydrophones and other sensors. Ray Deville had been hanging around him all morning. He had been informed of his impending evacuation and for the past few days had been making frantic efforts to convince Kurt of his competence to carry on, but he was not in sight at the moment.

There was the crack of a gunshot and I looked over toward the lab building. Someone practising on the target range. I was still working at raising the sensors with a hand crank, the motorized one having seized up yet again. A few more metres to go. Wyndham had his laptop out and was wiring it up to an array that measured changes in albedo—the reflectivity of the Arctic surface.

That, then, was our dispersal: Vanderbyl to the east of the landing strip, Rebecca and I to the west, Wyndham (and Hunter, still on his tractor) in a line straight north from the lab and the radio mast. Dahlberg, Washburn and Bélanger were inside. All of this I remember as vividly as if each of us were a pin stuck on a map.

More shots from the firing range. They sounded a little strange, but in that unpredictable acoustic environment I wasn't concerned. Arm aching, I finally managed to crank my sensors out of the drill hole. The problem was immediately obvious: an Arctic jellyfish had got itself wrapped around the fan. I pried the mess off with one of my trowels and it hit the slush with a smack.

The dogs had started barking and I looked around to see if there was a bear. I knew that Wyndham was armed that day, and also that Hunter—ex-military Hunter—was always armed. Rebecca was working reasonably close by and I could see the flare gun strapped to her waist. In most cases a warning flare is enough to make a bear think twice.

The dogs' barking transmuted itself into the yips and whines of canine paranoia. I pulled out my binoculars and focused first on Wyndham, who seemed intent on his observations. Hunter was ploughing at the near end of the runway.

Beyond the strip, Vanderbyl was hoisting a small pack onto his back. He usually headed inside about this time to spend an hour or two in the lab before lunch.

I took my radio out of an inner pocket. What's going on with the dogs? I said. Have we got a bear somewhere?

It was Wyndham who came back: All quiet over here.

A rumble of thunder cut him off. You get used to the sound of cracks shooting through contracting ice. Sometimes they make a deep squeal that ends with a gasp, a kind of breathy pop. I've heard fracturing ice wail as if a gate of Hell had suddenly blown open, and other times it sounds like nothing more than the slam of a washing machine lid. I had never heard one that sounded like thunder. The dogs began howling in earnest.

I turned toward Rebecca. I think I was hoping she would be perceiving some storm system visible only to her infrared. But she was not looking through her camera. She was standing in an attitude of anxious expectation.

I turned back with the binoculars. Wyndham had stopped work. He had his back to me in a posture of alertness, listening. Vanderbyl had passed him, heading toward camp, but stopped and turned around when Wyndham yelled something.

There was a tremendous crack and we all—everyone I could see—fell to our knees. Hunter was still on his tractor, still ploughing. It's possible he didn't feel that first tremor.

At first no more than a fissure, the crack that appeared was the otherworldly blue of the polar lead. From my vantage point, the lead seemed to run about three hundred metres, forming an amethyst wound that stretched from the edge of the camp to the foot of the radio tower. Hunter had seen it too and switched off his tractor, creating an envelope of silence.

Leads opening up like this were not uncommon. To reduce the risk of such a fracture forcing us to up stakes and move, we had erected Arcosaur in the middle of the widest ridge, in the middle of our island of ice. What no one had expected was that a lead might open up at right angles to the island furrows.

We got to our feet and looked around, one to the other. Ray Deville had emerged from somewhere, having changed from his parka to a lighter jacket. He was on his knees, as stunned as the rest of us. My radio crackled and I had to retrieve it from the slush where it had fallen.

Wyndham's voice, with a tremor in it: I've got a huge lead just opened up less than ten feet away.

Get away from it, Vanderbyl told him. It's probably over, but let's be on the safe side.

I can't move. My sledge is caught on something.

Uncouple your tether, man. Don't hang around.

I'm trying to. My bloody fingers won't work.

Even over the radio you could hear the laugh in Wyndham's voice—nervous, of course, but also self-deprecating. That was utterly in character, and it was one of the many reasons he hadn't an enemy in the world.

I don't think Wyndham, I don't think any of us, had yet registered true panic. We were not yet cognizant of the magnitude of the disaster. Vanderbyl, a tall, no-nonsense sort of man, easily six-three, moved toward Wyndham in long, efficient strides despite the slush.

Wings shearing off a jetliner. That was the sound that at that moment ripped through the atmosphere. Off to my right, our main building imploded, the roof crashing in toward the middle as the two sides were pulled away from each other. The crack in the ice widened with horrific speed, shooting like a pale blue bolt across the surface.

Vanderbyl was on the far edge of the split. With me, across from him: Wyndham, Rebecca and Ray Deville—and somehow Dahlberg. Dahlberg had no reason to be outside, but I had no time to wonder about that. Wyndham's sledge had disappeared. Wyndham himself was down, having been dragged a short distance until he caught on one of the buoys, and now he clung to it. I found myself running toward him. Rebecca looked unhurt. She was getting up, but Deville remained on his knees where he had fallen. His face bore the vacant, bewildered look of a man who has been pulled unhurt from a death-dealing car crash.

As I ran, I registered in my peripheral vision that Hunter had started up his tractor again, raised his plough, and was turning the ungainly machine toward Wyndham. And it was only as I ran that I understood exactly the peril Wyndham was in. The Nansen sled, with its freight of equipment, had tumbled into the lead with Wyndham still harnessed to it. The only thing keeping him from following it into the abyss was the buoy fastened into the ice and to which he desperately clung. I patted my pockets for my folding knife as I ran.

It looked as if Hunter would reach him first. Vanderbyl had come to a stop on the far side, halted by the blue gap that was now some twenty metres across. Hunter's tractor was slamming toward them.

It takes considerably more time to read about what happened next than the events themselves took to occur. We are talking a matter of seconds, somewhere between three and five.

There was a tremendous boom and those of us on foot were hurled to the ice. The impact sent the snot flying from my nostrils, and all the bony places of my body lit up with pain. As I pulled myself up, I saw that the crack had turned serpentine, opening a whiplash curve just in front of Hunter. He had no time to react. The tractor's port tread went over first, causing the whole machine to pivot and tip sideways, pitching him into the crevasse. What is most vivid now in my mind is not the image of his death—the sprawling, ungainly ugliness of it—but rather his absolute silence, the absence of any cry, the slightest protest at his severance from the living. The tractor tilted with agonizing slowness, halting for a moment on the precipice with the poise of a ballerina, before somersaulting with a roar over the edge.

I was getting to my feet, trying to regain my breath, and saw Vanderbyl doing the same. He would not be able to help—the gap had become a canyon. Behind him, the radio mast listed at a forty-five-degree angle. Somehow I managed to stagger the last dozen or so metres to Wyndham.

He was on his side, curled around the buoy. From his position he couldn't have seen what had happened to Hunter. He even tried to make a joke.

No rush, Kit, he said to me. Take your time.

I was on my knees. I had my knife out but was having trouble opening it. Some people, I said to him, will do anything for attention.

A squeal of metal and I looked up. I have absolutely no doubt that if we had had just another few seconds, I could have saved Wyndham. The radio mast lurched and fell another ten degrees, paused for a half-second, and crashed full length to the ice. The top third of the array snapped off and vanished.

I cannot say with certainty—no one could know for sure—but it seems likely that the top of the radio mast, in its plunge into the abyss, smashed into Wyndham's dangling sledge and tore him away from the buoy. Before I could so much as drop my knife to grab for him, he had slithered across the last few feet and over the edge.

Again, that terrible silence.

I crawled to the precipice, lay down and peered over the edge. In that blue and shimmering canyon, there was no sign of life. Sea water swirled and foamed as it flooded into the crevasse some hundred feet below.

Vanderbyl was stabbing at his radio, barking Mayday, Mayday. Get some rope, he yelled to me. We've got to get them out of there.

There was no rope to get. The fracture, serpentine to the north, had forked to the south. The lab hut hung in jagged pieces from either edge of the initial split. The rest of the buildings—the power shack, the vehicle shed, the sleeping quarters—were mostly intact on a shard of shelf ice that had become its own separate floe. I remember wondering what had happened to Murray Washburn, our facilities manager, and Paul, our cook. They rarely had occasion to visit the lab, and it seemed unlikely that they would have been in it the moment it was destroyed.

Ice island T-6 was now at least three ice islands, rapidly drifting away from each other. Kurt Vanderbyl was a hundred and fifty metres distant, adrift on his own shard, his dark silhouette rippling against the sun. Rebecca ran to the edge of what now amounted to our universe, calling her husband's name. The useless shortwave dangled from his left hand. He slowly raised his right in farewell.

14

AT LUNCHTIME, CARDINAL WENT OVER to D'Anunzio's and ordered a sandwich and a coffee. The place was a fruit store in addition to being a coffee shop, and while he was waiting he bought a half-dozen oranges and set them on the counter. Tony D'Anunzio was as chatty as usual, but Cardinal just grunted in reply. His ham and cheese sandwich came and he ate it in silence. He had looked for Delorme to see if she wanted to join him, but she had already headed out somewhere else. In thinking about her now, his mind went into split-screen mode. On one side, the image of her as she looked that night of the party—an image that reawakened the desire to kiss her. On the other, the image of her sitting on his couch with a bowl of popcorn on her lap as they watched a movie together. He missed the easiness of their friendship—missed it so much that he could not have said at that moment which side of the split screen he wanted to become the whole story.

He reached for a *Toronto Star* someone had left on the stool next to him. Half of page five was devoted to the Flint–Lacroix case. The article was accompanied by a still of their most likely suspect from the Broadview Motel's security camera footage. Beside it, they had reproduced the Identi-Kit composite. *Have you seen this man?*

Silver hair, regular features, large nose. Whether or not anyone had actually seen him, a lot of people were going to think they had. The calls would be many, time would be wasted, and they would be no closer to the killer.

Tony D'Anunzio refilled his coffee cup without asking.

"Thanks, Tony," Cardinal said. "What do I owe you?"

His cellphone rang. Jerry Commanda, detective sergeant at the OPP and a former city cop.

"Tell me something good, Jerry."

"You're not dead."

"Always a ray of sunshine."

"I've been cogitating." It was Jerry's habit to employ words that, while not exactly obscure, were not common conversational tender. "Pondering your question about possible similars."

"You said you didn't have anything."

"Which was correct at the time. I don't personally have anything similar, nor does anyone in the detachment—or on the reserve, before you ask."

"I already did ask."

"That's true, you did."

"I wasn't talking murders necessarily."

"I know. We don't have any attacks or attempts that might have been the work of the same guy. But . . ."

Jerry started flirting with one of his colleagues in the background, telling Deandra Couchie she was looking dangerously provocative today. Deandra was a good-looking woman old enough to be Jerry's mother, or nearly. Cardinal used to think it was just Jerry, but he had come to realize that First Nations people were not squeamish about proper office behaviour, at least among themselves. If Cardinal had ever suggested to Sergeant Flower that she was looking too sexy in her new jacket, he'd have to endure a lecture from the chief, if not a written reprimand.

"Leave her alone," he told Jerry. "She can beat you up."

"I know it—I was her kick-boxing instructor. Listen, I just heard back from the Parry Sound detachment. They had a thing, fifty-eight-year-old female, Brenda Gauthier, froze to death last February—record snow, remember? And near-record lows. Anyways, she suffered from early-onset Alzheimer's and had lately become peripatetic. Went AWOL a couple of times, way they do. So when she turned up frozen to death in the middle of the bush, it maybe didn't get the attention it deserved."

"What makes you think it deserved more?"

"Well, the age would fit, obviously. But here's what struck me in reading the report: when Brenda Gauthier was found, she was wearing clothes that didn't belong to her."

"I need to speak to the husband," Cardinal said. "How do I contact him?"

"You can't—and that's another reason I thought you'd be interested. He killed himself two days ago."

~

A stack of call slips was waiting for Cardinal on his desk. He tossed them on top of his bag of oranges and dialed the number Jerry had given him, the cellphone of Timothy Gauthier, home from his job in London's City district to bury his father.

He took the phone messages to Chouinard. "Why are all these call-ins coming to me?"

"That's exactly one-fifth of what's come in since this morning. Don't look like that. I'm not going to second-guess anyone at this stage, and it's Loach's case."

"I'm running Flint."

"So clearly the reasonable thing to do is for you to decide which of those messages relate to Flint and which to Lacroix and divide them up accordingly. Of course, in order to do that, you'd have to answer them."

Cardinal felt the anger rising in him and pushed it down. "I have to go to Parry Sound. I think we've got a third victim."

~

It was a two-hour drive to Parry Sound. Cardinal had lots of time to think about the reports Jerry had faxed. To the Parry Sound OPP, Brenda Gauthier was not a homicide but a case of unexpected death, and the case summary was accordingly laconic.

> Missing person, female 58 years of age and suffering from Alzheimer's disease, last seen 1 pm, Friday, February 15, 2010. LSW: cream blouse, navy blue cardigan, dark slacks.

Husband Frank Gauthier reports leaving for just over an hour for doctor's appointment. Upon return, wife missing. Has wandered off on prior occasions.

All-units alert and other obvious efforts unsuccessful. Grid search mounted the following day without result. Search expanded Feb 17 and body discovered 4:30 pm bottom of ravine 20 kilometres distant (near West Line Rd.). Foot of rocky outcropping, in heavy bush. Multiple injuries include broken leg, severe trauma to head.

Husband several times expressed concern/bewilderment that some clothes wife was found wearing not her own, specifically boots and blue down jacket, both new-looking. Accepts given victim's increasing dementia there are several possible explanations for this.

Coroner on scene found no evidence foul play. Autopsy also negative. Reports on file. Cleared: Death by misadventure.

The autopsy report found injuries consistent with a fall at the scene and put cause of death as intracranial bleeding. Toxicology showed high levels of donepezil and other medications for dementia but was otherwise negative.

Cardinal thought about that twenty kilometres. A long way for a woman to wander on her own, unseen, in heavy snow. And he thought about the clothes.

Five kilometres outside Parry Sound, a snow squall hit and he had to concentrate on driving.

~

"I'm going to ask you straight out, Mr. Gauthier. Did you find anything suspicious about your mother's death?"

"I certainly didn't. I've been living in England the past three years. I'd been painfully aware of my mother's illness, mostly from a distance. My father sent me anguished e-mails about it. It was horrible for him, as you can imagine. I knew she'd wandered off several times before. Typical for Alzheimer's, as I'm sure you know. Of course, I felt like shit for not coming home like a dutiful son and helping out."

"What about your father? Was he satisfied with the investigation?"

"Oh, Dad had a few questions, definitely."

"What sort of questions?"

"He said that after the first few times my mother wandered away, she became afraid to go out at all. She hadn't even left the house for a couple of months. So why would she take off all of a sudden? Personally, I didn't think it sounded all that strange. Horrible, but not exceptional, given the circumstances." He gave a deep sigh and rubbed a hand over his face.

"Do you need to sit down?"

"I'm pretty jet-lagged. Let's go sit in the kitchen. You want a coffee or something?"

"No thanks, I'm fine."

They went to the kitchen, where Gauthier poured himself a glass of water and drank it straight down. He put the glass in the sink and leaned against the fridge. Cardinal remained standing by the door.

"What about the clothes your mother was wearing when she was found?"

"That *did* sound weird. Apparently she went out wearing her regular boots and coat, but when she was found she was wearing a brand-new down jacket—bright blue—and a pair of hiking boots my father had never seen before.

"He got quite obsessed about it in his e-mails. '*Blue!* She never owned a blue coat in her life! And these heavy-duty boots, like she was some kind of bushwhacker.' That kind of thing. It's mysterious, for sure, but once you put Alzheimer's in the mix, I imagine anything's possible."

"How much did any of this have to do with your father taking his own life?"

"Oh, I don't think it was about that. Those weird details were just a bee in his bonnet. Something he couldn't explain. My father was a nuts-and-bolts kind of guy, very scientific, didn't like mysteries. No, he just got more and more despondent—it was something I'd worried about before. My parents were very close, always together, especially after Dad retired, which was a long time ago now. They were each other's world, you know, and . . ."

Gauthier turned his back and faced the bright window. He reached for a Kleenex and blew his nose. Cardinal gave him a minute.

"Mr. Gauthier, I have to tell you something that is not public knowledge, and it's very important that it stay that way."

Gauthier turned to face him, dabbing at his eyes.

Cardinal told him about the other two dead women, how they were dressed. When he was finished, Gauthier went very still.

"And they were murdered?"

"Yes, they were. No question. Which is why I'm hoping you'll let me look around a little. We need to know if there is anything else that connects your mother's death to these others."

~

Gauthier showed him to a large, sunny room. Neat rows of books on shelves, L-shaped work table that ran the width and breadth of the room. Wide-screen computer. Windows overlooking the white expanse of the sound, its evergreen shores and rocky islands.

"Looks like a serious computer," Cardinal said.

"My dad worked in medical tech, but my mother was pretty savvy too—this is hers. People think librarians are Luddites, but they have to keep up with information technology. You can see she was in the middle of a big project here, digitizing all the old family photographs. I don't think she'd done anything on it for a while. Even her long-term memory got quite impaired toward the end. I'm amazed Dad never even put this stuff away. I really underestimated . . ." Gauthier's voice broke and he had to stop for a moment. "Sorry. I'm still kind of in shock here."

"Take as long as you need."

Gauthier blew his nose again, sat at the keyboard and powered up the computer. A few Ouija moves with the mouse and he pulled up his mother's calendar, address book and e-mail programme.

"You said your father was in medical technology. MRIs and those kind of things?"

"Robotics. For robot-assisted surgery mostly. Also some prosthetic applications. He was super successful, but you'd never know it from his demeanour. He was not a flashy guy. Eventually he sold the company and moved up here from Montreal. My mother was from this area originally." He stood up. "I'll be in the living room if you need me. I've got a ton of arrangements to make."

"Thanks. I'll try to be quick."

Gauthier paused at the door. "I'm giving you access because if my mother was murdered I want to know. But I expect you to respect my parents' privacy in every way possible."

~

Cardinal looked around the room. Yellow note squares were stuck to drawers and cupboards: *Paper, Folders, Envelopes, Pens and pencils.* The books were all hardbacks and seemed to be evenly divided between fiction and non-fiction. Many of the authors were names Cardinal recognized but had not read: Richler, Shields, Munro.

The office furniture was all modern—pale wood, clean lines—but Brenda Gauthier's reading chair was plump and overstuffed, with a colourful blanket draped over the back. On a windowsill, a small plant hung, exhausted, over the edge of a pot that sat on a plate. The plate had a crest, blue on white, of a beaver, a tree, and books. Cardinal had a vivid memory of university, cheap meals dished out in the Great Hall of Hart House, the long-ago days before he had decided to become a cop.

He expanded the address book and scrolled down. After a few minutes he pulled out his cellphone and dialed Delorme. She didn't pick up.

"I'm sending you the address book of Brenda Gauthier," he told her voice mail. "She froze to death in Parry Sound. Nothing's jumping out at me, but maybe you could do a quick scan-and-compare with Flint and Lacroix and get back to me." He thought about saying he hoped she wasn't still mad at him but figured if she was, mentioning it wasn't going to help.

The woman's e-mails seemed to consist mostly to receipts from the Teaching Company, audible.com and online bookstores. In her Sent file, the only messages of any size were chatty e-mails to her son. They stopped some four months prior to her death.

Cardinal sat back in the chair and thought about Mrs. Gauthier's line of work. Librarian didn't seem to connect with either of the other cases. Her husband had been in high tech, as had Senator Flint quite a while back, though not medical like Gauthier. Laura Lacroix had been a hospital administrator, which might have some faint connection, but her former husband, Keith Rettig, was a CPA.

He dialed Delorme again and left another message. "Something else. We requested a CV on Keith Rettig. Did we ever get that? Let me know when you call back. Hope Loach isn't driving you nuts." He disconnected, thinking he wished Delorme was here to help him go through this room. She had a laser-like eye when it came to reading people's personal environments. Then again, he just wished she was here.

He started the web browser and opened bookmarks. Gardening sites, libraries, weight loss, and several folders devoted to Alzheimer's disease—patient forums, family forums, sites of famous clinics and universities. Mrs. Gauthier had subscribed to many listservs and newsfeeds and kept bookmarks for newspapers worldwide.

A folder called "Frank" caught his eye. He opened it and found sites for MRG Robotics, her husband's former company, and URLs for articles about it. One of these was a corporate profile of her husband that went right back to his childhood in Quebec and his education at Laval and later the University of Toronto, where he had done graduate work in engineering.

His cellphone rang. Delorme in her all-business mode. "I've checked, and there are no matches between Marjorie Flint and Brenda Gauthier. Laura Lacroix either. You sure Gauthier is related? She froze, but was she confined? Was she drugged?"

"Not according to the reports, but she was found wearing new clothes that weren't hers. What's going on there? It sounds noisy."

Delorme lowered her voice. "A bunch of us are balking at interviewing every French-Canadian male over the age of fifty in Algonquin Bay. You wouldn't believe the calls we're getting. Chouinard's yelling at everyone to stop yelling."

"Did Loach add 'French-Canadian' to the flyers?"

"Are you kidding? He gave the recording to the radio station. They've played it, like, five times already. The phones won't stop. Everybody knows someone who sounds like that caller. Loach wants us to check out every tip—he can't get it in his head that we are not Toronto."

As they talked, Cardinal was examining the boxes and albums of photographs that were stacked in neat piles, each one labelled with a yellow square: *History*, *Friends*, *Work*, several labelled *Vacation* and one *Ancient History*, her term for baby pictures, birthday pictures, Christmases. The Gauthiers, like Cardinal himself, were of the last generation whose childhood had been recorded in black-and-white.

"What I'm thinking," he said to Delorme, "is Lacroix and Flint were not our guy's first run at this. I think he went after Brenda Gauthier first and it didn't go the way he planned."

"What—she didn't end up dead enough?"

"Didn't look murdered enough. Clearly he wanted the others to look exactly like what they were. This one doesn't, it looks like an accident. So he changed his MO.

Did we get Keith Rettig's CV? If Laura Lacroix wasn't connected to these people, maybe her ex-husband was."

"Brunswick Geo swear they couriered it over the day we asked. They're going to fax it again this afternoon. I have to go. Get back here. This place is a circus."

Cardinal opened the box labelled *History*. High school graduation pictures, sports triumphs, the Laval lacrosse team—a muddied and big-haired Gauthier holding the trophy. Brenda Gauthier, svelte hippie in headband and bell-bottoms, clutching her books in front of the University of Toronto's School of Library Science. Gauthier on the field in King's College Circle, yellow hard hat over wild hair, clutching a Molson in one hand and an ungainly electronic device in the other.

And then there it was. Not a photograph, but a photocopy of an article from the *Varsity*, the university's student newspaper. Cardinal recognized the steps of the Sandford Fleming Building, where three grinning students stood behind what looked like a metal spider on wheels. Except for the colour of his hair, the senator had not changed much over the years. For the other two, Cardinal had to rely on the caption. *David Flint and fellow School of Engineering postgrads Keith Rettig and Frank Gauthier crushed the competition at RoboRama, held last month at MIT.*

From the Blue Notebook

In addition to the central camp, there were three remote sites on our ice island. Two of these, the AES weather tower and my core hut, were now lost to us, though possibly of some use still to Vanderbyl. There was a chance that the that seismic hut, which was located on a different ridge, might still be attached—which would mean shelter, extra clothing, perhaps fuel.

We took stock. None of us was adequately dressed for any drop in the temperature, which now hovered around freezing. Deville was the warmest in a blue down jacket over a light fleece. Dahlberg and I had fleeces over sweaters. Rebecca had a light shell over a fleece. We were all wet to varying degrees from falling to the slushy surface. Dahlberg had badly twisted his knee and was having great difficulty walking. He made no complaint, other than to point out the fact of his situation, but his face was grey with pain.

Rebecca put aside her panic for Kurt and adopted a calm, matter-of-fact manner. Ray Deville was the only one who still appeared to be in a state of shock. His responses to my questions were sluggish, his affect flat. But he nodded his understanding that we had best keep moving.

Who has a weapon? I asked.

Rebecca still had the flare gun.

Dahlberg shook his head.

I turned to Deville; I thought I could smell gunpowder. Ray? Do you have a gun?

No, me, I don't 'ave a gun.

We all carried pencils but none of us had any real food. Deville had some Juicy Fruit, Dahlberg had a pack of cough drops and an Aero bar. I had nothing edible, but I still had my field glasses strapped round my neck and a butane lighter in my pocket.

It was decided that we would walk south in hopes of finding the seismic recording hut intact. I say south, but what I mean is south in relation to our base camp. Maintaining a sense of direction is one of the hardest things to do in the Arctic, especially in summer months, when the sun just circles above the horizon—a horizon that is all white and, unless you are near shore, devoid of landmarks.

It was hard travel, let me leave it at that. If you have never had to cross an extreme environment without the proper gear, nothing I say will convey the agony of this venture. It was crucial to move just fast enough to keep warm. To stop moving would mean freezing to death in a matter of fifteen or twenty hours. But moving even slightly too fast would bring on increased hunger, sweat that would soon cool, and exhaustion that would sap body heat quicker than anything except wind and moisture.

Jens could not keep up, and I asked Deville to hang back with him while Rebecca and I moved as fast as we could toward the hut.

Jens protested. Just keep me in sight. I'll manage.

Don't worry yourself, Dr. Dahlberg, Ray said. I'll be wit' you.

Rebecca and I pressed on ahead with an awkward, high-stepping gait and made reasonable progress. The lenticular cloud had shifted, and the sunlight warmed us as we moved. We kept our hands in our pockets—I had only one glove—although we took them out often for balance in the manner of a clumsy skater.

I don't know how long we walked—long enough to leave Jens and Ray far behind. Perhaps two hours. I doubt if we exchanged more than a dozen words. Until we knew the status of the remote hut, there was no way to judge our chances of survival. Rebecca expressed no false hope, uttered no prayer. We just kept moving.

Where the seismic shack should have been, there was nothing but open water.

No good, I said. It's gone.

Are you sure? Even if it's broken off, shouldn't we still be able to see it?

I was sure. Rebecca had never been to the hut, but I had many times. I pointed toward two distinctive promontories some three or four kilometres distant.

That's still Axel Heiberg Island. A lot of ice gets pushed south as it jams up in the margin. With a little luck, we might make landfall somewhere near the Strand Fiord. The LARS research station should still be manned this time of year.

Rebecca stared at the claw shape of the two hills, their eastern sides of exposed rock, their western sides ice and snow.

15

Delorme opened her laptop on the dinner table and typed in *Assistant Crown Attorney Garth Romney*. She added *Régine Choquette* to the search, and the screen lit up with many articles. She selected Images, and the first one to appear, top left, was the picture of Romney holding up the hood found on Choquette's body.

That hideous leather object, black, dirty, a hole for the nose, a zipper for the mouth and the zipper shut tight. *Some women like to be scared.*

Romney held it at arm's length as if it were a dead rat. Behind him, a picture of the Queen, the Canadian flag, the flag of Ontario.

Delorme clicked on another image, then another, coming to rest on a picture of Fritz Reicher—a little thinner back then, blond hair a little thicker. Beside him, lawyer Richard Rota.

~

"It's a police!" Richard Rota said, coming out of courtroom three. "What have I done this time?" He set his briefcase on a bench and shrugged on his overcoat. He went about five foot four, even with the lifts, which meant

Delorme could look him in the eye without looking up, an excellent thing in a lawyer.

"I wanted to talk to you about Fritz Reicher," she said.

Rota closed his eyes and tilted his head back. "Reicher, Reicher . . . it sounds familiar . . ."

"The Régine Choquette—"

"I'm messing with ya. I know who you wanna talk about, and I also know why. We can talk in there."

They went to an interview room at the end of the hall. Rota dropped his briefcase on the desk and sat beside it. Delorme decided to remain standing as he started firing questions at her. Like many lawyers, he spoke louder than was strictly necessary. How's his good friend R.J. (the police chief), how's Ian McLeod, and what about this new guy, this Roach character?

"Loach," Delorme said. "He's fine."

"What about John Cardinal?"

"He's fine too. I wanted to ask you—"

"You could use a few more of him."

"I had occasion to talk to Reicher recently on another matter."

"Women turning up dead in the great outdoors?" Rota gave an exaggerated shrug. "Of course you want to talk to him. Makes sense. Cop sense, anyway. Not that I've seen mention of any sexual element in the papers."

"I was a minor witness in the Choquette case."

"I remember. I deposed you. I was very polite, as I recall."

"You were adequate."

Rota laughed. "Thank you. That's the best I ever get from women."

"In his original statement to Detective Cardinal, Reicher said the entire scenario was under the control of Leonard Priest. Priest chose the woman, drove all the way here from Ottawa specifically to arrange an encounter with her. To 'play some games,' as Reicher put it."

"That statement was made before he had benefit of counsel. What's your point?"

"He said Priest was there the whole time. That it was Priest who ordered him to shoot."

"It's a defence Germans seem fond of." He raised a hand to forestall Delorme's next question. "And you want to know why Algonquin Bay's finest defence counsel did not push for the arrest and trial of Leonard Priest."

"Well?"

"Because it was not in my client's best interests. That's the short answer."

"And the long answer?"

"It's the long answer too."

"Did Leonard Priest pay for Reicher's defence?"

"Fritz Reicher paid for his own defence. Whether Priest gave him a handsome severance cheque or not is none of my business."

"Did you ever meet a friend or associate of Leonard Priest's named Darlene?"

"Darlene? No, I've never met any Darlene. Until this moment my life has been Darlene-free."

"Did you not at least wonder why the Crown chose not to pursue Leonard Priest? The murder weapon was his gun. Found in his sex club. His prints were at the scene."

"What's to explain? Obviously, the ACA didn't feel he had the evidence. You know, you're not bad at this. You ever think of going to law school?"

"Way we saw it, the case looked like a total gift."

"Garth Romney saw differently. Look, Garth's a real go-getter. Mr. Avenging Prosecutor. A real pain in the ass for us innocent little defence lawyers." Rota suddenly snapped himself together. The gleaming shoes flashed, the white cuffs shot forward and he was sitting upright, pulling his desk chair toward her, elbows on the desk. "Look, we have to be mindful of lawyer-client privilege here, but I'll tell you this. If Leonard Priest came to trial, Fritz would have been called to testify. You've met Fritz. Have you met Priest?"

"Briefly."

"Then you know how that would have worked out."

"The Crown could have offered Reicher a better deal."

"No such offer was made or requested. Had Priest been brought to trial, he would have painted Fritz as a disgruntled employee looking for revenge—among a lot of other unpleasant things." Rota stood and picked up his briefcase. "Can I go home now?"

Delorme stepped aside and Rota held the door open for her. He was a polite little guy, she'd forgotten that about him.

"Let me walk you to your car, Detective. I'm intrigued by this Darlene character."

"You really don't know anything about her?"

"Not a thing."

"Me either."

—

Curriculum vitae for Keith Charles Rettig, born July 7, 1954. Joined Brunswick Geo in 2004. Previous employment: Toyota Canada, 1996–2004; Inglis Appliances, 1990–1996; GeoLogic Solutions, 1988–1990; Argus Aquatics, 1984–1988.

Cardinal looked up the last two companies on the Internet. He couldn't find GeoLogic Solutions anywhere, but Argus Aquatics had been bought and sold by several different companies, the latest being Neptune Corp., makers of submersibles ranging from three-man subs to the kind of remote-operated vehicles used to explore the *Titanic*. Rettig was a finance man, not a techie, but the early involvement in robotics was still evident.

Cardinal looked up Senator David Flint again in *Who's Who in Canada*. The entry was modest considering his business successes and his current position. He had begun to make his mark in the early eighties with a start-up called Momentum, which designed power systems for electronics in confined spaces such as aircraft and submarines. In the following years he had added several patents in photovoltaics to his list of achievements. A stint at Boeing apparently hadn't worked out too well, and he moved back to Canada after just four years in Seattle.

Frank Gauthier, he discovered from a similar search, had a long history with MRG Robotics. Twenty-five years with the company he had founded in 1986, its first triumph being a robotic assistant for hip replacement surgery. Before that he had worked two years for R-Tech, which went on to a troubled history with bionic limbs and thoroughly human lawsuits. MRG had been a prime contributor to the development of the Aesclepius system, which detects a surgeon's hand movements and transmits them, much reduced, to an array of micro instruments.

All this information was easy, if time-consuming, to collect. Cardinal, no tech whiz, took a blank sheet of paper and drew three columns, into which he copied the names and dates.

He entered all three names together in the Google search field: Keith Rettig, David Flint and Frank Gauthier. No results.

He spent the next hour accessing business databases. It was no problem to get executive lists for all the various companies that were still extant. But he didn't know where to find "historic" staff lists or where to look for information on companies that were defunct. Delorme would know. But Delorme was not here, and Delorme was behaving strangely, and Delorme was angry with him.

He opened the To Do list on his computer, and just below *Call Ronnie B.* he added *Lise re corporate histories.*

He looked again at his handwritten table. At the top of it, he wrote: *U of T, 1980.* That was the year of the photograph in the *Varsity,* three grinning postgrads with what looked like a tin insect. None of the three career columns had any entry earlier than 1984.

~

Leonard Priest opened the fridge, took a large bowl from it and nudged the door shut with his elbow. He took two large goblets from the cupboard and filled them both just under halfway and handed one to Delorme. He raised his glass and she clinked with him. They both took a sip.

"Very nice," she said. In contrast to Richard Rota, with Priest she had to look up to meet his eye.

"I didn't think you'd come."

"Neither did I," Delorme said. Thinking, Boy, is that the understatement of the year.

"What made you change your mind?"

Priest's calling her twice over the course of the day might have had something to do with it. Message one: He had some information relevant to her case that he wanted to share with her. Message two: He had failed to mention in his first message his most important attribute as far as women were concerned—no irony intended: he was a very good cook. The worst she could expect was a bang-up meal and a first-class bottle of wine.

"I was hungry," she finally said.

"Fair enough. I hope you won't be disappointed. Let's sit." He tilted his glass toward the living room, the couch. "Don't worry, I'm on best behaviour."

Priest sat on the couch. Delorme chose an armchair.

"I'm sorry I don't have anything for an appetizer. I'd given up hope."

"You don't seem the type to give up hope."

"Yeah, I'm probably an optimist, generally speaking—enjoy a challenge, admire commitment and determination. But I don't like feeling like an idiot, either, pursuing someone in the face of repeated rejection. Hard to tell the difference sometimes—between commitment and stupidity, I mean. How's work going these days?"

Delorme shrugged. "Challenging."

"In general? Or for a woman in a man's world?"

"Both."

"I can imagine." He looked at her and shook his head. "God, I'm an idiot."

"For which thing?"

"For behaving the way I did. I know you think I'm just playing you—"

"Yes."

"Right, then. Apology is on the table. Next business . . ." He picked up a remote from the glass-topped table and pointed it at the largest TV screen Delorme had ever seen. The logo of a cable station came up and he froze the image. "This is *Up to the Minute*—Toronto news show. Tends to be a little fluffy, but it does have the virtue of being live."

He hit Play and the announcer did his intro. "Today is Tuesday, January third, and you're watching *Up to the Minute*."

Priest hit Pause. "I'm assuming the date is of interest."

"The day Marjorie Flint was abducted."

"And the time, no? The show airs at five o'clock."

"And the time."

Priest reached for the wine and topped up their glasses. He hit Play again and the show continued.

"There he is," he said, "in all his glory."

The interviewer asked first about music, any plans for a solo album. No, but Priest said he was honoured to have been asked to play bass on Daniel Lanois's latest effort. There was no mention of Priest's clubs, and after a few more pleasantries they went into the nature and makeup of an anti-poverty group he was involved with.

"You don't need to hear the whole thing," Priest said, and switched off the TV. "Excuse me a second."

He went out to the kitchen and bent to peer through the oven door, putting on a pair of glasses to do so. He took them off and came back.

"Dinner is served."

—

Cardinal put his dishes in the dishwasher and sat down at the kitchen table again and scrolled through the contact list on his cellphone. He dialed Ronnie Babstock at home. He'd already tried him at work and been told he was on his way back from a business trip to Brussels.

"Ronnie. John Cardinal. Something I want to ask you. Give me a call back when you get a chance—it's kind of urgent. Hope Brussels was good."

He went into the living room and picked up the TV remote and just held it in his lap. He thought about his day. Loach coming in and yelling at him in Chouinard's office.

Loach: Am I lead on this case or not? Because if I am, then I want everyone to pull their weight.

Chouinard (to Cardinal): You didn't do your follow-up?

Cardinal: I'm working on something that actually promises to go somewhere. These women are all connected through their husbands, who were at school together. I think they must have worked together, too, at some point, and if we can find that point, we might be able to discover who exactly it is that they've pissed off so bad.

Loach: We have a recording of the guy's *voice*, D.S., the guy's *voice*. I say that trumps any ancient history between the victims' spouses.

Cardinal: Let me follow this, D.S.

Chouinard: They live in three different cities, these husbands. Do they have any recent connection?

Cardinal: Not that I know of. Not yet. But it may not have to be recent.

Loach: We have a voice on the line confessing to murder and you don't want to pursue it. That's your opinion, I don't care. D.S., we're going to need some manpower from OPP to make up for the slack around here.

At that, Cardinal had turned to Loach and totally lost it, calling him a pompous little twit and a prima donna and any number of other things until Chouinard booted him out of the office. In the movies it always looked so satisfying to tell someone off. Why in real life did it feel like shit? In the end, Loach got his OPP assistance. Cardinal couldn't wait to hear from Jerry Commanda on how that was going.

He turned on the television and it tried to sell him a Volvo and he turned it off and put the remote aside. Delorme would be good right now.

Have her sitting on that couch with her feet up. Small feet, white socks. She'd called in sick again and hadn't returned any of his calls. None of Loach's either. Loach was turning out to be an albatross, but he had reason to be frustrated with Cardinal and Delorme.

He picked up his land line and dialed Delorme's home number.

"It's John. Pick up, Lise. I'm worried about you. I got in royal shit today with Loach and Chouinard. Love to tell you about it. Hope you're okay."

He switched off the light and went to stand at the window. The moon hung low over the lake. It was nearly full and he could see the dark shadows of the Manitous out in the middle of the ice.

He went to the bathroom and turned on the shower and then to the bedroom to get undressed. He got his shirt off and stood there holding it. After a minute he put it back on and went back to the bathroom to turn off the water. Then he got his coat from the hall closet and headed out.

The night was clear and twenty-something below and the heater in his Camry was not as efficient as it once was. He drove up the hill across Rayne Street and up to Delorme's. Her lights were off and there was no car in the driveway.

"Stupid," Cardinal said—about himself, not Delorme.

He turned the car around and headed back down the hill. At the stop sign, he had a change of plan and made a left toward the downtown. It was a quiet night, not many cars about and too cold for many pedestrians except the odd dog walker. He thought about getting a dog, a living being to come home to, but he had never been much of a pet man. When Kelly was a little girl, they'd had a dog, a floppy-eared mutt named Gizmo that she loved passionately. But the dog developed a brain tumour that changed him from an affectionate goof into a biter. Cardinal had been forced to have him put down, and the memory of breaking his daughter's heart had spoiled dogs for him forever.

He pulled into the parking lot of the Quiet Pint and sat for a minute. He didn't recognize any of the vehicles.

~

Perfect beef tenderloin with a red wine reduction, arugula salad, and for dessert a lemon cream concoction that Delorme could have eaten four times more of.

"Well, you were right," she said, raising her glass. "You are one hell of a cook."

"Thank you," Priest said. "Why don't you go sit in the living room and I'll bring us some port. Much underrated, port is."

He had announced when they sat down that he wanted no discussion of police business during dinner, and they'd been almost entirely successful in avoiding it. Delorme asked him questions about the music industry, and they'd moved on from there to talk of movies and books. She was finding it a lot harder to believe Priest had ever killed anyone. She was feeling pretty comfortable, considering, and you would never have known, to look at her, that she was breaking every rule in the investigator's handbook.

Priest himself noted this at one point. They had shared a laugh over an amusing scene in a Tom Cruise movie and he suddenly said, "Seriously, Lise—aren't you being a little irresponsible? If you ever *did* bring a case against me, you'd be in a lot of shit, wouldn't you? Having fraternized with the accused?"

Delorme shrugged. "Algonquin Bay is small. There's not a single detective on the squad who hasn't had to arrest a neighbour or someone they went to school with."

"Not quite the same, is it?"

"I guess we'll find out."

He came into the living room now with a dusty bottle of port and sat beside her on the couch and poured them each a glass. When they were about to toast, Delorme's phone rang.

"Sorry. Hold on, I'll switch it off."

"I shut mine away in a drawer when I don't want to be bothered."

"I'd love to, but we have to keep them with us at all times." She put the phone back in her purse and set the purse beside her on the couch. She reached for her glass again. "Sorry about that. Cheers."

Delorme had never tasted port before, never tasted anything like it.

"Was this made by some monks high on a mountain somewhere?"

"Not bad, is it." Blue eyes flecked with firelight.

He set his glass down and reached for a slim green folder, then sat back and opened it. Delorme didn't know why, but his every move was attractive to her in some elemental way. To counter this, she thought of the black mask, Régine Choquette's contorted body, Fritz Reicher's "games."

"Take a look at these."

Delorme took the folder from him, careful that their hands did not touch. She picked up the first piece of paper. A receipt from Toronto's Windsor Arms Hotel.

"I thought you had a home in Toronto."

"Condo. Sold it. Look at the dates."

"I see the dates."

"Look at the others."

She went through the receipts one by one—dinners at expensive restaurants, tickets to a Cat Power concert, a car detailing operation, a dentist—and closed the folder.

"You can keep those. My lawyer has the originals."

"Thank you. Leonard, can we just clear up one more small item?"

"God, you're relentless. You're lucky it's sexy."

"Why does Fritz Reicher say you ordered him to shoot Régine Choquette?"

"He doesn't."

"But he *did*. Then he changed his mind—so that's actually two small items. Why did he say it, and why did he change his mind?"

"Fritz? Have you met Fritz? Fritz is an amiable idiot. I'm sorry, but he's mentally defective—very attractive qualities in a servant, but not much use for anything else."

"If he's so dim, why did he change his mind?"

"As I understand it, he was stoned when he was picked up and babbled anything that came into his head. Then he sobered up . . ."

He swivelled toward her on the couch and tugged at a lock of her hair. "Now, haven't I been a good boy? Haven't made a single move on you all night, despite the fact that you look absolutely gorgeous."

"Let's keep it that way."

"You can't really think I'm a cold-blooded killer."

"Maybe not cold-blooded. Maybe out of control."

"So why did you come here, Lise?"

"You invited me. I'm an investigator. You have information."

"Ooh, such a calculating little article you are."

"I admit I find you fascinating. In a clinical way. Sometimes you almost seem like a good person."

"Even when I'm bad, I'm not *that* bad."

"Hmm."

He grasped her elbow lightly and shook it as if rousing her from a nap. "Don't you ever have the urge to break the rules? Do something a little wicked? Just be bad?"

She nodded. "Sometimes I even give in to it."

"You smile like a cat, you know that? Not the warmest smile, must be said."

"What can you tell me about Darlene?"

"Darlene." He swivelled away again and poured himself more port. When he reached for her glass, Delorme put her hand over it.

He set the bottle down and took a sip. "I only know one Darlene, and I'm not going to talk about her."

"Come on."

"Sorry. Wouldn't be gentlemanly. How would you like it if I talked about you?"

"There's nothing to talk about."

"The night is young."

"It must be awful to be an addict. Be a slave. Feel out of control all the time."

"It's only an addiction if you can't afford it."

"Really? That your personal definition?"

"It'll do. Just out of interest, are you wearing your gun? Perhaps a neat little automatic strapped to your ankle?"

"Why do you want to know?"

"Because I desperately want to kiss you, but I don't want to get shot."

"Better be careful, then."

He leaned toward her and she didn't pull away—to pull away would look like fear—but she did turn her face aside.

"All right," he said, stopping halfway. "She doesn't want to be kissed. What does she want? Hmm, I wonder." A hand rested itself on her breast.

Delorme didn't move, the heat of his palm through her clothes.

"What does Lise want, he wonders." The hand sliding to the other breast and Delorme remaining utterly motionless, remaining that way, barely breathing, as the hand slides down her chest, across her midriff, and Priest leans closer so he can reach between her legs.

She grabbed his wrist and lifted it off and placed his hand back on the couch.

"Thank you for a lovely dinner."

"Tease."

"I didn't do anything."

"Silence means consent, darling."

"Actually, it doesn't. Check the Criminal Code."

"You don't have to go, you know. Not really."

"Yes, I do," she said, getting up. "Really."

Priest stood up and blocked her way. "Do you know what you're playing with?"

"I don't know what you mean."

"What I mean is, if you really believe I ordered that gormless German twit to shoot a defenceless woman, what does that say about you? That you come here and get all cozy, looking all hot and bothered—"

"Hardly. I'm leaving now." She pushed past him and headed for the kitchen.

"Ambition isn't the only pheromone you give off, in case you don't know. But you do know, don't you? You know very well. You want to play with fire, sweetheart, you better be ready for a little heat."

"I'll need my coat."

"Of course. Sorry." His tone had changed again. Once more he was the gracious host. He walked her to the door and retrieved her coat. She put it on, fighting with the zipper.

"Come on, Lise. Dinner's one thing, but you really can't still think I had anything to do with Marjorie Flint or Laura Lacroix."

"I don't." The zipper finally surrendered and she pulled it up. "But I do think you killed Régine Choquette, and I'm going to put you away for it. That's what Lise wants."

From the Blue Notebook

The low sun shining in Rebecca's eyes as she said, I think we're going to die. I just mean it factually.

Quite possible, I said, noting the lack of fear in her voice, a preparedness to meet fate head-on, on fate's terms. But let's try to do it on actual land rather than a chunk of ice.

What about staying where we are, waiting for the plane?

The arrangement was that a station radioed in to Resolute at agreed-upon days and times. In our case, every two days. If a check-in was missed and the station could not be raised, a plane would be in the air within a matter of hours. Unfortunately, we had checked in the day before.

It'll be hard for them to spot us, I said. Kurt may be all right—the radio mast is visible and he probably even has a beacon—but a single plane is going to have a hard time spotting us.

And there was the matter of keeping warm.

It was my idea to set out for what was now the western end of the floe. Although we were closer to Axel Heiberg, the current was taking us toward Meighen Island. The Polar Continental Shelf Project had once had a camp there, and there was a chance it was still operating.

My memory goes wading among the four of us like a ghost, reaching out to try to protect Rebecca, enclose her in my giant hand and keep her warm, but of course she does not see me, feel me. Nor does my younger self. I remember the fear, the panic in my chest, and an odd sense of guilt, as if I were the one, and not Kurt (or her own curiosity and ambition), who had lured Rebecca north of the eightieth parallel, where she was now very likely going to die. I was a creature of the High Arctic, went walking there even when I was not working there, studied the maps and journals of the great explorers. It was as if she were meeting my family and they were being hateful.

They say you haven't really travelled in the Arctic unless you've been lost at least once. I have been lost many more times than that, twice on Ellesmere alone, once in Greenland north of Thule. The fear was intense, but nothing compared with what I was feeling now. And yet my mind was skipping forward to some years in the future—a house, a quiet street and the smell of fallen leaves, Rebecca seated in a leather chair. A wall full of books.

That was one future. The other was gathering itself into a darkness in the west, not much more than a smudge at that moment, between the surface and the sun. I was about to point this out when there was a gunshot behind us. We turned our backs on the indigo water and scanned the horizon. Jens and Ray were no closer to us than they had been when we stopped. I took a look through my field glasses.

Something's wrong, I said.

Maybe they saw a plane or something. Trying to draw attention?

Give me the flare gun.

What for?

And the belt. Just give it to me. I reached inside my fleece and pulled out the radio and handed it to her. Keep this. Kurt may manage to get the mast working, or there may be a submarine in the area. If I don't come back, head west quickly—that means keeping Heiberg at your back—and try an SOS every half-hour. Keep it inside your jacket.

Kit, what are you doing?

Wait here. I won't be long.

16

AWAY FROM THE WARMTH OF Leonard Priest's hearth, not to mention the heat of his attentions, Delorme shuddered with the cold. The touch of the February night at her neck and wrists, the gaps in her clothing.

As she moved toward her car, careful in her dress shoes that were never meant to come near snow, she saw a car heading away from her and then making the turn off Crozier, a Camry. Too far away to make out the plate or even be sure of the colour, but it looked like John Cardinal's Camry.

Paranoia, she thought, starting her car. That paranoia was telling her to move fast, get a good look at that Camry. She took a deep breath and resisted the urge.

No doubt that shudder upon stepping outside Leonard Priest's house had to do with things other than the low temperature, the crystalline cold abrading her face. Guilt, all right, yes, tremendous guilt. Guilt of the Catholic girl gone wrong. Guilt for breaching her professional ethics. Guilt because she was pretty sure she was in love with John Cardinal and she had just allowed another man to touch her—and this less than a week after that night at the club.

"What's happening to me?" she said aloud in the car. She reached for the heat control and turned it up full. In any other circumstances, I would have broken the bastard's arm.

Some women like to be scared.

She hadn't been scared—not of Priest, anyway. But fear was definitely one of the intoxicants flowing in her veins, just as it had been at Club Risqué. Since Priest had not been particularly threatening, it could only be herself she was afraid of.

John Cardinal's got nothing to do with it, she repeated over and over to herself as she drove home. John Cardinal and I have no relationship.

She hadn't finished taking off her coat when the phone rang.

"Frank Toye on the desk. Hope I didn't wake you. Got a call from the hospital—one of yours is in Emergency, asking for you. The doctor was pretty insistent, so I thought I'd check with you before I sent—"

—

"She gave me this." The doctor, absurdly young, reached into his white coat and pulled out a key. "She said to give it to you and tell you top right drawer of her desk."

"Top right drawer." Delorme took the key and put it in her pocket. A gurney transporting an unconscious man clattered by, IV swinging. "Can I see her?"

"Not right now."

Dealing with a battered woman too dumb to get out of a self-destructive situation was not high on Delorme's list of priorities at the moment. On the other hand, she didn't want Miranda Heap to wake up and change her mind. She drove the few blocks to the woman's home and let herself in.

It was one of the contradictions of Miranda Heap's life that she was a very orderly person. Much more orderly than Delorme, who always had a pair of jeans hanging on the back of a chair and a stack of bills on the kitchen table. But this woman's trade was organizing people's offices and homes and work systems, and apparently she had a natural bent for it.

Vestibule with its neat double shelves of shoes and boots, living room with a four-square stack of magazines on a gleaming coffee table, cushions on the sofa just so. But then this emotional chaos in her life, a chaos against which she could apparently maintain no resistance.

As if I'm anyone to judge, Delorme thought. She felt again, in memory, the grip of Priest's hand between her legs. Lise Delorme, incipient slut.

In the kitchen, a platoon of appliances lined up on the counter. A dish-free sink and drainer. Set of cookware neatly suspended above the stove. Not the least sign of trouble in this sparkling little chamber, unless you counted the few drops and smears of blood on the counter, and the bigger smear on the floor. Beside it, a crushed and empty Kleenex box.

There was blood in the bathroom too, and blood on the telephone and desk.

Delorme pulled open the top right drawer and took out a large envelope with her name on it. It was sealed and taped, and she took a letter opener from a desktop canister of pens to open it. Inside there was a smaller envelope, also sealed, and a note written in violet ink on a sheet headed *From the Desk of Miranda Heap.*

Dear Lise,

If you are reading this, I am in deep shit.

Remember I told you he makes the most beautiful apologies? I've actually been saving them for my therapist, but I'd like you to hear them too—if only so you don't think I'm such an idiot. They're not all *apologies. He* does *have some redeeming features, you know.*

*Pick up my phone and dial *98 and when it asks for the PIN press 4252. Then hit 3 for saved messages.*

I don't know if I can bring myself to tell you his name yet. I'll have to think some more about that.

Miranda

—Oh hell. Listen to the messages and then take a look in the other envelope.

The voice that came on was so soft as to be almost a whisper. The words were close, muffled even, as if the mouthpiece were up against the lips. He was utterly sorry, his moods were getting the better of him lately, she mustn't ever think he didn't love her, she was the world to him.

The voice was not one she recognized. In that near whisper, it could have been anyone. He sounded educated, sincere, affectionate. As she listened, she opened the smaller envelope, which appeared to contain a handful of receipts and a photograph.

The next two messages were muffled, whispery, romantic in an overwrought kind of way—but neither of them seemed to Delorme's ears particularly inspired, particularly wonderful. Such was love. Passion anyway.

She swivelled the chair around and stared out the window as she continued to listen. A thin snow starting to fall, car lights travelling up and down the hill of Algonquin Avenue. And then the next message made her spin round and plant her elbows on the desk and stare at the base of the phone as if the caller might be visible there.

It was the same caller, the same man, but this time he had forsaken the breathy, into-the-pillow sibilants for accents more declamatory, flamboyant even. *Honey, I'm so sorry! I don't know what I was thinking! Sometimes, I swear, you just get me so excited I go over the top. But I've been soooooo bad! Darlene has been a bad girl, honey, and you're just going to have to punish her. You're just gonna have to take your little Darlene and put her over your knee!*

Then, in his normal voice, *Seriously, Miranda, I love you and miss you and I'm sorry if I went a little overboard. I'll see you soon, sweetheart.*

Delorme knew who it was.

—

Cardinal was brushing his teeth when the phone rang. He rinsed his mouth and spat and went to the living room to see if it was Delorme. It was Ronnie Babstock.

"How was Brussels?"

"Promising. Brussels was very promising. I'm tired as hell, though. Shoulda let one of the younger guys do it, but, I don't know, I'm *good* at this, you know? I don't trust anyone else to do as good a job. Not cuz they're not smart—they're smarter than me, some of 'em—but I don't think anybody *loves* it as much as me, and therefore . . . you get my drift."

"Thanks for getting back to me. You must be exhausted."

"Yeah, but also kinda wired, as I guess you can tell. What can I do you for? You had a question, your message said."

"You can't talk to anybody about this, all right?"

"Word of honour."

"I'm looking at David Flint, Frank Gauthier and Keith Rettig. Do you know any of them?"

"I know who they *are*—Flint and Gauthier anyway. Flint's the senator whose wife died and Gauthier is a very big deal in medical tech. Who was the third guy?"

"Keith Rettig. He's a CPA at Brunswick Geo."

"Oh, right, right—with the missing wife or ex-wife or whatever."

"She's dead, actually. Her body was found while you were away. In circumstances similar to Marjorie Flint's."

"God, you're kidding. That's horrible."

"I'm just wondering—you know the high-tech industry probably better than anyone—do you know if these guys have any history? They were all at U of T together."

"Yeah, Flint was a year or two ahead of me—or maybe behind. Gauthier too, as I recall. I don't think our paths ever crossed, though."

"Did they ever work together?"

"You mean, like at the same company? You could look it up easily enough."

"Well, *someone* could. I didn't get very far, other than the school thing. I'm looking at the years 1980 to 1984."

"Ah, yes, those dark ages pre-Internet. Did you think of asking Gauthier and the others themselves? I'm a big believer in the direct route where possible."

"It's not my best course of action just now. Gauthier's dead, for one."

"Frank Gauthier's dead? When did that happen?"

"A few days ago. Suicide."

"Oh, that's sad. I'm sorry to hear that. Well, I'm sure you'll find out whatever you need to know. Sorry I can't be more useful."

~

The jet lag alone would have been enough to destroy Ronnie Babstock's sleep that night, but Cardinal's questions had cranked his insomnia dial right up to ten. I should have gone to the lake house, he told himself. The lake house was not so full of noises as this ancient place.

When the voice came this time (3:14 by the bedside clock), he was certain he had not been sleeping. It could not be a dream, unless it was a waking dream—and that was just another name for insanity.

So cold. Dear God, I've never been so cold.

It was in the room with him. Babstock lay unmoving, sweat beading on his forehead, slick beneath his arms and on the back of his neck.

I'm not going to get through this. Shivers in her voice. Terror. *I'm not going to make it.*

Babstock sat up and swung his legs over the edge of the bed.

I'm so frightened.

He put on his bathrobe and slippers and switched on the light and stood listening.

Hold me. Hold me tight. Oh, God.

Babstock got down on his knees and looked under the bed. He reached for the bedside lamp and removed the shade and laid the lamp down on the floor and looked again. Nothing.

He put the lamp back on the table without the shade and went to the foot of the bed and pulled at it. He leaned back with all his weight, but it wouldn't move. He went to the side of the bed and put his shoulder to one of the posts. The bed shifted away from the wall at an angle. He pushed again.

He went back to the head of the bed and knelt again and placed his hand against the wall and waited. The bare bulb threw hard shadows, his head monstrous against the corner where the wall met the ceiling.

I don't want to die.

He ran his hand up and down the wall, feeling for vibrations. The wall felt like painted drywall, nothing more. He rapped a knuckle against it in various places and sat back on his heels.

The voice came again, but this time it was weeping. The woman, whoever she was, sobbed and shivered and it was hard to tell where the sound was coming from. He felt up and down the wall.

"Fuck you," he said, and grabbed the bedside lamp and laid it on the floor again. He lay down on his back and pulled himself under the bed. When he reached for the lamp to bring it after him, he banged his head on the box spring and cursed again.

The undirected light from the lamp made it difficult to see. He put one hand out to shade it and with the other felt along the edge of the box spring.

Please . . .

Her voice louder now, directly above him.

Dear God, don't let this happen.

An audio clip from a movie. He could hear the sound effects now—the howling wind, the flapping canvas—tinny and miniaturized.

He found a gap in the seam and pulled the fabric away, closing his eyes against the dust. His fingers travelled along first one slat then another, until they dislodged a small object that landed on his chest and slithered to the floor. He got out from under the bed, set the lamp on the table and looked at the thing in his hand.

A cellphone.

It hurts, the woman said, and Babstock hurled it against the wall.

~

Not even light out and there was someone at the door. Delorme finished drying off and put on her bathrobe. Then she went to the living room and made a small part in the curtains to peer out.

Cardinal pounded the door with the flat of his hand and leaned on the bell.

Delorme went to the door and opened it without taking the chain off.

"What the hell are you doing, John? It's six-thirty in the morning."

"Why haven't you been coming in to work, Lise?"

"I'm sick."

"You're not sick, and in case you haven't noticed, we've got several murders to clear."

"I'm sick. I'll be back as soon as I can."

She started to close the door, but Cardinal stopped it with his foot.

"I'm freezing, John. Get your foot out of my door."

"Why aren't you returning my calls?"

"You have work questions, I'll answer them—when I'm at work. But I'm not at work now and I have nothing for you. You wanted to cool things off, I'm cooling them off."

"Not like this. I just— Jesus, this is new territory, Lise. Can't you have a little patience?"

"We work together, John. End of story. That's the way you wanted it, that's the way it is."

"If you're so sick, why were you at Leonard Priest's last night?"

Delorme looked at him. "You followed me?"

"I was worried about you. This isn't like you, not showing up, being evasive, being cold to me—"

"You followed me. I don't believe it."

"I didn't follow you, Lise. Yes, I was looking for you, but I was not tailing you. We need you at work and I need your help with Flint and— What *were* you doing at Priest's, anyway?"

"Why—do you think I'm fucking him or something?"

Cardinal let out a gasp. "Uh, no, Lise. That had not occurred to me."

"What else could she be doing—right? She's such a half-assed investigator, it couldn't be anything work related. She must be fucking the guy."

"Lise, truly. Let's get past this and get back to work. You can't call in sick when we've got all this work to do. You know it's wrong. It isn't like you."

"Get your foot out of the way."

"Lise, come on."

"Move it!"

He removed his foot and she shut the door and locked it. She stood there, breathing hard. When she heard him drive away, she went to the bedroom and pulled her suitcase out of the closet.

~

After his fight with Delorme, Cardinal promptly had a fight, via telephone, with Chouinard. This was in order to avoid a fight with Loach. "D.S., he's got five guys from OPP to check out every French Canadian in the district—he doesn't need me for that. You don't need me for that. And you know I think it should not be our priority. I've been tracking down the history between the three husbands, and there's a lead I need to follow up. It's in Gravenhurst."

"What the hell's in Gravenhurst?"

"More connections, I hope."

Chouinard gave him a list of reasons why he had to come in for the morning meeting, the most compelling of which was: we're already down one man with Delorme being out sick—had he heard anything, by the way? Cardinal insisted he had not. The D.S. stopped just short of ordering him to come in.

The sooner I get to Gravenhurst, Cardinal had said, the sooner et cetera. But he hadn't even got to the highway when his cellphone rang and Jerry Commanda came on the line.

"John, I am nonplussed."

"I'm sorry to hear that. Have you tried Metamucil?"

"What is the story with this Lacroix case? We've got five guys on loan to you and they don't know why they're doing what they're doing. Interviewing people because of their accents?"

"No, no, it's much more fine-tuned than that, Jerry. It's only males, for example. And they have to be fifty years old or so."

"It's not funny, John. Seriously, you have to do something about this guy, it's imperative."

When he hung up, Cardinal thought about calling some of his old colleagues on the Toronto force. One or two of them would be bound to know Loach. Maybe someone would have some ideas on how to work with him.

The previous night's snow was melting in the morning sun. The highway was black and gleaming so that it looked brand new, as parts of it were, and Cardinal took it fast, all the way to Gravenhurst without stopping, arriving in under two hours.

Gravenhurst was the kind of town that quadrupled in size during the summer. In winter it made Algonquin Bay look like Manhattan. The snow was deeper here, the old-style parking meters buried up to their necks. Cardinal used the GPS to find the address he was looking for. He had been expecting a small office building, but it was a ranch-style house of cedar and pale brick in a sixties-era development that had somehow managed to avoid proximity to any of the numberless lakes in the region.

He was about to ring the doorbell when he noticed the hand-lettered sign that said *Side Door for Good Monkey Enterprises*, the final *s* squeezed in like the last passenger on a crowded bus.

The young man who answered his knock looked about thirty-five, with dark, almost black hair that fell dead straight past his shoulders. He wore a white T-shirt, much stained, that said *I Just Like New York as a Friend*.

"You must be Detective Cardinal."

"That's right."

"Only other visitor we're expecting is coming to pick up a Yoda doll, and you don't fit the demographic, among other things. I'm Jackalope—Jack, when I'm offline."

Cardinal followed him downstairs. Good Monkey Enterprises turned out to be a finished basement lined floor to ceiling with industrial shelving.

"This is my brother, Wally."

"Hi, Wally."

Wally, wearing a headset, was staring at a computer screen. He raised a pale hand by way of greeting. Cardinal had met a few identical twins in his time, but the matched proprietors of Good Monkey Enterprises took identical to whole new levels. When Wally yanked off his headset and stood up, he was exactly the same height as his brother, his dark hair was exactly the same length, and he even spoke with his brother's voice. Luckily, they were not dressed identically; Wally's T-shirt just said *Deadwood*. He shook Cardinal's hand and sat back down.

Cardinal looked around. The shelves were densely populated with dolls of varying size and physiognomy, teddy bears, action figures, board games, Bankers Boxes labelled *Post Cards* and *Photographs*. There were old toys, racks of DVDs and CDs, video games, and electronic gizmos that Cardinal could not have named.

"We're eBay masters," Jack explained. "We buy and sell pretty much anything that's easy to ship and isn't too breakable. No china, for example."

"I don't see any robots," Cardinal said.

"Oh, *lots* of robots," Jack said, his voice breaking like a thirteen-year-old's. He led Cardinal to the end of one shelving unit and pointed from one item to another. "All in boxes. We must have twenty Robbies alone."

"Twenty-three," Wally said from his desk.

"Some even have the original packaging. We have Gort, Robosapiens, couple of Daleks, a whole family of Tekno Dinkies—even a vintage Sparky. We don't even bother with Transformers anymore."

"It's not the toys I'm interested in."

"No, you said. How'd you get on to us, anyway?"

"You're the prime contributor to the Wikipedia article on Canadian robotics. I was expecting a professor or a grad student—"

"Not a web nerd—I get it. That's okay. Robotics is a hobby of mine—I got into it through the toys and movies and it just grew into, I don't know, a kind of useless expertise. I'm like a trainspotter, or one of those people who memorize bus schedules for cities they haven't even been to. Alfred Hitchcock did that, believe it or not."

"I had no idea."

"It's the kind of thing control freaks get off on," Wally called from across the basement.

"Don't mind my brother. It's been hard for him, growing up in my shadow."

"You had some material you were going to look up for me."

"On David Flint and Frank Gauthier. Yeah, I did the Wiki articles on them too. I dug out some stuff over here you might find interesting. Patent applications dating from the early eighties. God, I'm such a nerd."

"You *are!*" Wally called out.

Cardinal looked at the applications. There were drawings and schematics for micro-movement systems and micro-power systems for "applications in remote-controlled vehicles." Two of them had both Flint's and Gauthier's signatures. Several of them had a third signature.

Cardinal looked up. "They worked with Ron Babstock?"

"Cool, huh? Who knew? I dug up some stuff on LARS for you. I printed it out."

"Who's Lars?"

"L-A-R-S. Laval Arctic Research Station. They built it way the heck up on some tiny Arctic island. They test a lot of stuff for space exploration, to make sure it works in harsh conditions. Look at this." He pulled a clear plastic folder off a shelf and handed it to Cardinal. "Dates from 1992 or so. Pristine condition. I could sell it for a decent price, but I'll probably keep it."

Inside the folder was a glossy brochure, only a few pages long, describing the research outpost. "A summer-only facility dedicated to the exploration of remote and extreme environments on Earth as analogues for human exploration of the moon and Mars. Development teams will find the environment ideal for testing equipment intended for outer-space applications." Pictures showed a moon-like vista, smiling men in colourful parkas, arrays of electronic gear bristling with antennas.

"See there?" A bony finger, nail much chewed, pointed to a picture of four young men kneeling or standing beside a machine that looked like a mechanical praying mantis. "Brochure's 1993, so the picture's gotta be at least the year before. What you're looking at is an early version of what eventually became the famous Marti."

"Marvellous Marti!" Wally called across the room. "We love Marti!"

"We sell the models, when we can get hold of them."

Cardinal read the caption aloud. "'David Flint, Ron Babstock, Frank Gauthier and Keith Rettig with the prototype REV I exploratory vehicle.' Ron Babstock worked with all three of these guys?"

"Cool, huh? Dude got NASA excited and the rest is history. Little bastard's rolling across the Martian countryside as we speak."

"You'd think there'd be all sorts of stuff on the Internet about those early days, but I couldn't find it—not about these guys, anyway."

"Sometimes the Internet can be a little unpredictable—sorta like a woman. That's probably why we love it."

"You're darn tootin'!" Wally called out.

"He's using the expression ironically," Jack said. "At least I hope he is."

From the Blue Notebook

I left Rebecca standing by the open water that separated us from Heiberg Island and headed back toward Dahlberg and Deville. The sky was fretted with high cirrus and the low-hanging sun bathed everything in red and gold. At any other time it would have been beautiful, but there was that growing smudge of darkness rolling toward us, and there was the scene before me.

It is commonplace these days for a man to be well versed in psychology. I am not such a person. At that time, that year, I had had little experience of outright madness. My earlier incarnation as a bush pilot had been stress-free in that department. In academia, in field research, I had encountered overwrought students, hysterical faculty members, countless florid eccentrics, but I had no experience of violent psychosis, if that's what I was facing.

From half a kilometre off, I could see that Jens was down and Ray was standing over him. I won't even attempt to convey my emotional state. I tried to empty my mind, to be readiness made flesh. The sun threw my shadow in a long dark tangent, as if it were being torn from me toward the magnetic pole.

Someone with training in psychological matters might have opinions about what would have been the proper way to handle the situation. The situation was there, I was who I was. I began talking to Ray as I approached—a hundred metres away, maybe a hundred and fifty—I knew he could hear me. But I chose to pretend I had not heard the shot, that I had not noticed Dahlberg lying motionless at his feet.

We must head that way, I told him, pointing. The current should take us to Meighen Island. They won't send a plane for days. Ah, Jens—we'll have to do something about that knee. Ray and I will put our heads together and come up with something.

As I talked on in this calm-in-the-face-of-disaster way, Ray did not so much as twitch. He stood, feet apart, arms a little away from his sides, head tilted downward. He looked like a man who had just shot a raccoon, or perhaps a cat by mistake.

I kept talking as I approached, one hand gripping the flare gun under my fleece. The flare gun is not a weapon. It is a plastic single-shot pistol not designed for accuracy. I needed to be close for it to be of any use at all. But I was not going to let Ray near Rebecca. I was not going to let him kill or injure me. I was not going to let him live.

There may be a submarine, I said. We might have luck with the radio. Or the sovereignty expedition could come through.

This was a falsehood. The sovereignty expedition, made up of dogs and soldiers and Inuit reservists, had come up Nansen Sound and was by that time halfway across the top of Ellesmere.

If there's any sign of them, I went on, Rebecca will send up a flare.

I was within thirty or forty metres, close enough to see the gun in his hand, when Ray finally moved. It was perhaps not a direct threat, perhaps nothing much at all. He didn't raise the gun at me. He merely looked at me. There was something mechanical in the movement—perhaps the stillness in the rest of his body, or the way he lifted his chin and then turned his face toward me in two separate motions, as if responding to typed-in commands.

Another man, of a more heroic cast, might have waited until he aimed his weapon. Might have ordered him to drop the gun. Might have made a run at him. Still talking, I pulled the flare gun from my pocket and fired.

The flare made a tremendous hiss as it corkscrewed toward him. I feared it would miss him entirely, but it didn't. It caught in his down jacket and the phosphorus burned as white and brilliant as a comet. His coat was on fire and he turned this way and that, flapping his arms. I saw the gun fall and ran for it.

Ray managed to shake the flare from his jacket. The phosphorus hissed and burned in the slush, sending up clouds of steam. I had his gun now, and while he was trying to tear his jacket off, I shot him in the back. He fell at once to his knees and I shot him again, so that he toppled face down. I thought then and think now that his heart had already stopped, but I stepped closer and shot him in the back of the head to make sure.

The sight of his blood pumping into the snow made my gorge rise. I turned away and bent over the still form of Jens Dahlberg. Ray had shot him through the heart, and he lay on his back in a red cloud of blood. There was no breath, no pulse.

I checked the Glock's magazine. Two rounds left. Presumably Ray had used the others to shoot Paul Bélanger and Murray Washburn before his spree was put on pause by our disintegrating island. I put the gun in the pocket of my fleece and turned around.

Rebecca had followed me. She was standing at the edge of a throbbing circle of brightness cast by the still-hissing flare, one hand covering her mouth.

17

CARDINAL GOT INTO HIS CAR and shut the door and started it but didn't move. He sat there with the heater going full blast, thinking about Ronnie Babstock. After a while he took out his phone and saw that Loach had called him twice. He ignored that and dialed Ian McLeod.

"You and Delorme are turning into real assholes," McLeod said. "Loach is going to get you bounced off the squad—possibly *before* he's appointed Governor General, possibly after. Seriously, what the hell are you doing? It's lonely here without you. Nobody loves me."

"I don't love you either," Cardinal said. "I can't speak for Delorme."

"She *secretly* loves me."

Cardinal told him what he'd just found out.

"Wow. Ronnie Babstock. We gonna pick him up?"

"Not yet. We now know he worked with those three guys back in the late eighties, early nineties—and when I asked him about them, he made out like they had nothing to do with each other. The really weird thing, given how high-profile at least three of them are, is that there's almost nothing written about them having worked together. If there'd been super bad blood between them, you'd expect to see lawsuits and stuff like that on the Net, but there's nothing. Literally nothing. It's like it never happened. In any case, Babstock doesn't look anything like the description of the suspect. So I'm wondering about possible third parties. Maybe there was some kind of criminal activity up there at the same time. They could've crossed paths with the wrong people. We're talking way north here, like Arctic north."

"Oh hell, fucking Eskimos are killing themselves every five minutes. Killing each other too. It's cuz of all the vitamin A. Seriously, just between you and me, is Delorme really sick?"

"Delorme wouldn't call in sick without a good reason."

"Better be *really* good. I'm telling you, Loach wants to set up a fucking guillotine. You want to give me the dates and locations you have in mind? I'll check out the RCMP database."

"I'll take care of it. You've got French Canadians to interview."

~

Hayley had slept in that day, so she hadn't got to the health club until after dinner. Unfortunately, the only good times to work out were first thing in the morning, well before her first class, or late at night. Any other time you had to wait ages to get a machine, some tiny frond of a girl doing endless arm curls with the thing set at five pounds, or they got on the elliptical and covered the readout with a towel so you couldn't see that they'd been on it for three times the half-hour limit.

After twenty minutes on the treadmill and a half-hour of weights, Hayley could feel the tension of the day leaving her body. She would be alert enough to tackle some of the dreadful academic articles she had to read as research for her own academic article, should she ever get a week free from marking or makeup exams to work on it. She had the shower room to herself, and there was only one other person in the change room as she got dressed, a skeletal anorexic who came every day and spoke to no one.

Hayley dialed a number on her cellphone and told Kate Munk, her TA, she could come and pick up the papers she had to mark. Kate said she'd be there around nine.

Hayley snapped a flashing red light onto the rear fender, a white one onto the handlebars. The day's snow had melted, and Bathurst Street gleamed with the red smears of tail lights. She was tired after the workout and let three other cyclists pass her on the ride home.

As she turned into the alley, she saw a white van parked behind her house. A man opened the driver's door but stopped when he saw her coming. He raised a hand.

"Would that be Miss Babstock?"

Hayley braked but didn't get off the bike. She didn't recognize the guy, maybe a workman or something. He had an intelligent face, maybe a little hawkish. She waited with one foot on the ground, the other on a pedal.

"Sorry to appear out of the blue like this—especially this time of night. I slipped a card under your door, but when I saw you coming, I just thought . . ." He held up a photographic ID. "Ironclad Security. Your father asked us to look in."

"Oh, for God's sake. I told him I don't want a bodyguard. He's being totally weird."

"No, you're wrong about that. I assure you, the threat is both serious and credible."

"I don't mean to be rude, but aren't you a little old to be a bodyguard?"

He grinned. "Way too old. I run the outfit. You won't be seeing me after tonight. In the meantime, it would be very helpful if you would fill out this form. It'll only take a minute."

Hayley switched off her front light and put it in her backpack. Then the rear light. "If my father's already hired you, why do you need me to fill anything out?"

"We just need brief descriptions of people we should expect to see coming and going at your home and work."

"Excuse me, I have three hundred and fifty students."

"Let us worry about that. Just give us what you can." He handed her a clipboard. It had a small light attached to the top.

Hayley skimmed the first page. "I think I'd prefer to talk to my father again."

As she looked up, she saw his hand coming down toward her, something gleaming in his fist. It pierced her neck before she could grab his arm. She swung away from him and grabbed for the handlebars, and then her legs were gone and she could feel the bike falling away. Her eyelids slammed closed—once, twice—and she heard the clatter of the bike as a distant event, a tin can tumbling down a well.

~

"Can I get you another Stella, Stella?" The blonde behind the bar was wearing a black tank and micro skirt that showed off her annoying muscle definition. "Sorry. You must get that all the time."

"Yeah, I think I'll sit with this one awhile," Delorme said. "Is Len in tonight?"

"Len—you mean the owner? Don't think so."

"I saw him up in Algonquin Bay a couple of days ago. He said he was coming down."

"He comes, he goes. I'm just a peon. You expecting some friends?"

Delorme shook her head.

"Things should pick up soon. Still a little early."

The restaurant downstairs was hopping—Delorme had had a good Thai curry with a glass of Chablis—but the second floor was dead. A bare-chested man with a grey flattop stood behind a woman lounging on a couch and massaged her shoulders. His hands slipped in and out from under the spaghetti straps of her camisole. A languid couple kissed in an alcove. The look and feel of the Toronto Risqué Club was identical to the Ottawa one; it was just a lot less busy—at least at the moment.

"You look familiar," Delorme said. "Do I see you at Extreme Fitness?"

"Yeah, I'm there every day," the bartender said with a grin.

"It shows."

"Oh, thanks. My trainer's a total sit-ups Nazi. Have I seen you there? I can't say I really recognize you."

Delorme pointed to her head. "Wig."

"Ah, yes. Makes sense. Not everybody's so open-minded about these things."

"No kidding. I guess I will take that Stella now."

The Extreme Fitness had been a guess, though not a wild one: there was a branch right across the street from Risqué. Women pedalling their stationary bikes and staring into their smart phones.

The bartender bent to get the beer from the cooler and Delorme couldn't help noticing the silky legs, firm of calf and thigh. Thinking, great—lesbian cop. A single encounter and I turn into a total cliché. As a countermeasure, she called John Cardinal to her mind, their kisses on that winter night that seemed so far away. Picturing his face, those mournful eyes of his, brought an ache to her heart. She dismissed the image.

"Darlene been in lately?"

"Darlene! You a friend of his or you just know him from here?"

"I know him from Algonquin Bay."

"Is he from up there? Darlene. Boy, quite a character, that one. Was that you with him the night he had those three guys lined up and—oops. Forgetting myself here."

"Have to be discreet, huh?"

"Big time. Really, I shouldn't have said anything."

"It's okay. Take a look at this." Delorme opened her purse and pulled out the photograph she'd taken from the envelope in Miranda Heap's desk.

"Ohmigod, that was taken here!" The bartender clutched the photo to her tank top and looked around before leaning forward. "They're dead serious about the no photos thing. Really, I've never seen a picture taken here before. I mean, they throw people out if they catch them taking pictures."

"Well, you can see the club logo right behind him," Delorme said.

"Put that away, girl. I never saw that, okay?" She rushed away to serve some people at the other end of the bar.

The place was filling up. Delorme stayed at the bar waiting for, well, she didn't know what for. There was some kind of weird throbbing, a yearning inside her. People do things out of character all the time. I don't know why I did it, they say—it was an impulse. Or, I had way too much to drink and suddenly I just, I don't know, lost control. Police hear it all the time.

Out of character. Delorme thought about that. Across the room on a red plush couch, a woman lay back as two men kissed her and stroked her. If the woman felt anything other than lust, she wasn't showing it, kissing them right back, unbuttoning their shirts. A few more minutes and they'd be heading up to the third floor.

Out of character. Who doesn't want to be out of character once in a while? Junior detective on a small-city force with a reputation as a hard-ass, a decent worker but not much more. Single, and thirty-five a receding memory. Lusty, yes. Definitely fond of sex. But not promiscuous, at least not up until now, and about as unkinky as an average Canadian girl can be. Or so I thought. Why shouldn't I fuck my brains out? It's not like it's going to upset the husband, embarrass the children.

A man came up and asked her nervously if she'd like to join him and his wife in an alcove.

Delorme turned her head toward the dark nook. A small woman in a silver lamé halter smiled and gave a little wave.

"Let me think about it, okay? I'm not exactly used to—"

"I get ya. No problem. We just think you're really cute and you seem to be on your own, so . . ."

"I'll think about it."

"We don't come here a lot either. It's only our second time."

"Okay."

The guy went back to the alcove. His wife straddled his lap and his arms circled her waist. They were both attractive, and Delorme thought she could detect honest affection in the way they touched.

Maybe it's not out of character. Maybe it's just discovering another part of my character, like coming upon a secret room in a house you've lived in all your life. She looked at the couple again, the man's hands stroking the woman's back. Suppose she went over there and sat beside them, the man reaching over and touching her, or perhaps the woman. Just thinking about it changed the chemistry in her bloodstream—a light sweat breaking out on her forehead, heart rate heading to the high end of her aerobic zone—a dark cocktail swirling through her veins, of lust, of fear, of guilt, with notes, as a connoisseur might say, of despair.

She turned around and caught the bartender's attention, holding up her clutch purse. "Can I get a key? I think I want to lock this up."

The bartender brought a key with a rubber band attached to it. "Taking the plunge, huh?"

Delorme had to take her phone out of the purse to get at her money. As she set it on the bar, it lit up and began to quiver. She picked it up and looked at the screen. John Cardinal. Something like a sob welled up in her chest. She pressed Talk.

"Jesus, you picked up for once. Listen, how fast can you get down to Toronto?"

"I'm in Toronto. Why?"

"Hayley Babstock has been abducted."

~

When Hayley first woke up, she thought she was on her way to the beach. Her mother and father in the front listening to classical music or the news while she curled up in the back seat. Every year they went to Cape Cod in the States, drove there (when they could very easily have flown first class) because her father found the driving relaxing. They stayed in a perfect jewel box of a house in Wellfleet.

Her parents were both so happy during those vacations. It was the only time it seemed to Hayley that she lived in a family like the ones you saw on television. Everybody close and happy, especially her father. August was the only month she got to spend a lot of time with him. He would build sandcastles with her, put puzzles together on the huge refectory table, play board games. And the three of them reading, devouring stacks of books and magazines.

But this was not their car, and she was not a little girl. Her arms and legs felt thick and heavy. She tried to stretch, and found that her hands and feet were bound. There was a handkerchief or something tied across her mouth, tight enough that she couldn't dislodge it, push as she might with her tongue. But no blindfold.

She remembered the alley, the security man, the thing in his hand. A hypodermic meant planning, elaborate intentions, and she felt a strong urge to scream. She forced herself to take deep, slow breaths.

Highway—the road smooth, the speed steady—a major highway. Sounds of larger vehicles growing near, fading, but no whoosh of oncoming traffic. There were no windows in the back of the vehicle, but passing lights swept through the darkness at regular intervals. Highway 400, the 401, or the QEW. At any given time, half of Canada was on these roads.

Whatever he had injected her with was wearing off. She could wiggle her hands and feet and turn her head. Her fingers touched the metal side of the van. She pressed here and there as many times as she could, leaving marks. She would get out of this. She would get out of this and they would find the van, and she would be believed. Her fingerprints would convict him.

She craned her neck to see. Part of the profile, the strong nose, hair the colour of a grubby coin, slicked back from his face. He turned his head to look at her and she closed her eyes too late. Moments later, the sway of inertia as the van changed lanes. Another move to the right and then it slowed and stopped. Whoosh of cars rushing by.

Hayley backed herself up against the seats, expecting him to appear at the back of the van. But a side panel slid open and he was right beside her. He held the needle, point up, by his shoulder. She squirmed away and tried to kick at him with both feet.

From the Blue Notebook

I am a person given to the scientific and materialist view of existence. Not a man to dwell on concepts of fate, predetermination or tragedy. But concerning that chapter of my life that began with Rebecca's arrival at Arcosaur, I have been drawn again and again to the medieval idea of Fortune.

And yet not the wheel of fortune, which is a neat analogy to the common situation of being on top of the world one minute and utterly cast down—or at least on a marked downward trajectory—the next. But luck, yes luck, fair or foul, shows its hand in the affairs of man far more often than, say, effort rewarded or love conquering all. We commonly see fools come out on top and good men brought low.

My scientific training is of no use in explaining what had happened to us so far, let alone what was to come. To take but one example, what were the chances of these two catastrophes—one a disaster of geodynamics (actually, ice dynamics), the other of human psychology—occurring simultaneously? Individually, either event was quite likely. Ice floes crack and fracture every hour. And the stresses of cold and isolation will torment anyone whose psyche is not securely integrated. But the chances of their co-occurring are infinitesimal, and the fact that they did is offensive to common sense, not to mention any notion of justice. But there's nothing to be done about that. And Fortune was not done with us.

We were still standing over the bodies of Jens Dahlberg and

Raymond Deville when the sun dimmed. We looked toward the approaching storm.

We need their clothes, I said, and got down to remove Ray's jacket. I had to pull him up into a seated position and wrestle the sleeves off him. I got up and handed it to Rebecca, but she backed away.

I can't.

Put it on. The gale will kill us. Put this on. As long as the wet doesn't soak through, it will act as an insulator.

Kit, in God's name.

God is not available. We need every scrap of clothing we can get.

Rebecca helped me get Ray's trousers off, weeping the whole time.

Put them on over your jeans.

I can't.

You must. I'll help you.

I steadied her as she removed one of her boots and pulled on the pants. When she had that boot back on, we did the same with the other foot. Ray was a small person, but even so, the trousers were far too big. We rolled up the cuffs and, using my pocket knife, I cut a new hole in Ray's belt. The jacket was not burned too badly, and it had a hood—a thin one meant for rain, with no drawstrings. I took Ray's fleece and put it on over my own.

Are there any gloves in the pockets?

She shook her head. We scavenged everything else we could—the pencils, the Aero bar, the cough drops.

I'm sorry for crying, Rebecca said. I won't panic again, I promise. What are we going to do?

We have to head into it. Movement is the only thing that will keep us warm. And that end of the floe is full of pressure ridges—they may provide some shelter. Help me cut away the rest of their clothes—anything that's dry.

Even for someone wearing the proper gear, an Arctic gale is a terrifying experience. Winds unchecked by hill or tree and chilled by endless wastes of ice and freezing water, winds so powerful they suck the air out of your lungs. If they carry snow, one must also survive blindness and complete disorientation.

I cut pieces of cloth into strips for makeshift headbands and hand warmers, and we walked into it face first. At first the wind carried no snow. But it was a wet wind that soon rimed our eyebrows with frost. My arms, the core of my body, thanks to the double layers, conserved their heat. But my legs, the skin of my thighs, burned with the cold.

There was no question of stopping. When the wind was unbearable, we turned our backs to it and pushed against it. It was like trying to back a ship up a mountain. Then it would relent and we would turn and face it once more, moving the whole time.

We had already been fighting it for an hour when the snow hit, big flakes that clung and leached the body heat from our faces. Visibility sank to twenty, thirty metres. We had no compass. In any case, it would have been next to useless so close to the magnetic pole. We kept moving, guided by nothing but the direction of the wind itself.

The wind carried with it a massive payload of fear. You would not think mere disorientation could worsen the physical adversity we faced, but it did. When, over the course of the next few hours, the snow relented, it was replaced by fog—a fog so dense it clung to the eyeballs like blindness itself. The sun was reduced to a wash of paler grey amid the grey.

We had to tread that fine line I have already mentioned between losing heat to hypothermia or to sweat. Sometimes we had to slow our pace until we could no longer bear the cold and damp. Then we would move faster, staring at our feet the whole time (a smooth surface is extremely rare in the Arctic), until our own sweat threatened to kill us.

There was no telling how much of our ice island was left. I could not even work out what had caused it to break up—possibly a shoal on which the tides cracked us like an egg. Not that it mattered.

We walked through fog past the first edges of pain—the aches in hips, back, knees and ankles—and on toward exhaustion. We decided on a schedule of rests—three minutes every half-hour, five minutes every hour. The five minutes proved too long; we never lasted more than four. Rebecca did not complain. Neither of us voiced anything at all. We would stop, arms around each other, rubbing each other's back and arms, pressing close. I could dimly feel her breasts, her breathing, through the layers of clothing. Her courage in those hours pierced me.

After hours of walking, nearly seven by my watch, we reached a pressure ridge offering angles and corners that made admirable windbreaks. By then the wind had died down and we had less need of them. But with the sun shrouded in fog, the temperature had dropped. We could not remain still for long.

Her arms around me. Throb of her heart a distant, invisible sun.

She pulled back a little to look at me. Exhaustion in those eyes where before I had seen only youth—youth and a thousand shades of emotion I could not have named. She told me she was sorry she had been "so mean" to me.

I thought she must be being sarcastic.

There are two things I regret, she said. One, not being honest with Kurt, and with myself. Not admitting what I knew, that I mistook admiration for love and led him into a trap he didn't understand and couldn't escape. And two, being mean to you.

Being mean. It sounded so teenage, the way one regrets having been harsh to a pet, to the class dimwit, or to someone who sought nothing more than friendship.

I played games, she said. I shouldn't have. I wanted everything you had to offer but I wanted it for free. I've always been a selfish person.

But of course it was I who had been stupid and weak and selfish. I tried to tell her this and found I could barely speak before her purity of spirit. I should have been strong enough to admire you from a distance, I said.

It was all I could manage. I could only hope she understood there was more.

The fog clinging. We had to release each other and put our hands back in our pockets.

We have to keep moving, I said.

Yes. But which direction?

I pointed to the wash of paler grey. Given where we left Axel Heiberg, I think that must be south. There should be more ridges, if we need them. And it will take us closer to shore.

Despite the uncertainty, we headed in that direction. We were both very hungry but dared not speak of it. The fog began to thin and then we felt on our faces the first caress of sunlight.

Oh, God.

It was the first time Rebecca had spoken since we had spoken of regret. Her tone was new. A deeper level of despair. I already knew, having seen it through the field glasses, what she had just realized. I had been waiting for her to see it, couldn't bring myself to point it out.

Oh, God, Kit. Oh, dear God.

I know.

She stopped and I thought she would weep, but the realization had taken her beyond weeping.

I stopped as well and the two of us stood side by side, a few inches of Arctic between us, and looked toward the shore. The sun now lit the snowy western slopes of the promontories—the same two promontories from which we had set out hours before.

We haven't moved, Rebecca said.

The headwind had turned our ice island into a vast treadmill.

We haven't moved.

18

CARDINAL WAITED FOR DELORME AT the end of the alley where it opened onto College Street. She arrived in a cab, which was itself unusual, and there was something else about her that seemed a little . . . off. He could not have said exactly what it was.

"Are you okay?"

"I'm fine. Why wouldn't I be?"

"Well, you've been calling in sick and—"

"Who called this in?"Delorme headed down the alley toward the lights.

"A teaching assistant who came by to pick up some term papers. Hayley knew she was coming. When she got here, she found Hayley's bike lying in the alley and no sign of her."

"How'd they know to call you?"

"I used to work with Art Drexler, the lead guy at 52 Division, a century ago."

They were waved past the crime scene tape and Cardinal introduced Delorme to Drexler. He didn't waste any time on preliminaries.

"Don't bother with the bunny suits, we're just about done here."

Two cops were loading a woman's bike into the back of a van.

"That's hers," Cardinal said. "It looks like she never made it into her apartment."

"*She* didn't," Drexler said. "But he did."

He led them up the fire escape to a door on the second floor. Inside, the scene people were collecting their markers, putting camera gear away, snapping cases closed.

"I asked the wizards to leave some stuff out for you to see. First of all, check out her land line." He picked up the handset, which was wrapped in clear plastic and dotted with print powder, and pressed a couple of buttons. "It's got an automatic message retrieve function. I'm putting it on speaker." The phone beeped a couple of times and a synthetic voice said there were five old messages. Drexler skipped four of them. "Students and TAs. But get this."

Hi, sweetheart, it's me again. Why can't I get you on your cell? I suppose you were in class. Listen, I know you said you don't want anything to do with a bodyguard, but I've gone ahead and contacted a company anyway. Their top guy will come around in person tomorrow morning at eight-thirty.

"That's Ronnie Babstock," Cardinal said to Drexler. "I know him."

"He saw this coming?" Delorme said. "Why didn't he call us?"

It's crucial that you listen to him, the message went on. *These people know what they're doing and he won't waste your time. If you have any reason to fear for your safety—anything untoward—call the police. And tell them to call Detective John Cardinal at the Algonquin Bay police. Hayley, please, please, be careful.*

"Looks like someone else picked up that message," Drexler said. "Also, take a look at this."

Someone had scrawled a number on a small notepad next to the phone.

"79," Delorme said. "Could be anything. Is it her writing?"

"Not enough there to be definitive," Drexler said, "but the sevens and nines in her chequebook are quite different."

"We had numbers at two other scenes," Cardinal said. "25 at one and 45 at the other. We're not a hundred percent sure about those either."

"Well, I think we can be reasonably sure it's not an address where we can find him," Drexler said.

"No, but it might contain some other information."

"You're with 52 Division?" Delorme said. "I don't suppose you ever happened to work with a guy named Loach? He's with us now."

"Ugh. You can keep that prick."

"We might have got here sooner," Cardinal said, "but Loach has got everyone running in circles."

"Chasing this," Delorme said. She pressed the Play button on her phone and the mysterious caller told them in thick French-Canadian tones that he would soon strike again.

Drexler's face changed. "That's your suspect?"

"It's Loach's suspect."

"Caller have anything not general knowledge? He mention any of your holdbacks?"

"Yeah, he did," Cardinal said. "He mentioned those two numbers, 25 and 45, in an oblique sort of way. We don't know how he got them—obviously a leak somewhere. It's not that chasing down the voice is insane, it's just—"

"It's just not good prioritizing. That's Loach. Also, you've got a leak. And Loach, you may have noticed, is a real motormouth. Has a habit of yakking to people off the rez." He turned to the last remaining member of the scene squad, who was waiting by the door with hands folded and head bowed. "Jackson! Sorry! You guys can go. We'll be along in a minute."

When the scene man was gone, Drexler said, "I don't normally badmouth a former colleague, but in Loach's case I'm making an exception. The thing about Loach—well, there's a lot of things—but thing number one is, he gets something in his head, it don't leave."

"We noticed."

"Thing number two, Vernon Loach is not a team player. You have a big success, Loach is its daddy. No one else had anything to do with it. Thing goes sour, Loach had nothing to do with it."

"Our D.S. is pretty dazzled by the Montrose case," Cardinal said.

"I can't blame him, way it played in the media. But Montrose got cleared because two dozen detectives worked nights and weekends to follow all the boring little details that make a good case. Plus we got lucky—Mr. Montrose having used a firearm that matched a case from eight years ago."

"Was it Loach followed that up?" Delorme said.

"It was me. But it coulda been any one of us. I can't tell you the number of court cases went belly up with Loach. Chain-of-evidence crap. Witnesses who didn't pan out. My blood pressure's going up just remembering." Drexler laughed. "And the whole time he's yapping about how his ship's about to come in."

"At the moment," Delorme said, "he seems to be expecting a CBC biography or something."

Drexler shook his head. "It makes you want to roll on the floor laughing. Except it also makes me want to cry. I can't say I ever hated Loach. I try not to hate anybody. But a lot of people did. In particular, a sergeant named Chuck Rakov. Rakov used to make fun of him all the time. To his face. Refused to take him seriously. Eventually, Loach got him fired on some trumped-up thing—actually got the guy *fired*—which as you know is pretty near impossible to do. Listen, come on down to the div with me. The others should be wandering back with their reports, and you may as well get the stuff first-hand."

—

Drexler was everything Loach was not. He brought everyone to order quickly. He had Cardinal and Delorme stand up when he introduced them.

"Hayley Babstock was abducted in our town and this is absolutely our case," he told them, "but these two detectives are our total allies. They know *way* more than we do at this point, and I'll have them run through it for you once we get everyone debriefed.

"Now, there was a number written at the scene that may or may not be in this maniac's handwriting. That number is 79. Cardinal and Delorme are telling us there were numbers found at two previous scenes. Those numbers are 25 and 45."

"Could be a combination," someone said. "To a lock of some kind."

Someone else suggested a computer key or maybe a password.

"It could be a lot of things," Drexler said. "We're going to have to brainstorm it."

Detectives got up one after another and gave a summary of what they'd found. A security camera across College Street had picked up a white van leaving the alley. They had a techie trying to enhance the image so they could pull up a licence plate. But the alley had two other exits that were not covered by any kind of surveillance.

Cardinal got up and told them what he knew so far. When he was done, someone asked where he thought the perpetrator might be headed.

"Possibly Algonquin Bay—he's killed two people there so far, including one he abducted from Ottawa. But his first victim was in Parry Sound.

So, other than that . . . somewhere cold. Right now I'm working on the theory that this series of killings is aimed not at the victims themselves but at their husbands—or in this case, her father. All of these men worked together years ago, and all of them have managed to keep that fact quiet up to now. The minute I have any more, I'll let you know."

"For our part," Drexler said, "I want to put everything we've got onto narrowing down that white van. I want every one of those neighbours questioned in detail. Keep in mind it's likely this guy was hanging around scoping the place out, possibly following the victim. Somebody had to see him."

As his team scattered, Drexler took Cardinal and Delorme to a meeting room where a sleek black computer with an extra-large screen was set up.

"Gimme one minute," he said, and left them alone.

They sat in silence. Expensive equipment everywhere, and all the furnishings of a much higher grade than they were used to. Chouinard is right, Delorme thought. We're not Toronto.

"It's good to have you here," Cardinal said.

She looked at him. "Right."

"I don't like it when you're not around."

Delorme didn't feel like saying anything. Or maybe a lot of things. She became aware of a sudden longing for sleep. She wanted to be unconscious. She could see Cardinal was in full terrier mode, ready to go all night.

Drexler came back and stuck a flash drive into the computer. He picked up a wireless keyboard and put it on his lap. A couple of clicks and the screen lit up with a blur of people. Much clinking of glasses, laughter, lots of people talking at once. One voice skimmed above the rest.

"That's Loach," Delorme said.

No, I was talking with their backroom boys—they're seriously considering getting me to run.

Drexler grinned. "Hasn't changed, right? But watch—sorry about the quality. Guy who took this was hammered, obviously. Interesting thing from your point of view is, it's *not* Loach . . ."

The image blurred and swung once more, coming to rest on a bulldog of a man in a houndstooth jacket and cap.

"That's Chuck Rakov. Bit of a clown, Chuck, but a solid investigator. Definitely someone you want watching your back."

Rakov put a phone up to his ear. *That's right, honey . . . The Prime Minister . . . I know . . . Yeah, me personally. Gotta go.*

"Great mimic," Cardinal said, getting up. "Guy should be on late-night TV. Listen, Art, is there a desk I can take over for a few hours?"

"Hang on, hang on. You gotta see this." Drexler was fast-forwarding in jerks and hops. "Here we go."

A lot of shouting and then Rakov, still wobbling on his chair, launched into a new voice. *I'm tell you the troot—for shore! We get to de address and dis lady, she and 'er 'usband are sitting side by each on da porch swing. And da guy, he's got no clothes on—nudding!*

Cardinal and Delorme looked at each other.

"That's the guy," Delorme said. "He's the damn caller."

Drexler froze the image. "Loach annoyed everyone he worked with. As I'm sure you know." He pointed the remote at the screen. "But I guarantee you, nobody hates him like Chuck Rakov."

—

Drexler found an empty desk for Cardinal to use, and Cardinal stayed there after Delorme had gone back to the hotel and Drexler had gone home. He looked at the brochure he had purchased from the eBay brothers: the four young men and their prototype robot. Eventually the clatter and hum of the big-city police station vanished and he focused on the task before him.

He began working the search engines, beginning with *Arctic, crime, 1992*. With each response he narrowed it down a little more. *LARS research, robotics*. That didn't get him anything useful. Finally, he typed in *murder, Axel Heiberg Island*, and that brought up a JPEG of an old clipping. RESEARCHER ACCUSED OF MURDER IN DRIFT STATION DISASTER.

The article was brief, but a quick scan of it gave Cardinal enough names and dates to hone his search even further. What the bizarre story boiled down to was this: an enraged researcher's murder spree had been foiled only by the sudden disintegration of their camp on an ice floe. Cardinal had a dim memory of the events—very dim indeed, because that summer he had been working on an extremely difficult case of his own. And yes, Catherine had been hospitalized at the time. He had had no spare attention for cases thousands of kilometres from his jurisdiction.

Axel Heiberg Island was in the northern territory of Nunavut. He would have to wait until morning to call their corrections department. He switched off his desk lamp, left a note of thanks for Drexler and headed for his hotel.

~

It had been snowing for the past fifty or sixty kilometres. Big lazy flakes in no hurry to hit the highway. They swirled in the headlights and around the side windows and stuck to the windshield, except for the smeary arcs left by the wipers.

The traffic had thinned and he hadn't seen a single patrol car since Toronto. The girl was silent in the back and appeared to be in no distress. His main concern was catching the turnoff. Many of the signs were obscured by clinging snow. Eventually it came up on the right, and he saw it in enough time to signal and slow and make the turn.

Different road, different journey. Narrower—thick trees pressing up close—darker. No ploughs had been through, and the snow was falling more heavily now. Visibility dropping.

It would be fifteen or twenty minutes on this road, then one more turn. Beyond his headlights, blackness. No other headlights anywhere. He switched on the dome light and looked back at the girl. Still out cold. The sharp turn hadn't woken her, nor the new roughness of the ride.

He didn't know what hit them when it hit. He didn't even hear it. As he turned back from looking at the girl, the windshield came in on him and the van went into a spin. He couldn't see through the shattered glass and the wheel was slick with blood. Chances were good they were going to flip, but somehow the wheels held as they turned and turned.

Durie's eyes were blind with blood and he had no idea which way they were headed as the van spun or, when it finally came to a stop, which way they were facing.

His head was a sphere of black cloud and he couldn't think. He held his eyes closed against the blood, and when he tried to wipe them, his arm was stopped by something. There was no pain, but he considered that might just be a matter of shock. He was over on one side, something pressing heavily on his hips and legs. The driver's seat was totally disarranged, he could feel that much. Tilted way back so that he was nearly falling into the back of the van.

There was a snuffling sound from somewhere. He craned his neck to see forward. Windshield shattered and dark. Strange shapes bulging over the passenger seat. Antlers. That snuffling sound the beast's dying breaths.

The pressure on his side was the airbag.

He thought the girl should be all right, he had strapped her down pretty well. He forced his left arm free and wiped some blood away. Yes, she was twisted around a little and the blanket had been thrown clear, but otherwise she looked okay.

He reached for the passenger seat and pulled but didn't get anywhere. His fingers found the seatbelt buckle and released it and he managed to drag himself nearly free. Blood all over him, but that could be the animal's. The snuffling had stopped.

Slam of a car door.

Durie reached for the glovebox, opened it and pulled out the Glock. He freed the last of himself from the airbag and opened the passenger-side door and crawled out of the van hands first, snow a cold bracelet on each wrist.

"Ho-ly Christ," someone said, "are you all right in there?"

Durie heard no footsteps. He grabbed the door handle and pulled himself up, breathing hard. He pushed the gun into his coat pocket but kept his hand on it. The grip was sticky with blood.

Leaning against the van, he hobbled to the back end of it and shielded his eyes against the man's headlights, and now his flashlight.

"Holy Christ," the man said again. He stood still, shining his light. "Are you okay?"

"Yeah."

"You sure?"

"Yeah."

"You're covered in blood."

"Moose blood. I'm okay."

"The moose ain't. That's the third one this year." He gestured with the flashlight. "There anyone else in there?"

"No."

The man moved toward the van. It was on the side of the road, at an almost perfect right angle, with the dead moose half sunken into it.

Durie gripped the Glock in his pocket. His head was clearing a little, but even so, he was not seeing a wealth of alternatives.

"Not that big," the man observed, "as moose go. Van's a writeoff. Tell me what you need outta here."

"Leave it," Durie said. "Just take me somewhere."

The man pulled at the side-door handle.

"Leave it," Durie said.

The man pulled again and the door slid back. "What in the hell?"

He stepped back and looked over at Durie standing in the headlights.

He leaned back into the van, and when he came back out he said, "Girl looks okay, but she's out cold. You must of incurred a head injury, mister—you said there was no one in there. Shouldn't let people sleep in the back like that, even if they are strapped in."

He reached into his pocket.

"Don't."

"I gotta call an ambulance."

"We don't need an ambulance."

"I'm gonna call."

"Just help me get her into your car."

"No way. I'm not gonna risk moving an unconscious person." The man held his phone out at arm's length to shade his eyes. "Okay? Why don't you go siddown in my truck, eh?"

He held the phone to his face to dial. The screen lit up his features—doughy, harmless, middle-aged—and a surrounding nimbus of falling snow.

From the Blue Notebook

The headwind had driven us closer to the shore of Axel Heiberg, an island rich in glaciers and one I knew well. It provided the dedicated researcher with everything the Arctic offers: desert, ice cap, meltwater ponds and icebound lakes. Mountainous in the centre, much of it is also just above sea level. Not so many years ago I had taken cores from the Midden Ice Field, walked the Crusoe Glacier to its terminus and observed its new meltwater stream, which had only just started flowing. I discovered vast deposits of dead ice that had lain hidden for centuries beneath layers of tundra and soil—evidence of a previous glacier, and a glimpse into the far recesses of planetary time.

Rebecca and I were now drifting south of Iceberg Glacier, the only one on Heiberg that reaches the sea. But we were staring at thirty metres of open water that separated us from the pro-glacial gravel of Heiberg. Thirty metres we had no way of crossing.

The terror of hypothermia welled up in me. The fact is, few of the nineteenth-century explorers who came to grief did so by freezing to death. They were killed by scurvy, by malnutrition, in some cases by lead poisoning brought on by faulty canned goods. They had the assistance of Inuit hunters who knew the landscape intimately, whose hand-drawn maps may still be used to advantage, and whose clothing has never been bettered, except in terms of weight, for keeping the cold at bay.

The temperatures Rebecca and I faced were by Arctic standards not severe. As far as I could judge, the temperature swung from perhaps minus ten Celsius to a few degrees above freezing. But we were improperly dressed. Even so, the human body maintains its warmth very well until other factors come into play—wetness, which we had so far managed mostly to avoid, hunger, exhaustion. We had been walking for hours, without food. Our core temperatures were moving downward, and hypothermia, despite the layers we had salvaged from the dead, was imminent.

There's a promontory just above Strand Fiord, I said. Pack ice tends to jam up there—we may be able to make it to shore. If we can do that, we can make the LARS camp.

Rebecca's face was grey and there was a blue tinge to her lips—not a good sign. She nodded silently.

I pulled out the radio and scanned for transmissions. Nothing but the gasp and crackle of solar storms. I pulled the aerial out full and pointed it in the direction of the LARS station. It is sometimes possible to reach receivers normally out of range by doing a cloud skip or strat skip. There was small hope of success, but I put out another mayday all the same.

I don't know how long we walked after that. Polar conditions do nothing good for your sense of time. The fog had gone, but without time, one has no idea of distance. I knew we must be near Strand Fiord, but not how near.

Eventually, yes, there came a moment of luck. We were jammed, not against the shore, but up against another floe. The fit was not perfect, but we found a place where the gap was about four feet, perhaps a little less. That may not sound like much, but the surface was slush and we were ragged and worn.

How's your long jump? I said.

We can't. The edge will snap.

It's multi-year ice—you can tell by the blue. It'll be a couple of metres thick right up to the edge. Do you want me to go first?

I don't care.

She was shivering violently, her body becoming less able to generate heat.

I decided to go first. That way I could grab hold of her if she had trouble on the far edge. We both knew that even a few seconds of exposure to that water would mean death.

If I fall, she said, hold my hand if you can, but don't pull me out.

You're not going to fall.

We moved back a few metres and without preliminary I took my run. Landing on the far side, I stumbled forward and my hands and forearms plunged into slush—a sure sentence of maiming by frostbite. Then Rebecca ran toward me and leapt the gap and I made sure she crashed into me so she couldn't fall.

We tore Ray Deville's shirt into pieces to wrap my hands and forearms, and set off again. We made landfall in less than an hour. The tabular floe had been forced well up onto the rocky shore, and it didn't take long to find a spot where the drop to the gravel beach was not too high.

If we can make Strand Fiord, we can make LARS, I said. This time of year there's bound to be someone there. Even if there isn't, it'll mean shelter, supplies.

Rebecca said nothing.

Did you hear me?

What? Yes, I heard you, she said, but she remained still, staring at the gravel. She was shivering again, and I held her close and rubbed her arms. My own arms, particularly the left, were going numb. Heiberg is a forbidding landscape—from our present vantage point it was nothing but gravel and bald rock—but the feel of dry land under my boots was encouraging.

Come on, then. Let's move. You go first. And I want you to talk to me.

I'm going to die, Kit. I'm going to die and I don't feel like talking. I don't feel like walking either. I just want to lie down.

I made her walk ahead of me and browbeat her into talking. She told me about some places she had lived—a farmhouse in Saskatchewan's Qu'Appelle Valley, a small room in a house she had shared with five other people. She spoke of the colours of fields, the million hues of green and gold, and she told me of a split-log cottage she and Kurt had rented one summer on Georgian Bay, and about the white sparks that seem to fly off Lake Huron in certain seas, certain lights.

I wanted to keep her talking so that I could judge her state of mind. She talked well and coherently over the next two or three hours. Even as she wept.

It's not me that's crying, Kit. It's just my body. It's so cold, my body. It's never been so cold.

You mentioned another house you shared. Who else lived in the house? Where was this house?

Ottawa, when I was a grad student. One night I came home late—everyone else was away for holidays or something. I came home and the landlord was there sitting in the dark. He thought I might be lonely, and I was, but he terrified me.

Gradually Rebecca's mind began to wander. One minute she was telling me about a cat, a childhood pet, I think, the next about a man—a fellow student?—who used to dismantle his motorcycle and bring the engine into the kitchen to clean it.

Sounds like Wyndham, I said.

Yes, Wyndham was there. And Kurt too, eventually. Everyone was there.

In Ottawa.

Well, yes. I mean, I think so. What did I say?

Her rambling might have been just exhaustion, but I kept her talking, and it was more than that. A sign of deeper hypothermia. We had two possible sources of heat: the flare gun and the BIC lighter I carried everywhere to warm up frozen locks and so on. There was nothing resembling firewood. And Rebecca needed internal heat at this point. Using my lighter and the remains of Ray's shirt, we might have melted some snow and heated it and drunk it, but we had no receptacle, no cup, no can, nothing.

We were both extremely thirsty. A casual camper may eat snow for water, but that would have meant lowering our body temperatures even further. We came across some meltwater in the hollow of a rock and lay on our bellies to sip from it. It had been recently warmed by the sun and, while cold, it was far from freezing.

Rebecca's confusion came and went. Sometimes she thought she was alone and would suddenly stop and call for Kurt. Other times she spoke to me as if I were her father or brother.

Remember the time Mom took the boat out and got lost? Will Nana be coming this Christmas?

Then she would look at me, eyes aghast.

The wind was not strong but the numbness had spread to the backs of my hands and into my wrists. We stopped in the lee of two striated ice blocks and Rebecca pulled my arms into her clothing to warm them.

I don't want to steal your heat, I said.

You can't. It's already yours.

We lingered too long this time and fatigue all but devoured us. We had been walking for a day and a half with nothing to eat but a few cough drops and some pieces of Aero bar. We ate the last of them now. Then I started up the slope of a smooth rock formation and Rebecca followed. The gradient was mild, but it felt mountainous. When we reached the top, I pointed into the distance.

That's Little Matterhorn and Bastion Ridge, I said. We're not that far.

Rebecca lay face down on the rock.

Get up, I said. The rock will leach all of your body heat.

She said nothing. I went to her and took hold of her wrist and pulled at her. She wept and cursed me and told me to leave her alone.

I'm not going to let you die here. Get moving.

We moved on. My own gait was weak, trudging. But Rebecca's legs would no longer obey her. With each degree of body heat she lost, she was entering further into a hypothermia from which recovery became increasingly unlikely. She staggered and fell, staggered and fell, and each time, as with a boxer who has taken more punishment than any human is meant to endure, it took longer for her to get up.

I knew we would not make the LARS camp. A trio of boulders came up on our left, the closest thing we would find to shelter. Rebecca sat down on the gravel and rested her back on a rock and closed her eyes.

You should squat, I said. Touch as little rock as possible.

She didn't respond.

I pulled out the radio and spoke once more into static and silence and received no response. I ripped apart our bundle of rags and set some of them in a pile. I broke up the small collection of pencils we had salvaged and laid them on top. Using my lighter, I lit the fabric.

I had to shake Rebecca hard to wake her. She pulled herself away from the rock and lay down, curled around the tiny fire.

No, darling. You have to sit up.

A small moan. Dry weeping.

I had observed my own faculties flickering over the past few hours. For a time I had thought we were heading back to camp on Ellesmere—the memory of an event at least a dozen years previous. When I first became aware of a distant buzzing, I thought it was an inner sensation, tinnitus, and then a hallucination, because there was nothing moving in that landscape except the grey and purple clouds.

But the heat from the burning clothing and pencils, paltry as it was, had restored me somewhat. And when I thought I saw something flash on a ridge to the north, I snatched at the face of the rock and pulled myself up. Voices. A man's voice. Calling to others. Another flash, as of something metallic catching a ray of sun.

People, I said. There are people.

I knelt beside Rebecca and scrabbled through her layers of clothing for the flare gun and our last remaining cartridge.

19

DELORME KNEW SHE SHOULD BE with Cardinal. Before she left him at 52 Division the night before, he had said he would come by early to pick her up at her hotel. If they had no other leads, maybe they'd tag along with Drexler when he went to go talk to—and probably arrest—the former Sergeant Rakov.

But she'd told him she wanted to finish the Priest/Choquette case and was pretty sure she could do it in one day, two at the most. She had thought Cardinal might give her a talking-to. But he just looked at her with those sad, soulful eyes of his and didn't say anything for a bit. Then he said, "Lise, do what you have to do. I'll see you back home." Meaning, *you* explain it to Chouinard.

It was still dark as she headed out of the city. Even Toronto was quiet if you got up before six, and she drove up the Don Valley and hit the 401 and got to Kingston with no trouble at all. Even the prison staff were reasonable.

Fritz Reicher was brought in—manacled this time—and sat down opposite her, regarding her warily through a fringe of blond hair.

"I brought you a present."

She pushed a small shopping bag across the table. The manacles rattled as he reached inside and extracted a coffee-table book. *The Dogs of New York*. He laid it flat on the table and turned a few pages.

"It's for me?"

"You said you liked dogs."

"Yes, of course. I—you remembered. Sank you. It's beautiful." He examined a few more pages. He turned the book around to show her a photograph. "Poodles. Poodles are the best."

"Fritz, I wanted to talk to you about a couple of things."

"Hah! Look at ziss." He turned the book again. Photo of a woman walking five dogs in Central Park. "I love it."

"Fritz, I need your attention."

"Yes, of course." He closed the book, using a finger to keep the page.

"I wanted to tell you I've met Darlene."

"You have? Who is she? What's she like? She's some old rich lady, isn't it?"

"You've met her too."

"No, not me. I've never met ziss person."

Delorme showed him a photograph of Garth Romney.

"But that's the prosecutor. I don't know what you're saying to me."

"It turns out the assistant Crown attorney is a regular patron of Risqué—the Toronto club, not Ottawa—and has been for some time." She showed him the picture of Romney as Darlene. "He is well-known at that club—especially at their Thursday night Hellfire sessions. Well-known to Leonard Priest, of course."

"Yes, Lennet loves those evenings," Reicher said, still not getting it. "Sometimes he likes very much to be the one in chains. Likes to be frightened."

"Interesting tip. But listen, Fritz—this is why Romney never prosecuted him. He couldn't afford to have his night life as Darlene come out in court. That's why Leonard got a free ride and you're rotting away in here."

"Yes, of course. I see." Reicher looked at his hands holding the book. His manacles. Delorme gave him some time. He was clearly not the brightest criminal you were ever going to meet, but she hoped he would make the necessary connections. Certain synapses had to be crossed, and she sat there waiting for his neurotransmitters to work. Eventually they did.

"But if ziss is true, he could have let me go too. Lennet could have told him, 'Let Fritz go too, he didn't mean it, I told him to do it.'"

"There was too much against you—your initial confession, your prints on the gun, a witness who saw you with the victim."

"Yes, of course. He must have tried. I'm sure he tried. He is so good to me, Lennet. He sends me money, you know."

"Yes, you told me."

"It's true. We're not allowed to have much money in this place, but he sends me a little spending money and puts some aside for me in an account. He sent me a copy of the papers."

"Did you check if this account is in your name?"

"No, it's not my name. I was in here—I could not be signing the proper papers." Reicher's face clouded. "It's money for me, not Lennet. He's putting it away for me."

"If it's in his name, how does that benefit you, Fritz?"

"He's going to give it to me when I get out. You're not trusting anyone, I sink. You must be a very angry person, a lonely person. Or maybe it's you don't like gays, bisexuals, and you're not understanding. But Lennet loves me and we're going to be together again when I get out, and he has put ziss money away for me because he's a good friend and he loves me."

"Well, I'm sorry to tell you this, Fritz . . ." And it was true—in the face of his delight with the book, his gratitude, his simple belief in friendship and loyalty, Delorme really was sorry. She pulled out her phone—her second phone, the one she used strictly for recording—and set it to play aloud.

Fritz? Have you met Fritz? Fritz is an amiable idiot. I'm sorry, but he's mentally defective—very attractive qualities in a servant, but not much use for anything else. Delorme had once seen a film of a massive building being demolished, some public housing project down in the States. The blasts from the charges shooting out before you even heard the explosions, the face of the building rippling, sinking. A sag in the middle, clouds billowing out from underneath, and then the whole sorry structure brought first to its knees and then to nothing, a heap of smoking rubble.

It was like that now, watching Fritz Reicher's face. The mouth with its thin lips open slightly, the cheeks hollowing. A glance to one side, unseeing, and back to the cellphone spewing its poison. A rattle of manacles as the large hands rise to cover the mouth, and then the whole, surprisingly delicate, construction collapsing forward, eyes wincing closed, face lowering to the book as the murderer's shoulders heave with sobs.

~

Cardinal's room at the Delta Chelsea was grotesquely overheated and there was no way to adjust the temperature. He'd woken, seared and desiccated, at four in the morning. He'd drunk a glass of heavily chlorinated water, but it had taken him hours before he got back to sleep, and then he slept through his alarm—or switched it off, he wasn't sure which.

It was past ten o'clock. He put some water in the miniature coffee maker, set it to brew and got into the shower. As he was drying himself, he started mentally leafing through an extremely repetitious inner file labelled *Delorme, Lise (relationship with)*. He had always thought of Delorme as a strong person. Unshakeable. Now he was not so sure. Like you know so much about women, he told himself. John Cardinal, man of the world.

He poured his coffee and sat at the desk. His first call was to the corrections department for Nunavut—the vast northern territory that included Axel Heiberg Island. No, he was told, no one connected with a murder in 1992 had been incarcerated in Nunavut, for the simple reason that Nunavut had not existed in 1992. At the time, it was part of the Northwest Territories—would he like the number for Yellowknife?

Yellowknife was two hours behind Toronto; the parole office would not be open yet. Cardinal opened his laptop and googled corrections facilities for the area. There were four places for males—one of which was for young offenders and two that provided housing ranging from low to medium security. The only one that offered maximum security was the North Slave Correctional Centre. The name sounded like something from the Soviet gulag but actually referred to the facility's proximity to Great Slave Lake. The web page was rudimentary but it did provide a number for warden Bruce Saxton, which Cardinal promptly dialed.

"This is Saxton."

Cardinal introduced himself and apologized for calling so early. "We have a series of murders here and, between one thing and another, I'm coming up against a murder trial and conviction that occurred in 1992. A group of scientists were living and working on what they called a drift station and—"

"And you're looking for a suspect who has a noticeable limp, I bet."

"Well, yes, as a matter of fact."

"And maybe a prosthetic hand?"

"Right again, Warden."

"You're looking for Karson 'Kit' Durie."

"I am."

"I expect you know I can't put him on the line for you."

"You're going to tell me he was released."

"I'm pulling it up right as we speak. Karson Durie was released November 15, 2009."

"And the parole office didn't see fit to notify anyone?"

"Parole office has nothing to do with it. Durie's not on parole. He was sentenced to eighteen years and he served every last one of 'em, reason being he refused to ever accept even a tom-tittle of responsibility for the lives he took—one of which he doesn't deny and three or four more of which he shot down in cold blood. Other than his recalcitrance on that little point, he was a model prisoner. He taught a lot of classes here over the years. Toward the end he enjoyed about as normal a life as it's possible for an incarcerated individual to enjoy: all the books he wanted and almost unlimited computer access, though we kept an eye on his search histories and so on. As you know, an individual serves his full sentence, there's no parole officer checking up on him. He can go wherever he wants. Last note in the file says 'released to Northwest Territories,' so there was no reason for anyone here to inform Ontario or any other province of his release. He's done his time, he's a free man. Could be anywhere. Did you know he used to be a bush pilot?"

"No, I didn't."

"Yep. Before he became a scientist and a murderer, he ferried people in and out of some pretty inaccessible places. You want me to fax you his known contacts, et cetera?"

"Better to e-mail it—that way I can pick it up on my phone."

"It'll take an hour or two—clerical people aren't in yet—but you'll have it soon as poss."

Cardinal got dressed, put on his coat and went down to the parking lot. Crusts of filthy snow clung to the sidewalks, and morning light made everything look worse. Every time he came to Toronto he was surprised by how bad the traffic was. He took Bay down to College and then he got stuck behind a streetcar and had to inch his way past the university and the student pubs and the computer supply stores.

He turned into the alley and drove to the back of Hayley Babstock's building. There was nothing left of the crime scene tape or any other sign of police presence. He sat with the motor running, staring at the windows of her flat, thinking. After a while he thought he saw something move in the kitchen window. A shadow.

He got out of the car and shut the door quietly. The gate squeaked a little as he pushed it open. He pulled out the Beretta and went up the fire escape. No sign that the door had been tampered with.

He took a breath and held it and tried the handle. The door wasn't locked. He pushed it open a crack and saw across the wide single room the figure of a man seated on the edge of the bed. Elbows on knees, staring at the floor in a posture of exhaustion, a cellphone to his ear. Cardinal was about to yell "Police" when the man looked up.

Cardinal lowered the Beretta. "Ron?"

Ronnie Babstock spoke into the phone. "Thanks for calling, David. I have to go. My friend John Cardinal's here." He put the phone in his pocket. "I don't think you'll want to be my friend any longer. Not when you know what I really am."

From the Blue Notebook

There are environments where simply to be alone is to be at grave risk—desert, high altitude, open seas—and the High Arctic must be counted among them. The assumption in such places is that anyone you encounter who is alone is likely to be in need of help unless otherwise indicated. Certainly, any sign of distress is never to be ignored. On the open seas, to do so is a crime.

I devoted the next few minutes of my life to attracting the attention of the party up on the ridge. My mind was dulled, my movements clumsy. My first attempt—waving my arms and calling—was pure instinct and utterly worthless. Dehydration had reduced my voice to a croak, and in any case they were upwind and would not have heard me.

Despite my almost useless hands, I managed to fit a cartridge into the flare gun. I raised my arms as high as I could and fired.

The flare shot upward into the sky and burst into a bright green parachute of light burning against the cloud cover. It could not be missed. I watched through my field glasses and saw one figure, hooded, uncertain, pause as he climbed the ridge. He looked toward the flare and back in my direction.

I took my jacket off and waved it overhead.

I think they've seen us, I said—not that Rebecca could hear me.

I took the Glock out of my fleece pocket and fired once in the air. The shot echoed off the ridge and the mountains beyond.

Another figure appeared on the ridge and stood with hands on hips, looking in my direction.

They've seen us, I said. They've seen us.

I put the gun away and tried the radio. It was like a block of wood in my fingers. I stabbed at it and twisted the dial, repeating mayday into any frequency that seemed possible.

There was no radio response. The figures on the ridge disappeared and I heard the sound of machines starting up. All-terrain vehicles. It could not be long.

Rebecca was still unconscious.

They'll be here soon, I said. I'm going to walk a way to meet them. It won't be long. You're going to be all right. We're both going to be all right.

There was only one way for them to get to us: descend the ridge and come through the valley. I walked on shaking legs in the direction from which they must come. Depending on the terrain they had to cross it would be half an hour, an hour at most, before we would meet.

As I walked, my ears were straining for the sound of their engines. When the sound faded, I stopped and listened. Perhaps there was some logistical problem, an issue of geology, that was holding them up. Perhaps mechanical failure. But I had definitely heard more than one machine. They could not all have failed.

It may be that I have always had a propensity for dark thoughts, but I would not describe myself as a cynic or a pessimist. A scientist is always curious, always open, assumes the answer will be found, if not by him, then by someone else. In considering the many ways we might perish in our circumstances, it did not occur to me that anyone who held the chance of life in his hands would refuse it.

No sound but wind over the hills. My own laboured breathing.

I scanned the ridge with my glasses, the valley open before me. Nothing.

How long I waited I can't be sure. The temperature was not far below freezing, but it was unbearable to stand still.

No.

I remember saying the word aloud. Barely a whisper, a single syllable, and yet it hung in that silence, hung around me like a shroud.

I turned back. I rounded a small rise and the low sun warmed my face. I walked with my arms clenched around me, staring at the stony ground. I got back to Rebecca and burned another piece of salvaged clothing between us. I pulled Rebecca as close as I could. She did not wake or even stir. The heat, pitiful though it may have been, was like honeyed liquor, and I fell asleep while the little flames flickered between us.

I don't know how long I slept. When I woke, the fire was out and cold.

Rebecca was gone.

For one delirious moment, joy rose inside me. She must be all right, she must have recovered, she could not be far. Lying on the ground had done terrible things to the muscles in my right leg. It was torment to stand.

Rebecca? I said her name over and over again in my desiccated voice. I wanted to laugh. She must be all right. We would move on. We would reach the LARS camp and safety.

I found her a short distance away among a tumble of rocks. Rocks that would have been folded one on top of the other by the meeting of two glaciers centuries earlier. Rebecca lay in a shadowy gap, curled in a fetal position, and my joy went out.

This was "terminal burrowing," the final stage of hypothermia. Usually it is seen in bodies that are found indoors, huddled in a closet or under a bed.

Her eyes were open, staring. I curled myself around her as best I could. I hung one arm over her, pressed my face against her shoulder. She blinked once, twice. Her lips moved as though she would speak, and I waited, staring at her dry, cracked mouth, but no words came. A few minutes later, she stopped breathing.

20

Cardinal closed the door and took a seat at Hayley Babstock's small wooden desk. You would never know it was the residence of a person from an extremely wealthy family. The room, a former attic cheaply remade into a studio apartment, was sparely furnished with scraps of carpet and flea market items. There was nothing overtly feminine about it, and yet it was clearly the domain of a young woman. The one jarring note was the bottle of Jack Daniels on the desk.

"You want a drink?"

Cardinal declined.

Babstock reached for the bottle and poured a finger of bourbon into his glass. "I picked it up on the way in. Hayley doesn't drink. Well, not more than a beer or a single glass of wine with dinner. She's the kind of girl who gets giddy quickly and knows enough to stay away from it. Woman, I should say. You still think of Kelly as a girl?"

"Not really. By the time she finished university—"

"You're right. I'm just being—"

"We don't have a lot of time, Ron. Tell me the story. Tell me where all this comes from."

"The story. The story is about four young men. Four young men who did everything right. For a time. There was me, there was David Flint—it was David who called me just now—there was Frank Gauthier, and Keith Rettig. How we found each other, I don't know. It was incredible luck.

"I was robotic engineering with a special interest in software, David was robotics, but already had postgrad credits in electrical engineering, Frank was an ace in AI but also mechanical—a totally unique combination right there. And Keith was our finance guy. He had his accounting credentials before he was twenty, I think, before he got his MBA. Keith and Frank were roommates at one point—that's how they met. And David and I had the same theologian for an adviser."

"Theologian?"

"Artificial intelligence professor at U of T. We both hated him, but he was the top guy at the time. Anyway, the four of us just hit it off. There's nothing like shared ambition to forge a friendship—especially in a field where teamwork is essential. Robotics, computers, AI—these are not mathematics, not fields where loners are likely to shine.

"We knew we wanted to do something big, and we knew we wanted to do it together, we just didn't know what it was. But around that time—this was the early eighties—it was becoming clear that miniaturization was going to be the dominant factor, the equivalent of natural selection, in technology. It was also becoming clear that space exploration was going to be unmanned.

"David—aside from being an engineering genius—is a very political animal. Knows how to network and has a natural charm, which you know if you've met him. David developed good contacts at Caltech and through Caltech with NASA, and we knew for a certainty they were going to need remotely controlled vehicles, rovers, that would be light enough to transport, tough enough to withstand difficult terrain in extreme temperatures.

"So we put our minds to it. We were like the four musketeers. I'm telling you, John, you may think I'm successful—a lot of people think I'm successful—and David and Frank same thing. But there isn't a day goes by I don't think of myself as a failure, and I'll bet you anything it's the same for David and Frank too. We are what we are, but together we could've been much, much more. I'd say Apple, but there's something ultimately trivial about that company, something showbiz.

"By this time, the three of us on the tech side were super hotshots. We all had incredible offers—incredible. I'm amazed we had the nerve to turn them down. But we decided to bet on ourselves. Keith hit the venture capital circuit—a deal with the devil if I ever heard one—but we didn't want to deal with government at that point."

"But NASA and those places—surely they'd be pouring money into this themselves."

"They would—they would and they were. I know. We were just incredibly arrogant. We figured they didn't have *us*, and therefore they couldn't possibly come up with anything as good as we could. I mean, these were the people that were trying to *hire* us, right?

"So we get enough money to go to specs. Only thing is, our venture capitalist wants a timeline of three years, not five—for the finished goods, not the specs. The specs take a year, three of us working eighteen-hour days, seven days a week. I've never worked so hard in my life. I've never been so smart. I look back at that time and it's like my mind was a hand. I could pick a concept up and turn it around, turn it upside down, inside out, rearrange it, make it simpler, better, more beautiful. And *fast*. Same for Frank and David. We develop the specs, we wow the money men, we get the green light to go to prototype.

"Another year. You'd think three ambitious, egotistical guys would grow to hate each other, but it was quite the opposite. I've never been closer to anybody—except for my wife, but that's different. Shared effort, grand enterprise, there's nothing like it.

"You know, in the movies you'd see lots of explosions at this point in the story, fires-in-the-lab kind of thing. We never had anything so dramatic. Just endless fizzles. Just developing independently motorized wheels involved major intellectual effort. And the power systems—how do you build a rechargeable battery that'll last years, that's still small enough? Do you have any idea where rechargeable batteries were at that time? And the whole thing's gonna be computer controlled from down here on Earth? Where do you think wireless computing was back then? God, we were brilliant."

"I don't doubt it," Cardinal said. "But you'd better tell me what went wrong."

Babstock reached for the whiskey and poured some into his glass. He took a sip and said, "LARS."

"The Arctic research station?"

"It's a Mars analogue site on Axel Heiberg. The ideal spot would have been the Haughton Crater station on Devon Island, but NASA had that all booked up for themselves.

"Keith managed to book us a slot at LARS to test our prototype. To tell you the truth, none of us had any idea just how far north that place was. A lot of people don't realize this country is as tall as it is wide. We're talking twenty-five hundred miles. It's not as glamorous as Haughton—it's only a research and sleep hut and a couple of Parcoll tents and not much else—but we were excited as hell.

"The day we arrived, another team was leaving. They'd been testing spacesuits, I think, so we had the place to ourselves. Let me tell you, the High Arctic is not for everyone. Some people, they get a taste of it, they're totally addicted, they're home. But most people are going to find it unsettling to say the least, and others have to be flown right out. Basically, all your moorings are gone.

"We'd already had lots of test runs in Toronto, but in order to make an impact the rover had to work on hard terrain, cold terrain. This was it. There would be no more money, no going back to the drawing board. It was the proverbial throw of the dice—either we'd win, and win big, or we'd be four guys looking for work.

"The plan was to test Rocky—the prototype was called Rocky—on the various types of terrain up there. Rock, snow, gravel, ice. The three most important features were the camera, manoeuvrability and response to command. Obviously, response to command is the most important, otherwise what you have is a paperweight.

"We had set up a series of four tests, and I had put together a logging algorithm that would record what commands were input and where Rocky went as a result."

"How did you control it?" Cardinal asked. "A joystick?"

"No, no, no. This is not a toy we're talking about. Every move had to be done by keystroke. It's the same now. So we take a deep breath and send Rocky off on Mission One. A simple go there, turn left, turn right, pan up, pan down, make a circle, come back. There was no manoeuvrable arm at that point.

"Worked like a charm. This was pretty flat terrain, but it did involve several different surfaces. Let me tell you, there was much rejoicing at the camp that day. So far, so good. Next mission, we send it in a different direction. Pretty much the same sequence of commands, but the terrain was more challenging—a few hills involved—and we left it sitting out in the elements for twenty-four hours. You know what cold can do to batteries. I can tell you, David was sweating through that one.

"Again, went off like clockwork. We were gods, John. Gods. Mission Three was the toughest yet. We knew this one was likely to fail. There was twenty-four-hour sunshine, of course, and aside from slush, which we did not want to mess with, there were areas where the permafrost had melted and the surface was mushy at best. Idea was to test the independent wheel motors and range of motion.

"Well, it didn't take long for Rocky to bog down. But he came out of it better than any of us expected. Keep in mind, we can't see those wheels back at the shack—we can only see what Rocky sees, and the camera couldn't pan down to that angle, not back then. But the rpm readouts told us which wheels were stuck, and I could turn them and try again. It was mostly another triumph. We got him out of several jams and we knew we had a winner—even when we got him stuck in some foot-deep muck and had to go retrieve him. We were totally high by then.

"Unfortunately, we still had Mission Four. We decided to make this one relatively easy. We sent Rocky off in a westerly direction. We wanted him to travel down this long, slow hill, stopping for a video survey every now and then. Then he was to shut down for three nights and we would leave him just sitting there and start him up on the fourth morning. We had plotted out a fairly easy route back to camp on the fourth day.

"It wasn't cold, really, by Arctic standards, maybe two degrees C. But needless to say, it was a pretty tense few days. Finally the time comes, I fire up the programme, and . . . nothing. We couldn't raise him. There was a lot of solar activity that week, unbelievable. There was some storm activity off the western shore as well, but it wasn't hitting us, and anyway, it's not storms that screw up radio communications, it's solar activity.

"Rocky had a beacon on him and we couldn't even pick up the signal from that, but of course we knew where he had shut down. So we pull on our gear and head out toward his last known address, a few kilometres west. We hike for an hour, get to the spot, Rocky's not there. We have no clue where he is. The terrain is shale, no tracks. Very bad news.

"It didn't take long to narrow down the possibilities. Discounting human or animal interference, it was very unlikely and probably impossible that Rocky had gone in any direction other than due west. The question was, how far? How long? Depending on when he started up after we shut him down, he could theoretically be a hundred and fifty kilometres away.

"But that wasn't truly possible—Heiberg's not that big. Anyway, he would run into trouble with the first rocky outcropping, the first hummock, anything resembling a pothole. But the four of us hopped on a couple of all-terrain vehicles and headed west. Couldn't use snowmobiles because half the island was snow-free, depending whether you were windward or not.

"Our biggest fear was maybe he'd driven himself right into open water. At the very least, we expected to find him face down in a gully."

"Surely it would crash into trees or something," Cardinal said.

"No trees, John. This is a thousand miles above the treeline—anything taller than six inches is an animal. And there aren't too many of those either. Lack of trees worked in our favour, of course. It didn't take too long to find Rocky, and it turned out we'd named him exactly right. He'd got himself into a rocky area and got his front left wheel caught and run his batteries down to nothing.

"We were all relieved, but especially David and Frank, because electrical and mechanical had obviously performed fine. Clearly the issue was going to be software. Why did the little bastard not shut down? Why did he go rogue? In exactly two weeks we had to give our presentation and test data to NASA. There was no way they were going to be interested in a rover with a mind of its own. As we saw it, if this came out, it was a game-ender."

"I don't understand," Cardinal said. "It had performed so well up to that point, I would have thought you had a star on your hands."

"We were poised on the brink of massive success or massive failure—no middle ground. So by the time we found Rocky, we were in total panic mode. We couldn't budge the rocks around him. So David and I go up to the top of this outcropping with some rope to get some loft into the configuration. We were up there, I don't know, twenty minutes maybe, and I'm yelling things down to Keith and Frank, who are trying to rig the rope around Rocky so it doesn't pull his arm or his head off.

"Suddenly David says, 'Look!' I turn around and there's a flare in the sky. It's quite far off, four, maybe five kilometres. There's no denying it. The thing is there, burning bright green, arcing down toward the north.

"'They can't be signalling us, can they?' David says.

"'It's probably the sovereignty patrol running some kind of manoeuvre. Or it could be the RCMP practising rescue stuff,' I said.

"David had pulled out his binoculars and was staring out into this incredibly bleak landscape with them. 'Really? That what you think it is? That's your considered opinion?' David talked like a cowboy even back then.

"'Well, who the hell else is it gonna be? There's nothing else on this island.' You have to understand, John, we hadn't heard of Drift Station Arcosaur at that point. No one had.

"'Maybe it's someone lost. Maybe some party's trying to chase off a hungry ursine.'

"Well, of course we both knew you wouldn't fire a flare into the sky to scare a bear. The camp advisers had drilled us in all that stuff before we even set foot up there. You'd aim it at his feet or just over his head. I could hear in David's voice that he wanted to believe we were not needed, that there was no one in distress. So I said again that it's probably the sovereignty patrol and we'd better get Rocky back to camp or we were all of us staring into the face of complete failure.

"Then David says he sees someone. A man. I ask what he's doing, and he says it looks like he's hiking, climbing the rocks. He hands me the binoculars and I take a look. I saw him, John.

"You're the first person I've ever told. Twenty years now, all four of us have kept it secret. When we got back to camp, we all swore we would never so much as mention it, not even to our wives. It poisoned our friendship. We had been working together for years, fresh out of school to the edge of success, but after we got back home and heard that people had actually died, that there were people in serious trouble, well, we couldn't stand to look at each other, couldn't stand to be with anyone who knew what we had done—or not done. We decided we were all free to exploit our separate patents and went our separate ways. I called David the other day when his wife was found, and that was the first time we'd spoken in more than twenty years.

"I saw a man through those binoculars. He was hardly more than a blurry speck. Could have been part of the patrol, could have been anything. I saw him stumble, but he got up quickly and then he waved. Waved a cloth or something. That's the thing I saw that I have not been able to unsee. Not for twenty years. He was signalling us, John. I'm filled with shame as I say it. He was signalling us.

"Before I could say anything, David had called the other two to come up. The four of us had a powwow. David told them we'd seen a flare, we could see a man who seemed to be hiking, but we weren't sure if it was someone who needed help or if it was nothing. We kept coming back to the sovereignty patrol. It had to be them.

"The full responsibility, the blame, lies with me. I didn't tell the others I'd seen the man waving at us. I don't know to this day if David saw him do that. If he did, he kept it to himself. But the other two definitely didn't. And we couldn't find the man again in the binoculars.

"None of us were seasoned adventurers, but we all knew you don't turn your back on someone possibly in distress, not in those latitudes.

"We weighed the options, and it came down to this: no one knew we had been there and it had to stay that way. It would have come out why, that we had a malfunctioning robot, and it would have doomed Rocky and his descendants to oblivion—and us as well. Our little day trip had to be excised from the record if we were to have any future at all.

"It was just the patrol, we told ourselves. Just an exercise. Although I'm sure the others did the same as me later on, and looked up where the sovereignty patrol had been. It had passed Axel Heiberg a month earlier and by now had to be near the northern tip of Ellesmere.

"We did the wrong thing, John. *I* did the wrong thing. We turned our backs on a man in distress, and now that man has come to balance the account. He has my daughter, John. He's the one who has my daughter."

Cardinal reached into his pocket and pulled out his notebook and started flipping through it. "Which parallel did you say you were at?"

"We were at seventy-nine degrees north. Ninety north is the pole."

"Take a look at these." Cardinal showed him the page with his various arrangements of the numbers found at the crime scenes. "What do they mean to you?"

"None of these are right," Babstock said. "Hand me your pen." He took Cardinal's pen in his manicured fingers and copied out the figures in a different order. Then he tapped the page with the tip of the pen and read them aloud. "79 degrees, 25 minutes north, 95 degrees west. Add a few minutes west and you have the coordinates of our location. That's where we found Rocky, and where we saw that man."

21

CARDINAL STARTED THE CAR, AND while waiting for it to warm up he checked his phone. North Slave Correctional had sent the information he had requested. He forwarded it to Chouinard and Drexler, then phoned them both.

"And you think he's headed up there?" Drexler said. "To the exact spot where it happened?"

"Why else would he leave those numbers at the scene? He knows how to fly a plane, and I think he gave us the coordinates so we could attempt to mount a rescue—a rescue that would arrive too late."

"All right. I'll call the Horsemen. They've got outposts way the hell up there. Somewhere."

"We need people watching private airfields—the smaller the better. He's travelling with a person who's unconscious. He's going to avoid security as much as possible."

Cardinal drove over to Parliament Street and down to King, cursing streetcars the whole way. Then he had to fight a gauntlet of one-way streets, mostly grey with big-city snow, to find the address he was looking for. He parked on a filthy slag heap of old snow and walked up the front path of a red brick townhouse. In the front window, red curtains framed a grand piano.

Alison Durie was slim and elegant and not happy to be visited by an out-of-town detective. She looked about fifty-five—but still with a bloom in her cheeks and something regal about the way she carried herself, an easy grace. There was no wedding ring.

Cardinal asked if he could come in and ask a few questions.

"No, you may not. What's this about?"

"Maybe you could just tell me if you've seen your brother recently."

"I don't mean to be rude, but why should I answer that question?"

"He's wanted for questioning in connection with a major crime."

"Rubbish. What crime?"

"I'm sure you've read about the abduction and murder of Marjorie Flint and Laura Lacroix."

Ms. Durie laughed. "That's so preposterous I don't even have any response to it. Really, you have to find something else to do with your time, Detective."

"The man we're looking for has a limp, and probably a prosthetic hand."

The regal facade faltered. Alison Durie's slender, ringless hand levitated toward her throat, pale fingers touching her collar. "Even if he was the murderous creature you take him for, why would he do these things? How could he? Why? Many people limp, and my brother has no connection to these women." She started to close the door.

"Ms. Durie, wait. Did he ever talk to you about what took place up north? At the drift station?"

"Karson would never kill anyone. And if you think he would ever harm a woman, you're grotesquely mistaken. When he first came here after his release from prison, our mother was living out the last months of her life. He could not have been more attentive, more tender. Even two decades in prison had failed to destroy that. In any case, I haven't seen him for at least two months now, and I've no idea where he is."

"I think you do. Tell me where to find him. If he's innocent, that shouldn't be hard to prove."

"How dare you say that? We have no reason whatsoever to trust the justice system. My brother served eighteen years and was denied parole repeatedly. Repeatedly. Well, now he's out, he's a free man, and it's nobody's business—not yours, not anybody's—where he might be."

"He was denied parole because he showed no remorse."

"He showed no remorse because he was innocent. He was innocent then and he's innocent now."

She closed the door and Cardinal stood there staring at it. He reached into his jacket and took out a business card and put it through the mail slot.

~

When she woke up again, Hayley had the idea that she was somewhere near a place that sold motorcycles. Every ten minutes or so, from somewhere in the distance, there would come that ragged, ripping sound of an inadequately muffled engine.

She was lying on her back on a sofa, too tired and dazed to move. She tried to turn her head, but a rush of nausea stopped her. The ceiling, country pine, was awash with light. It was light of a very particular softness combined with brightness, and it took her a while to register what it reminded her of. The ski chalet at Collingwood. The light was coming from snow. The motorcycles must be snowmobiles. She must be somewhere up north, perhaps near a lake, with the sunlight bouncing off the snow and filling this room.

The terror came back as the drug, whatever it was, wore off. She could turn her head now. The man limped by her, shirtless, with a makeshift bandage around his rib cage. He sat down with a grunt of pain. After a while his breathing became heavy and slow. Sleeping.

Her wrists, underneath her, were fastened together. Ankles too. The moment she worked at the bonds, a bolt of pain shot through her. Her wrists were already torn from trying to escape. She remembered the truck. She remembered the needle. Then nothing.

The man woke up and rose from his chair with a gasp. Had he been shot? Could that have happened without her being aware of it? She listened to him moving about the house, or cottage. A fridge opening. A cupboard. Running water. And then the smell of toast, the clack of the toaster, the rasp of a knife spreading butter or jam. She had the feeling he knew his way around this cottage, this house.

Hayley wasn't sure if he could see her from wherever he stood at the moment. She worked at the gag with her tongue, strained her neck to stretch the fabric, worked at it again. It was the only thing that felt any looser.

Sound of a chair scraping. Something falling to the floor. A curse. Then footsteps and the sound of a bathroom cabinet opening. The rattle of a pill bottle, then water running.

She strained at the gag, lifted her head and turned her neck from side to side, forcing down nausea. Working at the fabric with her tongue, her chin, her jaw, she managed to get the gag out of her mouth. It was now tight against her lower lip. She would be able to scream.

A scream would likely go unheard. It would also bring what? The needle—or perhaps worse. She raised her head to look around. Large chalet-type room. Books everywhere. A baby grand piano.

The man came back, limping, slow. He came close, looking down at her. His eyes catching her gaze, moving to the gag. He leaned toward her, reaching for it.

Hayley shook her head. "Please. No."

His eyes assessing her, the short chain of her potential moves, his face hawkish, weathered. A professor, perhaps. A judge. The eyes closed and the face paled, a hand clutching at the bandage. His limp worse as he moved to an armchair and sat down again, this time silently.

Hayley gave it a few seconds. Then, "Is this your house?"

The words hung in the air, a neon sign with no connection to the human relationship in this room: victim and murderer. They might have been here for social reasons, two strangers at a party. Hayley kept her eyes on the ceiling. He might be looking at her, he might be asleep.

"So many books. I'm wondering if they're all yours, but a lot of them look old. I'm thinking maybe they belonged to your family, your parents, I don't know."

There was no response from across the room. A faint rustle as he changed his position, perhaps turned his head to look at her, or out the window. She was still afraid to look. A direct gaze might be too much, the shout that triggers the avalanche.

"Books have always been important to me. I may be the last person to avoid the social media sink. It's a problem for me sometimes. Students want you to be on Facebook, Twitter, but e-mail's enough. It's too much, in fact. Half my students seem to have no concept of a private world, and that seems sad to me, but maybe I'm just an introvert."

Hayley held her breath. If he was as intelligent as he looked, he would realize what she was trying to do. Poor little girl trying to make herself into a person, something harder to kill than a creature you know nothing about. But persons, people, full human beings, were exactly what this man had made it his business to kill.

She forced herself to turn her head and look at him. He was seated in an armchair across the room, at an angle to her. His hands gripped the arms of the chair and he sat erect, something Egyptian about the posture. His eyes were open—she saw him blink—but he wasn't looking at her. The expression on the sharp features—if it was in fact expression and not its absence—was one of incalculable weariness.

"I don't know anything about you—and maybe it'll sound like dime-store psychology or obvious self-interest—but it seems clear that something terrible has happened to you. Maybe recently? Maybe a long time ago, I don't know, but something terrible." She thought of a creature on the edge of extinction, the last *T. rex* on earth, gasping out its final breaths in a jungle sheathed in ice.

No response.

"My parents had a lot of books too—still do. My father, anyway. He's a scientist, but he never seemed to want me to be one, really. He always encouraged me to do artsy things. I used to write the most terrible poems and he would pin them up—even the depressing ones when I got into a Sylvia Plath phase, which is pretty funny when you think of it.

"Poetry is so powerful you'd think you could tell from someone's face if they read it or not. Respond to it. But I look at you and I have no clue. Do you read poetry? Have you ever?"

He turned his face toward the window, sharp features outlined against that brightness.

Hayley lifted her ankles and swung herself up into a seated position. The room tilted and lurched and the urge to vomit was strong.

Her moving got his attention, but he didn't get up.

"I read poetry," Hayley continued. "I have a father. I was a little girl at one time, then a teenager. Now I'm a teacher. In other words, you could say, I'm nothing special. But that's the thing about being human, right? You're not required to be special. You're only required to be human."

She talked on. The thought took hold that she would not die as long as she was talking. It was a common myth: the dancer who must keep dancing, the storyteller who must keep spinning tales, to keep fate at bay.

"I read poetry," she said again. "I tried to write it. I try to teach it, or at least the appreciation of it. I want to be a professor. I'd like to get married someday. At this moment, of course, all I want is to stay alive. Will you tell me your name?"

He sighed, and shifted his weight a little in his chair, but did not look at her.

"May I know who has imprisoned me, and why? No? I want to write a book. I'd like to write about Leonard Cohen. I would talk about Catullus and Villon, the Book of Psalms, poetry as song. But scholarly circles aren't so big on him. He's too easy and too popular. Atwood would be better. She's kind of one of them, one of us, an academic even, though she's not at a university. Of course, if I write about either of them, every English department in the United States will shut their doors on me forever after. Canadian literature is not a hot topic in New York or Chicago. But what can I do, I love poetry, and it's the only thing I know anything about.

"Except now I know how it feels to be terrified."

The man remained in his chair like an empty garment. Maybe begging was the best gambit, maybe get down on my knees and promise whatever sex or money or worship he wants. She could never have guessed, before this moment, the magnitude of her desire to live. It shrieked and shrieked in the room and yet the man did not hear it, seemed unaware of it—in no particular rush to harm, yet free of any desire to spare her little life. She was nothing more than any mosquito she'd ever swatted, any spider she'd ever drowned, tiny legs frantic as it circled the drain.

A sob escaped her. The last thing she wanted.

When his voice came, it was as dry as wind, wind through dry grass. He tilted his head back and closed his eyes. "Poetry. No. I don't read poetry . . ."

Hayley choked back her sobs, caught her breath, held it.

". . . but I knew someone. A long time ago. Someone who did."

~

Things happened relatively fast once Delorme got back to Algonquin Bay. Loach was on the phone when she walked into the station, but he hung up right away and pointed at her. "You! I want to talk to you right now."

"Good idea," Delorme said. "Why don't we go in here." She reached in and switched on the lights in the meeting room. "I'll be right back."

She went and tapped on Chouinard's door and he followed her across the squad room, baying the whole way. Delorme said nothing. She held the meeting room door open for him and closed it behind him, and then there were two of them baying at her. She held up a DVD, and they both quieted down as she inserted it into the player and switched on the TV monitor.

"What the hell are you up to?" Loach wanted to know. "I'm trying to run a major investigation and you go totally AWOL."

Delorme spoke to Chouinard. "I'm sorry, D.S. I know I called in sick, but I was actually working on the investigation. In Toronto."

"And who told you to go down to Toronto?"

"Cardinal," Loach said. "I know what's going on. I have eyes."

"It's ears you need right now," Delorme said. "You have to listen closely."

The image came up on the screen. The crowded pub, and one inebriated detective climbing up on a stool.

"That's Chuck Rakov," Loach said. "What the hell are you doing with a video of Chuck Rakov?"

"Who the hell is he?" Chouinard said.

"One of the worst cops I ever worked with. Took a while, but I finally managed to get that bastard gone."

Delorme had paused the video. "May I go on?"

Chouinard nodded. She hit Play, and Rakov went into his Loach impersonation.

"Hilarious," Loach said, "but I don't have time for this shit." He got up and reached for the monitor.

"Let it play," Chouinard said.

"Are you serious? Chuck Rakov is and was a total drunk."

"That's not the good part," Delorme said. "The good part's coming up."

On screen, Rakov went into his French-Canadian accent. Even drunk, he had mastered the mimic's art of instant transformation. The Toronto cop's body was possessed by the spirit—and accent—of a thorough Québécois.

"Oh, Jesus," Chouinard said. "Tell me this isn't happening. Tell me this is not the guy we've been throwing out a dragnet for."

"Wait a second," Loach said. "We don't know it's him who called. Rakov's a total asshole."

"An asshole who hates you," Delorme said. "An asshole you got fired. An asshole the Toronto police have now charged with obstruction of justice and interfering with an investigation. I gave them your recording—they've already done the voice print."

"Bullshit," Loach said. He appealed to Chouinard. "She's just trying to undermine me. It's ridiculous. I'm citing her for insubordination, for conduct unbecoming, for misusing police funds, for—"

"Go home," Chouinard said. "You're not citing anybody."

"No. This is wrong." Loach shook his head. "This is so, so wrong."

Chouinard looked over at Delorme. "Toronto Forensics confirms the voice?"

"It's definitely Rakov."

"You're off the case, Loach. Go home."

Loach stood up. "You're both wrong. I did the right thing. I made the right decision. Given what we had to work with at the time, I made the right decision."

"Go *home*."

~

After he'd put his business card through the letter slot of Alison Durie's door, Cardinal sat in his car and tried to decide what would be his next step. It seemed unlikely that the all-units would result in a street cop or a highway patrol pulling over exactly the right van. It would be the OPP, if anybody. If Durie was planning to complete his revenge on that Arctic island, he had to be headed for an airfield.

He opened his briefcase on the seat beside him and took out a photograph of Hayley Babstock. Twenty-seven or twenty-eight, a sweet age for a woman. Still enough of the student-age naïveté to be cute, but there was a confidence in those blue eyes as well. She would be a person with a good idea of her own capabilities. He took out his pen and wrote on the back of the photograph, *This is Hayley Babstock. She is a teacher—and also the daughter of someone your brother has reason to hate.* He got out of the car and went back up the steps to Alison Durie's house and pushed the photograph through the slot.

His phone rang as he was getting back into the car.

"Drexler here. Are you a hunter, by any chance?"

"No."

"I'm standing by the side of a road just north of King City, watching two guys rig a sling hoist under a dead moose. It wasn't shot, though. It was hit by a white van."

"What's going on? Is the girl okay?"

"She's not here. Neither is Karson Durie."

"Send me a picture of the van on my phone. Is there a logo on the side?"

"I'm sending it now. Jesus, you should see the antlers on this thing—they're winching him out of the windshield. Must weigh fifteen hundred pounds. I gotta say, I am often struck by the role of sheer luck in the lives of criminals—not to mention the lives of their victims.

"Mr. Perpetrator—heading for an airfield five kilometres from here, where it turns out he has reserved a Twin Otter under an assumed name—has the bad luck to hit a moose. But lo, the wheel turns again, and he has the good luck to have a good Samaritan show up. This is bad luck for Mr. Samaritan, who has stopped his truck to help. ''Preciate it—please accept my .45-calibre thank-you card.' The man is dead. He's got two kids under the age of twelve and a wife gonna be wondering why he doesn't answer his cell."

"We're sure it was Durie."

"Well, there's no prints from the gloved one, but this Babstock kid is one smart cookie. She left her fingerprints inside—they're all over the back. Perfect prints, like she pressed 'em and rolled 'em just for us."

"Do we know what he's driving now?"

"Our Samaritan's vehicle was a black Dodge Laramie."

"Should be easy enough to spot," Cardinal said.

"Should be. And was. OPP found it by the highway about forty miles up the 400, and now we have no clue what he's driving. And no clue where he's heading. At this point the man is an open case in at least three jurisdictions, and we have no idea where he is."

"Hold on, Art. I think we just got a break."

Alison Durie was crossing the street toward him.

~

Delorme couldn't wait to get out of the office again after her meeting with Loach and Chouinard. She could still hear them shouting at each other as she headed out the door. She drove up to the hospital and visited with Miranda Heap, who had regained consciousness. Her lips were swollen and she was groggy from the drugs, but her mind seemed perfectly clear. Perfectly clear, and perfectly made up. Did you listen to the phone messages? And you know who it is. Good. Did you get the receipts too? The photograph? Good. Son of a bitch thinks he's going to be a judge . . .

Delorme paid another visit to her house and found, as Miranda had expected, that Garth Romney had left another message. *Darlene has been such a bad girl, my darling . . .*

"Yes," Delorme said, "you have."

Then she went back to the station and made copies of everything.

She sat across from Chouinard in his office as he leafed, grim-faced, through the receipts, shaking his head at what he was hearing through his headphones. Finally he took them off and muttered, "Garth, Garth, Garth . . . Misuse of funds, dereliction of duty . . ."

"Don't forget assault."

"Assault. Jesus. Tell me something, Sergeant Delorme. Tell me how it is that such seemingly intelligent people manage to get themselves into so much trouble."

"I'd like to take this to Crown Attorney Hartman right away."

"No, no. This is far too hot for the local. We take it to Sudbury, to the regional crown."

"But that'll take so long."

"No, it won't. Believe me, they'll want this cleaned up fast—before Romney is actually installed as a judge. This is out of our hands, as far as jurisdiction goes—they'll want the OPP, or actually, probably Toronto police to handle the investigation."

"But the work's all done."

"I know. You've done it all *for* them. And now we know why Priest was never prosecuted."

She told him about her interview with Fritz Reicher.

"He's ready to testify?"

"Definitely. I'd like to arrest Priest as soon as possible. Why not tonight?"

"Hold on now. It won't be tonight. Order of business is we get the regional crown on board first. He's going to want to see—and hear—everything we have. He'll want to line up an outside investigator, and *then* he'll lower the boom."

Delorme got up to leave. As she was opening the office door, Chouinard pounded his fist on the desk. "*Damn.*"

"What, D.S.?"

"This is *good*, eh? This is *good*. This is what we get into this business for, isn't it."

"I'd say so."

He pounded the desk again. "Fantastic. Totally fucking fantastic—and you know I never swear."

"Absolutely, D.S. I've always admired that about you."

~

"After I sent you away so rudely," Alison Durie said, "I went to look at some things my brother left behind. But I need to tell you a bit about him before I show you."

Cardinal was sitting at her kitchen table, where a pot of tea was steeping. He studied her face. Wide brow, aristocratic neck, the regal manner undone by unbearable sadness.

"I flew to Yellowknife when Karson was released and brought him back here with me. He stayed for about six months."

"How did he spend his time? Did he have a job?"

She shook her head. "My father left us some money. Karson's share collected interest over the years. It generates enough income that he doesn't have to take a job—provided he's careful. He's not a man who requires a lot of material things."

As she spoke of her brother, she forgot about the tea and cups and spoons between them.

"He spent most of his days at the library—the university library. It broke my heart the first day he came home from an afternoon there. The joy on his face. Karson is not an effusive man, but he positively jabbered at me about advances in his field. He went back every day, got himself access to their online journals, and I saw—for a moment, anyway—something like happiness in his eyes. I know he also went because he didn't want to be a burden to me—which was silly, because he was very helpful looking after our mother. But I'm sure he wanted to be out of my hair. And the happiness was soon gone. Prison—or perhaps not prison so much as injustice—took that capacity from him."

"I'm surprised he didn't get his own place, rent an apartment."

"My brother is a man who is capable of walking across Ellesmere Island dragging a two-hundred-pound sled. Alone. He has lived entire winters with Russians, Laplanders and Inuit in places that are barely on the map and have numbers for names. He has been stranded for weeks in Good Friday Bay, saved an Inuit hunter on the pack ice of the Beaufort Sea. But eighteen years in prison? Eighteen *years*, Detective. Just going out on the street was disorienting. He was like a man afraid of heights stepping out onto a ledge forty floors up. He had to walk next to walls, step into doorways.

"The distances, the scale of things, were too much. Can you imagine? This is a man who has walked on icebergs the size of Manhattan. But after twenty years in prison he had to be accompanied everywhere. He needed time to find his feet, and he was intelligent enough to know it."

"That must have been hard for you."

"Not at all. Karson is three years older than me. I grew up absolutely adoring him. Even as a teenager, he absorbed knowledge the way the rest of us absorb pop songs. He used to speak of relativity, nuclear fission, differential calculus the way our contemporaries might speak of Led Zeppelin or the latest sitcom. That's probably why I went into the arts—music—to avoid competing with him."

Cardinal let her talk a little more. Then he said, "You mentioned some things you wanted to show me."

"Yes. When you first appeared, I didn't really listen to you. I couldn't really hear you. I didn't *want* to hear you. But I saw you waiting out there and I looked at the girl's picture, and . . . Karson left some things. Nothing much—he's always travelled light and actually doesn't own very much—but he left a small box of things in the garage."

"I need to see it."

"Tell me truly, Detective—are you absolutely sure it's Karson you want?"

Cardinal pulled out his cellphone and opened the photo Drexler had sent. He held it out for her to see. "Do you recognize the van?"

"Oh, dear God."

"The girl's fingerprints are all over the interior. It appears that both of them got away, but we don't know in what vehicle and we don't know where he's headed. I need to see his things."

"Yes, of course you do. It's this way."

She got up and put on a coat and boots and they went out the back door and through a small garden to a garage. It was brightly lit with fluorescent lights. There were gardening tools, a workbench and shelves along one wall. Oil stains on the floor spoke of a vehicle, but there was none there.

"I never come out here in winter—don't own a car—but I let one of the neighbours use it. He used to own a small business until he had a heart attack a few years ago. I don't know why he never sold the van. Anyway, a few weeks ago his son told me it was missing and asked if I had seen anyone in the garage. It didn't occur to me that Karson might have taken it."

"What kind of business?"

"A flower shop. You could still make out the logo on the van. But what I really wanted to show you . . ."

She pointed to the shelves along the back wall, a plastic storage container.

Cardinal prised the lid off the container and set it aside. Shirts, jeans, neatly folded. A pair of shoes. On top of these, several notebooks, the three-hole kind that schoolchildren use, with the map of Canada on the front and a blank class schedule on the back.

"I think it's the blue one you'll want first. Careful—the staples have been removed. Prison protocol, one assumes."

Cardinal opened the blue notebook. The handwriting neat, controlled, easy to read. He thumbed through the pages.

I dreamed I had to climb a glass mountain that glittered in the glare of a savage sun. I was in the company of a man and woman who claimed to know the way but did not . . . when I woke in the darkness, my eyes were wet as if I had been crying.

"I just noticed something else."

Cardinal looked up. She was contemplating the far wall of the garage.

"My mother—I told you she was living here the last few months of her life? She was in a wheelchair much of the time. She had a motorized one in the house, but she also had one of the basic push models. It was folded up and stored out here." She pointed a slim finger at the garage wall. "And now it's gone."

22

DELORME PULLED BACK THE GLASS shower door, thought about it for a moment, then closed it again. Instead, she went to the bathtub and put the plug in and turned on the water. She knelt there feeling the water until the mix of hot and cold was right.

She went into the bedroom and pulled the curtains and took off her clothes. For a while she sat on the edge of the bed listening to the water run in the other room. Now that she was on the bed, she thought maybe she should skip the bath and just get in between the sheets. You wouldn't sleep, she told herself. You'd just lie there running the whole day over and over again in your head.

She went back to the bathroom and poured a capful of foamy stuff into the water and swirled it around. She stood in front of the mirror to put her hair up and secured it with a headband, then put her left foot into the tub. Just hot enough to sting. She turned the cold on and swirled the foamy water around with her foot for a minute. Remembering the light, she stretched and reached for the wall switch and flicked on the night light near the sink.

As she lowered herself into it, the hot water rose over her up to chest level. She could see half of her reflection in the shower enclosure, and beyond that the open bathroom door. She soaked a washcloth and squeezed the water out, then lay back, covering her eyes with the folded cloth. Sound of water rattling into the overflow drain. She sank down so that her shoulders were submerged.

The steam felt good in her lungs and she breathed it in deeply, letting it out with a sigh. She lay there for a while commanding her muscles to relax, but she didn't really believe that kind of thing worked and gave it up after a while. The water began to cool and she sat up to turn on more hot.

While it was running, she thought she heard a floorboard creak, and turned the water off again. She sat listening, hand on the tap, water dripping. Clearly the hot bath thing wasn't an instant cure for tension. She soaped up the washcloth and went over her entire body, toes to shoulders, before lying back again for one last soak. She closed her eyes and the image of her bed, the cool sheets, drifted into her mind.

Another sound. Movement of some kind, not quite identifiable. Silently, she submerged her hands to stop any dripping sounds and listened. Her back was to the door, but the entire dark rectangle was reflected in the shower enclosure. The human instinct was to lie still, to wait for danger to pass, no matter how fast the heart might pump, and it was going full tilt already. Her bathrobe hung from the hook on the back of the open door.

She pictured rushing to the bedroom, the dresser, the gun. Fuck the bathrobe. On three, she told herself. One, two . . .

But then he was in the doorway. Leonard Priest—every toned, buff inch of him was standing in her bathroom doorway—wearing absolutely nothing.

"Christ," he said to her reflection. "I thought you'd never get undressed."

Delorme watched his reflection as he came into the bathroom. He stood near the tub, penis just above her head level, and folded his arms.

"Little de-stressing in the tub? Little home spa routine? Very nice. Very sexy."

Delorme considered a swift punch to the balls. He was just out of reach.

"You're scared, sweetheart. I can see it in your face. But a little bit of adrenalin at the right time can make just that bit of difference, turn a ho-hum encounter into something truly memorable. What are you thinking right now? What images are going through that wicked little mind of yours?"

"You mean other than the image of you driving over here in the middle of winter stark naked?"

"Taxi. Fully clothed."

"Or the image of you jimmying my back door?"

"Wax impression. When you came for dinner. Little trick I learned in Borstal. But we can discuss *your* back door if you like." He got down on his haunches so he was at eye level, looking at her. "I know you, Lise. Maybe better than you know yourself. Look at that—I can see your heartbeat in the foam. Amazing."

"I'll tell you what I find amazing, Leonard. I find it amazing that you can break into a cop's house—a cop who suspects you of murder—and wait in the basement with no clothes on until she comes home. What's truly amazing is that you can do all this and yet have no clue that you have a serious problem."

"No problem."

"You've never heard of addiction, I guess."

"Sex is not a drug. It's natural."

"You take a serious risk of getting shot and you don't consider it a problem?"

"Like I say, Lise—adrenalin. Part of the fun."

"Uh-huh. So it's not just the women who like to be scared."

"Definitely not."

In one swift motion, Delorme grabbed the sides of the tub and pulled herself up.

Priest stood up and fell back a step. "Whoa. Pussy alert."

"Hand me that towel."

"Very nice indeed."

Delorme reached past him and grabbed the towel. "Give me a minute."

"I'm not leaving this house until we finish what we've started. What *you've* started, to be brutally frank."

"Leonard."

"All right. But I'm taking this." He unhooked her bathrobe from the back of the door.

"Give me the bathrobe."

"Nope. Sorry."

"You're really asking for it, aren't you."

"Ooh, yeah." He held the robe out and twitched it a couple of times, toreador-style.

"Trying to provoke my dark side."

"I got news for you, honey. You're *all* dark side."

He left the room without closing the door, and a moment later the bedsprings creaked with his weight.

Delorme dried herself quickly. She wrapped the towel around her waist, had a second thought and took it off. She went into the bedroom, where Priest was sitting on the edge of the bed with her Beretta in his hands.

He looked up and said, "What a body. It's enough to make me believe in God."

Delorme put her hand out. "Give me that."

He raised the automatic in both hands and pointed it at her. "What if I said no?"

"Two things. First, I'll disarm you, which will be very unpleasant. Second, you won't get laid."

"Lots of women talk tough."

"It's something I know about myself. I would literally rather die."

"Really? Death? Death rather than have sex with me?"

"Rather than be forced." Delorme reached and gripped the barrel of the Beretta, not hard. The safety was on, but still.

"Ooh, you're very forward." He pulled the gun back. "Tell you what. Let's just put it over here." He swung his legs up and rolled away from her across the bed. He reached up and put the gun on the windowsill behind the curtain. Then he lay on his side and patted the bed beside him.

Delorme put one knee on the bed and sat on the edge, facing him at an angle.

He reached and touched her, resting his index finger on her knee. "I found your handcuffs too."

"I figured."

"They're under the pillow. Have you ever worn them for fun?"

"They had us put them on at the academy. So we'd know what they felt like. The tightness, et cetera."

"Did you enjoy it?"

"The context wasn't conducive."

"But you might."

Delorme took his hand and held it in both her palms. It was very cold. "Leonard, you know what I think?"

"No. What do you think?"

"I think you're the one who likes to be scared."

"It's true you make me a little nervous."

"So I see. I think I know what to do about that." She rubbed his palm with her thumb. "Warm you up a little."

"Oh yeah?"

She got up on both knees, giving him the full view.

"Oh my," he said. "Oh yes."

He started to slide his hand from between her palms. Delorme gripped tight and twisted.

"Jesus!"

He was face down now, Delorme on top with his wrist at the back of his neck.

"Fucking hell!" He reached back, flailing at her with his other hand. "Ease off!"

"I haven't even started yet. Did you go through my closet?"

"What? No."

She jerked his arm up.

"Yes! Yes!"

"Oh, you found the toys, then."

"What toys? There weren't any toys."

"The blue case. On the shelf. I've got some things in there that'll get your attention, Leonard. Some things that'll teach you respect for the law. But first I think I'd like to see you in a stress position. Give me the handcuffs, Leonard."

"Not bloody likely."

"Was that a no, prisoner?"

She jerked his arm, and he pulled the handcuffs out with his other hand. She knelt on his pinioned arm and snapped the cuff on the other wrist, looping the chain through the bars of the headboard.

"I can feel your pussy hair on my—"

She slapped him hard across the back of the head. "Other hand. You're not going to give me trouble, are you? Are you going to give me trouble?"

"Never. Wouldn't dream of it."

She loosened her grip a little. "Because the faster I get you cuffed to this bed, the faster I'm going to dig out those toys and really go to work."

"God, I knew you'd be good at this."

"Shut up. You have a choice here, prisoner: toys or gun. Take your pick."

"Toys. No question."

"Then put your wrist in that cuff."

"No. Ow! Christ, you're a total fascist bitch, you are."

Delorme pulled his arm down and around, relieving the pressure, and he let out a gasp. She pulled the arm up to the cuff, and he offered no resistance while she snapped it on.

"Happy now?" He waggled the bracelets. "Totally at your mercy. And I have a feeling you're going to make me regret it."

"Oh, yes."

"Your implements of destruction and all."

"I may even have to involve some other officers."

"No, I'd have to draw the line at that. I think we should agree on a safety word: *lawyer*?"

"Well, if you think it will stop me. But first I want to whisper something in your ear." She leaned forward and brought her mouth close to his ear. He would feel her breath, remember the moment always. "Leonard Priest," she whispered, "I am arresting you for the murder of Régine Choquette. You have the right to remain silent. Anything you say may be used against you. You have the right to an attorney . . ."

23

Ronnie Babstock goes to work. He cannot be at home. He cannot be alone. It might be smart to let us protect you, Cardinal had said. Durie hasn't come after the other men, but you're the last on the list and he might see you as the ultimate target.

"I hope he does come for me," Babstock had told him. "I'd be glad to die if it meant Hayley would live. Christ, John, she's so young. This is a girl who's never hurt anyone."

There is plenty of work to do. The next Mars launch is less than six months away. The wheels on the latest iteration of Marti are refusing to fully retract, making a landing impossible. And the developer of the alpha-particle spectrometer can't seem to keep the specs straight. In both cases, communications between team leaders and department heads have reached a pass where only a quiet talk at the top is going to move things forward.

He can't bring himself to make the calls. His daughter's face is before him. It is an obsession he has not experienced since the year he fell in love with her mother and it was far from certain she would marry him. His mind had held her close the way his arms could not. Time was erased.

Now his daughter is before him in all her ages, from burping, crawling infant to knobby little skater girl to trampy teen in torn sweatshirts to frightening Goth poet to student and scholar and teacher. From his office on Airport Hill he can see across Algonquin Bay to the frozen bay itself, blue sky, the strange, snowless expanse of the lake. He is seeing none of it. He is seeing Hayley's face. He tries to select favourite moments: his visits to Toronto, all too infrequent, when Hayley takes him to dinner with colleagues, drags him to the AGO, even a poetry reading. His daughter the adult, the person he is still just getting to know. This person he has known all her life, suddenly a new friend.

He couldn't stand sitting there anymore, he had to be out and moving. He put on his coat and had just opened the office door when his computer made the sound of an incoming Skype call. Few people knew how to reach him directly that way.

He looked at his assistant. "Grace, did you just relay something to my Skype?"

"We haven't got anything out here."

He went back into his office and sat down.

Incoming Call From: Hayley Babstock.

Hayley didn't have a Skype account, as far as he knew. He clicked on the answer button.

An image of a newspaper clipping appeared onscreen.

"Hayley? Hayley, are you there?"

The cops had a trace on his phone lines but they wouldn't be able to trace this, not in time. He clicked Record.

The image zoomed in on the sidebar to a main article from twenty years ago. SCIENTIST PERISHES AFTER SURVIVING DRIFT STATION DISASTER. There was a photo. The young woman with her beautiful hair and shy smile. Twenty-seven. A specialist in Arctic cloud formation and energy exchange. He had never forgotten her face, though he had seen it only once, the day the story broke.

"Mr. Babstock, this is Karson Durie." There was just the voice and the clipping. The voice was polite, calm. "I wanted to make sure you knew who she was."

"Rebecca Fenn. I know who she was. She was young and beautiful and full of promise."

"Much like your daughter."

"Mr. Durie, I will do anything you ask, pay any price, give up my own life—anything—if you let my daughter live."

"There's nothing you can do. You did it many, many years ago."

"I've regretted it ever since."

"That makes no difference to me."

"Look, hate me. Hate me all you want. But not my daughter. Not Hayley. She's not someone you could possibly hate if you got to know her for even five minutes."

"I don't hate her. I don't even hate you. I'm indifferent. Just like you were. You were indifferent to a man and woman who were dying at your feet. Indifferent as the Crusoe Glacier, the Piper Ridge, the Steacey Ice Cap. It's the natural state. The remarkable thing is that there was ever in the history of mankind an instance of anyone who *wasn't* indifferent."

"I wasn't indifferent. I was greedy, selfish, stupid, ambitious, reckless, immature."

"Mid-thirties by my estimate—hardly a child."

"I know. And I won't lie to you—we saw the flare. And I know you don't ignore a flare in the Arctic. We had a lot at stake, and we made the wrong choice. It was wrong, and I am sorry for it. I've wanted to undo it for many years, but it just isn't possible. I will tell the world about it, if that will help in any way."

"It won't."

"May I see my daughter, please?"

"Of course."

—

It had been a while since the squad had had occasion to open the "war room." This was a grand name for the closet that housed special operations *matériel.* Each detective was issued a shotgun and full Kevlar, along with backup magazines and speed-loaders for the Berettas.

In the middle of all this, Cardinal had to go out to the meeting room to try to calm down Ronnie Babstock. He'd showed up with a laptop that he opened on the board table to the video recording of his daughter. She was dressed like the other victims, in blue down jacket, new boots, no gloves, no scarf. Nothing else visible in the frame but ice.

Her breaths were shallow, visible intermittently as fog against the blue of her jacket. She appeared to try to speak, but no words came out.

"She's going to die, John. I need to know what is being done."

"Ron, we looked at this the minute you zapped it over. It doesn't contain anything we can use, and we have another lead to follow up right now—a strong lead. We're heading out in a few minutes. You go back home and I'll call you soon as we know."

"He's on Axel Heiberg, John. Tell me the Mounties are there."

"They're on their way. They don't have an outpost on that island, but they're in the air right at this moment. Listen, Ron, that is only to make sure. We don't think he made it up there."

"He left the numbers. The coordinates."

"Yes, it was his plan. He wanted us to arrive too late. But he was in a car accident. He's injured. There's no way he could fly a plane that far. We believe he's here now. There's nothing in the video that couldn't be right here in Algonquin Bay."

"This is a recording." Babstock pointed to the laptop, the image of his daughter curled up on the ice, a chain winding out of the bottom of the frame. "It wasn't even live when he sent it."

—

The cottage was near the tip of Cole's Landing. The assault had to be coordinated with Jerry Commanda and OPP SWAT. He had asked Cardinal what they could expect.

"We don't know. Durie's sister told us the cottage never contained any weapons of any kind when they were growing up. Their father wasn't a hunter or anything. But he's had plenty of time to stock it up with whatever he wants. We've had plainclothes get as close as they can. So far, there's no signs of life, no signs of recent activity. We don't know if he's in there or if the girl's in there alone, or what. If she's with him, he could shoot her the minute he sees us."

A stillness had settled over the lake, no trace of last week's freak wind, or any wind at all. Sun hanging low over the Manitou Islands, radiating nothing but cold. The quiet sawn in two by a snowmobile heading out through the fishing shacks. Not too many of those would be occupied on a day like this. Thirty below, and that was in the sun. It was hard to believe anyone could die on such a beautiful day, but if Hayley Babstock was out in this, she surely would.

"Jesus, this is hellish," Cardinal said, "and we're dressed for it."

Delorme said nothing. She had been keeping her distance all morning. He had congratulated her on the Priest case and wanted to arrange a dinner or some time they could catch up, but she had pulled out her cellphone and feigned sudden interest in a text.

Not that he could worry about that now. He had McLeod and Szelagy at the ready behind a rock cut on the west side of the cottage. From there, they had a clear shot at the walkout on the lake side should anyone decide to make a run for it.

He and Delorme were taking the front, but OPP would be first in. Cardinal had briefed them thoroughly and he had no reason to fear they'd blow it.

"I think I saw a curtain move," Delorme said.

"I didn't."

"I could be wrong. Staring too hard."

The curtains had been drawn all morning as far as the drive-bys could ascertain. There was smoke coming from the chimney, but that meant nothing. All houses kept some degree of heat on throughout the winter to prevent pipes bursting.

Jerry Commanda's voice over the radio. "Everyone in place?"

Cardinal told him they were ready.

"All right, then. Let's hope she's in there."

Despite their vantage point halfway up the hill, he couldn't see Jerry and the SWAT team until they emerged from the bush like so many ninjas—ninjas plump with parkas and weaponry. He saw the point team heave the boomer into the door and a split-second later heard the crash of it.

He and Delorme ran down the hill and into the house.

"They're not here," Jerry told them, "but it looks like they were."

There were dishes in the sink, bloody bandages in the bathroom. They found a coat in a heap on the floor that Cardinal recognized from photos of Hayley Babstock. He went to the wide front window and looked out across the lake. To the north, the blocky outlines of fishing huts silhouetted against the sun. To the west, the reflected sun was almost as bright as the real thing. It was a moment before Cardinal realized the reflection was coming from Babstock's lake house, those glass rectangles hurling the sun right back in bolts of fire.

"Do we have any idea where he might be headed next?" Jerry said.

"Somewhere cold."

"That could be anywhere."

"It could."

"And we don't know what he's driving."

"No."

"You gonna order up your ident team?"

"They're on the way," Cardinal said.

"What's wrong? What are you staring at?"

"Ronnie Babstock's house. Glass one over there."

"I thought he owned that huge place on MacClintock."

Cardinal was about to answer when there was a flash followed by a tremendous bang. All those bright reflections vanished in billowing clouds of black and grey.

"My God," Jerry said.

They both pulled out their phones. Jerry issued terse requests for fire and ambulance. "Is that Outlook Drive he's on?"

"Outlook, yeah."

Jerry told them Outlook, hung up and ordered everyone to head over to the fire.

Ronnie Babstock answered Cardinal's call and Cardinal asked him to hold on. He covered the mouthpiece. "Jerry, he's probably trying to draw us away."

"I know that. But we have to respond. She could be in that fire."

Cardinal stepped away and covered one ear to block out the mayhem around him. "Ron. No, we haven't found her yet. But I have a question for you."

"What's going on there? What's all that noise? Have you got the guy?"

"No. Listen, Ron. That day you were up in the Arctic. The flare. How far would you say you were from where that flare went up?"

"What? I don't get you."

"How far were you? Best guess."

"I don't know. More than four kilometres. Less than six."

Delorme grabbed his arm. "Are you coming?"

"Go with Jerry. I'll be over in a minute."

Delorme looked at him and he couldn't read her expression, this woman he thought he knew so well now an unknown quantity. She turned from him and followed the others.

"Why are you asking this, John? What's going on?"

"Karson Durie was aiming for some kind of symmetry. Wanted to take Hayley to the exact spot he nearly died, but got stopped. Four to six kilometres is your best guess? What kind of angle was it?"

"What?"

"From where you stood. You were on a ridge, right? From where you stood on that ridge to where that flare went up."

"You know about the ridge? I didn't tell you about the ridge."

"The angle, Ron. The angle. *Now.*"

"It was about two o'clock from where I stood."

"Two o'clock. So you'd say about ten degrees?"

"Two o'clock would be seven point five—but look, I didn't do a compass reading."

"Understood. Another question for you—is there anyone at your lakeside house right now? Cleaning lady? Caterer? Anyone like that?"

"No, I don't go out there when it's this cold. Why?"

~

Cardinal went to the nearest neighbour's place and banged on the door and yelled "Police." There were two cars in the driveway, one snowmobile trailer. Someone was home.

A man came to the door in his bathrobe.

"What the hell's going on? I was in the shower, for God's sake."

"I believe you own a snowmobile."

"Yeah. So?"

"The sooner you hand me the keys, the sooner you can get back to that shower."

Smoke was still unfurling in fat black thunderclouds from where Ronnie Babstock's house used to be. Cardinal was no master of snowmobiles, but he knew enough to get it moving in the right direction and at a speed that felt insane after the car.

The cold scorched his face, and by the time he'd got himself in line with the fire he was wishing he had a balaclava. He'd dropped his woollen cap in the cottage or somewhere else and his ears were already beginning to go numb.

At this moment, he was the only thing moving across the ice, the only thing making a racket. He cut across a rocky point and got within two hundred metres of the smoke. The fire trucks were there, but it was a question how well their pumps would work in this deep-freeze.

He spun the machine around to face south across the lake. He had to thumb the fog off his sunglasses to see. The shadowy humps of the Manitou Islands, the random fishing huts. With his back to Ron's house, two o'clock put him in line with the smallest of the islands. Five kilometres would definitely put him on the island. But there were a lot of huts in between.

He gunned it and the machine leapt forward. There were patches where the winds of the past week had blown the surface completely clean. It flashed beneath him in a jittery blur of black and silver.

Not all the fishing huts that had been blown from their original locations by the freak wind had been dragged back. Orange warning signs were posted near the exposed holes. The holes had frozen over again, but they would not be ready to hold the weight of a person, let alone a snow machine.

A slim, dark object off to one side caught Cardinal's eye, and he slowed and stopped. He got off the machine and went to the object and knelt over it. A small video camera, still fixed into its tripod. A smear of blood across the brand name.

You aren't carrying anybody to those islands, Cardinal said. You aren't anywhere far.

He left the camera where it was and got back on the snowmobile, heading for the huts that lay between him and the nearest island. He had to veer around exposed fishing holes. The cold sank hooks into his face. It'll be even worse, he thought, if that pain disappears.

Usually there was smoke curling from the roof pipes of the huts. Not today. He counted only three with smoke. Those he ruled out right away. If Hayley was in a hut, it would be one without heat, and if she was dressed like the other victims, she'd be dead or right next door to dead.

Cardinal had heard that the RCMP—or was it the military?—were developing a stealth snowmobile, and he was wishing he had one now. If Durie was in any one of these cabins, he was going to hear him coming. And he would hear that he was alone.

Sometimes, Cardinal thought, you have to pretend you don't know something. I'm not making a sound. Invisible, too.

He drove right up to the door of the first hut. There was no snow machine nearby; there wouldn't be if Hayley was alone. The hut was a crooked wreck not much bigger than a garden shed, but he came off the machine with his Beretta in hand and kicked the door open. Coleman stove, empty Labatt cases, porn magazines.

The next hut had windows blinded with frost. He broke one with his elbow and saw at a glance the place was empty.

He moved to the next one. His fingers were barely working and he had to put his hand with the Beretta in his pocket. Again no snowmobile. Windows opaque. Drag marks where the hut had slid out of position. An unmarked fishing hole nearby, the danger sign flat on the ice.

This cabin was bigger than the others and there was blood on the doorsill. Cardinal took his gun out and checked that the safety was off. The padlock on the door was big, but it didn't matter. Two kicks tore the hasp from the frame. He pushed the door open.

Hayley Babstock lay half-curled on a bench. Blue down jacket like the others. New boots.

"I have a Glock .45 pointed at your spine." The voice came from behind him. "Place the gun on the ice and kick it back here."

"Just let me help the girl," Cardinal said.

"Gun on the ice, Detective. You're not rescuing anyone today." It was a dry voice, an exhausted voice. The voice of a ghost.

"Look at her, Durie. She's young. A teacher, but practically a kid herself."

The shot ripped into the door frame.

"Gun on the ice."

Cardinal lowered the gun and kicked it back. He heard the man gasp as he picked it up.

Cardinal turned around. Durie's face was a perfect match with his voice—grey, drawn, desiccated—the face of the walking dead. "Let's at least get inside," Cardinal said.

"Not that one," Durie said. He gestured with the gun at the cabin behind him.

"I think we should go in here with Hayley. You should see exactly what you're doing. Exactly who you're killing."

"I've seen it before."

"You mean Rebecca."

The man flinched. Black spark in the hollow of his eyes.

"I've read your notebook. I know you had to watch her die. But I don't think you watched Marjorie Flint or Laura Lacroix or Brenda Gauthier."

"Ronald Babstock is the one who should be watching. Unfortunately... technical difficulties."

Cardinal pointed inside the hut. "Hate Ron Babstock all you want. He and his daughter are not the same person. Hayley never harmed you in any way."

"Everyone's accusing me of hate. Hate is not required."

"You're not like this. This isn't you. It's obvious from your diary—your blue notebook. You're an intelligent man, a passionate man. A man capable of love. A man who recognizes the good qualities in others. A scientist. Observant. Curious. You loved someone, remember?"

"That was in another country." The dry voice. A whisper among reeds. "You flip that switch, push that button. Love turns into something else, but it isn't hate."

"I also know—"

"You don't know anything."

"From your notebook. Rebecca was also passionate, loving, a scientist—curious, rational, brave. She loved you. Loved her husband too, I think. But she saw the good qualities in you."

"I frightened her."

"From what you wrote, I think it was her own feelings that scared her."

Durie shook his head.

"I believe every word you wrote. What I don't understand is why the jury didn't believe you. Why did they think you killed the others?"

"I was holding the murder weapon when they found me."

"There's plenty of reason for that."

"If you've read to the end of my notebook, you know her husband testified against me. Told them I'd gone on a rampage in a desperate attempt to steal his wife. Now there's hate for you. Odd thing is, I don't even blame Kurt, really. I didn't even at the time. I understood it completely. I'd like to tell him so, but he died of natural causes before I got the chance."

"You got a bad deal."

"Eighteen years for four murders. The judge was marvellously impartial, considering. Took Arctic stresses into account."

"The woman you loved died too young. Hayley doesn't have to."

"Nor did Rebecca."

"Honour the person she was, then. She would beg you to stop. It's there, in everything you write about her."

"Rebecca can't care anymore. Being dead."

"Durie, listen. Here we are in the exact same circumstances you were in twenty years ago. A young woman is about to freeze to death, only this time it doesn't have to happen. This time you can save her. In some ways, I think that's why you've been doing this—hoping that somehow, against all odds, this time it would turn out right. Well, it can. This time you can save her."

"And what about me?"

"You'll probably die in prison."

"I was joking."

"But you'll be a better man. A better human being. The one that young woman loved so long ago."

"Karson Durie died twenty years ago, Detective. I'm just a ghost."

"Fine. At least they have heating in prison."

"You imagine I'm afraid of the cold."

"I don't think you're afraid of anything."

"I'm made of cold."

Durie opened his parka. He shifted the gun from one hand to the other and back, letting the coat drop from his shoulders to the ice. Underneath, he was wearing a dark sweater, khaki pants.

"It's what I was wearing that day. You believe that? They actually gave them back to me in a parcel the day I was released. They're a little big on me now. Would've been nice if they'd given me back my toes and fingers."

Cardinal took a step toward him. A searing pain like a scalpel across his arm before he even heard the shot.

Durie took two steps to the side, his limp severe. Then he stepped onto the fishing hole as if he were stepping onto the down escalator, both feet firmly in the circle.

The briefest pause.

Over the course of the next month, Cardinal would have to explain many times why he thought Durie would suddenly choose this course of action. He said, every time, that he did not know. Durie could have killed Cardinal, and the girl would have died the way he had intended. Maybe his thirst for revenge had been slaked sooner than he expected. Maybe he was just tired of killing. His own injuries were life-threatening—the autopsy showed deep cuts, seven fractured ribs, a punctured lung, and a torn spleen—and he must have known at this point he was unlikely to survive them. Or maybe it was that Hayley Babstock was too much like the woman he had loved so long ago, and he couldn't, in the end, bear to take her life. Or maybe it was as he had said, maybe Karson Durie had really died all those years ago.

The ice gave way beneath him and he vanished. Cardinal crawled to the hole but could see nothing beyond shards of ice. Water like ink. He plunged his arm in up to the shoulder and the pain made him shout. He rolled back from the edge, gasping.

Durie appeared under the ice a short distance away. The surface was not perfectly clear, but the face, stunned and incredulous, was vivid, as were the gloved hands that pressed so uselessly against the ice.

~

Hayley was still breathing, her pulse faint. Cardinal called for paramedics—they would not have far to come from Babstock's house. He gave them the same directions Ronnie Babstock had given him. Then he called Ronnie.

"Oh, dear God. Tell me she's all right."

"She's hypothermic, Ron. Pretty bad, I'd say, but the medics are on their way. She'll be warm soon."

There was no way of heating up the shack. The stove's exhaust pipe was still in the roof, but there were marks where the stove had been dragged to the fishing hole. There was a toboggan hanging on one wall. Cardinal got it down and rolled Hayley onto it. He took her across the ice to the next cabin.

He got her inside and close to the stove. It was already going, although turned low. He turned it up and went back outside. The dead man's outline was still visible beneath the ice, but Cardinal looked away. He picked up Durie's coat and went back inside and wrapped it around the unconscious woman.

This whole time, he was speaking to her, telling her she was going to be all right, she would be warm soon. Her skin was palest blue, but she had not been exposed to wind, there was no sign of frostbite. He thought of the young scientist dying of cold so many years ago. He thought of his own distant daughter. And for some reason, he thought of Lise Delorme.

24

Delorme had been so strange for the past couple of weeks that Cardinal was surprised when she picked up the phone on the first ring, and even more surprised when she agreed to go out with him for a celebratory dinner.

"Where did you have in mind?"

"I don't know. Someplace nice."

"Not too nice, okay? And not too celebratory."

By which she apparently meant she was fine with celebrating the fact that Hayley Babstock was making a rapid recovery and would be out of the hospital in a day or two. And with celebrating the arrest of Leonard Priest and the fall of Garth Romney. But she would not clink her champagne glass with him to "Senior Detective Delorme."

"There's not even any such position," she said.

"No, but you'll be running your own homicide investigations from now on. Chouinard's your new biggest fan."

"That was before he had all the gory details."

"Come again?"

The waiter appeared and recited a list of richly detailed specials. Cardinal thanked him and said they needed a few minutes.

"Come on, John. You've heard the rumours."

Cardinal shook his head.

"You will. Priest's attorney is Bob Brackett, and you can be sure he'll bring them out. I had to warn Chouinard, and he'll probably have to warn the chief. I'll even have to warn the crown. That should be a laugh."

"What'd you do, Lise—sleep with the guy?"

"Not exactly."

And so she told him. The waiter came back to take their order, but they just ordered wine. When he was gone, Delorme told Cardinal about Priest breaking into her house, and how she'd put the cuffs on him.

"He broke into your house, Lise. It's hardly your fault how you were dressed. I don't see why you're so uptight about this. You didn't have sex with him, right?"

"No."

"Even if you had, you'd have every right to plead duress. He broke into your house, for God's sake."

Delorme looked down at the tablecloth. "I feel like I'm back in the confessional. I'm so afraid of what you'll think of me."

"You think I'm that judgmental?"

"There's more, unfortunately."

She told him about being at Priest's place. Beside him on the couch.

"I let things go too far. And I, uh . . ."

"It's okay, Lise. You don't have to tell me."

Her voice was barely a whisper. "I let him touch me."

Cardinal sat back. He looked away, across the tables and banquettes, the snowy tablecloths, the sparkling goblets. "But you were undercover, right? Recording the conversation, and all. We have leeway, you know, in those circumstances."

She reached halfway across the table. Her hand beside his wineglass. "I'm not telling you this because of the legal ramifications."

"No. No, I realize."

"So . . . do you have any other response?"

Cardinal nodded. "It doesn't feel good, Lise. It feels pretty awful, if you really want to know."

"I thought you didn't care about me. You regretted that night of the party, and . . ."

"I was confused, Lise. I was so afraid of losing what we had. What we have. But I'm not anymore." He sat forward and touched her wrist. She opened her hand and closed her fingers around his. "Ever since that night of the party, feeling you drift away from me. Turn away. Whatever. I can't believe it isn't obvious to you."

"It isn't."

"I am totally and absolutely in love with you. I don't ever want to be with anyone else. And I don't want to be just friends. I don't know why I haven't said it sooner. I'm just an idiot sometimes. As you know."

Delorme gave a tight smile and withdrew her hand. She sat back with a sigh.

"It's just like Chouinard."

"Chouinard. You're going to have to explain that one."

"You don't have all the facts."

"I know everything I need to know. Trust me."

"I do, John. It's me I don't trust."

"You don't have to tell me anything more. We're not kids. I'm not, anyway. You don't owe me anything. You haven't made any promises. You haven't broken any vows. Why don't we just start from where we are? Can we just start from here, and not make any more confessions?"

"I don't know. I need to think about it. I just—I'm not the kind of person I want to be. And I think you deserve someone better."

Cardinal laughed. "You say something like that and you have no idea how ridiculous it is. I can't take any more. Can we please just order some food?"

"Just one more confession and then we can order, okay?"

"Okay."

"I love you, too. That's it. No more confessions. Not tonight, anyway."

"Good."

Cardinal opened his menu. He was looking at it but not really seeing it. He couldn't have said what was on it. Lise was looking at hers too. The sounds of a dozen conversations hovered around them. Sounds of wine corks, glassware, laughter.

"Kind of weird, isn't it," she said, "after all these years."

"It certainly is. It's good, though."

"I definitely like it. But I have to say, I'm also scared, still. I mean, it's great. We love each other, but . . ."

"Uh-oh," Cardinal said. "We love each other. Now what?"

"Exactly. Now what?"

Acknowledgements

I think most novelists dream of one day writing a story that requires no research whatsoever. This was not one of them. I owe a considerable debt of gratitude to each of the following.

Janna Eggebeen, Anne Collins and Helen Heller all read the manuscript in its early stages and remained encouraging right through to the final draft.

For help with Arctic science, and with Arctic conditions generally, I am grateful to Richard Logan, Derek Mueller and Robert Sprachman, all of whom read relevant sections.

For details of Arctic medicine, I want to thank Mike Webster and Dr. David Johnson of Wilderness Medical Associates International.

Assistant Crown Attorney Paul Larsh was helpful on matters concerning his office, and Staff Sergeant (Ret.) Rick Sapinski, once again, advised me on police work.

Other technical or historical information was generously provided by Elizabeth Legge.

I am also very fortunate to have the assistance of a miniature Académie française: *mes vieux* Paul Girard, Breen Leboeuf, Daniel Johnson and Émilie Johnson.

All of the above have spared the reader numerous errors and are in no way responsible for any that remain.

The song Durie somewhat misquotes on page [64] is "It'll Be a Breeze" by singer-songwriter George Meanwell.

GILES BLUNT grew up in North Bay, Ontario. After spending over twenty years in New York City, he now lives in Toronto. He has written scripts for *Law & Order*, *Street Legal* and *Night Heat*, and is the author of the bestselling Cardinal crime series, which he is adapting as a television series for CTV. He has won the British Crime Writers' Macallan Silver Dagger and the Arthur Ellis Award for Best Novel. *Until the Night* is his sixth novel featuring John Cardinal and Lise Delorme.